THE DEVILISH LORD WILL

MACKENZIES, BOOK 10

JENNIFER ASHLEY

JA / AG PUBLISHING

CHAPTER 1

June 1747

S cotsman." The cool English voice cut through the darkened room like an icy wind ruining a fine summer morning. "Speak to us, and I will ensure that your death is less agonizing."

Lord Will Mackenzie opened his eyes.

Nothing had changed. He remained seated on a stool in the cavern of an old kitchen, hands bound behind him, ankles also roped. No fire filled the hearth in the freezing room, and the only light came from windows high in the ceiling.

That light fell upon a major in the British army who sat on a hard chair, legs crossed, the man elegant in the dark red and silver braid uniform of an infantry officer. His hair had been tamed into a sleek queue, and his polished boots bore no speck of the mud that lay six inches thick around the makeshift army camp.

Major Haworth, a highborn gentleman, would let nothing, not even interrogating a stubborn Scottish traitor in the middle of nowhere, lower his standards.

The captain at his side was another matter. A hothead—a man who'd clawed his way up the ranks and instantly despised anyone his commanders pointed out as the enemy. Red-faced and foul-mouthed, the captain lounged against the stone wall with coat unbuttoned, his light brown hair straggling from the tail he'd pulled it into.

Will looked straight into Major Haworth's blue eyes and said in Erse, *If you think I even know anything to tell you, you're a gobshite idiot.*

The major and captain didn't understand a word. Haworth knew Greek and Latin and spoke perfect French, but Erse was a barbaric language, in his opinion, that needed to be stamped out. He'd expressed this sentiment more than once during the interrogation.

The captain's cheeks grew redder. "Speak a civil tongue, ye bloody Scots pig."

He drew back his hand to deliver a blow, but Haworth's cool voice stopped him.

"As you were, Captain."

The captain glared at the major but let his hand fall and dropped himself onto a wooden stool.

Will found it interesting that while the captain vented his frustrations with violence—demonstrated by the many bruises on Will's face and neck—the collected major was the more dangerous man in this room. Except for Will himself, of course.

Major Haworth reached long fingers to a silver bell on the rustic kitchen table. "Perhaps a light repast."

The furniture in this room, plainly made chairs and stools, matched the table. The bell was an incongruity, cast by a master silversmith, with a crest etched on one side, its handle fashioned of entwined silver snakes. The major had brought the bell with him.

He rang it now, its sound more appropriate for an elegant drawing room than an abandoned crofter's cottage.

"Woman!" the captain bellowed. "Bring us ale and be quick about it."

Footsteps sounded, and the wooden door swung open. The maid-servant on the threshold bore a tray that held a delicate porcelain cup and saucer and tall silver pot—more of the major's belongings—and a dented tankard that obviously came with the house.

In the cant of a Londoner born and bred, the woman said, "I guessed ye might be thirsty, sir. It's hot work with these Scots, innit?"

Dark eyes swept over Will Mackenzie, and he did his damnedest not to react.

She wore the garb of a farm woman, a simple chemise covered by a laced overdress in drab homespun. Will had seen her in these kinds of clothes before, but he'd also known her in the sumptuous silks of a lady, her hair in soft curls, her bosom bedecked with jewels.

Beneath today's shapeless clothes lay the lush body he'd first seen in his brother's studio, when Alec Mackenzie had been scowling around his canvas at his newest artist's model, admonishing her not to move.

Will had been the one frozen as he'd beheld beauty lying before him, her scarlet drape covering very little.

In a sultry voice that had fired Will's blood, she'd said to Alec in her French-accented English, "*You* press your bum to cold marble for an hour, my lord, and see how much *you* squirm."

She was supposed to be in London. Supposed to be safe in the boarding house where Will had left her, looking after her daughter. Alec and Celia had said she was in London.

What on earth was Josette Oswald doing in the middle of Scotland in an army camp full of murderous British soldiers?

The major examined her in suspicion—clearly he'd expected someone else. "Who are you, madam?"

Josette poured a stream of dark liquid—drinking chocolate by the smell of it—into the porcelain cup. She handed the cup to the major before depositing the tankard for the captain on the kitchen table.

"Mrs. Smith," she said glibly. "Me man runs the tavern in the village yonder. Sent to offer the best ale to the lads here, bless them. Nice to see Englishmen in this back of beyond."

The captain grabbed the tankard, took a greedy gulp, and then spat out the liquid. "Ye call this the *best* ale? Horse swill will do for a name, madam."

"I'm certain it's the finest they have," Major Haworth said quietly. The captain subsided and took another sip, which he swallowed. Then another. He'd decided not to let it go to waste, Will saw.

"Thank you, good lady," the major said. "And thank your husband."

Josette curtsied, but instead of beetling off, she turned her thoughtful gaze to Will. Her cheeks were as round and pink as they'd been nearly a dozen years ago when she'd portrayed Helen of Troy rising from her bed the morning after she'd eloped with Paris. Alec had been full of grandiose ideas for paintings in those days.

"He don't look like much," Josette said critically. "You sure this was one what gave you so much trouble at Culloden?"

"Appearances are deceptive, madam," Major Haworth said. "He is tamed for now, but believe me, these Highlanders are the very devil. The sooner they are all hanged and their ways stamped out, the better." He took a sip of chocolate. "Ah, well prepared. Thank you. If you'd brought your own supplies, Captain, you wouldn't have to rely on village goods."

The captain snorted but he continued drinking the ale. Josette lingered while Major Haworth took several more slow sips of his chocolate, as though she would take away pot and cup as soon as all were empty.

"Now then, sir," Major Haworth said to Will, clicking his cup to his saucer. "Let us start again. My patience is wearing thin, and I will give you over to my men soon if you do not speak. Please tell me all you know. Or be drawn and quartered—alive—for raise … raising … arms against your … your rightful king."

His words began to tangle on his tongue, and he shook his head as though trying to clear it. Behind him Josette quietly closed the door and drew a bolt across it.

The captain took another long gulp of ale, and choked. The major turned to him, his movements too slow. The captain fell from his chair to his knees and then did a prolonged topple to the floor, landing on his face.

The major rose jerkily, drawing a long knife that hung at his side. He stumbled as he rushed at Josette, and his cup fell to the floor in a porcelain smash.

"Damn you." Haworth glared at her. "That was a gift from my mother."

The major might be prissy, but Will had seen that he was a deadly fighter. Josette quickly sidestepped as the major struck, but she would not be fast enough.

Will sprang from the stool, still bound, and slammed his body into Major Haworth's. The major swung the blade at him, but only caught Will's loose shirt as whatever potion Josette had put into the chocolate gripped him.

The knife went slack, and the major, all six foot three of him, tumbled to the dirt floor in a heap of long limbs.

Josette snatched the knife from his hand and had Will's bonds cut in seconds.

"God's balls, woman." Will kept his voice a whisper, but it rang with rage. "What the devil are you—"

"Shout at me later," Josette said softly but fiercely, the London accent dropping away. "Follow me now."

Will growled as Josette caught his numb hand and pulled him to the back of the kitchen, making for an alcove near the fireplace he'd already spied as a potential way out.

Before Josette could duck into it, Will caught her around the waist, pulled her to him, and kissed her hard on the mouth.

Josette started, then her lips parted and her hands landed on his chest, her mouth softening to kiss him back. Her body warmed his, moving the blood that had been cut off by the ropes. Will's limbs burned as her fire swept through him.

The kiss grew stronger, memories pouring in with it: Josette's shy look as she, as Helen of Troy in Alec's studio, sent Will a tiny smile. Will had winked at her, hiding his sudden and overwhelming longing.

Seeing her weeks later in regal finery at a salon held in Alec's honor by the cardinal who'd commissioned the painting. Josette's ready acceptance to help Will uncover the cardinal's secrets—for money, of course. Josette had been raising a daughter and was always in need of funds.

Years later in Salisbury, when she and Will had posed as man and wife to discover the plans of a certain high-placed English lord who could expose a Highland plot. Josette had been a fine actress, playing a slightly dim but devoted wife smitten with her husband.

Their nights in bed, when they'd forgotten about playacting and spying, and simply enjoyed each other, knowing their time together would soon be over.

The Salisbury ploy had been the last, and had ended stormily. The boarding house in London had been Will's gift to her, a safe place for her to make a living and raise the irrepressible Glenna.

Will tasted Josette's heat in this drafty farmhouse kitchen with his captors lying senseless on the other side of the room. She'd done that —for him.

Why?

He abruptly broke the kiss. Josette gazed up at him, her fists on his chest. She was a dozen years older than when she and Will had first met, but the passing time had turned the desperate young woman into a beautiful and capable lady. Josette's face was as soft as he remembered, her dark eyes as glowing, her hair as sleek, her lips as ripe.

The kiss and their locked gazes lasted only a few seconds, though time seemed to slow to a trickle.

But they had to escape before the major and captain awoke. Will seized Josette's hand and pulled her through the narrow door beside the fireplace to the tunnel beyond.

Josette shook off his grasp and slid past Will to guide him through the darkness with confidence. The cords had cut off blood to Will's feet, but at least the captain hadn't taken away the old shoes Will had found to complete his guise as a poor farmer.

Josette warned him of a short flight of stairs that delved into the earth before he fell down them. This must be a smuggler's tunnel, built to let the farmer who'd lived here move whisky, brandy, and even men—anything those in the village wished to hide from soldiers and the excise men.

Josette had obviously explored the tunnel, because she led Will unerringly through twists and turns, down more stairs, then up another flight.

When at last she pushed open a gate—hinges oiled and silent—and began to step into the cool Scottish night, Will stopped her.

"They'll be scouring these hills once they find me gone. Best we hide a bit."

"I've got transport," Josette said, her voice a bare whisper. Her breath warmed his cheek. "It will take us to safety."

In the darkness, Will squeezed her hand. The late evening air felt heavenly, but he had no intention of diving out into it, his red hair like a beacon to all those searching for dangerous Highlanders.

"We wait until dark," Will said. "I know a place where we can go to ground while they search. They'll give up after a time. The major is not one for living rough."

Once in hiding, Will would interrogate Josette as to what she was doing here, where she'd left her daughter, and why she'd been on hand to rescue him. The interrogation would be thorough and intense and might involve a night together, the pair of them wrapped in shared blankets.

"We go now," Josette said. "My transport won't wait forever."

"Then let him go. We'll compensate him later if need be."

"No, Will." Josette's voice turned hard. "Ye need to come with me. *Now.*"

Will blinked at her. In the half light, her face was set, eyes determined.

"Josette?"

"I'm sorry, Willie."

He knew there was someone behind him, stepping out from shadows before he could register the danger. He noted a flurry of movement and turned in astonishment before a single, very hard blow rendered him senseless.

CHAPTER 2

*Y*e shouldn't have hit him so hard, Lillias."

Josette applied the cold cloth to Will's pale face as he lay beneath the castle roof. He'd already been hurt and weak from the interrogation, and the flat part of a shovel to the side of his head hadn't helped. Josette knew he'd allowed himself to be laid out only because he hadn't expected the blow to come from a tiny young woman.

"Never trust a Mackenzie," Lillias McIver declared in sullen tones. "He wouldn't have come because of your tender persuading, Mrs. Oswald."

"You might have given me a few more minutes to talk him round." Josette dabbed at the stitched-up gash on the side of Will's head, buried deep in his red hair. "If you've gone and killed him, he won't be of much help, will he?"

Josette spoke lightly, but her heart hammered. If Will died ...

That could not happen. Josette would grieve if he left life behind, and she knew she'd grieve hard.

Under her hand, Will groaned. Josette lifted the cloth in worry.

Will's eyes moved behind his lids but he didn't open them. Emitting another soft grunt, he slipped back into sleep. True sleep, to Josette's relief.

He was a big man, his height making him appear lanky, but his body was solid with muscle. Josette had cut his tattered shirt from him, his skin warm despite the chill of the castle, his torso firm under her touch.

Will Mackenzie had always been larger than life, dominating any room he entered. He moved easily, that fluidity enabling him to appear and disappear before one could notice him. *Unreachable*, Josette said silently. Every time she thought she'd hold him, he'd slip away and be gone, leaving her bereft.

Her own fault, Josette knew. She understood the instant she'd first seen Will that this was a man who'd never stop moving. A woman would break her heart on him—dash herself to pieces if she didn't take care.

But Josette, with the confidence of the young, had believed she could weather him. She'd been wrong.

"Ye should rest, Mum," sixteen-year-old Glenna said as she slipped into the chamber. While Glenna had been born in France, she'd taken to London cant and thoroughly adopted it. "I can sit with him if ye'd like."

Lillias's hazel eyes widened. "*Ee*, I'd not let a daughter of mine anywhere near a Mackenzie. He'll gut us all."

"No, he will not," Josette said, her patience with Lillias wearing thin. "He's not a vicious man. He took care of Glenna when she was a babe."

"Well, she's not a babe now." Lillias, who was only in her early twenties herself, declared. "He's been a prisoner a while, and who knows what hungers he'll try to sate? We should bind him at the least."

"We'll do nothing of the sort." Josette rose. "We need him, Lillias. On our side, not against us."

Lillias's rather pretty faced screwed into sour lines. "Ha. A Mackenzie does what he pleases when he pleases. He'll hear you out and then leave ye stranded, taking everything you have when he goes. We can't trust the likes of the Mackenzies—not *those* Mackenzies anyway."

Josette kept her temper with effort. "We'll leave him to sleep. 'Tis what he needs most, without our chatter. Lillias, you come with me. You're as tired as I am and it's making you out of sorts. Glenna, you too. I need your help downstairs" She turned to her daughter, never failing to marvel at how lovely she was. "Yes?"

"Of course," Glenna replied in French, which spilled fluently from her tongue. "As long as I don't have to do what this old witch says."

Lillias didn't know French, but she had a good idea Glenna was insulting her. Josette gave her daughter an admonishing look and led the reluctant Lillias away.

Josette didn't give voice to the thought, even inside her own head, that Lillias might be right. Will would take what he wished and leave, as he always did. But it was worth the risk, Josette reminded herself with another glance at Glenna. Definitely worth it.

WILL SPUN IN AND OUT OF SLEEP. HE TRIED TO RISE, BUT HE GROANED and dropped to the pallet, pain exploding in his head. Dried bracken crackled beneath his back, and the scent of peat smoke invaded his senses.

It was the peat that made him believe he was in Scotland, not hell.

He tried to remain awake long enough to assess where he was and how badly he was injured. He could breathe—no hissing or gurgling in his lungs. His heart beat fairly evenly. He was hot, feverishly hot.

The pain that wracked his body radiated from the side of his head. Had the captain hit him again?

No—the flash came to him of a flight through a tunnel after a thorough and satisfying kiss. Then the business end of a spade swinging at his head, wielded by a small but fiery woman with flame-red hair.

Josette had led him into a trap, he dimly realized. Why, he had no idea.

They hadn't parted easily last time. Will took the blame, though Josette could be bloody-minded. He hoped in the intervening years she'd forgotten what a bastard he was.

One look into her entrancing eyes told him she hadn't forgotten.

Despite the fact that Josette had drugged the captain and major to help Will escape, he had no way of knowing whether he was in the hands of friends or enemies. Josette knew how to play both sides of a coin. Survival, she'd say, and she'd be right.

Will wanted to leap up, find her, question her, but his healing body took over, and he succumbed once more to sleep.

When he finally floated to consciousness again, the fever had faded, and Will opened his eyes, alert and aware.

He studied the roof over his head, beams and stone. Inside a castle, he concluded, one of the many that dotted the hills of Scotland like old ghosts.

He'd hoped for a nice bed in a warm manor house, like his father's rented home in Paris, but he ought to have known he wouldn't be that lucky.

Will sat up, stifling a groan, pressing his hand to the bandage on his head. Mal and Alec would laugh themselves sick if they knew he'd been felled by a stripling of a Scotswoman with a garden spade. That she was a Scotswoman, Will had no doubt. She'd wielded her weapon with the ferocity of a clanswoman defending her bairns.

He swung himself out of the bed, leaning on the cold stone wall while he steadied himself and got his bearings. He wore no shirt, but had on a pair of trews made of some scratchy fabric. He'd been lying on a plaid, which he snatched up and wrapped around himself in the approximation of a kilt.

The room did not have a proper door, only a blanket tacked over the opening. Will pushed it aside and found himself in a stone corridor.

This part of the castle looked solid enough—ceiling intact, wooden floor fairly even and not rotted as far as he could tell. His room was the only one on the short hall, which ended in a stone staircase spiraling down.

Unlike his brother Mal, who could put a name to every room, hall, and corner of a castle or keep, Will had only a vague idea where he was in the building.

Castles had been built as hiding places, refuges from wild lands and violent neighbors. This one seemed to have no windows at all.

Will followed the staircase down, one hand on the wall to keep himself from growing too dizzy.

At the bottom of the stairs, a flicker of firelight led him to a wide room with rounded walls. The enormous fireplace that lit the chamber looked to have been added at a later date—different stone— and it didn't fit quite right against the curved wall. Kilmorgan Castle, Will's family home, had been overhauled and updated with each generation, but this keep had obviously been left in the past.

Kilmorgan was no more, Will reminded himself with a rush of pain. Now it was a heap of burned rubble, courtesy of British soldiers. It was also the main reason Will had returned to Scotland. Kilmorgan's destruction needled at him, and he desired to put it right.

The kitchen—obviously what the room was being used for—was filled with women.

Glenna stood at a table shaping pieces of dough for a gray-haired lady to roll out. The red-haired wench who'd wielded the deadly shovel turned a spit at the fireplace. The spit was large enough for a whole oxen, but only two small roasting birds rotated above the flames. Josette seemed to be in charge, moving from table to table, supervising the preparations, reaching out to help sort greens or chop an onion.

Female voices washed over him like gentle rain. Will leaned on the doorframe, unnoticed in its shadow, and listened to their chatter.

"Are you certain you're well?" one woman was asking.

Will opened his mouth to answer, then realized she'd not been addressing him. The red-haired woman at the fireplace nodded. "I'll mend. Those soldiers only grabbed me for a moment. I move quickly."

The gray-haired woman slapped a round of dough Glenna handed her to the table. "As long as they never knew what you were about."

"They had no idea." The younger woman looked smug. "Thought I was another light skirt. As though I'd waste me time." She spit into the flames, which crackled.

Laughter and salty comments followed. Will was in the High-lands all right, where the women didn't withhold their opinions.

They spoke English, not Erse, likely so Josette could understand them.

When the ladies wound down, another asked the red-haired lass, "What did you learn?"

"Nothing," she replied, despondent. "The soldiers didn't know a blessed thing. From their talk, they've heard no more than we have."

"Doesn't matter," Josette answered, her tone brisk. "Finding out nothing is still helpful. Means it's not yet in the hands of King Geordie."

Will smothered a chuckle. He was the one who'd taught the French Josette to call George the Second of Britain "King Geordie."

The gray-haired woman cast her eyes to the ceiling. "What about our new source? Are we going to use it?"

Four of the eight ladies present nodded and the other half shook their heads.

"Ye can't," the red-haired woman wailed. "He'll betray us all."

Glenna burst out with indignation. "He will not. He's saved Mum and me countless times."

"Aye, but who put you in danger in the first place?" another asked.

She had a point. If not for Will, Josette would still be in France, perhaps the pampered mistress of a wealthy patron. She'd recline in her parlor in finery, telling her paramour which artists to hire and which models to have said artists paint.

Because of Will, she'd had to flee Paris, and now, apparently, London.

"He's a fine man," Glenna snapped back. "Better to me and Mum than my own pa ever was. *He* scarpered the moment Mum knew she was having me."

"Glenna," Josette admonished.

"'Tis true, Mum. I've never minded." The flash of hurt in Glenna's eyes said otherwise, and Will felt old rage flicker at the man who'd deserted Josette.

"Will Mackenzie's the worst ye could turn to, *I* say," the red-haired woman said. "He and any of his family. Where are they now, eh? Living well in Paris while their people starve."

The gray-haired woman broke in. "Because they'd be shot or

hanged on sight if they returned. Kilmorgan burned to the ground and all were turned out. And I'll remind you they lost two brothers to the fighting."

"All of us lost someone," the red-haired woman said hotly. "They likely will only come out to swing." She blinked and coughed. "Blessed smoke," she muttered.

She received looks of sympathy, nods of commiseration. She was correct—everyone in the Highlands had lost someone to the war that had torn families asunder and created so many outlaws.

Another took up the argument. "If we use him, what's to say he won't take it and rush back to France? Won't help us none."

"But if any can find it, it's Will," Josette broke in, voice firm. She was the only non-Highlander in the room besides Glenna, but the ladies went silent as she spoke, acknowledging her authority.

"He knows everyone in Scotland," Josette continued, "and could wile information out of the devil himself. We can either poke around until we're in our graves or we can locate it quickly—or know for certain it's long gone. It would be foolish *not* to ask him. He's an honorable man, whatever he may seem."

The red-haired woman stuck out her lip. "And all know ye were his lover. What's to say ye won't find it with him? And you and he run off to France and live in luxury?"

Glenna jumped to her feet. "Now, see here, ye two-faced—"

"Glenna!" The sharp word from her mother halted the South London foulness from Glenna's mouth. Glenna went scarlet, but she sat down, lips tight.

Josette faced the red-haired woman. "You all asked me for help, Lillias, and I agreed, for the Mackenzies' sakes."

The gray-haired woman held up a floury hand. "And we accepted that help because Lord Malcolm and Lord Alec vouched for you, Mrs. Oswald."

"We're trusting a lot of Mackenzies," Lillias growled.

Will chose that moment to step forward.

"Why don't you lassies tell me what it's all about?" he asked in easy tones. "And I'll decide whether or not ye should trust me."

CHAPTER 3

*J*osette had known he'd stood in the fold of darkness, listening. Will had taught her how to sense a presence, and she'd known exactly when he'd arrived. She'd also known he would reveal that presence only when he was ready.

Lillias, predictably, snatched up a poker, ready to strike. "Ye told us he'd be out at least another day."

"He ought to be." Josette glared at Will. "I wager he's barely keeping himself to his feet."

Will's sway told Josette she was right. He was gray around the edges, the plaid gaping to show tanned flesh with a wan tone.

Glenna had leapt from her stool with a glad cry and now rushed to Will and flung her arms around him.

"Are ye chuffed to see us, Uncle Will? We thought you were a dead man, but ye rose again, didn't ye?"

Will lifted Glenna and spun her around, much as he'd done when she was a mite.

"I am right chuffed, little lass," he said as he set her on her feet. "How have you been keeping yourself?"

Glenna bussed him loudly on the cheek. "I've been keeping well. Hear you've gone and been captured a number of times. Thought you were more careful."

Will dropped a kiss to the top of her head. "I'm always careful, little dove. I let myself be captured on purpose—what better way to find out what the enemy is up to than to hear what questions they ask?"

"Ha," Lillias said. "More likely he stumbled into their traps, probably sang all kinds of songs about our men and our families, who are being hunted down one by one."

Will regarded her without much surprise. "Lillias McIver. The little hellion who used to follow my younger brothers and get into much mischief. Mal was fond of you, I remember."

"And I'd be whipped because of that mischief." Lillias jerked the windlass, sending a spatter of grease into the fire. "Entirely their fault."

"Why'd ye keep following them, then? Thought you'd safely married yourself off and settled down. But there ye were, popping up behind me and whacking me with a shovel." Will gingerly touched the bandage on the side of his head.

"My man's a guest of His Majesty, isn't he?" Lillias snapped. "Captured on Culloden Moor. And the likes of you will get him killed, blundering about, giving up information to English soldiers."

"English soldiers didn't get a word out of me. Not even my name." Will's voice softened. "I'm sorry, Lillias. Where is your husband being held?"

"I don't know." Frustration and grief filled her voice. "But he won't come out except at the end of a rope. Or maybe gutted where he stands."

"If he's alive, I'll get him out," Will said with conviction. "Ye have my promise on that."

Lillias turned away. "Ha. The word of a Mackenzie. Does nae give me reassurance."

Will caught Josette's eye. He wished to speak to her privately, she knew, wanted her to tell him exactly what was going on.

But these ladies didn't trust him—didn't trust much of anyone—not that Josette could blame them.

Josette's entire world had changed the day Will Mackenzie had walked into his brothers' rooms in Paris, Will tall, strong, and nonchalantly arrogant. His whisky-colored gaze had rested on Josette, who'd reposed in her altogether, nothing between her and the world but a wisp of red cloth and the bend of her arm shielding one breast.

Will hadn't seemed much impressed. He'd winked at her, acknowledging she was in the room, but that was all. As though naked women draped about his brother's apartments was a common occurrence, which it had been. Alec had received commissions from cardinals, archbishops, princes, and dukes who wanted mythological and allegorical paintings, most of which involved voluptuous women with no clothes on.

Josette, desperate for coin to feed her daughter, had become a model—in truth, her landlord had more or less rented her out to neighboring artists. Then the artists, liking the look of her, had begun hiring Josette for more and more wages. They'd also appreciated the fact that she arrived at the appointed time and didn't mind holding uncomfortable poses for hours.

Will had taken her away from the indignity—and the discomfort and the chill—of posing and gave her another way to earn money for Glenna. She'd be forever grateful to him, but Lillias wasn't wrong that he always played his own game.

She made her decision. "We tell him," Josette said to the silent and waiting women. "Now that he knows we've gathered here, we can't let him go, so we might as well make use of him."

Will's brows went up. He knew good and well Josette could never force him to remain where he didn't want to be, but he did not contradict her. He was good at pretending to be a prisoner until he was ready to leave, just as he'd done at the army camp. The fact that he hadn't already vanished into the Highlands told Josette he was at least curious about why they were here.

"What is it?" he asked. "A plot to free all the men captured by the Butcher? A daunting task, but I'll help, if that's the case. I wouldn't mind tweaking the noses of the king and his dear son."

"Partly." Josette drew a breath, aware of all eyes on her, some filled with anger, others with fear. Mysie Forster's hands remained fixed in the dough. Lillias's spit halted, and the roasting chicken's skin crackled as it burned.

"We're looking for the shipload of gold that came to the Highlands from France before Culloden," Josette said in a rush. "The gold that vanished. It has to be somewhere, in someone's hands. We intend to find it."

Will listened quietly, his face a careful blank, then shook his head. "Lass, ye know the gold is long gone. Either captured by the king's men or stolen by Highlanders and used to get themselves out of Scotland. The French gold's a legend now."

Josette knew good and well Will didn't believe that. Last June, he'd discovered that English soldiers were holding and torturing Scotsmen in secret. One thing the English soldiers had been trying to discover was the whereabouts of the French gold, convinced the Highlanders they'd captured knew its location.

Will's brother Alec had rescued him, and Will had accompanied Alec and his new wife, Celia, to Paris. A few months ago, Josette had received a letter from Celia that Will had vanished again. Will often slipped away on his own, but he'd send word to the family that he was well—very likely so they'd leave him be. This time, however, Will had disappeared without a trace.

As Will frequently disappeared without a trace, the family was not yet worried, but Celia asked Josette to keep an eye out for him.

Josette had learned from Will how to be alert to any information that might chance her way. Most of the information that passed through Josette's London boarding house was innocuous—day-to-day life—but once in a while, she heard a nugget that was valuable.

Such as a Highland ghost terrifying army camps in Scotland, coupled with the rumors that the French gold was still floating about.

Conclusion—Will knew bloody well the gold was intact and he was looking into its whereabouts. What he hadn't known was that Josette and her army of ladies also wanted it.

Will leaned on the doorpost, folding his arms, his expression well masked. "How were ye thinking to find it? When it's gone forever?"

"We don't believe it is," Mysie said.

Lillias spoke in anguish. "If we tell him everything, he'll take it for himself."

"Now, now." Will settled in more comfortably. "I can't well walk off with a legend. And I'm not all that greedy. I have enough put by to live out my days in comfort."

"You have money on the Continent," Josette pointed out. "Not in Scotland."

Will shrugged. "I'm a dead man here. My name is blazoned on the rolls of the deceased. So, no, I won't be purchasing a grand estate and settling down in the Highlands."

He spoke lightly, but Josette saw bitterness in his eyes. She knew exactly why Will didn't remain in Paris, Amsterdam, or Basel, where he could do well for himself, why he continued to return to Scotland.

This was his home, a part of his flesh and bones. He could no more stay from here than Josette could banish herself forever from Glenna.

"Tell me why you think the gold still exists," Will said, sounding interested. "And why a regiment of women wants it."

"Ye don't need to know why," Lillias growled.

Will pinned her with his golden Mackenzie stare, and for the first time since Josette had met her, she saw Lillias falter.

Will's stare could wilt the most hardened soldier. Josette had watched him reduce brave men, who supposed a tall Highlander the equivalent of a backward fool, to babbling incoherence when he turned the might of his gaze upon them.

Likely this was why he'd never raised his eyes to his captors in the camp. They'd have realized they were dealing with a dangerous man, not a sorry specimen they happened to find wandering the fields in the dark.

Will flicked his gaze from Lillias, and she quickly returned to the spit before their supper burned away.

"We've heard things," Josette answered into the awkward silence. "Enough to believe the money is real. In one place, not scattered."

"All right then." Will scraped an empty stool from the wall and sat down. Josette knew he'd have kept to his feet had he not been tired and weak, but he'd never admit it. "Where is this one place?"

"We're not entirely certain," Josette said. "I've been piecing through the stories, most of which I'm sure are wrong. Somewhere on the west coast."

"Ah, a very precise location."

"Do not mock. It took quite a lot of time and care to narrow it down that far."

Will's grin nearly undid her. "And I admire ye for it. Now ye want me to help ye narrow it down further? Maybe lead ye right to it?"

Josette looked at him without flinching. "That was the idea, yes."

"Will you help us, Uncle Will?" Glenna had been good at curbing her impatience, but the girl had her limits. "Do say ya will. When we have the money, we can use it to free the ladies' menfolk and get them to France or Amsterdam, or wherever we can manage. Lillias can have her husband back, and Mysie her brother and sons. Mum and me can go live in a grand house in London and never have to grub for our bread again."

"Glenna!" Josette broke through her babbling. She had no idea whether Glenna knew Josette's true reason for wanting a bit of the gold, but Glenna was canny, and the girl never held anything back from Will.

"Why not tell him?" Glenna asked in irritation. "We don't want to overthrow the king or anything, just get back to home and family."

Will's piercing stare softened as he regarded Glenna, who watched him with great hope.

"I see," he said, his voice quiet. "In that case, ladies, I will see what I can do."

WILL RETURNED TO HIS SMALL ROOM TO STRIP DOWN AND TAKE STOCK of his injuries. Not so bad. The captain who'd captured him had punched and kicked him, but Will's thick coat and plaid—since confiscated—had helped cushion the blows. His bruises were still black, his ribs sore, but fortunately not cracked.

His ankles were raw from the ropes that had bound them, his wrists likewise. He'd nearly dislocated his shoulder leaping up, attached to the stool, to hit Major Haworth, but rolling it now showed it was flexible if sore.

The clout Lillias McIvor had given him still made his head ring.

Will usually healed quickly—his body did, that is. His heart and his mind—that was a different thing.

"If the likes of Lillias had been at Culloden," he said to the curtain in the doorway, "the Hanoverians would have run like deer."

He'd observed Josette peek in and then abruptly drop the cloth when she saw he was stark naked. She'd never objected to his bareness before, but the curtain remained stubbornly in place.

Will slid the trews that must have been made of the roughest fiber from the threshing floor over his hips and tied them at the waist. His backside was not happy with him.

"Enter," he called. "I won't offend ye now."

Josette's cheeks were red when she slid into the chamber, and she looked everywhere but at his exposed chest. "Are you feeling better?"

"As you saw." Will sat on the pallet and patted the blankets beside him. "Come, tell me what this is all about."

"I'll stand, thank you." Josette folded her arms.

Will grinned and splayed his hand over his chest. "Ah, ye wound me, lass."

"You have beguiling ways, Willie. I'll keep my distance, if you don't mind."

Will's heart squeezed as he leaned back on his elbows. "And no one has called me Willie in a long while."

"Your family ceased speaking to you, have they?"

In spite of her light words, Josette's hands clenched and unclenched, and her stance was rigid. What did she fear? Him?

"Let me look at ye, lass. I haven't seen ye for a time."

Josette lifted her chin. "That's your own fault."

"I know, but …" Will let the words linger as he ran his gaze over her. "Indulge me."

Josette frowned but unfolded her arms and let them drop to her sides.

She dressed simply, as always, her round gown modestly draped, a cream-colored stomacher embroidered with chocolate-brown flowers covering a butternut bodice and skirts. Lace trimmed the cuffs of her elbow-length sleeves, and a linen fichu wrapped her neck, the ends tucked into the top of her bodice. No wide panniers or plunging neckline, no wig or fussy cap, only Josette's dark brown hair in a simple knot.

Will flashed to the last time they'd played the game together—she'd worn a grand gown of blue silk dripping with lace, her hair tumbling over her shoulders in sleek curls. She'd been a luscious coquette, peering around her fan, a roguish twinkle in her eyes. Her bodice had shown a fair amount of shoulders and a bosom glittering with diamonds.

That had been their last venture together—the one that made Josette tell him she was finished and needed to raise her daughter in safety.

Hence, the London boarding house, where Will had thought her even now.

"Where exactly am I?" he asked.

Josette hesitated, as though debating what to tell him, then she beckoned. "Come with me," she said and turned and ducked out the door.

CHAPTER 4

*W*ill slid on a shirt that was almost as punishing as the trews, snatched up the plaid, and followed Josette down the spiral stairs. She led him without stopping through stone halls whose walls leaned toward each other, and up another, much longer, staircase.

He was winded by the time they reached the top, where Josette opened a trapdoor. She scrambled out with a flash of plump leg, and Will followed her more slowly onto a rooftop of crumbling stone.

Will paused to catch his breath, but Josette wasn't flagging at all. Of course, *she* hadn't been held for three days with no food or water or place to relieve herself.

Before Will had left the kitchen below, he'd feasted on bread, a hunk of cheese, ale, and a dram of whisky. The whisky had been indifferent, nothing like Mackenzie malt, but he'd drunk it thirstily. He'd left the roasted chickens for the ladies, not wanting to deprive them of their supper.

"Ye know your way about the castle," he observed as Josette wandered to the edge of the parapet.

Wind gusted from below, catching a dark curl that fell to her shoulder. "You taught me to learn the lay of a place, and quickly. I know every route in and out by now."

"How long have you been here?"

"A month, perhaps a few days more."

Will reached her side, her warmth cutting the chill. "Ye've stayed in this godforsaken place a month? Why?"

Josette didn't answer as she gazed over the wall to the valley below.

They were in the Highlands all right. A treeless land spread under gray skies, hills rising to misty mountains in the distance. A loch shimmered about half a mile from the base of the walls—at least the ladies had fresh water and fish to go with their meager chickens.

Will didn't recognize the immediate area, though it couldn't be far from familiar territory. Much of the northern Highlands looked like this, rust-colored land tumbling from stark hills as it reached for the sea. He peered at the sky, but the sun didn't penetrate the gray, and he could not make out a direction.

"The nearest town is …?"

"Ullapool." Josette pointed over the loch to the gray horizon. "About fifteen miles to the southwest."

That would put them near the river Canaird, which ran through empty country of rocky ground, bogs, and isolated farms. This castle, half ruined, could only be one place.

"Strathy Castle," he said. Which was in Clan Mackenzie territory, though very near that of the MacDonnells and MacLeods. "Or was. Been abandoned since the battle of Glen Shiel in '19."

Yet another ill-fated plan to put James Stewart, the Old Pretender, on the throne of Scotland, which rasher members of Will's clan had supported. Good men had been killed in that venture, as they had been in the 1715 uprising, and now the '45. Will wondered when Highlanders would realize God was trying to tell them something.

"Well chosen," he said in admiration. "Far enough off the beaten path for a hiding place. No one has lived here for years, and the nearest village is a day's walk."

"I remembered you mentioning it," Josette said. "And Lillias knew where it lay."

"She would." Will pulled his gaze from the land to Josette. "Watch her, love. She is a staunchly loyal Highlander—wouldn't betray a soul to the English—but you're not a Highlander. She plays by her own rules, has since she was a wee one."

Josette gave him a nod. "Lillias and I have reached an understanding. She has lost much, as they all have."

Will had no doubt of that, but he'd seen Lillias's desperation. Highland women were no less scheming, determined, and violent than the men, a fact many outsiders did not understand. Highland wives could inherit lands, be lairds, and lead men into battle. Didn't matter that she was female, only that she'd been left in charge.

"How did you manage to get me here?" Will lounged against the wall of the parapet, pretending to be relaxed, but he was alert, aware of every creature that moved in the grass below, every flutter of bird. "A journey over a mountain pass and through a few glens?"

Josette's smile sparked heat inside him. "In a cart, pulled by a donkey not very happy with us. We buried you under a load of turnips."

"Ah, that's why I've gone off the things." He remembered none of the journey, but Josette would have made it in silence, she and Lillias hunched in shawls like farm women delivering a load to market.

"You groaned a bit. We had to stuff a rag into your mouth. I'm sorry about that."

She didn't look very sorry, as the twinkle in her dark eyes betrayed. Josette must have been happy to at last find a way to shut Will up.

"Ye seem to have an able contingent here. What need for me?"

"Because if there is something dead secret that needs discovering, you are very good at it." Josette flushed, as though reluctant to admit this. "You can ferret out whatever you like, whenever you like, out of whomever you like. As soon as I decided to help the ladies, I knew immediately we'd need your skill, and started a search for you. I knew from some stories I'd heard that you must be in Scotland. We scoured the Highlands for a long time—you certainly know how to hide yourself. Then Mysie got rumor of a lone but tall Highlander having been captured by soldiers and dragged to an army camp. We watched that encampment, and then I got myself in and saw it was indeed you. You know the rest. Don't worry yourself about payment for helping us—we'll give you your fair share."

Will peered into a pocket of mist nestled into the gray land as he listened, impressed. Josette had learned very well how to seize opportunity. "Ye have much confidence in me," he remarked. "I haven't been able to discover where the gold is no matter how much I've listened at keyholes or tried to trick men into telling me."

"You believe it's still out there, then." Josette moved closer to him. "Else you'd not be listening at keyholes."

Will's body tightened, but he made himself keep his arms folded. He had no idea what was between them now or if she'd push him off the parapet the instant he tried to touch her.

"The French never got it back," Will said, as though her nearness didn't matter. "Mal or Alec would have told me—they're chummy with the French king and his new, glorious mistress. The gold never left the Highlands, is my guess. But I don't see any Highlanders parading about, spending it on luxuries. I see men and women barely surviving the winter. So it's well hidden."

"Maybe it *was* lost," Josette said. "Maybe it's lying at the bottom of the sea, or in a bog."

Will shook his head. "Then every fisherman and ghillie would be searching for it. What I believe is that someone is sitting on it, hiding it. Hoarding it. For what purpose, I don't know."

"For what purpose?" Josette flashed him a sudden grin. "Spending it, of course. Buying food and clothing, or maybe purchasing their way into the good graces of the king."

"Aye, maybe."

With Josette a step away from him, smiling her beautiful smile, Will was rapidly losing interest in the conversation. Her cheeks were pink from the cool air, and her mouth was soft and sensuous, lips parted. A mouth worth kissing. Often.

God's blood, he'd missed her. Will hadn't realized how deeply until this moment, when they stood atop the Highland aerie, miles of nothing around them. Josette was *here*, exposed to wind and weather, and to his longing.

He'd tried to push her from his thoughts while they were apart, to go on fighting battles and long-term, secret wars. But always Josette had been in the back of his mind—her dark eyes, the low note of her voice, her softness beneath him in the night, the joy of waking in daylight to find her beside him.

What she was truly doing here he didn't know, but he'd find out. Josette was compassionate, yes, but there had to be more to her decision to help these women. He'd need patience to learn all her secrets, and Will could be so very patient.

She stood too close, the dim light brushing her hair. Will couldn't stop himself reaching to smooth back a silken lock.

Josette stepped away before he could touch her, her smile vanishing. "I'm sorry, Willie—I'll tell you right now, this won't be like Salisbury."

Her words stung like a blow from that mad captain's fist. Damn, she knew how to kick him.

Will forced a shrug. "Of course it won't. There we had solid walls, glass windows, soft beds. Ah, Marsden House—so many memories. And the food. I recall that velvety smooth lemon bisque. Chef was a bloody genius."

Josette's eyes narrowed. "I believe you know what I mean."

"We were pretending to be man and wife." Will made his expression go reflective. "Sir William Jacobs and his bride, Anna. Returning to beloved Britain after a long sojourn on the Continent—ostensibly for Anna's health, but as she was in such fine fettle, speculation was they'd fled to the Continent to hide from creditors. An influx of income from a deceased distant relation had made certain all was well again. The guests at Marsden House winked and laughed behind our backs, just as I wished them to." Will twined his fingers and stretched his arms. "One of my finer creations, was Sir William."

Josette sent him a look. "'Twas not difficult for you to play a reprobate. Even a mostly reformed one."

Will leaned one elbow on the wall, feigning nonchalance. "And you were excellent as my frivolous wife, Anna, who loved to shop. Easy to understand why Sir William went bankrupt."

A hint of Josette's smile returned. "Those aristos were so distracted by feeling superior to us that they never tumbled to what you were really about. Yes, 'twas well done." She held up a hand as Will started to lean to her. "But not to be repeated here. You know why."

Yes, he did. Will had found the information he'd needed at the huge estate called Marsden House near Salisbury, which had caused one man to flee to the West Indies and saved a few Highlanders a pile of cash and stretched necks.

The mission had grown dangerous, both physically and to Will's heart. Josette had told him in no uncertain terms that it was the last time she followed him into peril. She had Glenna to take care of, and she could not risk her daughter being hurt.

Will had complied. He'd set her up as landlady of the boarding house in London, where Will had fondly supposed Josette still resided, with Glenna to help her run the place. Josette had assisted Alec and Celia when they'd eloped, and Celia, who never forgot a kindness, had kept up correspondence with her.

"If you're determined to search for the French gold I can't promise you'll be in no danger," Will said. "'Tis a dangerous business."

Josette scowled. "I meant, blast you, no liaison between you and me. The danger is comparable, I grant you, but this time, we'll be in separate bedrooms."

Will hadn't realized she'd been so angry at him. He'd granted her wish after Salisbury and walked away. That should have been that.

He hadn't walked away in his heart. Will could pretend all he wanted, but while he'd done everything in his power to make certain Josette was safe, happy, he regretted every moment apart from her.

He managed a faint smile. "Aye, well. A man can hope."

Josette didn't soften. "You *know* what happens when we come together. What always happens. I am weary of it. Never again."

"Truly, lass? I rather enjoy … coming together."

Her cheeks went a dark red. "When it ends, I mean. It's awful. I can't go through that again."

Ye think I can? Will wanted to shout. "I remember *you* asking to do the leaving." Will jabbed a finger at her, going hot when he imagined her seizing the finger and nibbling on it. "It's never me."

"Because of danger to my daughter," she said, eyes flinty. "And my sanity. You're a dangerous man, Will Mackenzie. You always will be."

That was true. But Will being dangerous had ensured his family stayed safe—that is, until they'd all run mad and joined Will's brother Duncan when he'd taken up with Prince Teàrlach in the Jacobite Uprising.

Will being dangerous had allowed his father and brothers to flee when hell descended, had ensured they'd been listed among the dead. Will continued to keep the king's men from learning they were alive, as he went about his business finding out secrets and taking vengeance here and there on those who'd murdered his fallen brothers, Duncan and Angus.

But one day ...

Will told himself that one day, he'd cease these wanderings and settle down, read books and keep his feet warm, hire a chef to make him lemon bisques, drink malt whisky, and go to bed with a fine woman.

That woman in his daydreams was always Josette. Children and grandchildren figured vaguely in this vision as well, and they had Josette's sable hair and deep brown eyes.

Will lifted his hands in surrender. "If ye don't want me near you, then why did ye bother rescuing me? You could have interrogated me about the gold and then left me tied to that stool."

"Because I didn't want to see you die." Josette's face remained uncomfortably flushed. "That major was going to kill you once he was finished with you. But that is not the point." She stepped back again, as though determined to put space between them. "You were the only one I could think of who could help us. Alec could perhaps, but he is in France, and he and Malcolm have families to look after. And I have to admit, you are the best of your lot when it comes to deception and intrigue. I had no choice but to ask you."

"I'm flattered." Will folded his arms once more, tamping down his frustration. "Major Haworth wouldn't have killed me in cold blood—he was a gentleman. He'd have tortured me until I was nearly dead and then given me over to his men to shoot, or had me sent to the

Tower to be tried, fair and square, before I was executed. But no matter. I had already planned my escape. I always do."

"You *thought* you had," Josette corrected with chilling patience. "They knew it, and were going to let you go, and then shoot you as you ran. Major Haworth was no fool."

He believed her. Letting Will slip away and then killing him as he escaped would put the major in a good light—he could boast that his captain and men had valorously shot a savage Highlander on the loose.

Will had had contingency plans even for that, but he'd come close to death in that camp and he knew it. He suppressed a shiver.

"How did ye discover all that, love?" he asked in a light tone. "Admirable work, by the way."

"No one pays attention to a serving woman. They say things in front of her they wouldn't speak about before their own soldiers. Helps if she's cheeky."

Most men completely underestimated women, Will had learned early in life, never believing that ladies could turn around and feed all they knew to people like Will. Josette had been instrumental in trapping the cardinal all those years ago, exposing his evil secrets and winning Will the gratitude of a king.

"I thank ye again, love." Suddenly he was tired of it all. He yearned to hold Josette and bury himself in her, forgetting the petty cruelties of the world. "Can I show you how grateful I am?"

Narrowly avoiding death always made his passions run high. Fever high. A mindlessness stole over him, and all he wanted was Josette in his arms. Best if he carried her to the relative softness of his pallet, but the stones at their feet would do.

Josette stepped from him again. They'd sashay all over the roof at this rate.

"Have you not heard a word I've said? I'm asking you for help, and that is all. There's no need for us to pretend to be man and wife this time—in any way whatsoever."

"Not even if I'm dying for you?" By heroic effort, Will stood his ground and didn't leap at her.

Josette's pretty throat moved in a swallow. "I'm sorry, Will. Not even if we're dying for each other. I can't. Not again."

That was the difference between men and lasses, Will's dad would say. A man could take comfort in lying with a woman and be done. A woman would want the comfort to continue and be crushed when it didn't.

Not that the old duke hadn't been madly in love with his own wife and nearly drowned in grief at her passing.

Will also knew he'd never be finished with Josette. Not now, not ever.

He made himself nod. "Ah well, lass. If that's what it's to be." He sighed like a man resigned, as though putting it behind him.

Josette knew good and well he hadn't decided to give in, but Will was wise enough not to pursue the matter at the moment. There would be time enough later. Will would make the time. He'd not let go of his dream, even if Josette didn't want anything to do with him at present.

He'd seen the spark in her eyes, the memories, the knowledge of what they'd had.

She didn't like the leave-taking at the end, she'd said. Neither did Will—it had always been stormy.

This time, it would not end like that. Because there would be no leave-taking.

He was Will Mackenzie, the best man in the world for covert campaigns.

He'd finish what he'd returned to Scotland to do, and when he was done, Josette and Glenna would remain with him. He'd make *them* his mission, and this one, he would not fail.

IN THE MORNING, AFTER A BREAKFAST OF LEFTOVER BREAD AND A FEW fried eggs, Josette led Will to the chamber where they did their planning.

Without expressly saying so, Will had decided to throw in his lot with them. Josette knew this from the way he'd charmed the ladies over the meager supper, he eating little so the others would have more.

This morning he'd risen in good spirits, helped Glenna gather eggs from the hens a few of the ladies had brought to the castle with them, and charmed them once again over a meal. Even Lillias didn't look as murderous.

The planning room had a carved table left over from when this castle had been a laird's grand home. The windows held real glass, though the panes were old and warped.

Will moved at once to the maps strewn across the tabletop and began studying them.

Sunlight through the thick window slid across the sharp line of his jaw and burnished his hair red. Will leaned his fists on the table, the linen shirt, too small for him, tight on his arms.

Josette saw when his eyes moved from the coves on the western coast—potential hiding places for the gold—to the north, above Loch Ness and Inverness.

"You can't go back there," Josette said in alarm. "You know you can't."

Will didn't look at her. "But I'll have to, love. It's what I came here for."

Josette moved to him and brushed her fingers over the map, touching the area that contained the lands of Will's family and his home, Kilmorgan Castle.

"Promise me ye won't," she said softly. "If you're caught … They'll kill you for certain. I don't think I could bear that."

"I can't promise." Will flicked his gaze to her, and Josette hid a flinch at the determination in his golden eyes. "I can't promise *never* to go. I need to." His look burned her a moment, then Will shook his head. "But I'll not do so now. Don't worry—I won't bring soldiers down on your ladies by doing something foolish."

Josette relaxed in relief. "Thank you."

His roguish look returned. "Only if you tell me how the devil ye came to be leading a bunch of Highland lasses in a lost cause. What pried ye out of your safe London boardinghouse?"

"If you believe London safe, then you're naive," Josette said.

"Mysie Forster was boarding at my house—she'd come to London to try to discover what had become of her sons. I couldn't help seeing how upset she was. After a time I convinced her to confide in me. Her sons are awaiting trial, she said, but they've been waiting a long time. Seems the Uprising was a bit of a mess for the clerks and lawyers who keep track of everything and everyone. There the lads sit, not being tried, but not let go either. She'd been told that a large bribe might get her sons released, but of course, she doesn't have that sort of money, does she? I remembered you talking of the gold, and I thought, if I could find it …"

She closed her mouth over any more words. The story of the gold had made her decide a few things, had given her a way out of a dilemma. But Will didn't need to know everything at the moment.

Will regarded her with his Mackenzie stare. "What are you talking about? I never spoke to you about the gold. Never saw you after it came to Scotland."

"Yes, it's been some time since you showed yourself in my doorway," Josette said dryly. "I meant you mentioned it to Alec and Celia, and Celia told me in her letters."

"Celia is perceptive. And a very good wife to Alec. He needs the peace she brings him."

Josette let herself smile. "Peace, you call it? They're very much in love, if I'm any judge. Couldn't keep their hands off each other. I suppose lying exhausted in bed every night is a sort of peace."

Will's answering grin flashed heat through her. "It is. I remember."

Josette stepped back. "None of that. We've agreed."

"You've convinced yourself we should have no truck with each other. *I* didn't precisely agree."

"*Will.*"

"Ye blush so hotly. 'Tis flattering, love."

His smile would unmake her. Josette remembered it over her in the dark, and how his eyes would drift closed when he entered her …

Will turned away, the air his plaid stirred chilling. He leaned over the map again, blunt fingers moving down the paper, tracing the line of the coast. Josette refused to think of how those fingers at one time had skimmed her body, her breasts, moved along her belly to the join of her legs.

She jerked her eyes open, having no idea she'd shut them, and sucked in a breath.

Will's hand stilled, and he frowned. "Hmm."

"What?" She stepped to his side. "What is it? Where are you looking?"

The maddening man only rubbed his chin, his eyes narrowing. "I wonder if—"

Outside, a dog barked. Will's head came up in alarm.

Their gazes met, Josette going cold with fear as a man's voice, raised in a shout, drifted through the ill-fitted diamond-paned windows.

CHAPTER 5

"here have ye got to, ye daft dog?" the man bellowed.

Will and Josette ran into each other trying to reach the window. Josette scrubbed at the pane to peer out, but the glass was too grimy and pitted to let them see much. The man below, whoever he was, began to sing.

Will headed for the door, his long legs taking him through to the stairs several strides ahead of Josette. She noted, as he plunged down the staircase and through the passages, that he'd already learned his way around the keep.

Ladies scurried from the kitchen and elsewhere, fear on their faces. Will signaled them to stay put. Glenna, poker in hand, tried to follow, but Josette shook her head.

"No," she whispered. "Stay hidden. Back to the kitchen with you."

Glenna did not obey, too curious for that, but at least she remained in the hall and did not try to follow Josette or Will.

The keep's main door was bolted with a stout piece of wood. It was a makeshift bolt, as Josette and the women had found the door lying smashed in the weeds when they'd first arrived.

Opening the door now involved lifting it from the frame, the hinges useless, but Will managed it with ease. He gave Josette a warning look and soundlessly slipped outside.

Josette saw no one in what was left of the courtyard. The walls surrounding the keep had fallen, except for the outer gate, which stood forlornly, guarding nothing.

Will moved to the tumbled stones of the ruined wall, silent as smoke. If Josette had ever thought she could keep Will here against his will, he now proved, before her eyes, that he could vanish whenever he liked.

A huge gray dog trotted around a clump of wall and made unerringly for Will. It was an enormous hunting dog, its wiry hair matted with grass and mud. Its tongue hung out as it gamboled to Will, tail wagging.

The situation might have been comical—the ghostlike Will Mackenzie easily spotted by a hound—except the dog barked in greeting, and the singing, which had warbled in the distance, ceased.

"Beitris! Where are ye, lass?"

The voice was thickly Scots, but speaking English. The owner of the voice ambled around the stones, a large walking stick propelling him.

He wore breeches of homespun cloth, a flapping linen shirt that had once been fine, and an open coat. The man had light brown hair loosely bound in a queue, tattered gloves, and boots that had seen much walking.

He called again to the dog, irritably, then spotted Will and hesitated, hand snaking to his side. Reaching for a knife or pistol?

Will stepped from the wall and stood fully upright in the sunshine. His plaids, once brightly dyed blue and green, floated on the stiff breeze that hadn't calmed since the ladies had arrived in this glen. Will looked like a warrior of old, ready to defend his castle from all enemies.

The man facing him stared, mouth open. The dog, oblivious to the tension, circled Will once then caught sight of Josette and ambled her way, joy in its brown eyes.

Will and the other man motionlessly assessed each other, while the dog bumped Josette's thigh. She absently pet it, her heart racing as she waited to see whether the man would attack before Will could strike.

Then the man threw open his arms. "Willie!" he yelled to the skies. "Will Mackenzie, as I live and breathe! I thought ye dead and gone, old son."

Will roared a wordless sound. The two men embraced, Will lifting the visitor off his feet as easily as he had Glenna. Will shook him like a bear toying with its prey, then dropped the man on his feet and thumped his shoulders with both hands.

Josette gripped the doorframe in worry, poised to rush to his aid. The thumping and hugging didn't mean Will trusted the intruder—he probably was checking him for weapons.

Will pasted a wide grin on his face. "Bhreac Douglas. What are you doing so far north? Or I should say, on this side of hell?"

Bhreac stepped back comfortably. "Roaming. The Borderlands are the devil of a place these days. Bloody British soldiers all over it. I thought you dead, my friend. Saw your name on the rolls—broke my heart. *No,* I said, *not old Will. It's a trick. Must be.* I knew it. I bloody well knew it."

He seized Will's arms and dragged him back against him.

Once the two had danced around again, Will untangled himself. "I *am* dead, Bhreac. Right? You've never seen me. Now that you've gone and shouted it to all the Highlands."

"Not a soul around to hear. Except ..."

The man's sharp blue gaze went straight to Josette in the doorway, with the dog now sitting at her feet. He laughed heartily.

"I see why ye've holed up here, Willie. Ye've found yourself a beautiful lass, Geordie's men are far away, and ye can live out your life in bliss. You always land on your feet, don't ye, old friend?"

"Aye, this is my Josette," Will said. "Come out, love. Meet a reprobate."

Josette left the sanctuary of the drafty doorway and walked carefully across the broken stones of the courtyard. She smiled in welcome, as though dwelling in a ruined castle far from anywhere was perfectly normal. The dog, which had latched itself to her, walked beside her, tucked against her thigh.

"Good morning, monsieur." Josette gave him a little curtsy, putting just enough coquettishness into the greeting.

"French, are ye?" Bhreac's eyes took on an interested gleam. "Very wise, very wise. Scottish lasses can be deadly."

Josette hid amusement—the Scottish lasses inside must be avidly listening.

"This is Bhreac Douglas, ancient enemy of the Mackenzie clan," Will said. "It's been so long, no one remembers why or what the original feud between our families was about. We celebrate it now. Another excuse for a dram."

"Aye, that it is," Bhreac said in a loud voice. Ye don't have one, do you, Willie? Roaming's thirsty work."

"Of course. Seventeen barrels of finest Mackenzie malt stored in the cellars."

Bhreac looked eager, and Will laughed out loud.

"Sorry to disappoint you, lad. Weak ale is the best I've got. I'm hiding out for me life, you know."

Bhreac's expression turned somber. "When I heard of you all dying, I shed a tear, I'm not ashamed to say. But you're well and alive. What about your brothers? Your dad? Is it all a lie? Please say it is."

Will shrugged, a bleakness in his eyes. "I wish it were. Duncan is dead—went down at Culloden. Angus in a skirmish in the north. The rest ..." He opened his hands.

Will was always adept at telling the truth while at the same time skirting around it.

"I'm that sorry," Bhreac said. "You Mackenzies are good men, no matter what others say of ye. I'm glad ye escaped—I take it Cumberland and his ilk have no knowledge?"

"And I'd be obliged if ye kept it that way," Will answered.

"Damned if I'll speak to a lot of British soldiers. Your secret is safe with me, Willie. And Madame." He gave Josette a flourishing bow. "Now then, I wasn't joking about thirst. Can ye spare me a bit of that weak ale? Maybe something edible? Haven't had a meal in I can't remember how long. I'm a stoic Scot, but even I have a limit."

Josette glanced at Will, waiting for his cue.

"Come inside." Will stretched out his arm to usher Bhreac into the keep. "Love, see what's in the kitchen, and we'll share it in the parlor. We live in the lap of luxury here, my friend—you'll see."

Josette nodded, understanding what he was telling her. Will would let Bhreac in—it would be strange to not offer hospitality to an old friend—but the ladies would remain hidden for now.

The wolfhound waited with Josette until Will and Bhreac had ducked inside. Bhreac turned to look for the dog and grinned when he saw it remaining with Josette.

"She likes you," he said. "Don't ye, lass? She's called Beitris."

Beitris wagged her tail, which was neither short nor long, the appendage banging Josette's skirt. She seemed happy enough to stay with Josette while the men disappeared into the castle.

Will gave Josette a look over his shoulder as he led Bhreac into a room that held a few stools and nothing more. He made a joke about elegant drawing rooms, but Josette caught the underlying message.

She hurried to the kitchen to explain what had happened and to keep the ladies quiet. The game had begun.

"ARE THEY TRULY ALL GONE, WILL?" BHREAC ASKED AS HE SIPPED THE ale Josette had brought in.

Josette had withdrawn, cheerfully saying she'd leave the menfolk to it, but Will knew she lingered outside, listening to every word. She didn't trust Bhreac, which was wise, but even more, she didn't trust Will. He knew he was considered a prisoner here, despite the fact he wasn't chained or locked in.

"Aye." Will decided to keep his answers simple. "Culloden finished us."

Bhreac took a thoughtful sip of ale. "That means *you* are Duke of Kilmorgan now. If you're the last."

Will looked horrified. "No, no. I'm not interested in any duking. The title has probably already been taken by the crown, King Geordie thinking 'good riddance to bad rubbish.' I'll stay plain Will Mackenzie, thank ye kindly."

Bhreac continued to study him, interest in his light blue eyes. "But if you prostrated yourself before the king, claimed ye never took up arms against him—I don't recall one man actually seeing you in battle

—ye might be granted the title in your own right. Ye could save your-self and your family's name."

Will shook his head. "They'd never believe me. And I'm not falling on my knees in St. James's Palace and begging for His Hanoverian's forgiveness. The words would choke me."

"Ah, I have it—ye dress up like a vacant-headed dandy and pretend you're a long lost Mackenzie come to claim the land. Cousin to a cousin. Ye've been in Canada or some such place, and don't even know who Charles Edward Stuart is."

Will pretended to consider this. Bhreac was always full of schemes and scams, getting away with them by the skin of his teeth. "What about all the Highlanders who'd recognize me on the spot?"

"Ye take a house in London, put on a wig, and mince about with lots of flowing lace. No one will twig it's you."

Will had to grin. "The point of being Duke of Kilmorgan is Kilmorgan. I'd want to go home."

As soon as Will said the word, longing gripped him. Unbidden came the memory of wind battering at the old castle, while inside, all was warm and filled with laughter—and because they were Macken-zies, shouting and arguing. The acrid odor of Alec's paints, the bite of whisky when a ten-year-old cask was broached, the sound of the pianoforte coming to life under Will's fingers—all flowed back at him and made him ache.

"Ye convince enough English lords you're the true heir, and you'd be able to go to Kilmorgan," Bhreac continued. "Your people there would know who ye truly were, aye, but they'd never betray you."

That was true. Kilmorgan men were loyal. "Why are you so adamant I take the title back?" Will asked him. "Looking to touch me for cash?"

Bhreac raised his hands. "I know I usually have something up my sleeve, but not this time. I just hate to see ye turned to a vagabond, eking out an existence *here*." He observed the bare stone walls and sticks of furniture in distaste. "Even when this was a proper home it was remote and melancholy. I remember it as a lad. If times are so hard, Will, go to the Americas. Always something for a resourceful man there."

"You're looking after me, as a friend, are you?"

"Why else?"

Will sent him a wise look. "When Bhreac Douglas gives ye fair words, beware."

Bhreac looked hurt. "I'd never betray you, old friend. I owe you too much."

Will sipped ale while he thought about how to answer, then he made a face and set down the tankard. First order of business—procure some decent drink.

"Yes, you would betray me if enough was in it for you," Will said good-naturedly. "You have before. But you do owe me, in fact. Now might be time to call in some favors."

"Ask away."

Bhreac waited, his demeanor affable. He had to be up to something, because he generally was.

His clothes were threadbare and travel-worn, but they'd begun as a costly suit, tailored for him, if Will were any judge. Bhreac's brown hair was thick and sleek, if dusty, the mane of a healthy man. He'd not fallen on hard times; he'd been wandering the Highlands for reasons of his own—with a giant dog Will had never seen before.

"Where did you get Beitris?" he asked.

"Won her." The answer was too matter-of-fact to be a lie. "Dicing with fools in Glasgow. They kept her muzzled and hobbled, that afraid of her. But they had it in their heads she was a guard dog—she growled and lunged at them often enough. Can't blame her. Poor thing just wanted a bit of a run in the open. She's a hunting dog with the sweetest nature, which they'd have known if they'd bothered to release her."

Bhreac had always been softhearted to animals and children, one reason Will had decided to rely on him on their first adventure long ago. Will had needed to warn a Highland man that the Black Watch was coming for him, but there were too many eyes on him. Bhreac, who'd sometimes worked for the Black Watch, had volunteered to take the message to the man to get himself and his wee daughters out of Scotland. Bhreac had completed Will's mission with skill, and the two had become friends.

"Very well, ye've won me over," Will said. "Ye can stay. First thing ye do is tramp over yonder hills and bring us back some decent ale and whisky. Maybe some oats so we can at least be eating bannocks. And if ye find any stray cattle, persuade them over this way. I'll make ye a list."

Bhreac laughed. He drained the last of his ale and wiped his mouth. "You're putting me on procurement duty? That I can do. And then ye'll tell me why you're holed up here instead of in a mansion in France with that lovely bit of stuff. What can ye be thinking?"

THE DOG REMAINED BEHIND. SHE STAYED NEAR JOSETTE AS BHREAC pulled a tricorn hat down over his eyes and tramped away with a stout walking stick he'd cut from debris in the courtyard. He took the donkey that had pulled Will to the castle with him, needing it to help him carry back supplies.

Josette and Will—and the dog—watched him go from what had been a battlement over the main door.

"You know you gave him our only means of transportation," Josette remarked, shivering in the cool breeze. She'd slung on a plaid shawl she'd found discarded in the castle, but it wasn't much help— the fabric had worn thin long before their arrival. Beitris leaned on Josette's legs and provided a bit of warmth. "Do you trust him?"

Will, characteristically, shrugged. "I have in the past. Doesn't mean he's entirely trustworthy, but he has no reason to betray me at the moment."

"I HAVEN'T HEARD YOU SPEAK OF HIM BEFORE." NOT THAT WILL WAS forthcoming about all his acquaintance. He'd told Josette much when they'd pretended to be married a few years ago, but the name Bhreac Douglas hadn't come up. Probably because it hadn't been necessary.

"He's a Borderlander," Will said. "His family has switched sides more often than your morning bacon. If it's expeditious to be loyal to the English, they are. When the Scots have the advantage, they're back over to the other side. His ancestor, Margaret Douglas, niece to the wife-killer, Henry the Eighth, was quite the intriguer. Bhreac's inherited some of that ability, though he mostly uses it to win at dice."

"A harmless trickster, then?"

Will watched Bhreac disappear into the mist. "I wouldn't say *harmless*. But he's a font of information. The trick is to pry it out of him without giving away what you don't want him to know."

"Like the whereabouts of a hoard of French gold?"

"Exactly, my love."

Will's flashing glance made her shiver again, but this time not from cold. "He sounds much like you," she said.

Will shook his head. "Not exactly."

"The trick is to pry it out of him without giving away what you don't want him to know," Josette repeated. "You try precisely the same strategy with me."

He blinked. "Do I?"

"You know you do," Josette said with conviction. "You tell me only what you wish. I've shared your bed and some of your life, and yet I know so little about you."

Surprise flickered in his whisky-colored eyes. "Do you think so?"

"I know so. Sometimes you're the Scot with the broad accent, wrapping yourself in plaid and rhapsodizing about bannocks. Sometimes you have no accent at all and dress in sober frock coats, going on about Latin historians and Sir Isaac Newton. Sometimes you speak as foul as a gutter urchin and gamble away your coins with tattered gloves. And then you'll quietly watch a sunrise as though you've never seen anything so beautiful." Josette took the sleeve of his shirt between her fingers. "Which of these is the real Will Mackenzie?"

A shadow crossed Will's face, elusive, gone before Josette could catch it. "All of them," he said softly. "And none of them."

His hand went to her cheek, warm against the wind tugging at Josette's hair and his frayed plaid.

Yesterday when he'd tried to touch her, Josette had stepped away. Today, Josette couldn't stop herself from closing her eyes and leaning into him.

She'd missed him, desperately missed him, though she'd been the one to tell him to go.

If things had been different—if she'd not had Glenna to protect, if Will hadn't insisted on chasing danger for the fun of it—she'd have gladly stayed with him. She'd have disguised herself as anyone he wished, joined him in his spying and intrigue, and laughed with him as they lay together in the night.

But she'd been a mother first and had known Will would never leave his perilous adventures behind him.

Will cupped her face with both hands. He traced her cheekbones with his thumbs, then his breath touched her mouth.

Josette snapped her eyes open. Will was so close, his eyes fixed on her like golden sunshine before his gaze flicked to her lips. Josette's heart pounded as Will closed the distance between them and gently kissed her.

His lips parted hers cautiously, as though he expected her to shove him away, turn her head, or tell him to leave her be.

Josette's reason said this was what she ought to do. Her heart and body, on the other hand …

She sank her fingers into his plaid and swept her tongue into his mouth, craving his familiar taste. Will stilled a moment, and then all his gentleness fled.

He dragged Josette against him, his hands hard on her back, and let the kiss turn fierce.

CHAPTER 6

*G*od's balls, how had he kept himself away from this woman? She was sensual heat, softness, all that was good in the world.

Josette closed her arms around him, anchoring him, as the wind tried to blow them from the wall, a Highland wind that couldn't be bothered going around them.

The cold couldn't prevail with Josette in Will's arms, heating him like the best fire, her mouth a place of warmth. Her lips were smooth and tender, her kiss coaxing him to surrender, to throw away the complexity of his life and simply be with her.

It was tempting. If they'd been born in another place, another time, he'd even now be in a cozy room, in a bed, with Josette, laughing, conversing, kissing, making love.

He slid his fingers under her cap, finding the silk of her hair. She dressed like a prim matron, but he'd known her in a filmy chemise, her hair tumbling down, a shy smile on her face.

He hardened, his need for her overtaking all other senses. Will pulled her closer, and Josette came readily. Her gown under the shawl was thin, only a skirt and a petticoat between her and the world. No panniers and other underthings in so primitive a place. She felt him— he knew she did—because she stiffened.

Their mouths eased apart. "Will," she whispered.

Admonition? Or wanting more?

Will decided he liked the second choice. He kissed her again, smiling into it when her hands moved down to his hips and then to his backside, which was bare under the scratchy breeches.

Her breasts rested against his chest, and all Will could think of was loosening her bodice and dragging it downward so he could kiss and lick her flesh.

Josette made a noise in her throat, her lips answering his, her body pliant under his hands. She wanted him, he realized with gladness. Wanted him the same intense way he wanted her. That had never changed between them.

A cold chill struck his side, and Will flinched, still tender from his earlier wounds. Josette pulled back with a gasp, and then began to laugh.

The dog had pushed between them, her blunt nose bumping Will through a tear in his shirt, clearly wanting her share of the attention.

Will's amusement died when he saw Lillias at the top of the stairs, her skirts held free of the loose stones, her glare in place.

She turned her angry look to Josette but did not begin a tirade, to Will's surprise. Perhaps she *expected* Josette to be locked in an embrace with Will as soon as she possibly could.

Josette flushed, tucking strands of hair back under her cap. She did not apologize, did not hasten to explain. One thing Will loved about Josette was that she never felt she needed to justify to others what she did.

Lillias made a noise of derision. "While ye're enjoying yourselves, did ye think that maybe that man is off to tell soldiers we're here?"

"He won't," Will said. "Bhreac looks out for himself and has no love for British soldiers."

Josette finished straightening her cap. "She has a point, Will. If he seizes opportunities as you say, he might take money from the soldiers in return for information."

"True. But if he brings the soldiers back, we'll know right away that he means to betray us."

Lillias's eyes widened. "And we'll be sitting ducks. The logic of a Mackenzie."

Will busied himself petting the dog, enjoying the warmth of her wiry fur. "He won't find us at all. There's a fine view of the glen from here, miles and miles—soldiers can only come from that way." He pointed across steep hills beyond the loch. "We'll see them in plenty of time to escape out the back way."

When Josette and Lillias looked at each other blankly, Will raised his brows. "Ye did scout out the escape route, did ye not? Och, ladies, you're lucky I decided to help you." He gave Beitris a final pat and headed for the stairs. "Well, come on then. I'll guide ye through it. But bring a lantern or two. 'Twill be deadly dark."

JOSETTE'S CURIOSITY ROSE AS WILL LED THEM UNERRINGLY THROUGH the keep and down a set of broken steps that led to the old kitchens. These rooms were too ruined for use, which was why they'd moved their cooking space to the upstairs chamber with the newer fireplace.

Will halted at the remains of an old hearth and removed blocks to reveal a rectangular opening supported by stout columns of wood, gray with age. The columns were solid, cut from whole trunks and kept moist beneath the earth.

"Where did they find trees?" Josette asked, touching a pillar in wonder. The surrounding hills were bleak, no forests to be seen.

"Hauled them from elsewhere," Will answered. "In the old days, Highland lairds had power, men, and wealth. We weren't always poverty-stricken wretches."

"I'm sorry," Josette said quickly.

Will shrugged. "'Tis the way of things. No one is rich forever. Or poor forever. The world moves in cycles. A sine curve, my brother Mal would say, as though we all know what the devil he's talking about."

He ducked beneath the opening and signaled her to follow.

Behind Josette came Lillias, and behind her, the rest of the ladies, and Glenna and Beitris. Not one of them had wanted to remain in safety while Josette and Will explored, and she'd known it would be fruitless to ask them to. The English considered Highland *men* strong-willed—it was clear they'd never met Highland women.

Josette of course had every right to order Glenna to stay behind, but she also knew that her daughter would wait until they were gone and follow anyway. Beitris stayed next to Glenna, Glenna already adoring her.

Will led them through the tunnel, the candle inside his iron lantern barely cutting the darkness. The feeble glow showed a passage of brick, strong and squared, running straight ahead of them.

"Every castle in these parts has a covert way out," Will explained as they walked. "Ye never know when your neighbors will decide to besiege ye and try to starve ye into submission. This way, ye can flee, or at least bring supplies in."

"If every castle has tunnels, doesn't everyone know where they come out?" Josette asked. "Wouldn't the neighbors simply be waiting at the other end?"

"Not if the castle dweller is clever. The ways are hidden, sworn to secrecy within the clan." Will sent her a dusty grin. "I, too, lass, always wondered about that. Secrets must have leaked. But now, no one remembers. These days clan wars are arguments across tavern tables —or long, silent grudges." Or Highlander betraying Highlander in the Uprising, but Will decided not to mention that.

"I'm glad I missed the old days," Lillias said. "I barely have patience with the new days."

"You'd have been pouring pitch down on the heads of rival clansmen with the best of them," Will said. "Ah, here we are."

They'd walked, by Josette's calculations, a mile, perhaps more. Her feet were beginning to ache, and Glenna, the most curious girl on earth, had wondered out loud how much longer it would be.

Will kicked aside rubble and started to climb what looked like steps cut into the wall. They seemed precarious, but Will scrambled up without worry.

"Not far now." He sounded undaunted, animated, as though he'd done nothing so entertaining in a long time.

Josette eyed the crumbling, rather slimy staircase in distaste. Will was clambering up in a merry way, and Josette did not want him to think her too fastidious to follow.

Holding her skirts high, Josette ascended after him, hearing the dog panting and scrabbling behind her.

"He could be taking us to our deaths," Lillias said, out of breath.

"Ye didn't have to come," Glenna said. "Go back and wait for Mr. Douglas to return with English soldiers."

Josette called down to her. "A grand idea, Glenna. You take Lillias back. 'Tis too rough here for the pair of you."

"Bugger that." Glenna grinned up at Josette around the bulk of an eager Beitris. "I'm coming with you. I'm sixteen now, Mum. Ye can't tell me what to do anymore."

"Ha. I will argue with you about *that* later. If you fall and hurt yourself, I won't be kind. And watch your language."

Glenna didn't answer as she picked her nimble way up the staircase. From the sound of it, none of the ladies had made the sensible choice of returning to the warmth of the keep.

The staircase rose a long way, the walls changing from stone to shored-up earth. Josette tried not to compare it to a tomb, but the similarities gnawed at her. They'd be climbing out through a hole as though emerging from a grave, if there even was a way out. The entrance might be buried, walled off, or closed with a locked gate, to which no one had a key.

No matter, Josette reasoned. They'd simply go back. But still, the walls pressed at her, the air becoming thick.

Only Will's strong legs in the awful breeches, large feet in shapeless shoes, kept Josette going. She let her gaze linger on his backside, which was as firm and interesting as she remembered.

The darkness lightened, and with light came a breath of air. Josette heaved a sigh of relief and hurried behind Will up the final steps. At the top was a small square room with a grate set into a stone wall, the opening just large enough for a person to climb through. Gray light and a breeze wafted through it.

"The grate will be locked, I suppose," Josette said as she caught her breath.

"It is. 'Tis also well rusted."

Will banged the grate with his shoulder. The iron bars creaked mightily before the entire grating popped free and landed in rocks and weeds outside the hole. The opening, about four foot square, looked out over a long stretch of tumbled land, not a house or farm in sight.

Josette had grown up in southern France, which had been rife with farmer's fields, vineyards lining the hills. All had been lush, green, growing. She'd lived in cities as an adult, but even Paris and London had parks and trees.

She had difficulty growing used to the forbidding land of Scotland, which could some moments be bleak and others spread forth the most beautiful glory she'd ever seen. It was wild, untamed, rugged, like the Highland man leading the way out of the hole, his long legs wriggling as he crawled free.

Will turned and reached for Josette, gripping her arms with hard hands as he tugged her with great gentleness out of the earth. She wanted to hang on to him as he lifted her, to kiss his warm mouth again, to wrap herself in him and shut out the world. She'd told him she'd keep herself distant from him, but his presence was already crumbling her resolve.

The opening led to the side of a hill that slanted sharply down to a swollen creek that rushed through a narrow valley. Will released Josette as soon as she was free, and she slithered around him to sit on soft grass.

Beitris, with a grunt of effort, scrambled out, helped by Will with his hands on the scruff of her neck. Beitris shook herself as soon as she was free and waited for Glenna to crawl out with Will's assistance.

Glenna stood up, surefooted on the slope. "Ain't it pretty?" she asked the world in general.

The Highlands spread before them, the tip of Strathy Castle, their erstwhile home, small in the distance to the south.

"A good place from which to watch one's enemy." Will stretched out on the grass beside Josette, propped back on his elbows. "You'd know when your attackers gave up on the siege and retreated, or you could round up loyal clans and come upon them from behind."

Lillias peered out of the hole, Mysie behind her. "At least we know we can escape. I'm going back. Work to be done."

She gave Josette and Will a disapproving look before disappearing into the dark. The other ladies must have decided to go with her, because none tried to emerge.

Josette had no desire to immediately return to the drudgery of cooking and cleaning. She'd done that enough in her life to enjoy a reprieve when she had one.

When she'd been a celebrated artist's model in Paris, she'd dressed in finery and done no drudging at all. In her boarding house in London, she'd hired servants, though she'd assisted with plenty of the work. But that had been different—she'd labored but she'd had tenants and income, the results of running a good business.

Now she was back to drudging, eking out survival in this place while they sought the impossible. She might never have come but for that knock on the door in the middle of the night, a message that had chilled her to the bone.

Glenna, who thought of this only as a fine adventure, wandered the hillside. "If the men of the castle were so clever to have this escape route," she asked Will. "Why's it a ruin? Why didn't they round up an army and return to save it?"

Will laced his hands behind his head and studied the cloud-strewn sky. "Now that's an interesting tale. Strathy was abandoned only recently, about thirty years ago. The laird of this land threw in with the wrong side of the uprising in 1719 that destroyed Eilean Donan Castle—the English blew up a huge pile of gunpowder stashed there —and ended at the battle of Glen Shiel. The laird of Strathy got himself killed, his men outlawed, his castle left derelict. I suppose this ruin is left as a lesson—though probably it's empty because the land around here is hard for farming, and even for running cattle."

Glenna sat down, arms around her slim knees, leaving the dog to wander on her own.

"Are Highlanders always so rebellious?" she asked Will. "How long before you have another uprising?"

"There won't be any more, I'm thinking," Will said. "World's changing. More Scots are finding out there are places beyond our glens and fields, more money in banking or trading or scientific discoveries than in trying to raise crops in the rocky hills. But I don't think Highlanders will be kept down forever. 'Tis in our nature to fight. We don't like others telling us what to do with our lands, our people. One day we'll throw the English out and go back to fighting amongst ourselves, which is what we do best."

A breeze fluttered Will's plaids against the brown green heather, making him look like an ancient clansman taking his ease before running off to another battle.

"How do you know so much?" Glenna asked. "All about the uprisings and the battles at castles? Were you there?"

Will gave her a startled glance then relaxed into a laugh. "I know I'm ancient to ye, lass, but I'm not *that* ancient. What happened at Eilean Donan Castle and Glen Shiel took place when I was a wee lad. But I listen to the tales, talk to people. And ..." He let his eyes go wide. "I read things. Sometimes a whole book."

Glenna wrinkled her nose at his teasing. She sprang to her feet, restless, and wandered off again, Beitris at her side.

Josette rested her cheek on her arm as she regarded Will, his dark red hair stirred by the wind. "Books, eh? You really have read Sir Isaac Newton and all?"

"His *Principea*?" Will nodded. "Every word. He goes on a bit, but it's interesting. And Galileo. Same thing." He sat up, pushing his hair from his eyes. "Makes me glad I live in these times, even with the brutal soldiers chasing us. Did ye know, in Galileo's day, you could be tortured and burned alive just for saying the earth goes around the sun?" He huffed a laugh. "The Inquisition forced Galileo to state that his ideas were simple mathematical pleasantries, not meant to be taken seriously. At least now we're only persecuted if we don't kiss the right king's boots, instead of for movements in the heavens we can't do anything about. If God wants the earth to race around the sun, I figure that's His business."

Josette lost herself in his voice. It had been a long time since she'd heard his baritone rumble, words washing over her as he whispered to her in the night.

Will could talk—about anything and everything. He'd ramble here and there, dredging up stories about old Scotland, then tell her bits of gossip about the King of France, or go on about the history of Chinese porcelain.

He carried so much in his head, Josette marveled. Will had told her once he couldn't help himself—he learned a thing and he remembered it forever. Crowded up there, he'd say, tapping his forehead, which was why he had to let it out in long streams of speech.

Josette didn't mind. She lay back, letting his words wash over her. No matter the dire circumstances that had brought the two of them together again, she blessed the Lord she could be with him again, and listen to his chatter while touched by his warmth.

WILL AND JOSETTE, WITH GLENNA AND BEITRIS, RETURNED TO THE castle to find the ladies cooking and Bhreac not yet returned. Will left Josette in the kitchen and returned to studying the maps, ideas niggling at him.

The problem with Josette being here was that Will had difficulty concentrating when she was near. Even now as he examined the map, the memory of kissing her on the battlement, her hands seeking, kept intruding. That and lying with her on the grass in the sunshine, as though they had all the time in the world to talk, to laugh, to become reacquainted in all ways.

If Lillias hadn't interrupted them on the wall, Josette might have let her hands wander more, finding Will hard and hot for her. They'd shared passionate moments in awkward spaces before, touch working wonders.

Damn. Will forced himself to focus on the map again. Something had caught his eye—a place, a name. He leaned down, shutting out the stone walls, the chill, the voices and laughter of the women below.

It would come to him. Will's memory lost little, but sometimes it took a moment for him to pull a thought from the depths. Focusing on one object, letting the rest of the world go dark, helped.

Ah ... perhaps ...

Josette rushed into the room. "He's back. Will, Mr. Douglas has come back. And he says he has news."

Her scent, her voice, her presence, swept over Will and broke his concentration once more.

He sighed, marked the place on the map with a stone, and straightened. "We'd best go see what it is, then."

CHAPTER 7

*B*hreac had gone straight to the kitchen and was seated at the table by the time Will and Josette reached it, spooning hot soup into his mouth. He seemed not at all surprised to be watched by more than half a dozen women, from which Will concluded he'd seen them or discerned them no matter how they'd hidden when he'd first arrived.

While he'd been gone, they'd decided they couldn't very well keep the presence of the ladies from him, but they could be careful what they told him.

"Wind's turned bitter," he said by way of greeting. His face was red and chapped, and his hands, now free of gloves, were a bit blue.

A large canvas sack lay open on the work table, Mysie unpacking it. She brought out two small casks and more sacks, which she peered into with satisfaction.

"Broach the whisky, love," Bhreac said. "Just the thing."

Mysie handed one cask to another woman and put the second under her arm. "Nay. When men begin the drinking, nothing useful gets done. You'll have them when the day is over."

Bhreac looked aggrieved. "Bloody hell, Will. Are ye going to let them get away with that?"

Will hid his amusement. "I'm here on their sufferance, so yes. Josette said you had news?"

Bhreac nodded. The women, including Josette, pretended to carry on with tasks, but they watched and listened.

"There's a few ships in Loch Broom, and they have plenty of guns. Not sure why the Royal Navy feels it necessary to patrol near Ullapool, but they're there. Villagers 'round about are not happy, but so far, the ships are hovering off the coast, not doing much of anything."

"Looking for someone?"

Bhreac shrugged. "Mayhap. But it can't be you—you're dead."

Probably couldn't be Will, but he kept this to himself. "I'm not the only Highlander that's a thorn in their side."

Josette sent him a worried look. How could they search for the gold with naval ships prowling? Will wanted to reassure her that he had another destination in mind, but he didn't want to reveal too much in front of Bhreac.

"'Tis good knowledge to have," Will said. "I thank ye."

"Are ye going to tell me now why you've gathered so many women about you?" Bhreac grinned, but curiosity flickered in his eyes.

"Can ye picture me in any other circumstance but surrounded by beautiful women?" Will asked with a serious expression.

Lillias scoffed, and a few others rolled their eyes.

Bhreac, finished with his soup, pushed his bowl away. "I'd say they barely put up with you. But it's all right. Ye don't have to tell me. That way I can't reveal any secrets."

Will leaned against the table and folded his arms in an unworried stance. He knew Bhreac felt the tension in the room, and Bhreac knew that Will knew he did. They'd danced around each other a long time.

The money the French had sent to help the Jacobite cause hadn't been a few caskets of coins. It had been enough to fund an army through a winter. The fact that such a huge sum had simply vanished was deeply suspicious.

And now Bhreac had turned up out of nowhere, worming his way into the castle in his good-natured way. Even more suspicious.

"I'm teaching them how to eke out a living," Will said. "Soldiers forced them out of their homes, and they had nowhere to go. What I'd like is to convince them to take what they can and go to the Continent, but you know what Highlanders are like about Scotland."

"Aye, Borderlanders are much the same." Bhreac scraped back his stool and stood up. "Well, I won't press ye. But know this, Will. If ye need me, I'm here to help. I promise you."

The look he gave Will held nothing but guileless interest. Will returned the look with one as ingenuous, and Bhreac grinned.

He left the room, saying he'd find himself a chamber out of the way and sleep. The merry tune he whistled drifted after him.

Beitris raised her head and watched him go, then lay back down with a grunt. She'd found a warm place by the fire, and had already learned that her mournful brown gaze would quickly send a scrap her way.

Will surveyed the eight Highland women who gazed back at him without fear. They'd come from all corners and clans—besides Lillias and Mysie, there were two Campbells, a lady who'd married into a branch of the Mackenzies, a Sinclair, and two MacLeods. Their men had fought and had been captured for a lost dream.

If any deserved that French gold, it was these lasses.

Will gave them a bow, an acknowledgment of their courage and determination. He'd retrieve that gold for them, and they'd all live to tell the tale. He swore it on his blood.

~

"YOU'VE DECIDED TO HELP." JOSETTE FOUND WILL IN THE MAP ROOM not long later, as she thought she might.

He glanced over his shoulder as she entered. "I've said so."

"I know you *said*. But now you've decided. Before, you'd planned to play your own game."

"Ah, she knows me so well," Will said to the wall above the table. "Frightening, that."

Josette let out a breath. "Well, I'm glad you've come to see it our way."

"What do *you* want the gold for, Josette?" He turned to face her in one of his quick moves, his golden gaze searching.

"To take Glenna back to France," she said quickly. "To live in a cottage with a garden and be done with drudgery."

Not a lie. Josette did plan to do so when it was all over. She'd seek a place no one could find them or threaten them ever again.

Will studied her, looking for truth. Well, he'd find it soon enough. Will Mackenzie was the best man she knew. And yet, she'd leave him behind to save Glenna. He understood that, and didn't hold it against her.

He turned away as though they hadn't had a mute argument and resolution.

"I have an idea where to start looking for the gold," he said. "You won't like it, but it's worth a try."

Josette came to the table and leaned to look where he pointed, trying not to enjoy the warmth of him so close.

She'd feared he'd be determined to go to Kilmorgan, no matter what, but he indicated a patch of land on the western coast. It lay across a loch from the Isle of Skye, very near the castle of Eilean Donan he'd told her about earlier today. Josette wondered if this was why he'd related the tale.

"What is there?" she asked.

"The estate of an Englishman who hates Scotland. Sir Harmon Bentley. He made a pile of money in the Caribbean and settled here to enjoy his gains. Was an MP and then in the Cabinet, and English to the bone. He surrounds himself with gentlemen he entices to fish on his wild Scottish estate, and ships in every bit of luxury he can."

Josette gazed at the innocuous spot. "Why would such a man need the French gold? Or know where it is?"

"He's a fraud," Will said. "He spends lavishly, but he's chosen this remote area because creditors in London stay home and go after easier prey. If he thought a shipload of gold was somewhere in the Highlands, he'd make it his business to know where it was and try to get his hands on it. Even if he doesn't have it, he might know where it's likely to be."

"I see." Will knew about people, and if he said this man could have information, then he probably did. "Why wouldn't I like it?" she asked.

"Because the only way into his confidence is to be covert. He'd never tell a Scotsman. But he might boast about the lost gold to Sir William Jacobs and Anna, his lovely wife."

Josette went cold as she stared at him in dismay. "You want us to pretend to be husband and wife again? But Sir William and Anna disappeared after Marsden House. Never to be heard from again."

"Returned to the Continent after they spent too much as usual," Will said, waving the difficulty away. "Sir Harmon, a fellow profligate will believe that. And if he has guests—and he will—if they happen to know our earl from Salisbury or by chance have met Sir William and Anna before, it will be much less dangerous if we play the same roles."

Josette folded her arms. "I take your point, but this is the Highlands. Won't those who live near Sir Harmon know you as Will Mackenzie? The servants who work at the house might recognize you at the very least."

Will shook his head. "Sir Harmon brings an English staff with him, won't even use a Scottish ghillie—thus incurring the wrath of every villager in the area. The English servants don't venture out much, terrified of the barbarian Scots beyond the gates. If villagers do happen to glimpse me, I doubt they'd betray me to a man like Sir Harmon."

"You are very certain I will do this with you." Josette hugged herself more tightly. The last time they'd gone on this sort of venture, things had become dire, and not just because the villain of the piece had tried to kill them. "Why can't you go in alone? Why do you need a wife?"

"More believable," Will said, the answer too quick. "A gentleman turning up out of the blue is suspicious. But a man and wife making a tour of Scotland, needing a place to stay, and blessing their stars they found a civilized Englishman, is much more credible."

"Yes," Josette admitted reluctantly. "It's impossible, though." She regarded him with triumph. "Where will we find a coach and good horses that can stand the Highland roads—or lack thereof—not to mention fine clothes? We look like laborers, at present, and we can't very well turn up with a donkey and cart. We'd never be let in the gate."

"That ye can leave to me. And Bhreac. Lucky he turned up so he can run errands for me—I don't think you and your ladies will let me out of your sight."

"Lucky," Josette repeated. "Strangely so."

"Aye, well, he comes and goes—this is as usual for him. Meanwhile, I say we make use of him."

Josette liked intrigue to be simple, but Will loved it complicated—the more so, the better. "What I understand is that you'll have your way, Will Mackenzie."

Will flashed her his wicked grin, the one she could never resist. "Aye. I'm glad you agree with me."

Josette threw up her hands in exasperation. "Very well, I'll do it—not that you've asked, or said please. I'll do it for the sake of the ladies and their menfolk, but not for your enjoyment. I'll pretend to be your wife, but *only* in the presence of others. When we are alone … I have already told you, this will not be like Salisbury."

"I know." Will's smile remained in place, his eyes holding an intensity that was difficult to meet. He didn't touch Josette or reach for her —he kept his hand on the table and several feet of space between them.

But he might as well have entwined her in his arms and not let go. Josette knew that accompanying him to this house would be walking into the lion's den. The most dangerous man in there wouldn't be Sir Harmon and his English friends. Not to her heart anyway.

"Blast you," Josette growled. "You keep your distance, understand?"

Will took a step back and lifted his hands. "I'd never do a thing you didn't want, my Josie."

He spoke the stark truth. Anything he and Josette had shared, she had rushed toward, welcomed, and held close. The pain at the end had been her own fault, her reward for trying to touch a shooting star.

However Bhreac managed to procure a coach and four, as well as a pile of satin and silk clothes, he did it. There was even a pouch of coins to go with it—they'd need to tip the servants if they wanted hot water in the morning, and also have money for cards and other games ladies and gentlemen would be expected to play.

Will told Josette it was not wise to inquire too closely how Bhreac had obtained everything. But like Will, the man knew everyone in Scotland.

Josette's difficulty was not the disguise but persuading the others that this was the best means of obtaining information.

"I should go with you," Glenna argued, sullen. "I can be your lady's maid. I'm a Londoner enough for them to believe it."

"You also look enough like me for them to believe you my daughter," Josette returned firmly.

"I can pry information out of the servants, you know that. Same as I do at home." To Glenna, "home" was the London boarding house. She adored London, and Josette knew it would be a wrench for her when they had to leave for France. But leave they must.

"This is far more dangerous," Josette said.

Glenna clenched her hands. "I don't want to stay here with these Scottish biddies. They talk so I don't understand them, and Lillias constantly scolds me."

"For heaven's sake." Josette rarely shouted at Glenna, but lately the girl, on the uneasy edge of womanhood, was driving her distracted. "I am not having you running about the house of a country squire filled with the Lord knows who. You are a pretty young woman, and if you dress as a maid, you will be fair game for any of them who want an easy tumble. If you fight them, 'twill be *you* they blame, and if ye hurt any of them trying to get free, they'll arrest and hang you. This is what happens in the houses of English country gentlemen."

Glenna's mouth hung open, her rebelliousness evaporating. "But Will and you will be there," she said faintly.

"And if Will betrays himself in attempt to save you, he'll be taken as a traitor, and they do horrible things to traitors. Do ye want that, daughter? To be the means of his death? Perhaps mine for harboring him?"

Glenna's eyes fixed, her breath coming fast. She silently shook her head.

Josette softened. "Now, I don't mean to frighten you, love, but all I say is true. It's best you stay here, out of harm's way. Lillias is only afraid for her husband. Try to see things from her point, and if you don't understand the Scottish talk, ask them to teach you. You pick up languages quick enough."

Glenna's bravado had evaporated, and tears stood in her eyes. Josette gathered her in an embrace, burying her face in Glenna's soft hair.

From the moment Glenna had been placed into her arms by a rather surly midwife, Josette had loved and felt a sense of intense protectiveness for this girl. Glenna was now tall and beautiful, ripe for a gentleman with no scruples to prey upon.

She'd die for this child. It might come to that, Josette knew. She walked a thin line, like acrobats she'd seen tumbling on a rope stretched tight ten feet above the ground.

She'd learned intrigue from Will Mackenzie. If Josette were to survive this, she'd have to have him teach her to be a master at it.

THE CARRIAGE COULD NOT CLIMB THE ROCKY, BOGGY PATHS TO Strathy Castle, so Will and Josette, with Bhreac, walked to a coaching inn near a village on the shores of Loch Canaird.

Will kept himself well cloaked with a hat pulled down over his eyes, stooping to hide his height. He let Bhreac and Josette deal with the man and wife at the coaching inn, pretending to be a servant in the background.

Bhreac paid the ostler for looking after their rig and Will climbed to the coachman's box. Josette emerged from the inn with the bundles of clothes Bhreac had procured and let Bhreac hand her into the coach, he joining her.

A few miles down the rutted road, with nothing but the sea in sight, Will stopped the carriage and leapt down. He and Bhreac changed their clothing behind a boulder, giving Josette privacy to dress inside the coach.

"I need a maid," she said through the open window. "It is impossible to lace myself. I ought to have relented and brought one of the ladies with me, I suppose."

Will, clad now in velvet breeches, silk stockings, and a brocade coat dripping with so many ribbons and laces the fabric could scarcely be seen, opened the door and heaved himself inside. The sight of Josette half-dressed, holding her bodice modestly over her loose corset, nearly undid him.

"Any of our ladies would betray themselves too quickly," Will answered to distract himself. "Even the gentlest of them. Sir Harmon quartered British soldiers last year and has handed every Highlander within fifty miles of his land over to the English, whether the Highlanders fought for Prince Teàrlach or not." He studied Josette in her undress, and grinned. "You'll just have to make do with me."

She did not like the prospect, Will could see, but Josette was ever practical. She sighed and turned around so he could lace her corset.

The carriage lurched forward. Bhreac, having donned coachman's livery, had taken the reins.

Josette landed on Will's lap. He enjoyed her soft body squirming there before he eased her away and continued with the corset. He knew to tighten the laces in the middle of her back, not top or bottom, to draw the stays to the natural curve of Josette's body.

The bodice went over this, a pretty thing of green silk trimmed with blue ruched ribbon, and a stomacher embroidered with entwined flowers.

"Lovely," Will breathed in her ear. "Bhreac did well."

"He knows much about women's clothing," Josette said. "Perhaps you ought to question him about that."

Will chuckled. "I know much about it too, my lady love. Do you need help with your skirts?"

Josette sent him a dark look and scrambled to her side of the carriage. She shoved the petticoat into place and slid into the overdress, tying tapes to connect the two.

Will couldn't cease watching her, bathing in every moment. "I am remembering the other times I've dressed you. At Salisbury, in Paris, and that small coaching inn outside London."

Josette kept her face averted, her loosened curls moving on her shoulders. She'd transformed in an instant from the matronly housekeeper to a lush gentlewoman used to finery and men's attentions. Josette took off and put on personas nearly as easily as Will did.

"I remember too," she said, her face flushed.

Will sat back, flipping ribbons out of his way. He'd be used to the ostentatious clothes by the time they reached their destination, but they certainly were annoying. How did dandies put up with them?

"Will?" Josette said, peeping up at him. "I need to tell you something."

"Mmm?" Will's imagination sent him all kinds of places, but he braced his feet on the floor and answered nonchalantly. "What is that, my love?"

Josette looked unhappy. Her eyes filled with anguish as she said, "I need to tell you the truth. I was not searching for you only because I needed your help. I was tasked to find you, and betray you. The ladies looking for the gold simply gave me the opportunity. I think it only fair that you know."

CHAPTER 8

ill went very still. Josette waited for his reaction—would he dismiss her warning or grow enraged and throw her bodily from the coach?

Emotions Josette couldn't read flickered through his eyes. Will was a man of deep feeling, she'd come to know, but he also hid those feelings well. Some thought him a ne'er-do-well who flitted through life not caring whom he hurt, but Josette knew better. He hid pain beneath his carefree nature, along with fears that his missions caused the misery of others.

He stretched out his long legs, clad now in finest silk, his shoes supple leather with diamonds on the buckles. His legs brushed her skirts, the warmth of him palpable.

"And who gave you this task?" Will asked quietly.

"Glenna's father."

Will jolted. After all these years, Josette had at last surprised him, but the victory was bitter.

"Glenna's father, the British army officer?" he asked.

Josette hid her own surprise. She'd never told Will exactly who had fathered Glenna, but she ought to have known Will would ferret it out. Not from Glenna, who likewise did not know.

"To be fair to *him*, I believe he had no choice," Josette said. "His wife's family is rather formidable." Indeed Oliver had been worried, haunted, looking far older than his nearly forty years when he'd met her in a public house in London. He'd sent a message late one night, and Josette, heart in her throat, had slipped out to see him.

"Fair?" Will's voice was calm and he kept his hands quiet on his lap, but his eyes glinted with anger. "Captain Oliver Chadwick, officer of the Seventy-First Foot Guards. In France with his regiment and couldn't resist a pretty young Frenchwoman fresh from the countryside. He has a passionate affair with her, which results in the beautiful Glenna. Except the captain has not mentioned he is married and leaves France immediately upon learning she carries his child, abandoning the lady. Her father has recently passed away, mother long deceased, and she is left to fend for herself. Tell me why I should be fair to this man?"

"You are well informed." Josette's breath came fast, old hurts rising. "He's Colonel Chadwick now."

"It is my way to be well informed. When I first looked at you, I was thunderstruck. I didn't trust myself near you. So I found out all I could, to make certain I wasn't about to commit a terrible blunder."

"What blunder was that?" Josette asked softly. "Having an affair de couer with me?"

"No, stealing you from someone else." Will drew a breath to say more, then she saw him check himself. *Never give yourself away*, he'd always told her. *Keep your innermost secrets secret.*

Josette had found that good advice—except she couldn't seem to abide by the rule around him.

"Never mind." Josette waved her hand. "He turned up after disappearing for sixteen or so years, and told me he'd come to take Glenna away."

Will sat up sharply, his nonchalance evaporating. "What? Why?"

"I don't know. He certainly had no interest in her before. I told him, quite adamantly, that I'd deny with every breath Glenna belonged to him. But he frightened me. He could take her away, and I wouldn't be able to stop him."

Will's tone softened. "I know."

A woman was not considered related to her own child by the

bizarre laws of England. The man's seed contained the whole of the baby, so they said, who nestled inside the woman for most of a year before she bore it. This made the child the father's, not the mother's.

"What did you promise?" Will went on. The anger had left his voice—he simply wanted to know.

"I didn't mean to promise anything. I asked Colonel Chadwick what he wanted, mostly so he would go away. I assumed money, as he didn't look particularly well. I'd find a way to get any sum if I had to. He told me his wife had passed away, which would explain his pallor —I also know he was very dependent on his father-in-law, and perhaps his father-in-law had tightened the purse strings once his daughter was dead. Then Chadwick took me to a corner, where no one would overhear, and told me he knew all about you and my connection with you. He'd read that you'd died but no body had been recovered. He told me that if I could produce you, alive, and hand you over to him, he'd go and never see me or put a claim on Glenna again."

She ceased speaking, and silence fell. Wind whipped past the coach, and wheels crunched on rock, thumping over tufts of hard grass.

"Well," Will said after a time. "That is interesting."

Josette glared at him. "Not interesting. Disastrous. He asked me to choose between you and my daughter." She sat back with a thump. "Bloody man."

Will let out a sound much like a laugh. "Do I understand aright that telling me was not part of the bargain?"

"Of course not. But I knew you'd be wondering why I arrived in time to rescue you and then locked you into a castle in the middle of nowhere. The castle is also a good place to hide Glenna. Chadwick knew where to find me in London, but he's not the sort who'll ride across the brutal Highlands in search of her. He prefers soft living, which is why he married so much money." She let out a sigh. "I knew you'd tumble to all this eventually, so I decided to save you the bother."

Will only watched her quietly. "What do you intend to do?"

Damn him. He lounged before her, perfectly at his ease, not worried that she'd promised to deliver him to his enemies.

"I don't yet know. I'll not give over my daughter. If Chadwick's filial feeling is so great, why hasn't he sought her out before? But how can I protect her?"

The thoughts woke Josette in the night, seized her by the throat, terrified her. She imagined Colonel Chadwick bringing Glenna into his house as a servant, or at best, a poor relation—what he'd tell his wife's family, Josette didn't know. Glenna would be vulnerable to the attentions of the worst sort, the same reason Josette had left Glenna behind in the castle for this venture. The Highland ladies would guard her fiercely.

Josette tried to say more, but her voice broke and she fell back against the cushions.

Will was next to her before she drew another breath. His strong body surrounded her, arms supporting her like a bulwark.

"Don't cry, love. I won't let him anywhere near Glenna, I promise you."

"But to ensure that, I have to betray you." Josette wiped tears from her eyes. "He'll not be happy until my heart is entirely broken."

"Aye, it seems so." Will held her closer, his lips on her hair. "Not that I intend to give myself over to him *or* let him take Glenna."

Josette didn't bother to ask how he thought he would accomplish this. He was a Mackenzie. As Lillias said, they were arrogant and duplicitous, not to mention full of unshakeable confidence.

"You may push me out of the carriage if you like," she said, feeling defeated. "I'll crawl back to Strathy, take Glenna, and try to run. But I'm so very tired of it."

To her surprise, and some irritation, Will laughed softly. "I know why ye told me. Not remorse—ye know we can overcome this together. As we always did before."

"Before did not involve my daughter. Now it does."

"Makes no difference. We're always better together, love. Ye know it."

"You are very certain of yourself. Perhaps I *should* give you over to Colonel Chadwick to take you down a peg."

"Do ye think that will work?"

"Not really."

Josette was so comfortable against his chest, his warmth dissolving her tension, as though he could take all her troubles away. He likely could, but then, there was no greater trouble in the world than Will himself.

"We'll keep Glenna safe, Josie." Will rested his cheek on the top of her head. "I love her like she was my own. Always have."

He had, that was true. Josette remembered the second time she'd seen Will in her life—Alec had arrived at her rooms unexpectedly to deliver a drawing he'd done for her, and Will had accompanied him. For the excuse of seeing her again, Will had confessed later. Glenna had burst upon them. She'd been five years old, dressed in nothing but a dirt-streaked chemise, her hair a tangled mess, and began screaming like a hellion.

Will, instead of being appalled, had laughed, caught Glenna as she tore about, and had her cleaned up in a trice and eating her milk and bread, which she'd been rebellious about taking from Josette.

From then on, Glenna had called him *Oncle Will* and flung herself into his arms whenever she saw him. Will hadn't minded—in fact, he seemed to enjoy taking care of a child. He read books to her, sang to her and taught her songs, took her for walks and rides on his horse, and helped Josette dose her when she was sick.

He'd done all the things a father should, and had explained, when Josette asked him why he was so good with Glenna, that as the second of six brothers, he'd taken care of the younger ones. Will's oldest brother, Duncan, had been too lofty and too conscious of his role as heir to have much interest in his younger brothers, so Will had taken the role as their leader.

"Trying to get Malcolm to settle down long enough to eat, bathe, drink, and even relieve himself was a pitched battle from morn to night," Will had told her. "Glenna is a calm little angel compared to what he was like." Josette had expressed her sympathy.

The carriage bumped over another rut and Josette pushed thoughts of the past aside. "I don't know how we can keep Glenna's true father from her, even if she's his by-blow," she said mournfully.

"Do you know a decent, sober, kind, practical, and well-off single gentleman who can marry her? Young and handsome as well—I'd not foist her off on a doddering man she has to grow weary nursing."

"Hmm. I'm not certain there are any decent, sober, kind, practical, well-off, single, handsome gentlemen in the world. Well, apart from myself. But I'm a bit long in the tooth for her at three and thirty."

And he could always make Josette feel better, even when they were plunging into peril. "Well, you can strike sober and practical from that description of yourself," she said, shaking her head. "I don't mean you're a drunkard, but you're hardly serious and solemn. Practical? Resourceful rather, but you'll go off on a wild tear if it suits you. Kind, I will give you, when you want to be. Single, unless you're hiding a wife you've not told me of." Josette hesitated, fearing he'd spring such information on her as Oliver Chadwick had that horrible day long ago. "And yes, handsome."

"Good, I feared ye'd leave off the last one. No, love, I have no secret wife or a string of mistresses. Only one lady has ever had my heart."

Will leaned to her and kissed her cheek, moving to her lips. Josette let her fears die away and turned to him, seeking his mouth with hers, unable to stop herself.

Will started, then gave in to the kiss, his lips parting hers. He slid his hand up her stomacher to cup her breast, his touch firm and hot through the fabric and boning.

The carriage, which had no springs to speak of, jounced over a road far too rutted. Their mouths bumped, painfully, and they broke from each other with a laugh.

Will did not release her, however. He continued to caress her breasts, pressing a kiss to the top of each, dipping his thumb behind the stomacher to the space between them.

Josette melted against him and enjoyed the pleasure of his touch, which stirred fire in her blood and in her heart.

She would not let herself succumb completely to him this time, but she'd learned to savor joy when she found it. In that carriage for a few more miles, she took the sweetness Will gave her, storing it up against lonely days to come.

Several miles before they reached the estate of Sir Harmon Bentley—optimistically named Oak View Park—the road improved immensely, straight and packed, like the Wade roads to the east.

Sir Harmon must have friends in high places, Will reflected, as the going became almost easy. Something to note.

He'd reluctantly left Josette's seat and resumed his own to put the rest of his disguise in place. The smoother road made easier the job of combing his hair flat on his head and donning a wig of dark brown. Josette helped adjust it, the lace on her sleeves brushing him most distractingly.

In the box of potions he'd had Bhreac acquire was a bottle of face paint from Paris, which dandies there used to smooth their complexions. Will peered at himself in a mirror Josette held up as he slathered it on, turning his wind-burned face pale as a pampered aristocrat's. The mirror wobbled a bit, because Josette insisted on laughing.

She was beautiful when she laughed. Her cares dropped from her, and her natural beauty glowed. So many people in her life—including Will—had given her the troubles that brushed faint lines about her eyes.

Will would rectify that, he'd already decided. Oliver Chadwick could go to the devil, and Will would send him there. Then he would install Josette in a lavish home with servants to wait on her hand and foot, provide Glenna a governess to polish her so that she could debut and have her pick of the best men in England or France.

Will would give Josette the choice of marriage to him or not—if all went well with his mission, he'd no longer be a fugitive. They could settle in France or London—Josette's choice—and grow middle-aged and peaceful together.

Such a lovely dream.

No matter what, he wanted Josette beside him in the night—and in the morning, and the afternoon, and every time in between.

Will smoothed the makeup on his face and finished it with a little white powder. Josette sneezed.

He handed her the powder box and told her to don it as well. They would be playing a silly young couple who wanted nothing more in life than to be fashionable and rich and run with fashionable and rich people. They'd be too foolish and gauche for the very best circles, so they'd make do with second best, but preen themselves for that.

"The insipid Anna Jacobs I become once again," Josette said, closing the powder casket.

The powder made her very pretty—she'd deftly applied it to give her cheeks a soft glow.

Will added a touch of rouge to her cheeks, but just a touch. Her natural blush was better than artifice.

Her warm skin invited lingering, but Will made himself sit back, smear the rouge on his own cheeks, and wipe off his fingers. At least the personas of William and Anna were besotted with each other— Will looked forward to holding hands, secret smiles, flirtation, a touch on the waist, promising looks for later ...

He carefully set a tricorn hat on his head. "There. Am I a vision?"

"You look awful." Josette's grin told him all he needed. "An overweening popinjay."

"Perfect. You, of course, are splendid. Much too good for the likes of your ridiculous husband. I will be perpetually in awe that such a lady married me."

"She was too foolish to know any better," Josette returned. "This Anna is a complete featherhead. I always believe I'll go cross-eyed with all her tittering and simpering."

"Anna and William deserve each other. They'll be happy 'til their dying day, and never realize what fools they are." Will lost his smile. "I envy them sometimes."

"They're not real people, you know," Josette reminded him.

"The trouble with being so many different people is that they *are* real." Will put away the mirror and box. "One is the vagabond Highlander who may or may not know secrets but is too untrustworthy to carry any real ones. He's very useful."

Josette gave him a wry look. "I believe I found him tied up in an army camp, being questioned and beaten."

"Yes, that is one drawback. But I have learned much through him."

Josette shook her head. "I hope one day—very soon, for your own good—that you become only Will Mackenzie and cease your nonsense."

What he wanted with all his heart. "I'm not sure I can be only me, love. Do I even know this Will Mackenzie, and will I like him?"

"Well, *I* like him." Josette gave him a glance that eased his heart. "I look forward to seeing him again."

Will winked at her. He longed to return to her side and kiss her, but forced himself to keep to his seat so he wouldn't smear the makeup he'd just slathered on.

No matter. He'd save up the kiss for later. Every touch, every kiss he had to miss now, he'd claim another time. That time would be most satisfying, and they'd reach it together. This he determined.

BHREAC HALTED THE CARRIAGE AT A GATE LEADING TO A WIDE LANE across a flat stretch of land. Josette could see that an effort had been made to grow oak trees in this park, but they were poor specimens, spindly and tired.

The road had come down from the hills, and the gate to the estate sat at the top of a slope. A low bank separated the park from a loch, which spread, flat and gray, to a rocky shore on the far side. This loch, Will told Josette, ran southward to the sea, which was not far away.

The house itself was fairly new. A rectangular structure made of pale brick, it rose several stories, its multi-paned windows crowned with pediments. Square towers flanked the main house, as though the owners wanted to acknowledge the ruined castles that dotted the hills around them—but these towers were decorative and had never held off an army of murderous clansmen.

A man in breeches and brown coat emerged from the gatehouse to peer at them suspiciously. Will dropped open the window.

"Oh, thank heavens," Will cried, his accent switching to that of a foppish English gentleman. "Civilization in the midst of barbarian wilderness—can it be true? Let us in, dear fellow. We are weary travelers, terrified and wandering. We crave admittance. Pray tell your master that Sir William Jacobs and his wife are stranded and plead for his hospitality."

The gatekeeper looked Will over and saw exactly what was intended—an arrogant Englishman, spoiled rotten and out of his depth, relieved he'd found what he thought was the house of a fellow Englishman.

The man's suspicious expression faded into one of faint disdain. He'd sized up Sir William, Josette saw, and didn't think much of him.

"I'll send my lad running to the main house," the gatekeeper said. "They'll be ready by the time you arrive." He lifted his hat and bowed. "Welcome to Oak View Park, sir."

"Thank you, good sir." Lace fluttered as Will took a coin from his purse and tossed it to the man. "You see, Lady Jacobs, I knew all was not lost."

Josette gave the man a vacant smile as he opened the gate, and Bhreac started the coach. The carriage jolted over a bump in the earth that marked the boundary of Sir Harmon Bentley's estate, and the gate creaked closed behind them.

Was this sanctuary from the wild lands? Josette thought idly. Or a prison?

Josette saw a boy skim from the gatehouse and run flat out across the park. By the time Bhreac pulled to a halt at the foot of the double staircase that curved to the front door, several footmen had hurried out to open the coach and set down a stool so the travelers could descend.

A man in a severe suit emerged behind the footman and gave Will a correct bow. "Welcome, sir. I am called Stelton, and am majordomo here."

"Oh, my dear sir, my dear sir." Will heaved a sigh of relief as he reached the ground and turned to assist his beloved Anna from the coach. "We thank you."

Stelton watched him without expression. "Lady Bentley requests you step into her sitting room once you have refreshed yourselves."

"Excellent." Will took out another a coin and pressed it into the man's hand. "Everyone is so kind, so kind. Lady Jacobs, my darling, are you well?"

"I will be." Josette took Will's arm and sank into his side. "Now that I am no longer rocking in that dreadful coach."

It dismayed Josette how easily her voice took on the higher pitch of Anna, how effortlessly she flowed into the role.

Stelton contrived a sympathetic look that did not reach his eyes, and ushered them up the stairs and into the house.

Josette had seen plenty of mansions—Marsden House near Salisbury as well as villas in the French countryside and of course, Versailles—and she knew at once that this one had been built with much expense.

The wooden floors were even and polished. On the walls, white-painted paneling framed wallpaper in a Chinese theme—pagodas and bridges over streams. The mahogany tables and chairs shone with polish, their curved legs elegant, the silk upholstery on the chairs matching the wallpaper.

A fireplace stood in this main hall, the fire crackling merrily, though there was none to stand by it—the master of the house boasting that he could waste fuel.

Will immediately went to the fire and held his hands near the blaze. "Ah, I thought I'd never be warm again. Do you know what they burn in this benighted country, Stelton? Peat. Mud they dig out of bogs. I ask you."

"Indeed, sir. The footmen will show you upstairs to your chambers." He gave Will a pointed look, and Will flashed him an abashed grin.

"Oh, right. Thank you, Stelton. Come along, darling."

They followed the footmen through a gallery to a staircase that wrapped its way around one of the towers. Josette was dizzy by the time they reached their floor—the third from the ground. She glanced over the railing to the stairs spiraling below her and turned away with a slight shudder.

The footmen led them across another gallery lined with windows to a long corridor. White pediments reposed over every door and window, and pleasingly symmetrical plasterwork adorned the cornices and paneling.

A door opened farther down the corridor as they trundled along, and a man in a cavalry uniform stepped into the hall.

Josette missed a step in momentary dread, but she drew a calming breath when she did not recognize the gentleman. He was not Colonel Chadwick, nor had this man been at the army camp from which she'd rescued Will. This officer was cavalry, while Chadwick and the soldiers at the camp were infantry, and besides, the camp was far from here.

Will, on the other hand, paused. His hesitation was infinitesimal, and none but Josette would have caught it, but it made her fears pour back at her. Will knew the man.

Will turned his head quickly and sent the ribbons and laces on his sleeves and coat fluttering, a move to distract attention from his face.

"Good afternoon to you, sir," Will said in his clearest, most English voice. "I will greet you properly later, but for now—the roll of the coach has taken its toll, and I desperately seek relief, if you know what I mean. In you go, dearest."

Josette gave the cavalryman a quick curtsy, and he returned it with a proper bow, his dark blue eyes watchful. Will lifted a handkerchief to his face and did everything but cup the join of his legs as he pretended to rush for the chamber pot.

The cavalryman bowed again, in some disapproval, and walked away in the opposite direction. Josette hurried into the chamber where Will had already disappeared.

The footman who'd led them upstairs showed Will into a small closet within the bedchamber that held a privy. Not a chamber pot, but a hole in a seat that emptied to a cistern far below.

"I am most grateful, my boy. You may leave us now—we'll ring for you when we need to trot to your mistress. My heaven, this house is grand—and they've provided for everything. Anna, darling, I will show you this wonderful mechanism when I am finished with it ..."

He slammed the door, shutting off his voice.

Josette let her smile wrinkle her nose and handed the footman a few coins. "Thank you, lad. Go on, now. We'll be well."

The footman bowed with some deference—Josette had given him

two shillings. The more extravagant they were, she knew, the more their disguise would be believed.

Josette waited until the footman's steps faded toward the gallery before she rapped on the door of the closet.

Will slid out, his face set in grim lines. He led Josette to the middle of the room and pulled her into an embrace.

"Damn and blast and bloody hell," he whispered.

"You know him, don't you?" Josette whispered in return. "Do you think he'll recognize you? If you met him in battle, in all the confusion ..."

"I was never in a battle, but he will recognize me without fail," Will said in a low voice. "His name is Captain Robert Ellis. He spent the winter before Culloden in my family's house, and all of us were there—he knows me. He was my brother Mal's prisoner, and was in love with Mal's wife."

CHAPTER 9

"What do we do?" Josette said quietly.

Will liked that she did not immediately panic, or ask whether he was certain of the man's identity. She understood the trouble and had moved to deciding how they would deal with it.

"I'll speak to him. The fact that he didn't denounce me the moment he saw me gives me hope."

"Perhaps *I* should speak to him," Josette offered. "He does not know me at all, and I am not Scots. I could plead with him to keep his silence."

Will was already shaking his head. "If he exposes me, I want you to be astonished and amazed. You declare that I tricked you, and you know nothing about me but agreed to this deception because I coerced you."

Josette scowled. "I should pretend to be a featherhead in truth, you mean?"

"The world has a low opinion of my family. They'll believe I could be so duplicitous to you."

Josette planted her fists on her hips, which made her panniers sway. "You wish me to stand by while they take you away? Without lifting a finger to help?"

"You'd only be dragged to the noose with me." Will reached for her hands, prying them open so he could twine her fingers through his. "I need to know you'll be free and unharmed. You can take Glenna and go to my family. My brothers will help you. Tell them your story and they and my dad will defend you with all their strength."

"Meanwhile, you swing from a noose or are drawn and quartered," Josette snapped. "Hanging is the kindest thing they'd do, and you know it."

"Believe me, I'll do my damnedest to get away. I'll have more impetus to escape if I know you're safe."

Josette gazed at him with her sweet brown eyes, the ones that could turn seductive or ferocious in the space of a heartbeat. "How much in love was this cavalryman with your brother's wife?"

"Quite a bit. Though he did help them escape together."

"For her sake?"

"Oh, aye."

"Damnation," she said softly, but with feeling. "Best corner him soon, then. *I* will decide what I will do if he arrests you."

Will started to argue, but Josette lifted his hand to her lips. She kissed his fingers, then gently bit his knuckle, flaring his need for her to life.

"Lady Bentley is waiting," she said.

Will smothered an impatient sigh. He disentangled his hands from hers, pressing a kiss to her fingertips before releasing her.

Another thing he loved about Josette, he thought as they straightened clothing and prepared to descend to Lady Bentley's private sitting room, was that in their quiet tête-à-tête, Josette never once spoke his name out loud. She was careful, even in a whisper in the center of a room.

LADY BENTLEY ROSE TO GREET THEM FROM A PINK DAMASK SETTEE placed beneath a large chandelier in a room filled with mirrors. They lined the walls, filling every possible space.

The ceiling, in contrast, was painted to depict a summer blue sky with clouds floating across it. No frolicking cherubs or naked gods and goddesses. This was very modern decor, where plainer themes took the place of overblown mythology.

The chamber held no paintings, only the mirrors in gilded frames, each one sized to fit between and over windows. It was as though the architects had pried the Hall of Mirrors from Versailles and left it to shrink in the rain before installing it in this house.

Or perhaps Lady Bentley simply liked her own reflection. She was a regal and handsome woman, Josette guessed in her forties. Her unlined face was well shaped, marred only by a hardness put there by life.

Lady Bentley looked them over as they neared her. "Sir William Jacobs? And wife?"

Will presented her his most flamboyant bow. "Indeed, we are. How thrilled we were to hear that *Sir Harmon Bentley* lived here. How fortuitous. How wonderful. A beam of light in this howling wilderness. We cannot thank you enough for rescuing us."

Lady Bentley's smile turned satisfied. "You have heard of us, then."

"I pity the dismal fools who have not." Will gave her another, only slightly less fluttering, bow. "Sir Harmon Bentley, who won so much for himself in Antigua, and advises his Majesty on trade. Quite a reputation."

As Lady Bentley preened, Josette curtsied. "Your home is beautiful, my lady. How did you manage it, here, of all places?"

"One learns to be resourceful." Lady Bentley eyed Will thoughtfully. "Jacobs? As in the Berkshire Jacobses?"

"Beg pardon?" Will looked blank, then he dissolved into a smile. "My dear lady, nothing so lofty. My pater was a humble country squire—fell off his perch years ago, poor soul. The Jacobses of Berkshire *might* be distant cousins, but they'd never admit to such a thing. They do have a lovely house." He trailed off wistfully.

Lady Bentley's mouth pinched. "So, I do not know your family."

"Oh, mine is nothing to speak of," Will said, waving them away. "My wife is the one from the good family. She's a Garfield, of the Garfields of Wiltshire and Virginia."

"Ah." Lady Bentley's manner changed swiftly.

Will had labored over the antecedents of Josette's character long ago, providing a precise family tree that was intricate enough to be believable but convoluted enough that only a dedicated member of the Garfield family could unravel it.

Anna's "father" had almost the same name as a Garfield cousin who had emigrated to France decades ago and hadn't been heard from since. There was no record of the man's marriage, and he had passed on twenty years before. Easy to invent a French wife for this man—now also deceased—and say that his wife had brought him a fortune to leave to their half-French daughter, Anna.

By the time letters could be sent to check their story—and most people wouldn't bother—Will and Josette would be long gone.

The real Garfields had dismissed the cousin Will had chosen to be Josette's father as inconsequential, and showed no inclination to look for any descendants he might have left. Will Mackenzie was painstaking in a deception.

The connection seemed to please Lady Bentley, however, and she would be unlikely to meet the Garfields or Jacobses Will claimed as relations if she remained in this remote corner of Scotland.

Will exhaled a dramatic sigh. "Yes, dear lady, it was a misalliance. Many claim I pursued my darling Anna for her fortune, but I had no idea who she was when I saw her across the room at that soiree in Lucerne." He faced Josette, taking her hands. The false light dropped from his eyes as he spoke only to her. "I looked upon her and saw a great and beautiful soul. I knew at that moment, she was the lady I would marry."

Josette did not have to feign her deep blush. The memory flashed of Will strolling into Alec's studio, rumbling a greeting to his brother in his velvet voice. Sunlight streaking through dusty windows had brushed his tall, well-formed body and burned his hair red.

He'd moved with confidence that stopped just shy of arrogance, and possessed a self-deprecating manner that told Josette he didn't take himself too seriously.

Everything about Will had seared itself into her heart—a keen glance from his golden eyes, the bow he'd made her when Alec had introduced them, his half smile as he'd roved his gaze over her exposed body.

This is Josette, Alec had said. *Do not annoy her—she's the best model I've ever had.*

Will had raised his hands as though annoying Josette had been the furthest thing from his mind, and had dropped her that sly wink.

Gazing into his eyes now made Josette's breath stop and her knees weak. She'd tumble into a swoon if she wasn't careful.

"How pleasing for you," Lady Bentley said. Her tone and manner had softened considerably—perhaps she was a romantic at heart.

"Oh, and you can send word to the Earl of Marsden," Will continued in the tone of a man who liked to boast of his connections. "We stayed with them one summer in their marvelous home near Salisbury. It was delightful, was it not Lady Jacobs?"

Josette regained her senses quickly enough to nod and smile, as though dreaming of the golden days in that mansion.

"Well," Lady Bentley said, even more mollified. "You will find that, out of necessity, we live much more simply than Lord Marsden, but we will strive to make you comfortable. One more impertinent question, Sir William—your father—was he also 'Sir?'"

"A baronet, you mean?" Will looked aghast. "Dear lady, that would have been too much trouble for him. No, Papa was never a baronet, and I inherited no title, more's the pity. I was knighted for bravery in battle—I forgive you for not guessing that." He gave a high-pitched laugh. "But apparently, I was very brave. Pulled a chappie out from under a horse and took shards of artillery in my arm meant for him. Turns out, chappie was the son of a duke and quite grateful to me. His papa put in a good word for me to the king, and here I am, a *very parfit, gentil knyght.*"

He laughed again, and Josette, as Anna, giggled with him.

Again, Will had borrowed the story from a real young man of obscurity who had fought the French at a battle on the Rhine. A grateful duke had made certain the young man had been knighted.

"An army gentleman, are you?" Lady Bentley asked with interest. "We have a captain staying with us as well."

"I spied him, yes. He's cavalry, and I was infantry. That means we don't speak." Will shook his head mockingly. "But I will endeavor to be civil."

Lady Bentley tittered with him. Josette kept the smile on her face as she watched Will charm his way into yet another woman's confidence.

THEY DID NOT SEE CAPTAIN ELLIS UNTIL DINNER, WHICH COMMENCED at three that afternoon in a lavish dining room. This chamber had been copied almost exactly from Versailles, Josette saw as they entered. Sir Harmon must have sent his architect over to France with a measuring stick and a notebook.

Will had tried to run down Captain Ellis to confront him in private but hadn't managed it. Partly because their host, Sir Harmon, had returned from a muddy fishing expedition and taken Will aside to question him almost as thoroughly as his wife had.

Josette had wandered the house while Will was closeted with Sir Harmon, searching for Captain Ellis herself while she pretended to be fascinated by the decor, but the captain had remained elusive.

Captain Ellis's chair at the dining table was next to Sir Harmon's at the head, but Will had been placed by Lady Bentley at the foot, with Josette across from him and one down.

The remaining guests, three couples and an older widower, were spaced up and down the table, ladies between gentlemen, no married pairs together.

All guests were English, from the Heartland, they called it, meaning Staffordshire, Shropshire, Derbyshire and several other shires Josette could not remember at present. The gentlemen wore brightly colored and well-embroidered frock coats much like Will's, though he surpassed them in number of ribbons along the sleeves.

The ladies likewise wore bright colors, their gowns decorated with cascades of lace. Jewels glittered on bosoms, wrists, fingers, and earlobes.

They were an unlikely group to be found in the remote country-side of Scotland, but Sir Harmon's lavish house strove to shut out the landscape. If one did not look out the windows, they might be dining in the gentle parkland of Berkshire or Kent or on the plains of the Ile de France.

The ladies and gentlemen all knew each other, and chattered like the old friends they were. They were curious about Will and Anna and bombarded them with probing questions. Josette was grateful to Will's thorough preparation, so she could easily answer about her life on the Continent, her marriage to Will, and their sojourns in Basel and Lucerne.

Captain Ellis said not a word. He glanced down the table at Josette from time to time, brows drawn. He clearly wondered who the devil she was and why she was with Will, but to her relief he said nothing.

Waiting for a dramatic moment to denounce them? Or was he a friend to Will after all?

Will, meanwhile, flirted shamelessly with Lady Bentley. She blushed and simpered, enjoying every moment.

Josette did not like the jealousy that flitted inside her. Will played a part, she knew, and his behavior with Lady Bentley was to some extent Josette's doing. Before dinner she'd overheard one of the gentlemen wonder if Will, with his myriad laces and high-pitched giggles, was really a molly, his pretty wife a blind.

When Josette had conveyed this to Will in a whisper, he'd been neither surprised nor offended.

"Hmm. Could be useful, though I don't want Sir Harmon, who seems a bit prim, to decide to have me arrested for it." He grinned. "Never fear, love. I'll be a silly young man, but randy for the ladies."

Now he focused on Lady Bentley, making it obvious to stare at her ample bosom as often as possible. He did not neglect Josette, taking every opportunity to rake his gaze over her, or hold her attention while he touched his tongue to his upper lip. She found herself growing far too hot when he did that, and was thankful she'd brought her fan.

Lady Bentley might have claimed they lived simply, but they'd imported a chef who'd managed to find plenty of beef, poultry, and other very English comestibles to supplement the fish from Sir Harmon's catch today. The fish, being the freshest thing on the table, was excellent, served with a cream sauce flavored with dill and pepper. The meat was indifferent, but again excellently sauced.

The overly pampered ladies and gentlemen complained, of course, that no good thing could be found this far north of the border, in lands full of crazed barbarians.

"They're said to be very handsome," one of the ladies said. "The Highlanders, I mean. Tall and robust. *Very* robust."

"If you like them murderous and hairy," her husband answered with a sniff into his handkerchief.

"Their women are the same," the gentleman next to Josette said. "Hairy and murderous." The table roared with laughter.

Will joined the laughter, but Josette saw the dangerous glint in his eyes.

"I wouldn't mind a look at these robust gentlemen," Josette broke in too loudly. "What is the word they use to describe them? *Braw?* A braw Scotsman, dancing, big knees tossing up his skirts?"

"Kilts," another gentleman corrected her as more laughter ensued. "You won't see those, my lady. They are forbidden to wear kilts and plaids, or to have claymores and whatever other fool things they gather to themselves."

"A pity." Josette fingered her wine glass. "I don't object to a fine pair of legs." She sent a merry look to the young man next to her, and he all but leered back at her.

Will's laughter died into a scowl. "I see nothing beauteous in a man's bare legs, my love. A bit disgusting, I'd think. A lady's legs, now …" His face softened, his smile returning. "Ladies are the most wondrous creations, are they not, gentlemen? As Milton says, *Heaven's last, best gift.*"

He looked straight at Josette as he spoke the words, and then reached for a strawberry from the bowl between them. Holding her with his golden gaze, Will lifted a berry and dragged it through a bowl of sweetened cream, swirling the cream to a point on the strawberry's tip.

"Poets have compared a lady's bosom to the finest strawberries, nestled in cream," he said softly.

Will laced his tongue around the tip of the berry, drawing the cream inside his mouth. He then bit down on the strawberry itself, closing his eyes to savor it.

The heat inside Josette curled into flames. He teased, he played, he pretended, but the true Will looked at her when he opened his eyes, the promise and the wanting unfeigned.

As laughter floated up and down the table, Josette lifted her fan and flapped it before her scalding face. "Husband, you are unseemly. What will our hostess think?"

Exactly what he wanted her to think—that Will had a healthy appetite for the ladies, including his own wife. Indeed, Lady Bentley stared at Will in fascination, her lips parted as he finished the strawberry and licked cream from his fingers.

Captain Ellis, on the other hand, drank wine in silence. Sir Harmon, a red-faced man with his wig canted on his round head, looked slightly perturbed. Prim, Will had called him.

"Do you write poesy yourself, Sir William?" Lady Bentley asked, eyes bright.

Will shook his head. "Nay, I am only an indifferent poet. If I could pen lines about my lady's breasts, I would." He waggled his brows up and down at Josette. "But alas, I am no Bard of Avon. I can only borrow from others, like the good Herrick and the other Will. Shakespeare, I mean."

The ladies and gentlemen chortled, probably more at his feeble attempt at a joke than any appreciation of his wit.

Josette kept up her side of the play, closing her fan to tap Will's hand. "You are both overly flattering and mortifying at the same time. I can only blush."

And look very pleased that this handsome, virile man had singled her out to be his wife.

Will's wife. Josette pushed aside the temptation of this vision and hurriedly finished off her wine.

The other gentlemen then tried to be witty and complimentary to the ladies, some more successfully than others.

Dinner finished at half past five. It was full daylight, this being June, despite the efforts of the clouds to blot out the sun. As the guests slowly drifted from the dining room, Will peered through its long windows to the lush grounds beyond.

"I heard you have a water garden, Sir Harmon," he said. "Of all things."

"That is true." Sir Harmon joined him at the window, his shoulders straightening. "Fountains and little jests, and so forth. Marvelous things, hydraulics."

"I don't understand in the least how they work, but they can be so amusing." Will turned to him eagerly, his gaze taking in Captain Ellis, who lingered behind their host. "Do say I can view them. Captain Ellis, wouldn't you like to see the water gardens? Oh, perhaps you have already."

Will's crestfallen look was perfect. Captain Ellis, with the air of a man forcing himself to be polite, bowed and said, "I would, of course, be happy to observe them with you."

Sir Harmon eyed the mist outside with distaste. "I'll send one of my chaps with you. He knows what's what on the estate. Best put on some wraps, though, or you'll catch your deaths. Sun never shines in this blasted country."

In a quarter of an hour, Will, Josette, and Captain Ellis were assembled to roam the gardens. A lad of about eighteen or so summers, with black skin and in footman's attire, led the way, pointing out features as they went. His tone was weary, as though he'd given this tour once too often and was thoroughly tired of it.

"Roses cover the south terrace along with blooms from every part of the empire," the young man said in a flat voice. "The first fountain is Apollo and his chariot, which is the same as the one at Versailles."

The entire garden, like the house, reflected Versailles, Josette saw as she strolled at Will's side. She was glad Sir Harmon had suggested wraps—her gown hardly cut the chill of the mists, but its matching cloak helped.

The fountains marched along in perfect order to the end of the garden, although none were turned on—no spray filled the air.

Large yew hedges had been planted at the end of the fountain walk, creating a series of narrow paths that hid more fountains a stroller could stumble upon—often quite literally. One fountain was concealed in the bricks on the path itself, another beneath a hole in a garden bench. Josette imagined Sir Harmon gleefully starting up the fountains as the unwary walker stepped on the holes or sank down to the bench for a rest.

The fountains also grew more naughty the farther they were from the house. One depicted a maiden standing behind another, her hands on her friend's breasts, spouts for the water coming from the first maiden's nipples. Will stopped to ogle this, keeping in character, declaring it the best in the garden. Josette fanned herself as though discomfited. Captain Ellis only glanced at it coldly.

They reached a fountain where three stone little boys had their bare backsides facing the bowl, no mystery where the water would sprout from.

Will halted in delight. "Oh, I want to see this one run. Make it go." He burst into hysterical laughter. "*Make it go*—I declare I did not say that on purpose."

The footman barely restrained his disgust. He gave Will a bland bow and jogged back down the paths toward the shed that contained the mechanisms, the ribbon tying back his wig fluttering.

"Now then, Ellis," Will said as soon as the lad was out of earshot. He maintained his mannerisms, in case any from the house saw them, but resumed his own voice. "Will ye betray me to Sir Harmon or whatever generals might be lurking in the heather? Or will I have to confess to Lady Mary that I've killed ye? She will be most put out with me if I murder you, I think."

CHAPTER 10

*W*ill assumed a nonchalant stance while waiting for Captain Ellis to reply, but he was very aware of the comforting weight of the dagger he'd slid into his pocket.

"I haven't quite made up my mind." Captain Ellis looked Will up and down. "Or decided what you are supposed to be."

"A fatuous beau." Will made a bow, extending his leg, while at the same time carefully watching Ellis's hands. "Mal would also be annoyed with me if I killed you. He is fond of you."

Ellis's dark brows lifted. "Is he?"

"You let him run away with Mary instead of capturing him and dragging him off to be executed," Will said. "Gave him a soft spot for you."

"They were married," Ellis said stiffly. "By a vicar, whether I liked it or not. I had no grounds for standing in their way."

"Ah, but Mal had been declared dead, so Mary was officially a widow."

Ellis took a step toward Will. He had not changed much in the year since Will had seen him—his hair was deep brown without a thread of gray, his dark blue eyes hard as steel, his face set in quiet determination.

Captain Ellis brooked no fools, and he'd proved himself intelligent, well mannered, and fair-minded. Though he'd stayed at Kilmorgan as the Mackenzies' prisoner, Will's brothers and father had begun to consider him a friend.

"Is Lady Mary happy?" he asked. "If she is not, then I will find Malcolm and cut out his heart."

Will did not doubt it. Ellis would have to go through Will, Alec, and their father to get to Mal, but he was the sort who would die trying.

"She is," Will answered. "I give you my word on that. She and Mal are madly in love, and faring well in a comfortable house in Paris. She bore him a bairn not long ago. They call him Angus."

Captain Ellis flinched and looked away. "After your brother," he said. Angus Mackenzie, Alec's twin, had been killed in a skirmish in Scotland during the Uprising.

"Aye." Will nodded. "Angus was the best of us. The mite so far is more like Mal, unfortunately. Never ceases talking, even if he can only make unintelligible noises at this point."

Ellis smiled tightly, a man hiding his pain. "And you, madam?" He turned to Josette. "Are you well? Do not be afraid to tell me if not—I will let no harm come to you."

"He speaks true," Will said to Josette. "If you'd like Ellis to protect you from me, love, he will. To the death, I imagine."

"Just so." Captain Ellis gave Josette a bow.

Josette closed her fingers around Will's arm, her warmth a bright spot in the chill. "You are very kind, Captain, but Will and I are old friends."

Will shot him a grin. "Meaning she knows how to manage me."

"I would not quite say *that*," Josette returned. "But I am at his side for a reason and by my choice."

"I would love to know those reasons." Captain Ellis regarded Will's frippery with blatant disapprobation. "Something under-handed, I assume."

"Or I might be entertaining myself," Will answered. "I'm considered a bit mad, you know."

"Cunning, more like," Ellis said. "Will you give me your word that you intend no harm to this lady? Or to the persons here?"

"No harm at all. If a man comes at me with a knife or pistol, I will of course take the liberty of defending myself, but I have not come to instigate violence or take my vengeance. Well, not in blood, anyway."

Will had already learned much about the other guests—none of the gentlemen had had the courage to be part of Cumberland's army. They were feeble sprigs of the squirearchy who'd made money on the backs of others and hid here from creditors, bookmakers, and respectable society. One of the gentlemen had been socially ruined by refusing to pay debts of honor and then nearly killing a duke's son in a duel. The son had lived, the gentleman boasted, thus sparing him from a charge of murder.

"I am equally curious as to why *you* are here, Captain," Will went on. "I can't imagine you befriending these people."

Ellis made a small shrug. "I have a connection through my mother to Sir Harmon's sister's husband. I was asked to make use of that connection and spend some time at Sir Harmon's home."

Meaning Captain Ellis had been sent to find out what Sir Harmon was up to out here in the wilderness. There might be a good reason why Sir Harmon was no longer in the Cabinet.

"I see," Will said. "If I can be of any assistance …"

"I will inform you," Ellis said firmly.

"Meaning I should stay out of your way? I, on the other hand, would welcome any help you chose to lend me."

Captain Ellis gave him a nod. "If it comes to it."

The fountain behind them gurgled profusely. Water abruptly spurted from the marble boys' naked bums and streamed into the bowl. Staying in character, Will laughed and applauded, and Josette covered her mouth as though giggling. Ellis looked thoroughly repelled.

"At least I don't have to pretend to enjoy Sir Harmon's entertainments," Ellis said.

"Ah, but flattery goes a long way, Captain." Will changed his voice to the fop's as the servant returned. "Excellent craftsmanship. Please show me more, lad."

The footman barely hid his irritation as he turned and led Will and Josette around the next bend in the hedges. Captain Ellis, Will noted, quietly retreated.

THE HOUSE PARTY COMMENCED WITH TIRESOME PREDICTABILITY, AT least to Josette. No one was much for tramping or riding that evening, as they were terrified that savage Scotsmen would creep up on them and attack them.

Therefore, they remained stolidly indoors. The guests played cards for ruinous stakes as the hours wore on, gossiping madly—Will joined in without hesitation. No one bothered with the library full of books, and Lady Bentley teased Josette when she asked to choose one to read.

The guests sat up far into the night, the men drinking brandy, the women wine or sherry. One lady snuck in nips of gin from a flask. She offered the flask to Josette, who pretended to sip, but Josette abhorred the stuff. She'd seen firsthand how gin rotted people from the inside out.

Captain Ellis seldom spoke. He played cards without much animation, and the large stakes did not seem to bother him—mostly because he won. The ladies and gentlemen were quite bad at games, Josette noted, probably why they'd run into trouble with creditors.

Around midnight, the company decided to play at riddles—they made up a silly rhyme and dared the rest to guess its meaning.

The answers were always lewd, as in "copulation" or "cock's crowing." Captain Ellis vanished during these proceedings, and Josette concluded he'd wisely gone to bed.

When finally the ladies and gentlemen, yawning and half asleep, decided to go upstairs, it was three in the morning. Scottish nights were short in the summer, and the sun would be up within the hour.

Will and Josette were the last. As they strolled up the square tower stairs, Lady Bentley popped out onto the second-floor landing and laid her hand on Will's arm.

"Do let me speak to you a moment, Sir William." She beamed

Josette a sharp smile. "I promise, Lady Jacobs, I won't keep him. Not long enough to cause a scandal, anyway."

Will gave Josette a helpless Sir William look as Lady Bentley latched her fingers around his forearm and towed him off. Josette had no choice but to continue up on her own, pretending she thought nothing of it.

Josette warmed herself before the fire in their bedchamber and tried to still her uneasiness. She and Will were playing roles, and if it meant Will had to seduce Lady Bentley, then Josette would have to live with it, no matter how much she disliked it.

The knot in her chest urged her to run downstairs, discover where Lady Bentley had taken Will, and drag him away. Wouldn't a jealous and besotted Anna do so? Perhaps, but then she might interrupt whatever interrogation Will had begun.

It was all Josette could do to remain in their chamber, breathing hard, and try not to speculate what they were doing.

To her intense relief, Will banged into the room not long later, a white crockery bowl in his hands.

"I am here, my chicken," Will said, keeping to his Sir William persona. "Our lady hostess only wanted to give us a gift."

Josette peered curiously into the bowl. It held a mound of strawberries, with cream artfully arranged in a scalloped pattern around it.

"Lovely," Josette said. "They must have a large patch in the garden."

"Yes, isn't it kind of our hostess?" Will slid off his frock coat and loosened and unwound his cravat. "She noticed how I relished a strawberry."

Josette flushed, remembering how he'd curled his tongue around the berry at dinner, and his comparison of strawberries and cream to a lady's breasts.

"Yes, very kind of her," she managed to say.

"I believe she wants us to enjoy *all* of these. And the cream."

He stuck the tip of his finger into the bowl, swirled up a tiny blob of cream, and licked it away. Josette's chest went tight.

Will slid his finger back into the cream, and this time held it out to Josette.

She eyed the white dollop standing up in a soft peak on his finger-tip, her mouth drying. She ought to shake her head, tell him the charade was at an end for now, and go to bed, banishing him to the settee in the dressing room.

Josette swallowed hard, leaned to him, and laced her tongue around his finger.

Will's eyes darkened as she suckled the offered cream. He bent to whisper into her ear, "Peepholes."

Josette started, but she covered the move with a little gasp, as though he'd said something risqué. With great effort she kept herself from darting glances around the room, searching for said peepholes.

She knew that some people installed such things in their houses, perhaps to keep watch on those they did not trust, or for the purpose Will implied Lady Bentley used them for—to spy on those having connubial relations.

Oh, dear. If Josette and Will simply went to sleep, especially in separate rooms, the illusion of them being a besotted married couple would be at an end. Of course, many married couples of the upper classes did not share a bedchamber, but Lady Bentley had pointedly given them a only one chamber and only one bed.

They could pretend to have a tiff, but then both might be vulner-able to unwanted attentions from the others. Lady Bentley had already formed a great interest in Will.

However, Josette had no intention of allowing their hostess, and who knew who else, watch Will seduce her senseless.

Will's cheekbones stained red as Josette licked his finger. "We need to give them a show," he murmured. "Just for a little while."

Josette fought to keep the dismay from her face. "No," she whis-pered, the syllable nearly silent.

Will took her hand and kissed each of her fingertips. "They won't see you," he said quietly as he began to unbutton his waistcoat. "Only me."

Josette didn't like that any better, but now she felt another emotion—gratitude. He was protecting her.

Will dropped the silk waistcoat on top of his frock coat and cravat and untied the tape that closed his shirt at the neck.

"I've dismissed the servants, love," he said as Sir William. "We'll have to be lady's maid and valet for each other." Will caught Josette's hand and pressed a burning kiss to the inside of her wrist.

"No servants?" Josette said as Anna. "Well, I suppose we shall have to make do, husband."

"I suppose we will, wife." Will slid his loosened shirt down until it exposed his suntanned shoulders, a pale scar cutting across his collarbone. "Now ... I seem to be hungry."

Josette drew a breath, reached into the bowl, and plucked out a strawberry.

CHAPTER 11

*I*t was the most decadent thing Josette had ever done, and at the same time, so simple.

Josette tried to keep her hand from shaking as she dabbed the strawberry into a little cream and held it to Will's lips.

He bit down, a trickle of juices caressing the corner of his lips. He licked the trickle away before taking the rest of the berry from her fingers. Someone had thoughtfully trimmed off the hulls, and Will drew the whole thing into his mouth, chewing it slowly. Josette watched his throat move as he swallowed, her fingers going hot.

"Another, love," he prompted.

Josette quickly dug out another strawberry. She continued to feed him from her fingers, dipping some berries in cream, giving a few to him bare. Cream dotted Will's lips, and strawberry juice stained his chin.

He never touched her. Will lounged on the chair at the dressing table, the mirror reflecting him as he took the berries from her, licking her fingers in the process. His shirt slid to his waist, baring back, torso, and strong arms.

He was a beautiful man, skin bronzed by sun and wind. Sir William's tale of being in the army accounted for his scars, and muscles made tight by carrying rifle and sword. Will truly had carried such things and marched over the Highlands, if not in uniform.

Josette gave him every strawberry in the bowl, taking a few for herself—they looked too delicious to resist. Fresh and ripe, they burst into bright, sharp flavor in her mouth, softened by the sweet cream.

Before the bowl was empty, Josette found herself on Will's lap, forgetting they played a game, forgetting that anyone might watch. They enjoyed the berries together, Will kissing juice from her lips, she tasting cream on his.

He cradled her with arms trailing the linen shirt, his satin breeches warmed by his hard legs. Josette cuddled against his chest to feed him the last finger-full of cream.

Will closed his mouth over her fingertip, suckling gently. The heat inside her became incandescent and wove around her heart.

He licked the underside of her finger, taking his time. "We should to bed, my love. 'Tis already dawn."

Gray tinged the slits around the window's draperies, announcing another long summer day.

Disappointment stung Josette, and she slid reluctantly from his lap. "I'm not used to the sun rising so quickly."

"For the Highlands, there is day in summer, night in winter."

Will freed his arms from the strawberry stained shirt and tossed the ruined thing into the corner. In breeches and stockings, he doused the candles.

Only the dying fire lit their way to the bed. In the deep shadow near the bedcurtains, Will unlaced and unhooked Josette's clothing, his hands deft and sure. He stripped her down to her chemise, then held the bedcovers so she could slip under them. His body blocked her from the rest of the chamber, and the darkness finished hiding her. An observer—if any watched—would see only a flurry of bedclothes as Josette slid in and covered herself to her chin.

Will more leisurely removed his stockings and breeches, and then, in nothing but his skin, reached for a nightshirt that had been left to warm near the fire, along with a nightgown for Josette.

The sight of Will, tall and naked, half hard from their playing in the chair, should have satisfied any watcher. It certainly made Josette fix her gaze to him.

She'd told him there would be no liaison, that they would be in separate bedchambers. Fate and Lady Bentley had dictated otherwise. Josette's resolutions were dissolving, crumbling, and she wondered if he'd known they would so quickly.

Unhurriedly Will pulled on the nightshirt and climbed into the bed, shutting the curtains around it, giving Josette privacy to don the warm nightgown.

He spooned into her as they lay down. "Sleep well, love," he said, pulling her back against him. "I won't let anyone near you."

His strong arm around her waist was reassuring, his body at her back a wall of protection.

But who protects me from Will? Josette wondered sleepily, as exhaustion from the journey and the night of entertainments took over.

As she drifted off, the answer came to her. *He does.*

WILL DIDN'T MEAN TO SLEEP, BUT TIREDNESS AS WELL AS THE COMFORT of Josette overwhelmed him. He'd learned to control his sleep—to go without for long stretches, and then hole up and slumber for days to recover—but when he was with Josette, his self-discipline deserted him.

He had no dreams, for once, and woke hours later. One glance at a crack between the bed's drapes and long experience told him it was about noon.

Josette slept on, curled up against him, her face relaxed. He loved her like this, when all tension left her, and she simply enjoyed the sweet release of sleep.

Today Will would search the room and stop up the peepholes or any other openings. He hadn't had time to do it yesterday, and there had continually been one servant or the other in the chamber whenever he'd entered it—unpacking their clothes, turning down the bed, keeping the fire going. He wouldn't have known about the peepholes if Lady Bentley hadn't been so transparent.

"You will enjoy these," she'd said when she'd pressed the bowl of strawberries into his hands. "You and your lovely wife. And I will enjoy you enjoying them."

She'd looked mysterious and departed, and Will had concluded she must have a way to watch them.

Poor woman. She obviously craved bodily satisfaction, and her husband looked to be uncomfortable about anything to do with bed. No wonder there were so many young men here, including a few clearly out of love with their wives.

But while Will felt pity for Lady Bentley, he would not give her the voyeuristic satisfaction of watching him with Josette, or let her look at Josette at all.

Will lay with his head on Josette's pillow, basking in their closeness. Soon this would be over, not only the intimacy in bed, but their time together. They'd discover things, or discover nothing, and return to the castle, where Josette would again keep him at arm's length. Best to soak up what he could.

Josette stirred. She murmured as she stretched, then she rolled over, landing against him. Her eyes fluttered open in confusion.

"Good morning, darling," Will said, adopting Sir William's tones in case of listeners. "Did you sleep well?"

After the first startled glance, Josette realized where she was and why, and why Will lay next to her. He readied himself for her to leap from the bed or suggest he leave it, but she relaxed and nestled into him.

"Amazingly well, sir. Fresh air, good strawberries …"

"And a fine bed. Remarkably comfortable. With you." The last he said in a low voice, the truth.

Josette's face went red. "What shall we do today?"

Will sent her a slow smile, liking that her blush grew stronger. "Sir Harmon says there's excellent fishing. As evidenced by the tasty fish at dinner. Perhaps I'll catch our next meal."

"Oh, men and their fishing." Josette pushed at him playfully. "I suppose I must remain behind and embroider?"

"Do you embroider? I never knew. Perhaps our hostess and other ladies will provide some entertainment for you."

Will made himself sound exactly like the sort of husband who pursued his own interests and neither knew nor cared what his wife got up to in his absence.

He vowed then and there that when he persuaded Josette to marry him, he'd make it his business to discover what she enjoyed, all her interests. He'd drive her distracted with it. The man who ignored his wife, in Will's opinion, shouldn't be amazed when she began to ignore *him*.

For now, Josette was nestled against his nightshirted body, she only in a nightgown. The bed's thick hangings were pulled closed, and shadows prevailed, never mind that outside it was bright midday.

Will cupped Josette's face with one hand and kissed her.

Instead of pushing him away as he feared, Josette rose into the kiss, her body warm from slumber. She was a loving woman, never holding back. She showed it in her obvious love for Glenna, and whenever she'd been with Will ...

They'd been unstoppable.

Will sank down to her, hungry for her. Josette's smaller frame fit against his big form, and she stretched against him, as though wanting to touch every part of him.

Her mouth held heat, as did her fingers on his back, his hips, his backside. It had been too long, too many years. Will caressed her as she touched him, savoring her kisses.

She cradled him in softness, and at the same time, strength. Josette was beauty, kindness, resilience. Everything terrible in Will's life receded, becoming distant and unable to reach him, defeated by the magic of Josette.

She held him against the tumult that roiled around him, the danger that struck him from every side, somehow deflecting pain so that it could not hurt him.

The nightshirt bared Will's thigh as he slid it between her legs, the thin cloth of the nightgown moving aside to let him touch her heat. He knew how to pleasure her even when they were both half-dressed, always had, knew what made her lose control and composure.

Her face tightened at his touch, and then Will watched Josette let herself relax. They were in a place of aloneness, the thick curtains around the bed shielding them from would-be watchers.

Will's kiss hid her soft moan. She clutched him, rubbing herself against his thigh, taking her joy in the hot friction. Will ached for her, his hardness bumping her and the bedclothes as he pleasured her.

The action made him want to come, to drive inside Josette and fill her, but Will clamped down on his instincts. Josette had consented to this charade, and he wouldn't repay her by simply taking what he wanted.

On the other hand, this was punishing. Will was about to lift away, drag himself from the bed and her, when Josette seized him and pulled him down to her.

She squirmed against him, and he saw when she let reason flee and pure sensation take over. Damned if Will would move then. Josette opened her eyes, her smile wide as she cried out her release.

She took her pleasure for a very long time, Will shaking with effort to hold her and keep himself from simply thrusting into her. He was dying, but he was a strong man. He'd learned to live with disappointment before.

"You're beautiful, love," he whispered, his words drowned out by her cries. "So beautiful. My J— My sweet."

Even now, he couldn't say her name. They couldn't be Will and Josette.

One day—one day, he vowed it—they'd shut out the world and be only themselves.

"William," she gasped.

Josette held him to her in a crushing grip. Will fell onto her gladly, embracing her strength. This lady was worth loving. He'd protect her with all his might, and one day soon she would be his.

ANOTHER TEDIOUS DAY OF TEDIOUSNESS. WILL BEGAN TO WONDER HOW the inhabitants of this house existed without killing each other.

The Scottish land beyond the gates was vividly beautiful, the loch an ever-changing glory, yet these people shut themselves inside and scarcely bothered to look out the windows. To them, Highland Scotland was a place of barely tolerable exile, while Will fought to call it home.

Sir Harmon invited Captain Ellis to join him and Will fishing. Ellis started to accept, then realizing Josette was staying behind, changed his mind.

Will had almost changed his mind as well, but Josette's covert glare sent him on. Josette had the courage, intelligence, resources, and ability to take care of herself—Will knew. But it was a relief that she also had the watchdog of Captain Ellis guarding her.

Will kissed Josette good-bye, letting the kiss become warm enough for others to exchange either disdainful or knowing looks. He left her striving to be polite to the ladies who were, as she'd predicted, embroidering, and shouldered fishing poles to accompany Sir Harmon out into the damp summer day.

The wind was fresh, the day warm in the brief glory that was the Scottish summer. Mist hung in the air, tatters of it streaming over the loch.

Will tramped toward the loch behind Sir Harmon and his retinue —the man couldn't move without two or three servants surrounding him at all times. One was the young man who'd guided Will and Josette around the fountains the day before. The footmen had at least shed their red satin coats and breeches and wore sensible drab-colored wool against the damp.

Will's thoughts of Josette distracted him from the business at hand. Mostly those thoughts were of her warmth, her scent, her body beneath him. The beauty of her invaded his soul.

How the devil had he stayed away from her so long? Simple—Will had known that if he went to her, he'd toss aside the rest of his life to remain with her, no matter if they ran a boardinghouse in London, or retreated to France, or camped in a hut in a remote part of Scotland. The two of them being together would be the point.

Josette didn't necessarily want that. She agreed they were companionable, and fell into the game with ease. But she didn't like the variable wind that was Will Mackenzie, and the constant peril he brought that might risk her life, or more importantly to her, the life of her daughter.

Would she believe him if he said he would abandon his dangerous pursuit of secrets, of covertly hunting down dangerous men? Very likely not.

He'd just have to convince her, then.

While Sir Harmon had proved to be a feeble conversationalist, he seemed to know much about fishing. He picked the spot on the shore Will would have, and instructed his servants to set up stools and poles, and also a rather elaborate tent a little way up the hill where they'd dine.

Sir Harmon didn't speak as they cast their lines. Will, as Sir William, began to chatter, but fell into an embarrassed silence when Sir Harmon glowered at him.

"Right—fish." Will turned his gaze to the slowly rippling loch. "Must be quiet."

This gained Will an approving nod. He gained more approval from Sir Harmon by fishing competently and catching a few quickly.

"Not much else to do in Switzerland," Will said when Sir Harmon laconically praised him. "Well, that and climb about. Good fishing there."

"You were in Lucerne?" Sir Harmon asked.

"And Basel. Lovely city." Will had spent a year of his life there, which was why he'd chosen it for William and Anna's sojourn.

"I had friends in Basel." Sir Harmon cast his line across the water. "Lived in Hottingen."

Will contrived to look confused as Sir Harmon named a town near Zurich. "I don't believe that's in Basel. But we stayed mainly to the south of the Rhine. Near the Basler Münster."

Sir Harmon raised his brows. "Ah. Well, perhaps I mistook him."

He'd been testing Will. Interesting. Perhaps the man was not as feeble-minded as he seemed.

They fished for a time, no sound but the soft swish of lines being cast, the splash of a fish as it investigated the bait. In the quiet mist, the fish bit well, and the two men accumulated a nice pile.

"No need to return to the house for a meal," Sir Harmon said.

"Unless you wish to rush back to your wife." He gave Will a disapproving look before handing the string of fish to the dark-skinned footman.

Will sent him a rueful grin. "My darling girl is no doubt glad to be rid of me for a bit. I do tend to live in her pocket."

"Want to be careful your house isn't run by petticoats." Sir Harmon shouldered his pole. "Trust me."

"But my wife's petticoats are things of beauty. Especially when they are coming off her." Will guffawed, and Sir Harmon sent him a disapproving look. Definitely not a man fond of bodily passions.

They reached the tent. The dark-skinned footman began to clean the fish behind it while another had a fire going, ready for cooking. They'd set a table with linens and silver inside the tent, and the third footman was pouring deep red wine.

"No whisky?" Will inquired cheerily.

Sir Harmon frowned in distaste. "Won't have it in my house. Filthy stuff. Destroys your gut."

Will thought back to the tasting days in his brother Malcolm's distillery, breathing the scents of copper and steam in the stillroom, the mellow scent of oak in the aging room, the acrid, smoky smell of the coopery, where wine barrels were charred and rebuilt to be used for the whisky.

Mal would broach the first cask that had come out of its three-year hibernation, and the brothers would lift their glasses and taste. They'd sprawl about Mal's tasting room, laughing, drinking, telling horrible jokes, happy without realizing it.

I'll give it all back to you, Runt, Will vowed in silence. *I promise you.*

Sir Harmon and Will strolled out of the tent again and now Sir Harmon wandered back to the loch, shielding his glass of wine from the mist as he looked out over the water.

Will caught the dark-skinned footman watching him, eyes sliding sideways while he worked on the fish. The lad's gaze went to Sir Harmon, the hatred on his face unmistakable.

Will moved to him while the other footmen followed Sir Harmon in case he might suddenly want something.

"Wicked-looking knife," Will remarked.

The young man started and glanced down at his knife—a long thin blade with a small hook on the end.

"Best for gutting," he said.

"I imagine. What's your name, lad?"

"John."

Sir Harmon called every footman in his house "John." "I mean your real name."

The footman gave Will a sullen glare. "Henri."

"You'll never do it, Henri," Will said softly. "Too many witnesses."

Henri didn't protest or grow indignant. He only looked at Will with fear and rage so entangled Will knew he'd been nursing his fury for some time.

"You going to arrest me?" Henri's voice went defiant.

"For gutting fish? Not if that knife stays only in the fish. What did you plan to do? Creep up on him? Or simply attack him? The other lads won't let you, you know. Most likely they'd hang too, for not stopping you."

Henri blinked, as though he hadn't thought of that. When a servant killed a master, often other servants were blamed as well. A powerful man could have those innocents tried and convicted.

"I don't know what you're talking about, sir," Henri said stubbornly. "I'm cleaning fish, like the master asked me to."

"I understand vengeance, Henri," Will told him in a quiet voice. "Believe me. But there are better ways of going about it. Ways in which you won't get caught."

He saw that he'd gained Henri's interest, if not his trust. "Don't know what you mean, sir."

"I'd like to speak to you about it. Not now," Will put in quickly. Sir Harmon had turned back toward the tent. "Later. I'll have another hankering to see the gardens. Tell me then."

He didn't wait for Henri to acquiesce. Will resumed his Sir William face and joined Sir Harmon as they ducked into the tent and sat down to wait for their meal.

"Sir Harmon," Will said companionably as another of the footman poured them more of the blood-red hock. "What should a young man —such as myself—do if he needs money quickly? *Very* quickly? Do you have any advice?"

CHAPTER 12

Sir Harmon froze in the act of lifting his glass to his lips. "Are you touching me for money, young man?"

"No, no, no," Will said quickly, with a breathy laugh. "I would never presume. But …" He shrugged. "You know how it can be. My wife, bless her boots, had a nice fortune when we married, but with one thing and another … The dear gel must have the best of everything, you know."

"You lived extravagantly and ran through the principal," Sir Harmon said with brutal bluntness. "Foolish."

"Agreed. Neither of us is exactly wise. On the other hand, our man of business let us down. One's man of business is supposed to keep one out of difficulties, isn't he?"

Sir Harmon snorted. "A man of business only wants his fee. Good sound investments are the way to wealth, sir, but there are few to be had. The colonies are where I made my money, as you know. My advice is to go there. Land is cheap—the king wants men to reap the bounty of the New World and bring it home. Become a planter. Tobacco or sugar—cash crops. You'll have your wife in pretty new frocks in no time."

"Planter?" Will raised his brows. "I haven't the vaguest notion how to farm, especially in a foreign clime. I barely understood my father's little fields of barley and potatoes."

"You hire men who do know about it," Sir Harmon said impatiently. "They understand when to sow and when to harvest, where to get the workers, and how to sell the crops."

"I suppose, in the colonies, these workers are enslaved?" Will blenched. "I'm against slavery, myself. Don't approve of men in bondage."

"You find someone to deal with that side of things as well."

Never have to soil my hands, Will thought in disgust.

"I'd make a meal of it." Will sighed. "I was hoping for something that involved less travel. I am miserable on the journey between Britain and Amsterdam. I can't imagine weeks at sea." He pulled out a handkerchief and dabbed his forehead, as though already seasick.

"You're a bit of a milksop, aren't you, son?" Sir Harmon asked.

"I'm not ashamed of it. The ladies still love me."

"Hmph." Sir Harmon looked him over. "I suppose they do. Females haven't much sense. Well, then, you'll have to find money here. For investing, you understand."

Sir Harmon snapped his fingers, and one of the footmen stepped forward with a box. Will half expected Sir Harmon to open it and pull out a handful of gold, but he only lifted out two pipes and a pouch of tobacco.

He handed Will one pipe and began to fill his. Will decided that his character should be man enough to enjoy the occasional pipe, and accepted the tobacco pouch. He tamped the fragrant tobacco, soaked in brandy, into the bowl and let the footman light it.

"I might be able to help you," Sir Harmon said after they'd puffed a few moments, the tent filling with pungent smoke. "In return for a favor, of course."

"I'd be most grateful," Will said, putting just enough earnestness into his voice. "Though I have no idea what I can do for you."

Sir Harmon fixed him with a sharp gaze. "You travel much, you and your wife. I imagine you hear things, see things."

Will contrived to look nonplussed. "We do. We like to take in the sights, visit people. I am astonished at the hospitality we find wherever we go."

"Exactly. And you have no trouble falling into conversation. If you listen well, you might learn something that could benefit yourself—hints about shipments or what politicians are up to, or where battles are about to be fought on the Continent—that might help you know where to invest."

Will frowned, and then sat up straight as though enlightened. "Ah. You mean what ships are coming in or how many guns our troops seek. Or French troops seek for that matter. Everyone needs to purchase something."

"You are an intelligent young man," Sir Harmon said in an encouraging tone. "There is also benefit in knowing who is moving where on the Continent and what they plan. That way we know what they need and what ships might be taking them things, who provides their supplies ... that sort of thing."

Dear God, he's trying to spy on the British Army, Will thought in exasperation. *And not very ably.*

"I see," he said, as though working it through. "You mean, we can invest with these people supplying and shipping for the army and make our money back, and then some."

"You have grasped the thing, my boy. But it does not do well for you to bring others into your confidence about this, not even your wife. Ladies don't understand about money matters, do they?"

Will happened to know a woman from Edinburgh, who, when bequeathed a small amount of cash, had turned it into a vast fortune through skilled investment. She was a constant visitor to the Exchange in London and advised the boards of many companies.

Will nodded. "Yes, the ladies are lovely creatures, but not adept with finances."

"I am pleased we understand each other."

"Again ..." Will hesitated artfully. "I am willing to help you decide where to invest, but I have few coins with which to do it."

"I am coming to that. I have a friend who might be able to lend you a bit. To be paid back at the earliest possible instant, of course."

This all might mean nothing—Sir Harmon might be a petty trickster happy to pull another into his net, but then again, he might be selling secrets about British troop movements and sitting on a horde of French gold.

Will had to find out. For the sake of the ladies waiting in the castle, his family in exile, his friends in prison or in hiding, himself, and most of all for Josette, he had to follow this lead.

"Of course," Will said. "I place myself into your hands." He bowed from his chair and raised his glass to Sir Harmon.

JOSETTE SPENT A DULL AFTERNOON, CHAFING IN HER CONFINEMENT. As she'd feared, Lady Bentley wanted nothing more than to sit in the drawing room, embroidering on silk and gossiping. The other ladies followed suit, wishing to please their hostess, and proceeded to cut to ribbons every lady and gentlemen not present.

The husbands wandered about when they weren't playing cards or dice, one idly picking tunes on the clavichord. They didn't look particularly happy about being penned up in the house, but any suggestion they go out walking, even in the vast garden, was met with horror.

Josette stifled her impatience and listened carefully to the chatter. Women often knew quite a bit more about what went on in households, businesses, banks, and in the political arena, than gentlemen understood or gave them credit for.

Lady Bentley, however, seemed obsessed with the male anatomy, especially the size of one part of it. A man who was tall, or had large hands or a large nose—or even large elbows—was meant to have other attributes of corresponding size.

Lady Bentley gave Josette blatant looks when she made these jokes. Will was indeed tall, his hands were large, and his nose was proportional to the rest of him, as were, of course, his elbows.

But if Lady Bentley believed Josette would relate the exact dimensions of Will's cockstand, the lady was much mistaken. Josette hadn't had occasion to measure it exactly, in any case, though she could probably approximate it with her hands.

Much merriment was had from Sir William's name, and Josette was asked if she blushed whenever she called him Willie.

"Merry William, happy Will," Lady Bentley chanted. "But stiff Willie makes his wife happiest of all."

The ladies burst into laughter. The men in the next room glanced at them in perplexity, which sent the ladies into even more merriment.

Josette laughed with them, and wished she'd stayed at the castle. Not that the ladies there did not carry on with bawdy talk, as had her lodgers in London. But they didn't joke about Will, didn't have hunger in their eyes for a man Josette … loved?

The startling word broke through the inane chatter and made Josette suck in a sharp breath.

Will had squelched her good intentions of being cool to him this morning when he'd so easily brought her to joy. She might as well never have declared she'd keep him at arm's length. Josette wished she had said nothing—it would be less mortifying now that he'd seduced her with only his touch.

Abrupt noise announced the return of Sir Harmon, Will, and the servants, and Josette breathed out in relief.

Lady Bentley gave Josette a sly smile when Will appeared in the drawing room, cleaned up from the expedition.

"I say, old thing, a turn in the garden?" he asked Josette. "The weather has grown almost warm. Well, as warm as this benighted part of the world ever is."

"The corner by the summerhouse is quite lovely," Lady Bentley said with an arch glance at Josette. "And secluded."

Will looked bewildered at the giggling ladies but held out his arm to Josette.

The sight of his elbow sticking out increased the laughter. "Bundle up warm, Lady Jacobs," one of the women said. "And make sure you wear your gloves, Sir William."

Will lifted one hand, covered with a fine leather glove, and stared at it in bafflement. The ladies collapsed in mirth, and Lady Bentley's eyes shone with delight.

"Thank heavens none of them dare to set foot outside," Josette said as she more or less dragged Will down the path between the fountains. "I thought I would scream."

"Dull, was it?"

"Frightening, rather. Do not wander alone in the halls of this house, I beg you. Who knows when you might be dragged into a room and your cock-staff subjected to measurement."

"What's that, lass?" Will gave her a startled look, then he chuckled. "Terrifying."

"I'm not joking." Josette pulled him closer. "The ladies are cooped up and the gentlemen pay little attention to them. All are desperate for diversion."

"We may not have to stay much longer," Will said. "Sir Harmon indicated he'd send me to a friend who will lend me money. It might have nothing to do with the gold, but I must take the chance."

Josette perked up. "Even a chance is excellent news. What did Sir Harmon say about this friend?"

"Little, but I did not come out here to tell you about that."

"Oh, then what did—"

She broke off as Will halted near the fountain of the three bare-buttocked lads.

A footman waited there in the sturdy clothes he'd worn to carry the fishing gear. He was young, in his later teen years, Josette estimated, with the lankiness of youth that would soon turn to bulk and muscle. At the moment, his face held fear, distrust, and hope—as far from a servant's blank countenance as could be.

Will gestured for the lad to follow and led the way to a small building that looked as though it had been plucked from a Greek isle and deposited here. The summerhouse Lady Bentley mentioned, Josette assumed.

"This is Henri," Will said when they reached it. He pronounce the name the French way, *Ahn-ri*. "My wife can be trusted, lad."

Henri did not look reassured.

"I can be," Josette said. "What is this about?"

"Henri is going to tell me why he felt it necessary to contemplate Sir Harmon's death," Will said, to her astonishment. "I want to know why."

"Because he's a killer," Henri said without hesitation. "He killed my family in Antigua, then he murdered the Scots family who took me in. He's murdered my family twice, and he should die for it."

CHAPTER 13

*J*osette flinched at Henri's savage words and the violence they described, so incongruous with the beauty of this corner of the gardens.

"What happened?" she asked softly.

Unashamed tears filled Henri's eyes. "My family were slaves in Antigua. Sir Harmon took over the plantation where we worked. He does not know I lived there—he never noticed us. He worked my parents and sister until they were sick, and when they could do no more labor, they were turned out. I did what I could, but my parents and my sister were too ill, too starved. They died."

Josette listened in horror. "Oh, lad. I'm so sorry."

"I ran away. A Scottish family helped me. They brought me here and made certain I was freed. Papers to prove it. I worked for them— here. It was not like this."

Henri waved his hand at the summerhouse, the gardens, the vast mansion in the distance.

"And then *he* came," Henri went on. "Sir Harmon hated the Dunbars—the Scottish family—had been their enemy in the Indies. They were missionaries, and he believed they'd cause a slave revolt, and he'd lose all his land and money. When Sir Harmon returned to England, he lied to the government and said Mr. Dunbar was a Jacobite who sent money to the King over the Water. But they were not. They were innocent. They were arrested and taken away, and I'm sure they are dead. Sir Harmon seized their property and built all this. I stayed here to work. He does not know. Now I will kill him and throw myself into the sea, and they will be avenged. Why did you stop me?" He glared at Will.

"Because I need Sir Harmon to stay alive just a bit longer," Will said. "He's a rotten bastard, I agree. But killing him won't solve matters, and drowning is an unpleasant death. The man's not worth dying for."

Henri gazed at him in disbelief. "What reason do I have to live? Anyone I ever cared for is gone. Taken away from me."

"I know." Will put a kind hand on the youth's shoulder. Henri winced, but he didn't pull away. "I can help you, lad. How would you like to bring down Sir Harmon? Possibly get him arrested and hanged, free the Dunbars, if they are still alive, and live the rest of your days on his ill-gotten gains?"

Henri remained unconvinced. "Killing him will be quicker."

"Not necessarily. The cavalry officer who is staying in the house, Captain Ellis, would feel obligated to arrest you, no matter how much he agreed with you. He is an honorable man and follows the rules. I, on the other hand, do not."

Henri jerked from Will's touch. "Why should I believe you? You are one of them."

"I'll thank you not to insult me." Will's voice held a touch of humor. "I am not one of those trumped-up English brats. I'm not ready to tell you exactly who I am, but trust me, lad, I want Sir Harmon. I came here to finish him."

"How?" Henri's tone was suspicious, but he at least waited for Will's answer.

"I will make him betray himself, and then the honorable Captain Ellis will have no choice but to take him into custody."

"And his friends will get him free again," Henri sneered.

"Not if he's the traitor I believe he is. I sense in Sir Harmon a man who'd sell his own mother if he could make a penny. Probably has already."

Henri listened impatiently. "How can this help me find the Dunbars?"

"I know people. Those people know people who know many things. Or at least can find them out." Will didn't boast or even speak with great confidence. He simply stated facts that Josette knew to be true.

Henri's scowl returned. "Who are you really? Not Prince Charlie himself, are you?"

"Good Lord, no. My dad would skin me if I waltzed about like that overly arrogant coxcomb. I'm merely concerned with justice—and Sir Harmon might have knowledge that would help me greatly. Tell me, lad—as a servant you'll have learned the ins and outs of this place. Is there somewhere Sir Harmon hides things he wants no one to find? From his guests, his servants, his wife?"

"Here." Henri jerked his thumb at the pseudo Greek summerhouse. "There's also a secret room in the wine cellar at the main house. He thinks it's secret anyway."

"Ah." Will headed for the summerhouse, mounting the stone steps to its door. "An easy place to start."

"It's locked," Henri said as he and Josette trailed after him. "Only Sir Harmon and the majordomo have the keys."

"No matter."

Will drew a pair of thin wires from his pocket, knelt before the lock, and proceeded to pick it. Josette watched with interest, Henri in skepticism. In less than a minute, the lock clicked and the door creaked open.

"Not very formidable," Will said. "A baby could pick that. Anyone at home?" he sang out in his fop's voice.

Silence met them. Josette doubted any of the house party were here—they'd have had to venture outdoors.

The interior of the summerhouse had been simply furnished, without the grandeur of the main house. A table and chairs, a bookcase with a smattering of tomes, a chair and a desk, empty of papers. It was cool here, no fire in the small fireplace.

A search turned up nothing. Will was thorough, and he'd taught Josette to be. Henri watched them before joining in.

The floor was solid, no trapdoors leading to tunnels. "Too new," Will said in derision. "No escape route, priest's hole, or smuggler's tunnel. No self-respecting Scot of the old days would build a place like this."

"Sir Harmon had it put up," Henri confirmed. "Was finished six months ago."

"He would. Well." Will wiped his brow with the back of his hand and continued his search.

They turned up no caskets full of French gold, either in coins or bars, and no papers or maps that would lead them to such a find. The room seemed to be Sir Harmon's hideaway, with books on horses and fishing and not much else.

Will rubbed his palms, looking more animated.

"All right, then," he said. "On to the wine cellar."

NEITHER SIR HARMON NOR LADY BENTLEY NOR THE MAJORDOMO questioned them or tried to stop Henri from leading them to the cellar of the main house, which Will took to be a sign they'd find nothing.

A man skilled at concealment would not show concern about a person approaching his hiding place—betraying nervousness only gave a hiding place away. Sir Harmon did not seem skilled, however; therefore, his lack of worry told Will he had hidden nothing in his cellar. But Will would never forgive himself if he didn't search anyway.

Sir Harmon did have many casks of wine and brandy. Again Will thought of the whisky Malcolm had labored on every day of the year, how he'd hover over the mash like a mother hen, and wander among the kegs of aging brew, touching them, *talking* to them. Will imagined the British army's joy when they chanced upon the distillery and all the barrels in the aging room, and his deep anger simmered.

He tried to press Kilmorgan out of his thoughts, shut out the intense pain of the memories. Ironic that Will had been avid to leave home as a lad, weary of living with a horde of irascible men. Now he'd give anything to bring those days back.

A small door behind a stack of barrels intrigued him, as well as the fact that the racks of barrels were on tracks and could easily be moved. Henri helped Will slide the racks aside, and another picked lock later, the three of them peered into a small chamber—empty.

"Well, that is disappointing," Will said with a sigh. "But worth remembering."

He closed the door, locked it with his picks, and he and Henri shoved the barrels in front of it again.

"Are you playing a game?" came the voice of Lady Bentley.

Will quickly motioned for Henri to duck into the shadows as Lady Bentley swept toward them, the feathers in her bag-like cap swaying. "You hide, and I find you?"

Josette, bless her, let out a high-pitched laugh. "How delightful. No, my husband was curious about your husband's brandy. So much of it." She spread her hands and looked about at the racks of kegs.

She played the insipid Anna so well, Will thought with an inward grin. He wanted to kiss her. Again.

"Sir Harmon likes his drink." Lady Bentley's tone turned irritated. "He has friends bring it to him—never more delighted than when another shipment arrives. He won't be able to drink it all in his lifetime."

"He is kind to share it with guests," Will said. "I look forward to more at supper."

"There won't be supper," Lady Bentley announced. "That is, it will be served, but we won't sit down to it. I've ordered a feast to be spread in the dining room while we dance in the ballroom. But you look surprised, Lady Jacobs—I forgot, you ran out to walk with your husband before we decided." She clasped her hands like an excited girl. "We're having a masked ball. Hurry upstairs now, or you'll have no time to get your costumes sorted."

"OF ALL THE DAFT IDEAS ..." JOSETTE TRAILED OFF AS WILL LACED HER into the blue and pink gown covered with silk roses she had chosen from Lady Bentley's wide-ranging wardrobe.

Will, having spent a few years coming and going in European courts, had grown used to impromptu parties dreamed up by a bored queen or official mistress. Spontaneity counted as entertainment in their cushioned worlds.

"More time to learn things, my dear," Will said into Josette's ear.

He pressed a kiss to her neck. The smile she flashed him made Will want to consign the Bentleys to hell and take Josette to bed for the rest of the night.

Will finished lacing Josette's gown and helped tie on her mask, a lace affair with a spray of silk flowers on one side.

Will had fashioned his costume from a banner he'd found hanging in the gallery, taken with permission from Stelton, the majordomo. It had been easy for him to sew seams at the shoulders and tack the banner—a gold cross—to the front to make a surcoat.

"You are handy with a needle," Josette commented.

"Forced to be. Grew to manhood without a mum and not enough servants willing to sew clothes for six lads. We learned to shift for ourselves. A handy skill to have, stitching."

He finished and pulled the surcoat over his regular clothes.

"A knight of old," he said, studying himself in the mirror. "Sir William of ... Who knows where?"

"Unfair," Josette said. She wore flowers in the wig she'd donned over her knot of hair. "You only have to throw that off when the evening is over. I'll have to struggle out of all this fussiness."

"I don't mind helping you struggle." Will laced his arms around her waist from behind and pressed a kiss to her exposed shoulder.

Josette touched his hair, and Will's blood pumped hot. He was already thoroughly sick of Sir Harmon and his wife and their equally unpleasant guests.

At the moment, he wanted to bury himself in Josette and forget his pain. Damn men like Bentley and idiots like the zealous High-landers who'd thought it would be easy to throw King Geordie's armies out of Scotland. If not for them, he could be curled up around Josette without a care, the two of them wrapped in a warm plaid.

Josette's touch brought Will back from his vast well of regret. "Are you all right?"

Will shook his head. "No. But I'll weather it. I always do."

Josette watched him, her beautiful eyes troubled. Will raised her hand to his lips, kissed it, and clasped it to the cross on his chest.

"Shall we go down, my lady?"

"Of course, my knight."

Lady Bentley must have sent word to other Englishmen in the area, because the ballroom had filled with about a dozen couples. None were Scots—a quick scan told Will that—and all were masked. They spoke and laughed in the bright way of people determined to enjoy themselves, no matter that they were in the middle of a hostile wilderness.

Captain Ellis's only nod to a costume was a black mask and a tricorn pulled over his dark hair. He looked Will up and down. "Knight of what order? I don't recognize it."

"I'm sure no one does," Will answered. "One can buy banners of obsolete orders for decorating one's house. My many times great-grandfather was a famous knight, so why not?"

Old Dan Mackenzie had been a savage man who'd fought every enemy of his clan with a ferocity that even now flowed through Mackenzie veins. He'd been given a dukedom for being unstoppable —or perhaps the Scots king had simply tried to tame him with it. Hadn't worked, from what Will had been told.

Captain Ellis frowned. The man liked caution, and he believed Will was never cautious. Not that Captain Ellis hadn't charged out of smoke, alone, against a handful of Scottish soldiers, in an attempt to take back captured artillery. Mal had fought him down, but only with great difficulty.

"Speak to me later," Will said to Ellis under the cover of musicians beginning to play. Couples formed into squares for a minuet.

Will led Josette out, bowing to the other two in their square. He and Josette were skilled at the minuet—they seemed to end up dancing it whenever they came together.

Josette was graceful, her feet moving daintily, her skirts swaying enticingly as they went through the many steps. Her face was flushed, her eyes sparkling, and the smile she flashed at Will as they met and clasped hands held genuine pleasure.

Will was sorry when the minuet wound to an end. He and the second gentleman bowed to Josette and the other lady in the square, and the ladies curtsied prettily.

Josette took Will's arm, and they strolled the room to catch their breaths as another dance formed.

Something caught Will's eye, a flash of familiarity that broke through his disguise and struck the heart of the true Will. It was a jolt of incongruity, past rushing forward to meet present like a hazy phantom.

"A moment." Will made an abrupt turn to a window alcove, which contained a settee with delicate, curved legs. "I think that's one of mine. Yes, I'd swear it."

The settee was a graceful thing of gilded wood, upholstered with a petit-point scene of lords and ladies that had been expertly rendered.

Josette peered at it, bewildered. "One of yours? What do you mean?"

"I had it shipped from France to Kilmorgan. It sat in the front drawing room." Will bent to it, finger going unerringly to a hole in the upholstery above its front left leg. "Yes, here's the tear where Dad threw a whisky tumbler at Duncan. I tried to deflect it, but it caught the edge."

His breath came faster as the phantom rose to blot out his vision. Will had made himself stay away from his burned home—he'd only once returned to the ruins and then never gone again. But to see this piece of furniture, given to Will by the French king when Will had praised it, stirred the red rage inherited from Old Dan Mackenzie.

This was plunder, spoils of war, taken by those who'd destroyed his family. The fact that it had ended up *here*, in the possession of the idiot Sir Harmon, was more than Will could take.

"Will." Josette's soft voice cut through his anger.

Will forced himself to look down at her. Josette was warning him, but her dark eyes were full of understanding. She *knew*.

Josette was the only person in Will's life who grasped what he did and why. Gone were the days a Highlander could muster his clan and protect his lands—Scotland was now one country, gathered into the kingdom called Great Britain with a stroke of a pen.

Will had defended his family the only way he could, inside the nebulous world of intrigue. By becoming a dealer in secrets, he knew what truly went on behind the closed doors of the British government and used the knowledge to protect his family and friends.

In the end, it hadn't been enough. Kilmorgan had fallen, his family scattered into hiding. All because Will hadn't been quick enough, hadn't understood soon enough what would happen when the Jacobites joined Prince Teàrlach when he came home from across the sea.

"Will," Josette whispered again.

"Come with me," Will said, fierceness in his voice. He swept her abruptly out of the room and into the cool garden.

CHAPTER 14

*J*osette had to jog to keep up with Will as he pulled her down the long path, around the silent fountains, past the yew hedges and the folly, and out a far gate.

It was still light outside, daylight lasting to midnight now. The long twilight bathed the sky in dusky blue edged with gold.

Will found a path that wound up the hill, the house soon lost in the folds of green and brown. Behind them was the loch, glittering and gray, hemmed in by hills on its west side, winding to the sea to the south. A soft rain fell, not so much pattering on the earth as filling the air with liquid.

Will halted when the house and formal garden were out of sight and let out a long breath. "God of gods, Josette, what am I doing here?"

The plea was genuine, his voice filled with anguish.

Josette took his hand, which was cold without his gloves. "Saving your family. Your friends."

"Am I?" he growled. "I'm playing a damned game, as I always do. So caught up in the game I forget what the end is supposed to be."

"It is easy be lost in the role," Josette began.

Will jerked from her. He spread his arms, letting the breeze from the loch lift the surcoat and stir the tail of his wig. The disguise couldn't hide what he was from Josette—a Scotsman in his own lands, wild and free.

He spoke to the sky. "When Alec told me he'd almost gone berserk in a crowd of highborn Englishmen, I thought him a fool. He should have put on an inane smile and made digs the English idiots couldn't understand. I didn't realize …" He swung to Josette. "I ought to let Henri kill Sir Harmon and to hell with the rest of them."

"You'd not find the gold, if you did that."

"The gold." Will scrubbed his face with his hands. "I don't believe it exists, Josie. It can't, at least, not in one place. It's a dream." He gazed over the loch, body outlined by dying light.

"If it's true it doesn't exist, what will you do?" Josette asked softly.

"End this charade. Have Captain Ellis arrest Sir Harmon on suspicion of being a spy and possible traitor. Take my damned settee and return it to Kilmorgan. At least I'd have something to sit on."

"No."

Will went still, the wind lifting the curls of his brown wig to let his own red locks escape. "What was that, lass?"

"I said, no." Josette squared her shoulders. "Sir Harmon has promised to send you to a man to give you funds. Who knows? He might have the French gold."

Will shook his head. "A very long shot. He'll likely be a simple moneylender Sir Harmon has in his pocket."

"A chance I am willing to take. We have come this far, and I have put up with much. I'll not run back to the castle and tell the ladies we failed them because you saw a piece of old furniture."

Will glared at her, the anguish in his eyes naked and raw. Josette knew that finding the settee, blatantly pillaged from his father's house, had struck a nerve, had ripped off the bandage he kept over his deepest wounds.

Josette began to apologize for speaking too harshly, but Will's anguish abruptly fell away and he burst out laughing.

"Bless you for the fine woman you are." He seized Josette's hands and pulled her to him, then he reached up and swiftly untied her mask. "No one cuts to the heart of the matter like you, my Josie."

He tossed the mask away as his arms went around her. Josette's breath left her as Will drew her up and kissed her hard on the mouth.

He tasted of brandy and spice, anger and laughter, the complexity of Will Mackenzie. His strong hands braced her as the kiss turned forceful, Will's torment and determination coming to her like fire.

They stood on a craggy hill in an untamed land, its Highland son firmly rooted. The land flowed up through Will and out through his touch, his kisses, his embrace. Josette had sensed the solidness that was Scotland in him when they'd first met, and now that he was home, it filled him, welcomed him.

The rough of his whiskers burned her lips, his fingers bit into her back, his hard body pressed aside her skirts. Josette drank him in, knowing she could have so little of him. Will was strength, desire, a mountain she needed to steady her but one she could never ascend.

She expected him at any moment to break the kiss, straighten their clothes, and lead her back inside to take up the game once more.

Will rose from her, the light in his eyes like stars against the night. He removed the fake surcoat in one rapid movement and dropped it on the ground like a carpet.

He lowered her to it and Josette went willingly, tugging off her irritating wig on the way. Will's skilled hands easily found the laces and hooks of her stomacher, bodice, skirts. He wore almost as many clothes as she did, and began to laugh as Josette fought his cloth-covered buttons, ribbons, and profusion of fabric.

"'Tis so much easier with a kilt, lass," Will said. The front piece of his breeches came undone, letting his cock, thick and hard, tumble out.

Josette caught it in her hands, and Will drew a sharp breath.

She hadn't been properly with him in an age, but she remembered the feel of his cock, every long inch. The rigid cap, the smooth, tight skin of the shaft, the intoxicating weight in her hand.

Will braced himself over her to kiss her. He took his time, kissing her thoroughly while cool breezes blew across her exposed legs.

Josette wasn't cold, though. Will kept her warm, sheltered from the weather.

He'd bared her breasts, and they tingled as he kissed them. He licked her skin then nuzzled his way to her nipple, dragging it into his mouth.

Josette savored the pull of his lips, the scrape of his teeth, how his eyes closed as he concentrated on suckling her. She stroked his cock, swirling her thumb over the tip in the way she remembered he liked.

When Will looked at her, his eyes held fire, but his smile was slow and wicked.

"I've *missed* you, lass."

Josette had missed *him*—she'd hadn't known how much, until she'd seen him again. Now she realized she'd waited for his return with every breath, wanting him to bound back into her life, send her his smile, and ask in his rich Scots voice, "How are you, love?"

She couldn't speak, words catching in her throat. *I missed you. I want you. I need you.* The sounds seemed inadequate for the emotions that gripped her.

Josette laced her fingers through his hair, as Will stretched on top of her, a comforting weight.

Their gazes met, time flowing away. Josette was young again, three-and-twenty, swept off her feet by Lord Will Mackenzie. He had an easy way with him, a ready smile, a spark she'd wanted to touch.

Will brushed back a lock of her hair, his intense gaze on her, all smiles gone.

"I dreamed of you so long, lass." His whisper melded with the wind. "I scarce dared believe I'd see you again. And then ye came strolling in to my interrogation, cool as you please."

Josette touched his cheek. "I didn't want them to kill you." She'd scolded him about this before, but now her voice caught on a sob. "I couldn't let them."

Will's answering look, and touch, burned fires in her blood. "You are the bravest woman I know, my Josie."

"I was terrified."

"No." Will brushed his finger down the bridge of her nose. "You have the heart of a lion."

Josette had been prepared to strike those men down if the laudanum she'd dosed their drink with had not been strong enough.

She'd have done anything to get Will away from men who wanted to rip him to shreds.

She wrapped him in her arms, pulling him down to her. Their mouths met, and there would be no more discussion. They always knew when they were ready.

Josette felt his hand, warm and bare, at the join of her thighs. Then his hand vanished to be replaced by his cock, blunt against her opening, which was hot with longing. Will lifted from the kiss, his golden eyes sharp on her, and then he pushed inside.

Time lost all meaning. Josette no longer felt the chill Highland wind, or saw the sky brushed with its pink-edged clouds, or felt the hard ground at her back.

She knew only Will, the shape of him inside her as he stretched her in the exact way she remembered.

He began slowly, as though concerned he'd hurt her, then when her seeking hands found his bare back, pressing him on, he drew partway out and thrust again, harder this time.

Josette stifled a cry, but they were alone, a long way from anyone. Josette let the shout tear from her throat, her glad cry that the man she loved was loving her, as hard as he could.

It felt *right* for him to be inside her, for her to rise to him in urgency. Joy came out in Josette's cries, her laughter. Will wrenched out a groan, his eyes closing as he continued, his hot kisses falling on her flesh.

"Josette. Love. Beautiful." His words were disjointed, broken by groans. "Missed you. Need you. Love …"

I love you, Will. Josette wanted to yell it to the wind.

She rocked her head back and cried her love without words, rejoicing in the dark, wicked sensations pouring through her and blotting out all else. Nothing was real but the point of need where she and Will joined.

The friction of his thrusts was hot and bright. Will shouted her name at the same time she cried his. They were finishing together, in a crazed frenzy, the two of them locked in wildness. At this moment, nothing mattered but Will, and Josette, alone in the dusk and rain.

Will gave one last frantic thrust, shuddering. The misty rain, which had picked up, slammed into his back, drenching him. He bowed his head, rain dripping from his hair. He'd spent himself inside her, with the madness he'd told her he lost himself in whenever he was with her.

"Will," Josette whispered.

Will lifted his head and opened his eyes. They burned gold, the color of Mackenzie malt, filled with fire and passion.

They lay still, letting the rain fall, Josette's body relaxing in a way it hadn't in years. She touched Will's cheek, and he kissed her palm, his mouth slow and hot.

"My Josette." Will's voice was broken. "My Josie."

He kissed her lips, lay down on her, and was still.

WHEN THEY RETURNED TO THE BALLROOM, CLOTHING AND WIGS restored, rain splotches on their clothes hastily rubbed dry or hidden in folds of fabric, Will realized with surprise that few had noted their absence. Lady Bentley was the exception, of course, and she sent Will a broad smile. She noted his missing surcoat—it had been too muddy and stained to don again after serving as a bed—and her smile grew predatory.

Will ignored her. His whole form felt lighter, his determination returning. Josette had given him back his courage, lifted him from despair.

She was incredibly beautiful, sailing into the crowd with great poise, charming all as she went. Her wig and mask disguised any disarray their lovemaking had caused.

Will's blood thrummed, his body crackling like a charge of lightning. Everything looked brighter, sharper, cleaner-edged.

Henri served the ladies and gentlemen around the room, his face a careful blank, poor lad. Will had never met the Scots family who'd been turned off this land—he'd only become aware of the place since Sir Harmon had been given it. He'd find out, though, and do everything in his power to give the Dunbars their home back and sling Sir Harmon out.

Will kept an eye on Henri in case he erupted, and also on Sir Harmon and Captain Ellis who were speaking at length.

Most of all, his gaze went to Josette as she swayed through the ballroom, chatting, flirting, laughing, fluttering her fan like a coquette. She was an amazing actress, fitting in exactly with this overly-dressed throng, though Will liked her better with her body unfettered, her hair spread in its dark glory.

When Will finally dragged his attention from Josette again, he found Sir Harmon beckoning to him.

Will forced an ingenuous smile and made his way across the ballroom. Captain Ellis was planted at Sir Harmon's side, and his eyes narrowed as he took Will in.

"What happened to the surcoat?" Ellis asked.

"Spilled wine on it, wouldn't you know," Will answered glibly. "Looked as though I'd been gored by a lance, so I tossed it away somewhere."

Captain Ellis didn't believe him, but Sir Harmon made a dismissive gesture. "A servant will find it. I have fixed an appointment for you with my colleague, my boy."

"Excellent news," Will answered, hiding his unease. He'd prefer to speak to Sir Harmon about this without Captain Ellis near, but no help for that now. "Where am I going?" Will glanced eagerly about, as though ready to dash off at once.

Sir Harmon looked amused. "Tomorrow will suffice. You're a restless lad, who'd rather be roaming the hills instead of cooped up here, am I correct? You'll be visiting one of my friends in the Highlands. Name of Clennan Macdonald. Don't worry—he's not a brutish Scot. He's very civilized and fought against the Jacobites."

Will knew damned well he had. And he couldn't go anywhere near Clennan Macdonald, because he'd know Will Mackenzie on sight.

Captain Ellis, who might or might not have any idea of what was going on, waited for Will's answer.

Will beamed a wide smile at both men. "I'd be happy to, sir. You are correct—it will do me good to ride about the hills and breathe this clear air. I'll leave whenever you wish."

CHAPTER 15

*W*ill didn't come to bed. Josette let the maid Lady Bentley had sent up undress her, hoping Will would enter, dismiss the lady's maid, and take over unwrapping Josette himself.

He did not. The maid set Josette's wig aside and brushed out her dark hair, saying nothing about the few pieces of grass she picked out of it.

She buttoned Josette into her comfortable nightrail and helped her settle in the bed warmed with hot bricks. The maid doused all lights but one candle and departed. The light flickered between the crack in the bedcurtains the maid had closed, Josette in a cozy tent.

Alone.

She turned on her side and thought of Will stretched next to her on the ground after their lovemaking, the rain dwindling to nothing. He'd smiled his lazy smile and wrapped his surcoat around her to keep her warm.

Everything had fallen away—their mission, their past, any anger, expectations, disappointments, fears. It had just been the two of them, Will and Josette, no barriers, no regrets.

He'd cradled her in his arms, but she'd known she could no more hold on to him than she could the wind.

The short night ticked by, dawn breaking, and still Will did not come.

Josette's exhaustion took over and tumbled her into unrelenting sleep. Dancing, making love under the dusky sky, and worrying about Will induced deep slumber.

When she woke, Will lay next to her—snoring. His long body was wrapped in the blankets, his bare thigh touching hers under the covers. His red-brown hair lay tangled on the pillow, eyelashes of the same color against his skin. His face was relaxed in a way Josette rarely saw it.

He was beautiful. And loud. His snores could make the bed curtains flap.

"William," she whispered, nudging him.

Will continued to sleep. Josette nudged him again, harder.

"Mmphmph." Will's large hand came up to rub his face, and after a few more snorting sounds he awoke.

The smile he turned on her more than made up for the noise. "Good morning, love. If it is morning."

"Sun's up ... Well, sort of." The light through the crack in the curtain was weak, and Josette heard the grainy sound of rain on the windowpanes.

"That's bonny Scotland for ye," Will turned on his side, broad shoulder flattening the pillow. "Rain's good for the whisky."

He wasn't bothering to be Sir William. Josette raised her brows at him.

"I found all the peepholes yesterday," Will whispered to her. "Stopped them up. All the places a person could listen as well. Not many of those. The mistress of the house is more interested in her guests' bed play than their intrigues. Every spy in Christendom could dance through here and she'd only care how many positions they used when they copulated."

Josette pushed at his shoulder, laughter bubbling inside her. "You are awful."

"I know, lass. That's me—Sir William the Awful." He lifted a lock of hair from her cheek, his touch tender. "Ready for a bit of travel today? Or would ye prefer to remain in Lady Bentley's warm house?" He smiled as though he already knew her answer.

"No thank you." Josette shivered. "A ride across empty lands in the rain sounds grand. Where are we going?"

"To see a friend of Sir Harmon's. But we'll speak more later."

Josette understood. In spite of finding the holes in the walls, Will still wouldn't risk anyone overhearing anything vital. She'd have to wait.

Will kissed her throat, his hair tickling her skin. When he raised his head, his expression was serious.

"Love," he said softly. "We do have to talk about one thing." He slid his hand under the covers to her abdomen. "When we were out in the hills, I forgot everything but how beautiful you are. I wanted nothing to exist but us. But I might have given you a babe."

Josette's heartbeat sped in hope—she'd also realized the possibility. When they'd shared a bed in the past, they'd taken precautions, both knowing their time together would not last. Will had once told her that he had no intention of saddling her with another child.

"Or might not," she said, shrugging. "I'm rather long in the tooth."

"You aren't. Doesn't matter that I'm elderly, either. If we have the strength to love each other in the heather, we have the strength to conceive. If so—I won't leave the bairn fatherless."

Josette blinked. "What do you mean?" she asked lightly. "You'd find one of your many friends to marry me?"

She broke off as his face went dark, blood flooding his sunburned cheeks. "Is that what you think?"

She'd been teasing, but it was the sort of thing Will would do. "You have the resources and the friends to do any number of things for you." Josette tried to make the words nonchalant. "Why should this be different?"

"Because it's *you*." Will cupped her face, his hand strong. "The hell I'd let another man touch you, or marry you, or raise my wee one."

"Oh." Josette's mouth went dry as she realized what he had meant.

If she fell pregnant, he'd marry her himself.

Josette's heart pounded until her body was hot. She imagined herself with a babe, with Will at her side as its father—it was a glorious, exciting thought.

Or perhaps not. He might marry Josette to give the child a name and make certain he or she was looked after, but that did not mean they'd live as man and wife. Will Mackenzie was a bird in flight, a hawk ever moving, rarely lighting.

If Josette did *not* conceive, she'd be spared the days of waiting and wondering when he'd come home. But why did that thought make her cold?

"Will…"

"We have time to think about it." He stroked her cheekbone with his thumb. "Babes don't announce they are imminent for some weeks. We'll wait and see."

Where would Josette be in a few weeks? In France, hoping she and her daughter were safe? Or still hunkering in Strathy Castle, deciding what to do next?

Josette could only nod. She would not turn down Will's proposal if one became necessary. She wouldn't be so heartless to deny their child a father because her feelings might be hurt.

Will's touch became slower, more seductive. "While we wait…"

Josette should push him away, tell him once was enough, spare herself more heartache at the end.

Instead she pushed back the covers, slid her hand under his warm hair, and pulled him down to her.

Sir Harmon insisted they take a meal before departing. Will chafed with impatience, but he readily accepted, like a young man more interested in his comforts than anything else.

Will could barely focus on the lavish breakfast of partridge, coddled eggs, ham, sausages, soft breads dripping with butter, strawberries, and more cream. It wasn't the season for partridges, but a plump one had been roasted and divided for them.

All Will could think of was Josette under him this morning, warm from sleep, her arms welcoming. Last night he'd fallen in love all over again. They fit so well, the two of them complete together.

The possibility of a child made Will flush with excitement. When he'd touched her soft abdomen, he'd been filled with longing as he envisioned Josette smiling at him with a curly-haired daughter on her knee. Or perhaps a red-headed son with Mackenzie-gold eyes.

Why not both? Or a handful of children? Josette might object to all that childbearing, but they could try for as many children as was safe for her.

Sudden fear seized him. Childbirth was anything but safe—many mothers and children did not survive it.

Will attacked his food. He'd do everything in his power to make sure Josette was well and remained well, including finding a heap of gold so she could live in comfort.

He finished all his breakfast—why waste decent grub? And poured a glass of hock down his throat before Sir Harmon finally thumped his goblet to the table and agreed Will should depart.

Lady Bentley did her best to dissuade Josette from accompanying him, but Josette remained firm. She skillfully portrayed a young woman reluctant to let her husband out of her sight for too long, and Lady Bentley relented with understanding.

Will imagined not all of this was playacting—Josette likely believed Will would tuck the boxes of gold under his arms and disappear into the mist if he found them without her.

He preferred to have Josette with him. He'd have talked her into joining him if she hadn't already agreed, because though this house offered protection from the wet Scottish summer, he didn't trust the inhabitants to leave her be. The other gentlemen guests were restless, Josette was so very beautiful, and she'd be all alone ...

Anger smoldered through him.

Sir Harmon gave Will painstaking directions to Shieldag Castle to the north along the coastal road. Will already knew where the place lay but listened as though with great concentration.

Bhreac, who'd been keeping himself hidden in the stables, slouched on top of the carriage like a sullen coachman not happy to be out in the rain. Will handed Josette into the coach, shook hands with Sir Harmon, and climbed inside.

Sir Harmon shut the door himself and gave them a wave. Will lowered the window to pump his arm out of it, then they turned out of the gate and headed up the road.

When they were several miles from the house, Will threw himself back against the seat and let out a long breath.

"God save us."

Josette, across from him, lifted her feet to rest them on his seat. "I concur. We ought to feel sorry for the poor things confined there today, but I can only be glad we escaped."

"Their own bloody fault." Will heaved himself up and thumped on the ceiling. "Ye can stop now, Bhreac."

The coach slowed to a halt, sliding as the back wheels found mud. Will opened the door, letting in a gust of rain, and jumped down to the sodden road, not bothering with the steps.

Bhreac looped the reins around the seat, climbed to the ground, and moved to the horses. He spoke to them a moment, then left them to doze and came back to Will. The horses wouldn't budge, Will knew. Animals tended to listen when Bhreac spoke to them.

"Where are we really going?" Bhreac asked him. "Someplace with softer beds than those boxes of straw I've been sleeping in, please tell me. Master of the house is lavish with his own comfort, but not his servants'." He rubbed his backside with a grimace.

"Sir Harmon would have to spend money," Will said. "We are making for Shieldag Castle to speak to Clennan MacDonald, as intended. But there's a problem."

"Och, what might that be?" Bhreac asked the air.

"He knows me, and knows me well. Once upon a time, me mum was to marry his brother, who had the interesting moniker of Horace. Mum threw Horace Macdonald over for Dad. Been hatred between the families ever since. If Clennan sees me, he won't bother to call for soldiers to arrest me—he'll pick up the nearest pistol and shoot me."

Josette, listening through the open door, drew a sharp breath.

"And you still mean to go to his house? I am right about you, Will. You are completely mad."

"He's never heard of Sir William Jacobs," Will answered. "Doesn't know anything about him other than what Sir Harmon put in this message." He touched the paper in his coat Sir Harmon had handed him, then he eyed Bhreac. "Can ye pretend to be an idiotic Englishman?"

Bhreac cleared his throat then said, his face tight, "I'll bloody well have a go."

Josette and Will stared at him, then each other, then groaned.

"That is the worst English accent I have ever heard," Will said.

"Perhaps you should try to be French," Josette suggested. "Or a Spaniard, or Portuguese. From some country Mr. Macdonald likely hasn't visited."

"Why can't Sir William be from the Borderlands?" Bhreac asked. "If this Macdonald don't know anything about him?"

Josette answered. "Because Sir Harmon would never trust a Scotsman he'd just met."

"No indeed." Will ran his thumb over the seal on the message for Clennan—he'd have to warm it open and read it.

"Mr. Macdonald has never met *me*," Josette said. "I can speak to him as Anna Jacobs, and we can say Will is indisposed. Something he ate, perhaps. I can deliver the message as easily as you can."

True. They could pretend that Sir William had eaten bad fish and was laid up at the nearest tavern and sent his wife to run his errand as a last resort. Josette would play her role thoroughly, and Clennan would never tumble to the ruse.

The solution was excellent, except for the fact that Will did not want Josette alone in Shieldag Castle, at the mercy of a Highlander who'd sold out members of his own family. Macdonald had disapproved of the Uprising, but unlike Will, who'd protect his family to the last breath of his life, Clennan had his cousins and other clansmen arrested.

Bhreac came alert. "Rider."

Will looked around to see a horse coming over the rise, a man in a British uniform moving easily with his mount.

"Captain Ellis," Josette said.

Will shaded his eyes. "Ah, good. I wondered what was keeping him. I mentioned to him last night I'd be glad of him on this venture."

Mutely the three waited for the horse and rider to reach them. Captain Ellis tipped his tricorn hat to Josette and gave Bhreac a sharp look.

"Fine day for a ride," Will said to Ellis, indicating the rain-drenched land.

"I told Sir Harmon I wished to accompany you. He thought it a good idea, as there is danger on the roads."

"There is," Will said in a quiet voice.

Bhreac laughed. "Ain't none more dangerous than us, Captain."

"I worried about the lady," Ellis said sternly.

Josette gave him a friendly nod. "We welcome your company, sir. Angry Highlanders might form the wrong impression of Will."

Will had to agree. As Sir William, he'd dressed in light blue and yellow for this outing, lace dripping from his coat and even the cuffs of his breeches, his silver shoe buckles large and glittering.

"They'd run me through with the nearest claymore," Will said. "Never mind claymores have been outlawed—they'd dig one up for me. Maybe the presence of a cavalryman will keep me from having to explain myself." He grinned at Josette. "But I suggested he come along because Clennan Macdonald has never met *him*."

Captain Ellis nodded. "That is true. Macdonald is known to the British government as a man who hands over traitors. He's led Cumberland's men to many a Jacobite in hiding. But I've never made his acquaintance."

His tone held contempt. Captain Ellis was as loyal an Englishman as was ever born, but he also was the most fair-minded man Will had ever met. Ellis despised turncoats and had been appalled during the Uprising at how Highlander could turn on Highlander.

Will and his brothers had tried to explain about clan rivalries that went back centuries, where anyone outside your glen was a deadly enemy. While Scotland was now united in theory, those rivalries ran deep, even within clans themselves. The Scots had been scheming, plotting, battling, and turning on one another since men had walked these hills, and a few years being in one grand nation with England wouldn't change that.

"Which is the reason I can't appear in his drawing room with my hand out," Will said. "He'll be begging you to arrest me on the spot, possibly even rush out to build my gallows himself."

"Then why are you going?" Ellis demanded. "And why bring Mrs. Oswald into the danger?"

"Mrs. Oswald is not one to stay tamely at home, and anyway, it's easier for me to keep an eye on her if she's with me."

"I came to keep an eye on *him*, Captain," Josette corrected Will. "But I understand Will's point. If Mr. Macdonald has never seen you, Captain Ellis …"

Ellis looked pained—but one reason Will found success as a spy was that he took advantage of opportunities.

Will stuck out his arms to show off his garish coat. "It might be a bit large for you, Captain. But we'll do our best."

CHAPTER 16

Captain Ellis was red-faced and uncomfortable in the long yellow-and-blue frock coat with belling peplum, clocked silk stockings, and velvet knee breeches. He refused the wig but combed his hair until it was sleek, wearing Will's light blue tricorn hat with long feather.

"I look the veriest macaroni," the captain growled.

"It doesn't suit you," Josette agreed. "But it's just right for fooling Mr. Macdonald."

Even less did Captain Ellis's uniform suit Will. He stood in it as though his skin wanted to shrink from the fabric. Ellis was slightly smaller in build, and Will had to hunch down so the fit didn't look too wrong.

"Just don't injure my horse," Captain Ellis warned as he climbed into the carriage with Josette.

"Never fear," Will said. "Let Josette do most of the talking, and nod idiotically. Sir William is too stupid to be anything but what he is—a weak man who only wishes to keep himself in his comforts."

"I understand," Captain Ellis answered. "But I won't use that inane laugh you concocted. Your father would be horrified."

"Aye, well, he's already horrified enough at me and my antics.

Mary would kiss you, though." Will laid his hand on the open window, his face turning serious. "Be careful."

"I'll protect Mrs. Oswald with my life," Ellis assured him.

"Ye damn well will."

Josette saw that Will hated letting her walk into this snare alone, even with the captain to protect her, but he was doing so because they had no choice. Will didn't want her anywhere near Macdonald, or the Highlands, or Scotland altogether, she knew. The look on his face was what she felt on her own when she worried about Glenna.

"I'll take care, Will," she said softly. "I promise."

He didn't look any happier, but he straightened and waved the carriage on. Bhreac, already on the coachman's box, clucked to the horses, and they jolted down the rutted road.

～

SHIELDAG CASTLE WASN'T A CASTLE. IT MIGHT ONCE HAVE BEEN IN ITS distant past, but now it was a manor house along the lines of Sir Harmon's.

The house's wings stretched across the hill like a dam, windows glittering between tall columns of golden stone. The whole thing might have been lifted intact from a corner of Berkshire and dropped into the middle of the Highlands. A large gate separated the estate from the road, and when that gate clanged shut behind the coach, Josette felt distinctly uneasy.

Will had left them at the gatehouse, astride Ellis's horse, pretending he'd been an armed escort, a soldier guarding them from the Scottish barbarians. Josette didn't like the empty feeling that struck her as she watched him ride away.

"Better that he goes," Captain Ellis said in a quiet voice.

Josette realized she was craning her head to keep Will in sight as long as possible. Captain Ellis, awkward in the finery, studied her with understanding in his blue eyes.

Josette turned from the window and sighed. "I know, but I'll be happier when I see him again."

"Why are you helping him?" Captain Ellis asked her, concern in his tone.

"He is helping *me*," Josette said quickly. "You might say we are pooling our resources."

The captain did not change expression. "I've seen young women fall in love with Mackenzies before. The Mackenzie men are not the sort who marry a woman respectably and tuck her into a comfortable house while they go about their dangerous business. They drag the lady into that dangerous business with them, no matter what the cost to her."

"I know," Josette said. "I've met Lady Celia and had letters from Lady Mary."

Captain Ellis's politeness fell away, and for an instant, Josette saw anguish. "Is Lady Mary truly happy? Or must I sail to France and tear Malcolm Mackenzie's limbs from his body?"

Josette didn't hide her smile. "I'm pleased to tell you she is very happy. Lady Celia with Alec, as well. They are a close family," she finished wistfully.

"I spent many months in the Mackenzie house," Captain Ellis said. "Malcolm will eventually settle down, I believe, no matter how many mad schemes are in his head. Alec has a child and his painting commissions to keep him steady for his wife. Will is a different man entirely."

"I've met his brothers." Josette tried not to sound defensive.

"Will is restless," Captain Ellis went on. "Both he and Malcolm have it in their heads that they are the protectors of their family— their father and eldest brother were too busy with their own needs for that. Malcolm fulfills this obligation by finding ways to make money and keeping a close eye on the family. Will does it by absenting himself and fighting the rest of the world to keep his brothers and father free. He won't have time for a wife and children."

Josette let her eyes go wide, even as a lump tightened in her throat. "Goodness, who said anything about that?"

"I see how you watch him. I see how he watches you. He cares for you—have no fear—but do not expect him to buy a cottage and raise sheep while he looks after you. He will not stay home long."

"This I also know," Josette said, deflating. "I am not a silly young woman stupidly in love with a handsome man, Captain. I've known Will a long time, and I've learned exactly what he is like."

She swallowed and folded her hands in her lap. Will was a stone who gathered no moss. He never remained in one place long enough to put down roots.

But then again, neither did Josette stay in one place long. The pair of them might roll along together ...

Josette pushed the thought firmly from her mind. Will would never be hampered by a woman in skirts dragging a nearly grown daughter and a baby with her.

Will's baby ... Her heart gave a lurch.

The coach also lurched, plowing through a water-drenched rut before skimming between two massive doors pulled open to admit them to an arched portico. The carriage went right inside the house, the roofed passage clearly made for guests to descend out of the wind and rain.

A footman, a sullen Scotsman, opened the carriage door and set down a cushioned stool without looking at Captain Ellis or Josette as the captain handed Josette down. The footman ushered them into an echoing, slate-floored hall and held up a stilling hand, indicating they were to wait there. He then waved the coach off, and Bhreac, in keeping with his persona, clattered it away.

Unlike Sir Harmon's home, where guests wandered at will and servants darted about amid music floating from Lady Bentley's clavichord, Clennan Macdonald's house was deathly silent.

A staircase encircled the wide hall, whose walls were covered with paintings of haughty Scots in tartans and bonnets, ladies in stiff ruffs, horses posing as stiffly as the human beings, and landscapes of wide green spaces. One picture depicted a craggy castle that might be the predecessor of this house. Weapons from various periods in history interspersed the paintings, reminding the viewer that this was the home of warriors.

Josette had learned in her roaming life what wealth looked like and what it could buy. Every item she saw in this hall—paintings, swords, rugs, tables, chairs, candelabra, statuettes—had cost a nice sum of money.

"He's got a bob or two, hasn't he?" she whispered to Captain Ellis.

She said it in her Anna voice, in case they were overheard. Her words slithered up in a soft hiss, the syllables lost in the space above them.

A door banged somewhere on an upper floor. The footman who'd admitted them reappeared and jerked his head to indicate they were to follow him up the stairs.

The footman never spoke. Was he a defeated Jacobite, angry he had to grub for Mr. Macdonald? Or was he a loyal member of Clan Macdonald, surly toward all outsiders?

More riches were evident as they went up one flight, two flights, a third. They left the staircase, the footman leading them down a hall that was long enough to allow Josette to catch her breath. Captain Ellis, not winded at all, walked beside her in silence.

At the end of this corridor, the footman opened two carved double doors. Beyond this lay a series of small chambers, one leading to the next. Each room was filled with paintings Alec Mackenzie would enjoy.

So would their original owners, Josette realized as she walked beneath them. She'd known enough artists and art collectors in her life to have learned something about paintings. Two pictures from the collection of Louis of France hung in the second antechamber—Josette had seen the depiction of indoor life painted by Mr. de Hooch and the turbaned man by Mr. van Rijn blatantly displayed by his majesty.

In the third anteroom was a painting done by a more recent artist, and a very good one—Alec Mackenzie. The model dancing as a nymph near her forest pond, clad in only a translucent drapery, was Josette.

Josette stopped in her tracks. Captain Ellis nearly ran into her and then saw what held her gaze. Her face heated as Captain Ellis stared at the painting then quickly averted his eyes, cheekbones staining red.

"Should we retreat?" he whispered into her ear.

Josette shook her head. In the picture, she was a small body in a trailing cloth, her head half turned from the viewer. A cascade of curls further obscured her face.

She'd only recognized the painting because she remembered the long sessions in Alec's studio while he worked on it, small Glenna playing in the corner. Alec and Will had been ingenious at procuring toys for the girl.

Josette also knew that an artist's model dressed in ordinary clothing was not often recognized, unless she was extremely famous. Josette, while she'd done well for herself, had been relatively unknown—her modeling career had not lasted long, a few years only. The artists of France had forgotten her by now.

Captain Ellis looked unconvinced, but he continued walking. The footman had neither noticed their exchange nor slowed his pace.

The last of the series of rooms was flooded with light from four tall windows. A fireplace loomed on the opposite wall, lit against the cool air. A desk sat nearer the fire than the windows, its top littered with books and papers.

The man who rose from behind the desk and waited for them to enter was clearly their host, Clennan Macdonald.

He was about fifty, stout with good eating, but hard-muscled like many Highlanders. He'd have been at home in a plaid, but he wore a well-tailored suit of dark blue, his waistcoat pale ivory silk, no laces or ribbons in sight.

"Good afternoon," he boomed in a rumbling voice as he looked them over with keen blue eyes. "Welcome to Shieldag. My friend Sir Harmon said I could be of assistance to you."

"Sir." Captain Ellis swept him a bow, taking off his hat. "It was kind of you to see us."

"Sir Harmon and I often trade favors," Macdonald said. "Sit down, man. Let me pour you some whisky."

He did not include Josette in the invitation. Captain Ellis escorted her to a chair while Macdonald picked up a gilded bell from his desk and clanged it as though summoning the clan to a moot.

Macdonald did not speak as they waited but he looked Captain Ellis over thoroughly then turned the same assessing gaze to Josette. She made certain her expression remained interested but vapid, a woman who followed her beloved husband wherever he went but didn't want to clutter her mind with the details.

Another Scottish servant entered, thunked a tray with decanter and glasses on a side table, and stalked out.

Macdonald moved to the decanter. "A wee dram, Sir William? The one Scottish thing allowed to continue, the *uisge beatha.* I closed down all the unlicensed distilleries in the area—the one that brews this belongs to me."

Captain Ellis accepted the glass of amber liquid Macdonald handed him. Macdonald did give Josette a glass as well, with the tiniest amount of whisky in it.

Josette doubted that Mr. Macdonald had succeeded in completely shutting down the unlicensed stills. From what Will had told her about illegal whisky brewing, a tiny still would spring up in a cottage in the next glen, and another, and another. A crofter only needed to hammer together a copper vat and some tubing, hide a portion of harvested barley, and begin. The crofters might not produce the best whisky in the world, but they could sell enough to get them through a winter as well as warm their own bellies.

"Thank you kindly," Captain Ellis said. His voice had lightened, though it held nowhere near the silliness Will achieved. "Sir Harmon won't have it in his house."

"Nothing but French wine and brandy for him," Macdonald said, relaxing as though Captain Ellis had passed a test. "He turns up his nose at anything made on his home isles. Strange man. To your health."

Captain Ellis lifted his glass. "*Slàinte.* As you say in the Highlands."

Macdonald looked startled then burst out laughing. "Your accent is deplorable, but 'twas a valiant effort. Only don't speak that word in these halls. The Erse language is outlawed, don't ye know?"

"Yes, I knew that," Captain Ellis said somewhat stiffly. "A joke."

"A joke that will have British soldiers stringing you up by your balls, sir," Macdonald said jovially. "What would your pretty wife do then, eh?"

Josette managed a giggle and sipped her whisky. Will had given her a taste of his family's malt long ago—a soft and smooth liquid that tasted of Scottish winds. What was in her mouth now had a harsh bite, almost like vitriol. She swallowed and couldn't help a cough.

"Fair and strong," Macdonald said, resuming his seat. "Like you, Lady Jacobs."

Josette wiped her mouth with her hand, managing to look flustered.

"Now then, sir, I don't have much time for niceties," Macdonald said, turning back to Captain Ellis. "Sir Harmon sent you to me for capital." He tapped the letter Will had managed to unseal, read, and reseal before they'd resumed their journey. Will had shared the contents with the rest of them, filling in Captain Ellis with any information he did not yet know.

Captain Ellis cleared his throat. "Afraid I'm rather up against it. Investments not what they were."

Macdonald watched him with a wise air. "Never are, lad. What makes you think you can invest what I might give you any more skillfully?"

"I intend to take direction," Captain Ellis answered, as Will had coached him. "Sir Harmon will help me, as will his man of business."

Another loud laugh. "Watch yourself there. Sir Harmon is not the shrewdest mind on the Exchange. There is a reason he lives in the middle of nowhere and refuses to leave his house. Take advice from *me*, laddie, and only me. I'd like to see my coin again."

"Of course, sir," Captain Ellis said with respect in his voice. "I realized long ago I had no head for business."

Macdonald slid a gaze over Josette. "Distracted, no doubt."

Josette contrived a blush. Captain Ellis looked pained, and Josette saw him struggle to maintain his composure.

"Where did you meet your wife?" Macdonald asked him abruptly.

Josette answered before Captain Ellis could. She knew by heart the story of Anna and William that she and Will had concocted, embellished, and built over the years. "In France. Paris."

Macdonald nodded. "You're French, aren't you?" he asked Josette directly.

"My mother was," she answered as though slightly ashamed of this fact. "My father was Mr. Garfield of Wiltshire—"

Macdonald raised a beefy hand. "Spare me the pretty lies, Lady Jacobs. You might fool the world—you might have even fooled your husband, I don't know. You're a common tart, aren't you? If a beautiful one. What possessed you to take off your clothes for Alec Mackenzie, of all people?"

CHAPTER 17

*W*ill rode slowly around Shieldag Castle's grounds, watching the house and the road beyond. The rocky hills were trackless, and he guided the horse with care to avoid holes that could break his mount's leg or even kill it.

He saw no one else about. The narrow road they'd traversed, which Macdonald had no doubt improved at his own expense, was the only way in or out of the glen. A hardy clansman could hike over the hills on his own, but food, drink, and luxuries would have to come by that road.

This place could be cut off at a moment's notice—probably was in bad snow or rain. A man could be trapped here, or he could defend it against all comers. Macdonald had chosen well. If the British had been defeated, the Bonnie Prince's father now on the throne, Macdonald could easily have holed up here until he made his fellow Scotsman believe he'd really been on their side.

But the Jacobites *had* been defeated, and now Macdonald had blocked himself off from Highlanders seeking vengeance.

Not that he'd remain secluded for long. Macdonald was a schemer, always had been. The plan to have Alison McNab marry his brother Horace, who'd died this past year, had been Clennan's.

Alison's father had possessed plenty of lands, cattle, and money, plus she'd have brought the loyalty of many McNabs with her.

Clennan had been livid when Alison had met Will's father and decided to elope with him. It had been a love match, the two of them besotted. Alison's father had forgiven them, but Clennan Macdonald never had. He'd encouraged his entire clan to hate the Mackenzies.

Will studied the massive house below him. Palladian style, as so many manors were these days, every wealthy man wanting to replicate an Italian palace. Mal would know exactly what date the pile had been built and exactly what each feature was called.

He saw Bhreac, small and far away, lounging against the wheel of the coach in the drive outside the house. No worries that any would recognize him—though Bhreac traveled extensively, he'd stayed well away from the Highlands during the Uprising. Playing both sides of the fence, as usual.

Will also spied a tall man striding over the hills, coming straight for Will. He'd not seen anyone exit the house, but now the man climbed over the rocks, steps quick and sure, as though he'd been born and bred here.

Will was off the horse before the man reached him. The intruder was tall and lanky, with a shock of graying red hair, and light blue eyes in a long face.

The man halted in front of Will, studying him in silence. Tears beaded on his lashes as he reached a shaky hand to cup Will's face.

"God save you, lad," he said hoarsely, and then dragged Will into a hard embrace.

Will closed his eyes as he returned the embrace, remembering this man's strength from his days as a toddler. His long-fingered hands had steadied Will's steps and stopped him from plunging down the sheer hill on which Kilmorgan Castle was built.

"Naughton," Will whispered, unexpected joy rushing through him. "What the devil are you doing *here*?"

Naughton, the tall, thin retainer who'd been with the Mackenzies since before any of the brothers had been born, straightened. Tears wet his cheeks and a gust of wind tugged his hair.

"I knew your brothers and dad were well in France, but you …"

Naughton's grip on Will's shoulders was as strong as ever. "None knew whether ye be alive or dead."

Will patted Naughton's shaking hands. "You know I always come back. But you didn't answer me, man. What are ye doing at the home of Clennan Macdonald, of all people?"

Naughton released Will and stepped back. "Not serving him. I'd never … I remember when your mum threw over his brother. Clennan came after her with clansmen and pistols, the bastard. His Grace had more loyal men and a legal marriage, but Clennan vowed revenge. I'm here to see he don't take it."

"Why? What is he planning?"

Naughton looked regretful. "I'm not sure entirely. He's a close one. He don't remember me, probably never noticed me with your dad— he ignores servants. But he has his eye on Kilmorgan. It's lying fallow, avoided by most. Some say there's a curse on the place. The British are trying to sell it."

"Sell it?" Will balled his hands as fury and fear washed over him.

Will had known the land had probably already been taken from them. Whenever the line of a family died out, no more heirs to be had, the title and lands reverted to the crown. Now that Scotland and England, in theory, were one, that crown was British. Kilmorgan had been a dukedom for four hundred years—Will imagined King Geordie's men salivating at the prospect of a lucrative landholding falling into their laps. Sometimes the land was given to another favored courtier; sometimes it was sold to an up-and-coming man like Sir Harmon.

"Bloody bastards," Will continued. "Macdonald is trying to purchase it, is he?"

"I believe so. But the British don't want a Scotsman to have that land, unless there's no choice, so they're slow to grant it to him. They'd prefer to put in an Englishman to keep an eye on the country north of Inverness. They're building a great fort there, and they don't want Jacobite Highlanders too near. Fear they'll blow it up or some such."

Will nodded. He'd heard about Fort George, on the point where Moray Firth spilled into the sea. The post would be massive, if the plans he'd seen were anything to go by. The Black Watch, Scottish troops who watched over the Scots, would man it.

"They don't want a scheming Highlander living across the firth," Will said, understanding. "Wise of them. Macdonald likes getting his own way, though."

"Aye, but he'd need a lot of money to have it. They'll not give all that land away, even if no Englishman so far wants it. Too remote, too dangerous." Naughton sighed. "Too full of ghosts."

The ghosts were there, yes, Will thought with sadness. So much laughter and life—gone.

Will paced as he thought. "I wager Macdonald wants to walk where the lady who defied him trod. To gloat. The hell he will, Naughton. I'll not let him."

"I agree, my lord, but what can you do? Your dad and brothers are far away. You're dead—if ye forgive me being blunt."

"Yes, but being dead gives me a slight advantage." Will rubbed his chin as ideas formed.

Naughton looked him over, taking in the uniform, brows rising. "Are ye trying to be the wraith of a downed British soldier?"

"Not quite. I'm staying out of sight, blending in, while ..." Will glared at the distant house. "I couldn't go inside, for obvious reasons. So I sent a man I hope is a friend and the woman I love most in my life to do my work for me."

"You mean Mrs. Oswald?" Naughton asked at once.

"Did you see her? Is she all right?"

Naughton shook his head. "No, but ye'd never speak of another woman so."

Will's eyes narrowed. "What do you mean?"

To his annoyance, Naughton sent him a knowing smile. "Ye have a way with the lassies, my lord, but usually only as means to an end. Not with *her*. I saw how ye were with her when ye brought her to Kilmorgan long ago. I don't imagine anything's changed."

"It hasn't." Will clamped his mouth closed before he said too much. The trouble with Naughton was that he knew everything about the Mackenzies, sometimes before they knew it themselves.

"Why aren't you in France with my father?" Will countered.

Naughton shrugged. "Someone's got to look after Kilmorgan. I never took up arms, and none paid much attention to me. I lived there, in the distillery, until I learned Macdonald was nosing about after the land."

The distillery had been a house on the Kilmorgan grounds in the 1600s, a home away from the more grim castle. After the castle was modernized and made more comfortable, the house had been turned into a distillery for the new, licensed whisky business. Will and his brothers and father had moved into the distillery last year after British troops had burned the castle and reduced it to rubble.

"Hmm." Will's thoughts churned furiously. "You were wise to find out what Macdonald was up to. As to where he's getting the money, I have some idea." He shot Naughton a sudden grin. "How would you like to help me take it all away from him and have Kilmorgan back for ourselves?"

CAPTAIN ELLIS AND JOSETTE STARED AT MACDONALD IN TREPIDATION while Macdonald's amusement grew.

"Did he not know you were an artist's model?" Macdonald asked Josette, jerking his chin at Captain Ellis. "For a Mackenzie, no less?"

Captain Ellis shot a glance at Josette, waiting for a cue, but Macdonald was watching her too closely for her to give one.

"Of course he knew," she said hastily. "That is how Sir William met me. What of it?"

"Were you Alec Mackenzie's lover?"

"No." Josette's word rang with truth. She and Alec had been friends, nothing more. He'd been preoccupied with painting, and Josette had met Will …

"No?" Macdonald didn't believe her, but Josette had no intention of arguing with him.

"We do keep my … er … past … from Sir William's acquaintance," Josette went on, striving to look chagrined. "It would be too scandalous. Please, please say nothing to Sir Harmon."

Josette did not like the glint in Mr. Macdonald's eye. She'd assessed that Macdonald was the sort to use knowledge like this to his advantage—whether to have a hold over "Sir William," or to coerce Josette into things she'd rather not think about, she didn't know. Both, most like.

Macdonald studied the two of them sharply, but Josette saw him assume their uneasiness came from the secret of Josette's modeling days. He took on a look of smug contempt.

"She spends many a penny, does she?" he asked Captain Ellis.

"I'm afraid so." Captain Ellis made a helpless gesture. "But so do I. Hence our need for funds."

Macdonald rose and rested his wide hands on the top of the desk. "And what do I get in return? For keeping your sordid secret and loaning you cash?"

Captain Ellis widened his eyes. "Your money back with interest?"

Macdonald snorted a laugh. "Not good enough. Sir Harmon told me you travel much, and are in the position to observe many things. I think him too sanguine—you are probably too absorbed in yourself to have knowledge I could use, but I'll take the chance. Our proposal is this—I will lend you money for your investments. You put the money into the businesses *I* tell you to, never mind what Sir Harmon said, so you won't lose all of it. Then you and your pretty wife go to the houses I tell you to and talk to people. I know Sir Harmon has explained this contingency to you, and that you are willing to follow it. Then you return to Sir Harmon and tell him what these people have discussed. I believe he indicated the sorts of things he wants to know."

Josette had half-feared he'd demand payment in form of her person, in which case she'd have had to take up the fine bronze horse statuette on his desk and bash him with it. But all he wanted was for them to spy. Interesting.

Captain Ellis feigned consideration, then he shrugged, exactly as Will might do. "It seems so little to ask. Gives us a place to stay wherever we go, doesn't it, Lady Jacobs?"

"Very convenient," Josette agreed, sending Macdonald a smile.

Macdonald studied them, his opinion apparent. Fools, he thought them, but gullible and easy to manipulate. Exactly as Will had predicted.

Macdonald drained his cup in one swallow, told them to enjoy more whisky while he fetched the funds, and departed the room without looking back.

Josette spied another rather large footman in the next room, who scowled at them then closed the door for his master. She heard him take a stance near the door, standing guard.

Captain Ellis sipped his whisky without speaking, and Josette kept to her seat, setting her glass on the table beside her.

Sir William and Anna, to remain in character, would chatter to fill the silence, happily speculating on how they'd spend the money. Captain Ellis said nothing, probably knowing he could not be convincing.

Josette thought it significant that Mr. Macdonald had left to run the errand himself, instead of sending a servant. Nor did he want his two visitors tagging along. Some secrets, it seemed, he did not entrust to others.

She hoped he was doing nothing more than fetching the funds he spoke of. There were too many other things he could be getting up to out of their sight—summoning soldiers, questioning Bhreac. What if he caught sight of Will?

No, Will had ways of making himself invisible. As much as she worried about him, Josette knew Will was the most capable man alive at ... well, remaining alive.

Before her fears could escalate, the guarding footman opened the door, and Mr. Macdonald came back in, a small box held in both hands.

"Leave us," he told the footman in a warning voice. The footman did not respond, but after he closed the door, Josette heard his footsteps retreating.

Macdonald sat down at the desk and thunked the small casket to its surface. He didn't open it.

"What I'm about to hand you is the equivalent of five hundred gold sovereigns." He gave Captain Ellis a stern look. "But to use it as such, you'll have to take it to my man of business in London. He will make an account for you and invest the sum of five hundred as I instruct him. You will not simply take the money and spend it, thinking yourself clever, because I will know if you do. Do you understand?"

Captain Ellis nodded. Josette did as well.

"When you've visited my friends on the list that is also inside this box, you will make the journey to Scotland again and stay with Sir Harmon. You will tell him everything you have learned, and I will visit you there. You are never to return to Shieldag Castle."

"I understand, sir," Captain Ellis said with the right amount of eagerness. "Thank you, sir."

Macdonald regarded him with poorly concealed derision. He glanced at Josette, and a sly expression came over his face.

"I will give this to *you* to carry, young woman," he said. "You like pretty trinkets, I think. You'll guard this with your ... *virtue*, won't you?"

Josette managed a light laugh and made herself not flinch in disquiet. Macdonald rose—Josette and Captain Ellis got to their feet as well—and he handed Josette the casket.

It was heavy. The compact box, about six inches long and four high and wide, was made of inlaid exotic woods and had a brass catch with a stout lock.

"Where is the key?" Josette asked, examining the lock.

"My man of business has it," Macdonald said. "Take it to him, and he'll open it up for you."

"Oh, I see." Josette gave another laugh. "So we won't spend it between here and there."

Macdonald laid a hand on the casket as she held it, weighing it down. "I told you, lass. I'd know."

"Of course." She tittered again. "We'll be good, Mr. Macdonald."

"See that you are." He pressed the box, driving it against her chest. He didn't touch her himself, but the pressure from his hand through the box made Josette feel slightly sick.

Captain Ellis gave him a bow, as though he noticed nothing, but Josette sensed his tension. They needed to leave before Captain Ellis exploded.

Fortunately Macdonald lifted his hand away and made a motion for them to depart. Josette curtsied, hoping her smile was fatuous enough. Captain Ellis bowed to Macdonald then gestured Josette to precede him, and she swept from the room.

Macdonald followed them out, his steps echoing heavily behind them.

"It's a lovely house," Josette said. She tried not to look at Alec's painting as they passed it, but she couldn't help herself. Macdonald saw, and chuckled.

"How did you manage to find that picture, Mr. Macdonald?" she asked, as though merely curious.

"Jacobites," Macdonald answered with a grunt. "Mackenzie's father was Duke of Kilmorgan, as you no doubt know. They took up arms against the king and were slaughtered to a man at Culloden Field. Their home, what's left of it, was open for the crows to pick over. I rescued several paintings from the rubble, one by Rubens, if you can believe it. They'd fled when the castle burned, and left it all to rot. Traitors and idiots, the lot of them."

His voice filled with so much venom that Josette glanced back at him. Macdonald's face was brick red, cords standing out on his neck. A portrait of rage.

When he caught Josette's eye on him, he softened his tone. "Aren't you glad I rescued the painting for you, lass? I have half a mind to give it to you, as you're so pretty. But no, I believe I'll keep it. To remind me of you."

His leer was unmistakable. Even a fop like Sir William would be incensed.

"I say, sir," Captain Ellis began, exactly like an outraged but uncertain husband.

Macdonald laughed. "I am joking of course. When you pay me back my money, I'll turn it over to you, Sir William. Of course you'll want your wife in your own bedroom."

Captain Ellis hesitated, as though ready to seize one of the many weapons hanging on the walls and run the man through. Josette sent him a warning look, and Captain Ellis subsided, if his face remained stiff.

Somehow, they made it all the way down the stairs to the ground floor without murder being done. Josette clutched the box to her bosom and hurried with Captain Ellis toward the coach Bhreac had pulled under the portico.

The sullen footman was there to lay down a step for them, but Mr. Macdonald handed Josette into the coach himself. She did not at all like the feel of his hand through her glove—hard strength and ruthlessness.

Captain Ellis sent him a frown, and Macdonald bowed to them both, his enjoyment huge.

Captain Ellis ascended into the coach, and Macdonald slammed the door for them, nearly catching Ellis's foot. Bhreac started the carriage and they rolled out through the arch to open air, the sky shrouded in gray.

Captain Ellis at least waited until they'd passed the gate—opened by another attendant—and were a mile along the road before he pulled off his hat and threw it to the floor.

"Of all the disgusting, boorish, cruel vulgarians I have met in my life, he is the master of all!" Fury darkened the captain's face and made his eyes glitter. "I will call him out for all the things he said to you—I *might* even let him pick up a sword before I kill him."

"You are kind," Josette began, but Captain Ellis cut her off.

"It is not kindness, lady, but common decency. You are the friend of a family I hold in the highest regard, and I'll not let a brutish lout like Macdonald insult you. I'll wager he picked through the ruins of Castle Kilmorgan like a rat, pouncing on the choicest bits. The fact that a man like him is trusted by the crown while the Mackenzies are reviled is coarse injustice. It must stop."

Josette, her hand on the box of gold next to her, waited while he vented. She recognized a man whose principles had been thoroughly trampled upon.

If he hadn't had to play the part of Sir William Jacobs, ridiculous dandy desperate for money, she knew Captain Ellis would have told Mr. Macdonald exactly what he thought, challenged him, and possibly been killed for his pains.

"You are indeed kind," Josette repeated when he finished. "And a good man. Mr. Macdonald will be punished in time—which is why we came here today. To discover what he is plotting with Sir Harmon and what they know about the French gold, if anything." The weight of the casket by her side hinted they knew plenty.

Captain Ellis's mouth was a bitter line. "I know, but I have no patience with the Mackenzie hole-in-corner methods. I would rather face a man straight on and explain to him why I am killing him."

"You might have the chance. Ah, we are stopping—and there is Will."

CHAPTER 18

They'd traveled a few miles from Shieldag Castle, which was now hidden by a crag the road had laboriously climbed over. Josette's heart warmed when she saw Will waiting next to Captain Ellis's horse, but worry touched her as she realized another man stood with him.

Will didn't seem to be bothered by the man's presence at all. As Bhreac halted the coach, Will stepped forward, tore open the coach's door, and hauled Josette out and into his arms.

He smelled of warm wool and the outdoors, and the bite of whisky he'd drunk to stave off the cold. Will pulled her into a strong embrace, his body like a wall of comfort.

He held Josette then eased back and gazed at her as though nothing else existed but the two of them. The Highlands, the gold, and Mr. Macdonald could blow away on the breeze. Josette wished they would.

"Mr. Naughton," Captain Ellis was saying, gladness in his voice. "Well met."

Josette now recognized the man called Naughton from her visit to Kilmorgan, but she wasn't certain whether to be relieved or alarmed. Why was the Duke of Kilmorgan's trusted majordomo here?

"He's keeping an eye on friend Macdonald," Will answered her unspoken question. He tucked Josette's hand under his arm as they faced the others, including Bhreac, who'd jumped down from his perch. "You remember Naughton, Josie."

"Mrs. Oswald," Naughton said politely, though his eyes betrayed happiness at seeing her. "I trust you are well?"

"As well as can be expected, Mr. Naughton. And you?"

"Aye, well." In England, a man might make light of his troubles or hide them to be polite, but Josette had learned that if she asked a Highlander how his day had gone, he'd tell her. "'Tis much trouble fetching and carrying for Clennan Macdonald, I will say."

"I'm sure Will would send you to the family in Paris if you wished," Josette said. "There's no need for you to stay."

Naughton gave her his faint smile. "Then I wouldn't be here watching what Macdonald gets up to. I serve the family better if I remain."

"Macdonald is out to get his hands on Kilmorgan," Will announced. "I will stop him."

The words weren't spoken in anger or with vehemence but with quiet certainty.

"Shall we see what he gave us?" Captain Ellis asked. "Or wait until we're back at Sir Harmon's?"

"Might as well have a look," Will said, sounding cheerful.

Captain Ellis lifted the cask from the coach seat and handed it to Will, whose eyes widened slightly at its weight.

Will touched the lock, which was new and bright, contrasting the aged patina of the box's wood. "He doesn't want us to know what's inside, does he? Bhreac, keep a lookout."

"What d'ye *think* I'm doing?" Bhreac growled. He scanned the road and the lands beyond, glowering as though the very rocks had better take care.

Will nudged stones with his boot until he found one that fitted well in his hand. He set the cask on a boulder, hefted the stone he'd chosen, and then bashed the innocent hasp with all his strength.

The lock broke, and Will opened the lid.

Josette leaned over his arm, her heart pounding as she saw what lay inside. "Oh ... my ..."

The box was filled with shimmering coins. Josette reached in and plucked one out, holding it up to the weak sunlight. The profile of Louis of France winked back at her.

"Louis d'or," she said in awe.

One of these could feed all the ladies holed up at Strathy Castle for a week. The lot in the box could purchase the freedom of their husbands, brothers, and sons, with enough left over to pay Colonel Chadwick so he'd forget about capturing Will or threatening to take Glenna away. Or to let Josette and Glenna flee to a far corner of the Continent where Colonel Chadwick would never find them.

Will plucked out a folded piece of paper that lay beneath the coins. This proved to be, when unfolded, the list of names of people Macdonald and Sir Harmon wanted Sir William and Anna to visit and spy on.

"No wonder Macdonald said that if we opened it up and spent what was inside, he'd know," Josette said. "Word would get around if we tried to exchange a cask full of Louis d'or or use them in a shop."

"Aye, the shopkeepers and bankers would talk," Will said, his voice holding an undercurrent of excitement. "My love, I believe we've just found the French gold. Well … some of it, anyway."

WILL HELD HIS GLEE IN CHECK WITH DIFFICULTY AS THE COACH ROLLED down the road, returning them to Sir Harmon's.

Naughton had said his good-byes and trudged back toward Macdonald's large home, his back straight with new strength. Captain Ellis and Will exchanged clothes again, and Captain Ellis now rode alongside the carriage as their escort.

Ellis had told Will as they'd dressed all that transpired inside Shieldag, including Macdonald recognizing Josette as Alec's model, though not by name. Ellis also relayed the disgusting things the man had said to her and his own wish to call Macdonald out.

"How you let Mrs. Oswald into circumstances where men can be so loathsome to her is beyond my understanding." Captain Ellis had scowled at Will. "Kill the man and have done."

Will had no answer for this, because he knew Ellis was right. He should never have let Josette into that house, not even for the great cause of finding the gold.

"We'll have him," Will said tersely. "He's likely sitting on much more than he gave us. Cheer up. Soon you can have the satisfaction of hauling Macdonald in for treason."

"If we can make it stick," Ellis pointed out. "He *might* have the French gold, he *might* be keeping it from King George, and he *might* be handing secrets to British enemies. At this point, we only know he's an unpleasant man who has no respect for ladies."

"Oh, he's conducting dirty deeds all right," Will said. "It is his way. Macdonald doesn't know how *not* to be involved in chicanery. I promise that if you can't convince a magistrate he's a traitor, then I will kill him myself. I won't bother calling him out and following the prissy rules of dueling—I'll simply shoot him."

Captain Ellis wasn't satisfied, and neither was Will. But Macdonald had made a mistake insulting Josette, and he'd pay for it.

As the carriage made its slow way over the narrow road, Will watched Josette in the dying light. Shadows brushed her face, which was lined with tiredness. Josette was resilient, but the sooner they finished this, the better.

"Is Mr. Macdonald a fool?" Josette asked. "To hand us what is obviously gold coins from France? To the idiot Sir William Jacobs and his wife, who once knew Alec Mackenzie well?"

Will shook his head. "These coins could plausibly have come from his sound investments in France, which no doubt he'd claim if we grew too curious and opened the box. If we spend the money without bothering with his man of business, I have the feeling Macdonald would send lackeys to visit us in the night and explain why it's a bad idea to disobey." He stretched his arms, the lace on his sleeves making strange patterns on the coat's velvet. "And while he found a connection between you and a Mackenzie, he truly believes us all dead and gone, and he also has no idea that women can think, reason, or speak coherently. Not that he wouldn't make use of you if he decided to, but he does not believe you'd tumble to his schemes. Last, what better way to hide the gold than have a lackwit gamble with it on the Exchange and take the payout in English money back to Macdonald?"

Josette listened thoughtfully. "I suppose that is logical. To him, I mean. Sir Harmon must pass Macdonald likely dupes to gather information for him and wash his money clean—I wonder how many of Sir Harmon's other guests are under a similar thrall. If those dupes are caught, *they* answer to the law, not Macdonald or Sir Harmon, two prominent men who can spread their hands and be amazed such simpletons accuse them."

"Very likely," Will said. He looked forward to turning the tables on Macdonald, especially given the man's obsession with Kilmorgan. *That* worried him far more than Macdonald's need to buy himself unwitting spies.

"How do we find out if he has the rest of the gold?" Josette asked. "Dig up his cellar?"

"If it comes to that." Will fixed her with his gaze. "*You* won't be doing any digging at all. I want you to put this money to good use and take Glenna to Paris. You'll stay with my family, who'll look after you and keep Glenna's father at bay."

Josette's dark eyes widened. "I will, will I?"

Will's temper, which he'd managed to keep in check all day, burst at the seams. "Damn it, lass, I won't have ye roaming the countryside for one of my dangerous schemes only to be insulted by lechers like Macdonald. My brothers have a comfortable house in your native land and plenty of friends. You and your daughter will dine well and be protected for the rest of your lives. If you're worried about Colonel Chadwick, never mind about him. I'll deal with him and be done, have no fear."

Josette's eyes sparkled dangerously. "Are you finished?"

"Not really, but I have a feeling you're going to shout at me. Go ahead—but you're off to France, and that is the end of it."

"My high-handed friend, you are *not* my husband. I agree about using the money to send Glenna to safety, and I will do that. But I'll not leave you behind in these isles where you are captured and tortured by British officers and risk your life looking for the rest of the gold. If you want me and Glenna in France, then come there with us."

Come with us. Will gazed out the window, his anger dropping away. He knew, at that moment, why he traveled to Scotland so often, despite the danger, why he'd never, ever settle down in France, and why he'd do anything in his power to keep Josette here with him. The conflict between wanting that and needing her to be safe tore at him.

"I cannae," he said softly. "I must stay."

The astonishing thing about Josette was that she understood. Will did not have to explain that Scotland was a part of himself, and he was a part of it. That he could no more not come back here than cease breathing.

And he could not let Macdonald have Kilmorgan.

"He wants my home," Will said abruptly. "To prove to the world that the Duke of Kilmorgan and the Mackenzies are defeated and gone. If we do nothing, then he is right, and we are finished."

Josette leaned forward and put her hand on his knee. The strength of her touch came through his finely woven velvet breeches with a vibrancy Will loved.

"Do you think I can leave you to fight him alone? I learned from talking to Mr. Macdonald for less than an hour that he is a crafty devil, maybe even as clever as you. But I'm crafty too, Will. I don't want him walking over your family's estate, or your ancestors' bones. I'll send my daughter to safety and fight him with you."

Will dragged his gaze from the hills and focused on Josette. She looked back at him, determination glowing from her.

Mackenzies needed strong women, Malcolm liked to say, so they wouldn't be dashed to pieces on them. Old Dan Mackenzie, so the legend went, found such a woman in the lass who'd risked all to run off with him, and who'd been instrumental in helping him win the lands of Kilmorgan in the first place.

Down the centuries, Mackenzie women had bred strong sons, and daughters too, had taken up arms to fight beside their husbands. They'd fought for Kilmorgan, for their families, for their lives.

Will would never let Clennan Macdonald, or some English

lordling—anyone—take what those men and women had so furiously fought for.

Will closed his hand over Josette's, gripping hard. He hadn't realized he was shaking until he found Josette's steadiness.

"I do want ye to stay with me, lass. For now and for always. Can ye do that, do you think?"

CHAPTER 19

*W*ill's hand on Josette's was hot and solid, his strength unnerving.

What was he asking? To continue with him on his travels, by his side, as his partner? Or as something more?

Josette did not dare wish for more. She'd want to hang on to him, and Will was not a man who took well to clinging.

But who was she to turn up her nose at his offer to keep her by his side? For how long was a question for another time.

"I believe I can manage," Josette said. "But Glenna must be safe."

"We'll send her to Celia and Mary." Will's face set with new determination. "Glenna will kick up a fuss, I predict, but send her we will."

"Of course she will—she's sixteen. But I'll not have her running about the Highlands while men like Mr. Macdonald are in them. Nor will I let Chadwick take her away from me." Josette said the last with a tremor.

"Neither will I, believe me. And no, he'll not have me either." Will touched the box by his side. "I have plans for this gold, love, and for Clennan Macdonald. Help me carry them out?"

Josette squeezed his hand, glad he'd ceased talking about sending her away. She made her choice, and would take the consequences. "I'd be happy to."

By the time they reached Sir Harmon's, midnight's dusk hung in the sky.

The restless guests roamed the house—they'd barely noticed Sir William's and Anna's absence, though they greeted them with interest upon their return—anything to relieve the ennui.

Will gave the casket to Captain Ellis for safekeeping. He trusted the captain, and knew even the hardiest soul would think twice about robbing a British cavalry captain who'd been decorated for bravery.

Not that Will would mention to the other guests what his errand had been about. Will only shook his head when asked why he'd gone off into the wilderness.

"It's beautiful country," Josette said when pressed. "Not civilized by any means, but lovely in its own wild way."

"Did you tramp about like Scotsmen?" one of the gentlemen asked, wrinkling his powdered nose. "How awful."

"Good heavens no." Josette looked shocked he'd suggest it. "We had the coach."

Henri did not look happy with Will, but he fortunately kept his resentment to himself. He was young and wanted things to happen *now*, Will understood. He understood all too well.

Soon, lad.

Sir Harmon cornered Will on the terrace in the rear of the house while the other guests settled down for cards.

"Satisfied?" he asked Will.

"Oh, yes." Will let his voice grow fervent. "You and Mr. Macdonald are giving me so much for so little."

"The terms are to your liking?"

"Of course. I'm your man."

Sir Harmon's eyes held a sparkle of triumph. *He thinks he's just snared his fish,* Will thought. *He's probably snared every man and woman in this house.*

"Good. You'll understand then, when I ask you to leave tomorrow. To begin your visits," Sir Harmon added curtly to Will's wide-eyed stare.

"Oh, yes, yes, I understand. Tomorrow? So soon. I'm not certain my wife will be ready as early as tomorrow. The ladies, you know, with the packing …"

"The next day then, at the latest." Sir Harmon pretended indifference, but Will saw his impatience.

What secrets did the people Macdonald and Sir Harmon want him to talk to hold? Will had glanced at the list and recognized several of the names—one had stood out in particular—but he didn't know all of them, which was odd. Will knew so very many people, or at least of them. Captain Ellis might know those Will didn't—he'd ask him about the rest.

"If you do not mind, I'd like to take your footman, Henri, with us," Will said. "I'll need someone to carry things for me, and he's a sturdy lad."

Sir Harmon's brows furrowed in true confusion. "Who?"

"I believe you call him John. The West Indies lad who carried our fishing things."

"Oh, him." Sir Harmon waved him away. "The boy's a bit ham-handed, but I suppose there's no harm in you borrowing him."

The man had absolutely no idea who Henri truly was or where he'd come from. For that, Will should have gutted him with the fish knife himself.

Will forced himself to beam at Sir Harmon. "Thank you, sir. I'll return him in one piece."

Not until after breakfast did Will manage to escape with Josette to the summerhouse where they met Captain Ellis. Will insisted Henri join them, and the young man did so with great reluctance. He didn't want to attend anything so tame as a conference, and was doubly unhappy that Will had persuaded Sir Harmon to let Henri accompany Will when they departed.

"Don't want to go," Henri said stubbornly. "What'll he get up to while we're gone, eh?"

Will gave Henri a stern look. "Lad, I'm not leaving you here to murder Sir Harmon and then be tortured and executed for it. When the time comes, Sir Harmon will have his comeuppance, and you can tell the world all the things he has done. Preferably in front of elderly, bad-tempered, long-wigged judges who will sentence him to the worst."

"No judge in a court is going to listen to the likes of me," Henri said with a scowl.

"They will if *I* have anything to do with it. They do not like trumped-up, new men who have lied, cheated, and slaughtered their way into the soft life. Sir Harmon will not last, I promise you."

"It's the best way," Josette told him in her gentle tones. "You will be a hero and go on to live your life. That is the best revenge of all."

Will agreed with her—partly. Living well after trouncing your enemies and making certain they *stayed* down was even better.

"She is right," Captain Ellis said. "Let the law take care of Sir Harmon."

Henri glowered but subsided. He wandered to the door to be a lookout, and Will turned to Captain Ellis.

"Do you know who these people are?" Will asked him, indicating a few names on the list. "I've never run across them."

Captain Ellis nodded as he tapped the paper. "*He* is the uncle-in-law of the Lord High Admiral. And this is the second cousin of the war minister. Not men of extreme power themselves, but they have connections and are powerful within their own families."

Will understood now why he didn't know them. They were some-what distant relations of prominent men, and Will had the tendency to deal directly with the prominent men themselves, without going through their families. He did not make use of innocents, as Sir Harmon and Clennan Macdonald obviously liked to.

"Not the sort of gentlemen who'd welcome Sir William Jacobs into their homes, I'd think," Will remarked. "Why does Sir Harmon believe I can get close to them?"

"You have a tie through Lord Marsden, with whom you stayed in Salisbury—Sir Harmon told me about that. Lady Bentley will have pried your connections from you both on your arrival, as she did me, and passed the information to her husband. Lord Marsden will likely vouch for you. So would a few other names on this list."

"Yes ..." Will drew out the word as he thought. "I certainly will visit *one* of them."

Ellis knew which he meant. "Are you certain? Do you trust him?" Ellis did, but Will's encounters with the man in question had not always been friendly.

Will nodded. "He's a wily old goat, but fair-minded, as you know, and he'll do anything for his daughter's sake."

"Including give you information you can feed Sir Harmon and Macdonald? To get them arrested?"

"Maybe." Will continued to study the paper. He felt Josette's eyes on him—she wondering what he was up to. "I'll visit him, no matter what."

Josette watched him sharply, suspicion in her gaze. Before he could tell her not to worry—not that she'd believe him—a shout sounded outside the folly.

A moment later, Henri hauled a small lad into the summerhouse, one with wiry red hair and equally wiry limbs.

"Let me down, ye great lout!" the lad shouted. "I have t' speak to Lord Will."

"And you need to keep your voice down," Will said severely. "Let him go, Henri. Thank you for your vigilance."

Henri thumped the smaller boy onto his feet but watched him closely, ready to grab him if he made any wrong move.

"He sent me t' warn ye," the lad said, out of breath. "Mr. Naughton did. The Macdonald has left his house, and he's heading *here*, to pay a visit to Sir Harmon Bentley. At this very minute, m'lord. I came straight across the hills, while he's meandering on the road, but he won't be long behind me." The boy's legs buckled, and he fell to the floor before Will or Henri could catch him. He sat up and rubbed a hand over his sweat-soaked hair, making it stand up in spikes. "Lord, I could murder a pint."

◦≈◦

Josette was amazed how well frightening news focused her mind. Instead of worrying about what they *might* have to do, she knew exactly what they needed to do. Immediately.

So did Will. They exchanged a glance, which said everything.

"Henri, run for Bhreac and tell him to bring the horses," Will said. "Coach will be too slow. Ellis …"

"You'll need to come with us, Captain," Josette finished for him.

"Or hide myself," Captain Ellis argued. "When Macdonald is gone, I'll return to the house and tell Sir Harmon the pair of you begged me to escort you to the next town, afraid to travel the wilderness alone. He'll believe that."

Will was already shaking his head. "If Macdonald and Sir Harmon compare notes too closely, they'll start to wonder why you had to take on Sir Jacobs' identity, and I do not want them to put you to the question. Better to let them think, at worst, that we're a gang of confidence tricksters running off with a bit of gold."

"He'll chase you for that," Ellis said. "*I* can't disappear. I am known by name to them."

"If they believe we're robbers, yes, they'll give chase, but not as enthusiastically as they will if they find out who I *really* am."

"And the longer we debate, gentlemen, the closer Macdonald comes," Josette broke in. "We need to go now. You too, Captain Ellis."

Captain Ellis did not look happy at the abrupt end to his mission. "I was close to finding hard evidence that Harmon is up to no good," he growled.

"No worries about that," Will said with confidence. "I'll let you make the grand arrest when the time comes. You'll have to leave your things behind."

Captain Ellis's mouth pinched, but he nodded. "I have learned to travel light. They'll find nothing but my shaving gear."

Not long later Bhreac appeared in the open land beyond the summerhouse, leading sturdy horses, one of them belonging to Captain Ellis.

"Do ye know what it cost me to procure that carriage?" Bhreac growled to Will even as Will lifted Josette to a mount. "And all those clothes?"

There was no saddle—no time for it. Will sprang up behind Josette, his body a warm bulk, arms coming around her to take the reins. Captain Ellis got himself onto his horse with the ease of long practice, but Henri stared up at the beast he was to ride with complete distrust.

Naughton's lad gave Henri a leg-up, and Henri, after sliding around a bit, found his seat, but remained uneasy.

"I'll pay ye for them," Will said to Bhreac, letting the tones of Sir William depart forever. "I'm always good for it, aren't I?"

Bhreac sent him a dark look.

Josette reached down and handed the Scottish boy a coin—not one of the French ones, but a silver crown. "Thank you, lad. You rest yourself, and enjoy your pint."

He snatched up the coin and gave Josette an elegant bow. "Thank ye, ma'am. Best I be off. Don't worry, lass, I can get back over the hills easy as pissing."

He waved at them and launched himself into the heather, his face bright with smiles.

"Regrets, Lady Jacobs?" Will said in Josette's ear as he followed Bhreac unerringly up the track into the boulder-strewn slopes.

"For my wardrobe?" Josette touched her cheek to his. "All I need is a simple garment, Sir William, and I'm happy."

"A wisp of red to float over your bosom, perhaps?" His voice held warmth, comfort.

Josette flushed, remembering his lazy smile the day he'd walked into Alec's studio. A happy time, an innocent time, when the world was full of possibilities.

"'Twould need to be a bit larger now," she said. "I've grown stout."

Will laughed, the rumble pleasant. "Ye are the most beautiful woman I know, my Josie. That hasn't changed."

"Flatterer," Josette said but let herself enjoy his words.

Josette closed her hand around the horse's thick mane, leaned into Will, and used his warmth to cut the chill of the summer rain as they rode into the Highlands.

∼

JOSETTE ASSUMED WILL WOULD TAKE THEM BACK TO STRATHY CASTLE where the ladies and Glenna waited, but he turned them south instead. This worried her more than a bit, but he declined to tell them where they were going. Bhreac didn't seem to mind, and even Captain Ellis let Will lead them without argument.

The horses were compact and strong, bred on the Highlands to navigate these hills. They rode straight up mountainsides and down into glens, avoiding any roads, Will finding paths Josette would never have known were there. Captain Ellis and Henri followed closely, as though fearing to stray a step Will didn't take. Bhreac, on the other hand, rode easily, holding the reins negligently while he hummed lively tunes.

Josette didn't fancy camping out with no blankets in her now rain-splotched finery, but Will had provided for that as well. The point between day and night was confusing in the summer light, but as Josette's body drooped in exhaustion, Will led them into a hollow that contained a black stone house with smoke trickling from a hole in its roof.

The man who emerged to challenge them with a wicked-looking sword took one look at Will, lowered the weapon, and walked back into the house without a word.

Unconcerned, Will slid from his horse, helped Josette down—her legs buckled until he steadied her—and strode into the house. A woman's voice rose, speaking in Erse, the syllables gliding pleasantly through Josette's tiredness.

Worn hands closed around Josette, and an elderly woman led her into a place of warmth. The cottage was very small, but the rain stayed outdoors, and the wind almost did.

The man spoke little, the woman volubly, but only in her own language. Josette didn't mind her chattering as the woman took her behind a blanket that divided a bed from the rest of the house and helped Josette out of her clothes. She slid a nightdress made of scratchy homespun fabric over Josette's head and wrapped her in a length of faded wool plaid.

Josette wanted to ask questions, but sleep took her too quickly. She never remembered lying down, but the next thing she knew she woke to light trickling through stones. She lay on a hard mattress with no pillow, but she was warm wrapped in the plaid.

As soon as she stirred the woman popped around the blanket. She had a drab brown gown over her arm that she fitted onto Josette with the skill of a lady's maid. She spoke only Erse but managed to make her point clear—Josette was to keep this dress, the leather breeches that went under it, and the soft leather boots she tied on Josette's feet.

The woman was tiny and wizened, and far too small for the clothes she gave Josette, but Josette didn't argue or question. She thanked the woman in both French and English and hoped she understood.

Will waited with their three companions and host out under the sky, all eating a makeshift breakfast with their fingers. Bannocks, Josette realized as the woman thrust a cloth at her containing the oat cakes. Josette had learned to make bannocks herself and sometimes served them at her boarding house dripping with butter and dollops of cream. These were plain and dry, and a bit gritty, but Josette ate them gratefully.

Josette noted that the woman and her husband were accepting of Henri and only slightly wary of Captain Ellis—they seemed to not be overly worried that a British army officer stood among them. They were wariest of all, interestingly, of Bhreac.

"Because I'm from the Borderlands," Bhreac explained to Josette. "The devil in breeches. Will vouched for the captain and Henri, so they'll trust them—or at least they trust Will. He won't vouch for me."

"Why not?" Josette asked in surprise. "I thought you were friends."

Bhreac winked at her. "Don't mean he trusts me. We go a long way back, me and Will. He knows better. I don't trust him either."

"You two lead very complicated lives," Josette said, licking crumbs from her fingers.

"Not really. Will knows everyone in the Highlands. I know everyone in the Lowlands and the Border country. Sometimes we pool our knowledge; sometimes we're at odds. We know which is which."

Josette let it go and finished her bannocks.

They mounted up soon after breakfast and rode off, Will slipping the woman coins on his way.

"Friends of yours?" Josette asked lightly as they headed southward, she doubling with Will once more. Bhreac had brought an extra horse, which they used to carry their meager belongings, including the casket of gold. Will kept hold of the packhorse's lead rein.

"Aye. They have a daughter, who married a man in Edinburgh. I helped get her there safely during the Uprising. They're grateful."

"I'm certain." Josette's gown and boots must have belonged to their daughter. Will had given up their finery in exchange—the man and wife would sell the clothes to a secondhand shop the next time they ventured to a city.

The breeches under the skirt ensured Josette could sit astride the horse, giving her more stability, though she didn't mind Will encircling her with his arms.

Their journey progressed much the same in the following days, Will taking them across difficult hills and down into steep-walled glens, around lochs and over rivers, arriving at a tucked-away farmhouse as night fell, to be welcomed as friends.

They met no one on the tracks—saw no other person outside the stone houses where they spent the nights. The occasional clump of shaggy Highland cows turned their heads to watch them pass, as though wondering why humans had wandered this far into the wilderness. As Will and party journeyed south, the cows gave way to sheep, who gave them the same stare through similarly long forelocks.

If Sir Harmon or Macdonald pursued them, there was no sign of it.

Will moved easily, leading them up the steepest hills and fording chilly rivers without concern. He wore shirt, breeches, woolen coat, and a length of plaid that had once been dark green, obtained from the same couple who'd given Josette her gown. The clothes fit him suspiciously well—the man had been as tiny as his wife. Josette guessed the clothes were Will's, left there in case he needed them.

He'd left things for himself at all the houses in their path, Josette learned as they went. Will was always greeted as a friend, the surly expressions on the crofters' faces lightening as soon as they recognized him.

Will shrugged when Josette asked him about it while they lay together one night.

"You do good for people, they don't forget," Will said. "Whether Highlander or Lowlander. Not much difference between us but old prejudices. Well, that and wars. Battles. Bad blood. But even so, we're all struggling to get through life the same, aren't we?"

Because they were in a bed together, Will and his plaid wrapped around her, Josette had no impetus to argue.

After five days of hard travel, Josette discovered Will's destiny. The city of Edinburgh lay before them, gray and beautiful in the sun-dappled mist.

"Will," Josette said in trepidation as they gazed down the last hill toward the city walls. "We can't go to Edinburgh. That is, *you* can't. Especially not you."

"Mmm?" Will brushed his lips to her cheek. "Why not? You'll sleep in a softer bed tonight."

Josette glanced to make certain Captain Ellis, Bhreac, and Henri, who was riding better now, were out of earshot. "Because Colonel Chadwick is in Edinburgh," she said softly to Will. "This is where he told me to bring you to him."

CHAPTER 20

*W*ill, to Josette's annoyance, did not jump, exclaim, gasp, or do anything else that betrayed shock and concern. He nuzzled her neck instead.

"I must speak to a man there," he murmured after an exasperating pause. "I don't have time to deal with Chadwick at the moment, so we'll just be careful he doesn't see us."

Josette turned so she could glare at him. "This is no jest. He is serious about wanting to get his hands on you."

Will's absent-minded mien vanished, and he focused on her, golden eyes sharp. "I know, love. He'll never have me, or Glenna. For now, we will slide into and out of Edinburgh like the mists that continuously coat it. What I need to do is too important to let him drive us away."

"You are very confident."

Will's arms around her tightened. "No, lass. I'm desperate and determined. Besides, I'm cold and tired of riding around in the rain. He'll never notice us."

Josette didn't answer. Will could indeed be unrecognizable if he chose, and Colonel Chadwick had never met him that she knew of. Bhreac and Henri would most likely be strangers to him, and Captain

Ellis was cavalry, not infantry, so their paths probably hadn't crossed. But Chadwick would know *her*.

"You'll have to disguise me well."

"Never fear." Will laughed softly. "I enjoy disguises."

"That is not something to boast of," Josette said.

"You enjoy them too—do not tell me you don't." Will kissed her hair. "Never worry. We'll conclude our business quickly. But I will see to your colonel, love." Steel entered his voice. "I promise you that."

Josette believed him. But she eyed the city in worry—she wouldn't feel safe until the Channel and a good amount of land was between Colonel Chadwick and the ones she loved.

IT WAS CAPTAIN ELLIS WHO LED THEM INTO EDINBURGH. WILL PACKED away his plaid and then shrank down into a hooded cloak and muttered like an old man with a toothache.

Will had bundled Josette into a thick shawl, pulling a battered straw hat low over her eyes and tying a threadbare cloth around it and under her chin. Josette walked with the pack horse, head down, like a servant woman following the respectable-looking British officer.

No one challenged them, the soldiers at the old arched gate not much interested in the band of peasants with Captain Ellis. The Uprising had been put down a year ago, the unruly Scots rounded up or killed off, and business rolled on in the great city.

Josette had been to Edinburgh only once, but had admired its tall houses and narrow streets, and the long boulevard from castle to palace, packed with people, horses, carts, and carriages. Holyrood no longer held Prince Charles Edward Stuart, the charming young man come to reclaim the throne for his father. Most of the people here, Josette noted, hurried about their business, pretending no interest in Charles, Jacobites, battles, or plaid.

"Gone underground," Will said into her ear. "The yearning for freedom still exists, but from back rooms and cellars."

Josette glanced about to get her bearings. The house Colonel

Chadwick had told her to bring Will to was on the west end of town, near the castle and new houses built near it. Captain Ellis, following directions Will had given him, took them toward lavish abodes on the other side of the city, closer to the palace.

They arrived at a house off a main thoroughfare, a tall and neat affair with black-painted shutters and a well-swept front step. This was not the very tall and thin house Will's family hired for their stays in the city—Will had taken Josette there when he'd brought her to Edinburgh, when only Malcolm and Alec had been in residence. Josette remembered what a fine time they'd had, how Alec and Mal had made her feel so welcome. As she thought of that house, not many streets from here, tears touched her eyes.

Captain Ellis rapped on the front door. A pale, dark-haired young footman, very English, answered the knock and gazed down his haughty nose at them. He showed a bit more respect at seeing Captain Ellis in his uniform, but didn't waver.

"I regret to say his lordship is not at home, sir."

His lordship, if the aristocratic-looking person were he, peered down at them from a first-floor window. When he caught Josette's eye on him, he stepped back and vanished.

There was a flurry behind the footman, and a retainer with white hair and more seniority pushed past him and wrenched the door wide open.

"Forgive me, Captain. We did not recognize you. His lordship would be pleased to speak to you."

The footman, abashed, stood back to admit the captain. He tried to close the door on the rest of them—servants either used the staff entrance or should wait in the street—but Will ducked inside and gently moved the footman out of the way.

"They stay with me," Captain Ellis said.

The butler raised white brows in disapproval, but Will ignored him. Bhreac strode in without worry, and only Henri hesitated, uneasy.

Josette gave Henri a reassuring look and spoke quietly to the footman. "Perhaps you could take Henri below stairs and give him an ale. It's been a thirsty journey."

Henri brightened at the suggestion, and the footman, recognizing the voice of authority and a lad of his own status, jerked his head for Henri to follow him to the back stairs.

The severe butler led the rest of them up the staircase that bent around the narrow entrance hall. He behaved as though only Captain Ellis existed, clearly unhappy that lowly servants were accompanying the captain upstairs.

The master of the house waited for them in the center of a lavishly furnished study—behind him lay the window Josette had spied him through.

He was a small man and rather thin, with a neat wig with three white curls on either side of his face. His suit was of the latest fashion, but unlike Sir William's layers of ribbons and lace, his coat was plain and dark brown, his breeches the same.

The understated clothes went with the compactness of the man's face and the watchfulness of his blue eyes.

"Thank you, Upton," his lordship said. "You may leave us."

The butler gave a cool bow, bent a sharp eye on Will, Josette, and Bhreac, as though admonishing them to behave themselves, and departed.

Captain Ellis began, "I must beg your pardon, your lordship, for springing upon you in this fashion. Had I known this was our destination, I would have sent word ahead."

"Which might have been disastrous," Will put in.

The aristocrat gave Captain Ellis a civil nod before moving his pinched gaze to Will. *"You,"* he said. "You turn up in the most interesting places, looking like a beggar and a thief. What is your game this time?"

"Ah," Bhreac said, brows rising. "You're well acquainted then."

"We are indeed," Will said smoothly. "Josette, my dear, may I introduce you to his lordship, James Lennox, the Earl of Wilfort. His eldest daughter made the rash decision to marry my brother Malcolm. Wilfort, this is Mrs. Oswald, an extraordinary woman who can ride across the whole of Scotland without a whimper and then glide into a banquet full of the highest in society and speak with ease."

Lord Wilfort was every inch an English aristocrat. He made

Josette a formal bow, respect in his bearing, and then returned his attention to Will.

"I have no doubt you coerced your friends into coming here," Lord Wilfort said. "You must have a reason. You do not make social calls."

Will pressed his hand to his heart. "You wound me, Wilfort. How do you know I haven't longed for a chinwag with my brother's father-in-law about their new wee bairn? He's a bonny lad."

"I know. I've seen him." A fond light flashed in Lord Wilfort's eyes, quickly suppressed. "What do you want?"

From what Will had told Josette when she'd asked about Captain Ellis's confinement at Kilmorgan, Lord Wilfort had been a prisoner of war in the Mackenzies' castle along with him. It had been a civilized sort of imprisonment, Will had said, with both men given their own bedchambers and joining the family for meals. Wilfort and the Mackenzies had become friends during his captivity, and then family when Mary had wedded Malcolm.

"I crave a boon," Will answered. "But first, can ye give Mrs. Oswald a soft bed and a decent meal? The poor woman has been living on bannocks and sleeping in boxes all the way across the Highlands."

WILL ADMITTED THAT A BATH AND CLOTHES THAT DIDN'T RUB HIS SKIN raw was a nice change. He emerged from a chamber in a brown coat and breeches he'd had Henri run and purchase for him secondhand—nothing Lord Wilfort owned would ever fit him. The clothes were a bit tight, but Will couldn't complain.

Josette was lovely in a pink and gold gown Henri had procured, the colors suiting her dark hair and eyes. So lovely that Will wished he could shut himself into her bedchamber with her and never mind about the business at hand.

Wilfort, being Wilfort, invited them to stay for the night and served them a lavish supper. Will had a quiet word with him before the meal, telling him about the gold, the ladies at Strathy, and the list

Macdonald had given him. Wilfort listened without changing expression, typical of him.

Though the man lived alone here—his sister and second daughter and son-in-law were currently in the Lennox ancestral home in Lincolnshire—the dining room was laid out with fine porcelain and gleaming silver, glowing in the light of dozens of candles.

After days of nothing but oatcakes and the occasional fish from the clear rivers, Will found it difficult not to shovel the food into his mouth—turbot in lemon sauce, hens stuffed with sausage, a saddle of beef, and rolls so soft they melted on the tongue. Everything a highly bred Englishman could want.

The wine was delicious too, straight from France. Will detected Mal's hand in that—he always knew where to find the best.

Josette ate with grace, as though he hadn't half-starved her for a week. She so easily glided between worlds, but he preferred to see her like this, comfortable and content—herself.

Characteristically, Wilfort conversed on anything but why they'd come. He and Captain Ellis spent an agonizingly long time asking about each other's families and what each had done in the past year. Bhreac, almost respectable in unpatched clothes and combed hair, listened as he inhaled food. Josette ate quietly, politely answering when Wilfort spoke to her.

Finally, after the footmen whisked away the last plates, and Upton, betraying no surprise that the peasants turned out to be highborn friends of his master's, served sweet wine and withdrew, Wilfort bent his eye on Will.

"What is this boon?"

"Something that will please you." Will lounged back in his chair and savored the mellow sauterne. "Return your daughter and Mal to Britain. Scotland to be precise. Kilmorgan."

Wilfort eyed him intently. "The duchy of Kilmorgan has reverted to the crown."

"So I understand. But not if you prove the last heir is alive." Will turned his goblet on the lace tablecloth. "And that he is not a traitor. Malcolm Mackenzie isn't to blame for what his brother Duncan got up to. Brothers in many families fought one another in this skirmish."

"True, but Malcolm Mackenzie captured guns and a cavalry officer at the Battle of Prestonpans." Wilfort shot a pointed look at Captain Ellis, the officer in question. "He also fought at Culloden, on the side of the Jacobites, and was killed there, according to the accounts."

"Do you have witnesses to this death?" Will asked. "Culloden was a mess." The vision flashed to him of himself standing by a wall at the end of the field, watching helplessly as British soldiers shot and skewered his friends and family. Men he'd been fond of, men he'd disliked, and men he'd barely known had died the same, with bullets or bayonets in their chests as they'd tried to surrender.

His eyes grew moist as though smoke from the battlefield still stung them. "Did anyone actually see Malcolm there?" he went on.

"Captain Ellis fought your brother hand to hand at Prestonpans," Wilfort said dryly.

"And lost," Ellis put in. "I remember quite clearly."

"Perhaps your memory can be allowed to fade," Will said to him. "Duncan was at Prestonpans, definitely, in all his glory. No denying that. Mal only went to latch on to Duncan's cloak and drag him home. Perhaps Duncan captured the artillery and the captain, while Mal only observed."

Captain Ellis sipped his wine and barely hid a grimace. He preferred whisky and brandy to sweet wine. "I have difficulty lying," he said. "I'm not certain I could stand up in court and claim a bad memory."

"We won't make ye take an oath, then. Wilfort, you were a guest in our home for a time and came to know Malcolm well. You know he did not have Jacobite sympathies. In fact, I recall him railing at the Uprising for needlessly killing so many and disrupting our lives—so often, we started leaving the room when he began a rant."

"I do remember," Wilfort conceded.

"As do I," Ellis said with a wry smile.

"Mal was dragged into the conflict against his will. He escaped Culloden by clawing his way to the edge of the field—true. He told me. Knew he could not go home and so sailed with his wife to France and self-imposed exile. Also true. I helped them get there. But Mal belongs in Scotland, and at Kilmorgan—more than any of us. He'd begun building his manor house there, which the army destroyed. If you could see him in his rooms in Paris, pouring over his plans, dreaming of the day he can return … It would break your heart, gentlemen."

It had broken Will's the last time he'd visited. Malcolm had shown Will what he and Alec had come up with for the gardens, the two of them pleased with themselves. Will had been admiring the drawings, when abruptly Mal had crumpled them and thrown them across the room.

Don't know why I'm bothering, he'd declared in a red rage. *I'll never have a chance to use the bloody things.* Alec had stood quietly by, his unhappiness and commiseration apparent.

"I know," Lord Wilfort said quietly. "Mal showed me."

"My father has let the past go," Will went on. "He'll live out his days in Paris with the cronies he's made there, and be as content as he can be. Since our mother died, he hasn't much cared where he was. Alec is happy being the toast of Paris as the next great artist, beloved by the king. Madame de Pompadour is now sponsoring him, and making him fashionable. Me, I'm a roamer and always will be. But Malcolm." Will lifted his glass to his absent brother. "He needs a home. Put him back in Kilmorgan to build his house, fix up his distillery, and repopulate the family with Mary, and he'll be happy. And so will the rest of us be."

Will drank to Mal and thumped his goblet to the table. He felt Josette's eyes on him, understanding in her gaze.

"I agree with you," Wilfort said. "I comprehend that you are asking me to use my influence at the court of St. James's to clear Mal's name and allow him to return to Scotland as Duke of Kilmorgan. The rest of the family is officially dead, and Malcolm can be brought to life as sole heir. But it may take more than my word, and Captain Ellis's. Malcolm will have to prove himself—somehow make clear he was never a traitor."

"I've thought of that." Will leaned back, stretching out his long legs. "My solution is simple. Malcolm can give me up as a spy and a traitor, and the king, bolstered by your word and your support of Malcolm, will embrace him and give him back our land."

His words were barely out of his mouth before Josette sprang to her feet with a cry of fury. As Wilfort and Ellis stared at Will as though he'd lost his wits, Josette faced him, her eyes flashing fire.

"The devil I'll let you do *that*, Will Mackenzie."

CHAPTER 21

*J*osette shook with anger, the too-rich meal roiling in her stomach. Will, damn and blast him, lounged in his chair as though none of this mattered.

"Will has a solution, and all is well?" she demanded, voice resounding. "And we are to jump to it and obey, no matter how ridiculous it is? Give yourself over to the *king*? When the horses are pulling you from limb to limb, will you rejoice that your plan worked?"

Will came slowly to his feet. Wilfort and Ellis had risen when Josette did, polite to the letter. Bhreac was the exception. He remained seated, drinking his wine, enjoying the drama.

"I never said I'd *stay* a prisoner, love," Will said quietly.

"Oh, yes? How many times can you escape? Your luck will run out sooner or later—they'll put you in a dungeon so deep you'll scarce be able to breathe, and they'll keep you chained until they cut you to bits."

"It doesn't matter how stout the lock—it matters who guards the door," Will said, sounding too reasonable. "I've taught you that."

Josette thumped the table with her fists, making the silver cutlery dance. "What you've taught me is you do as you please, devil take the hindmost, because it suits you. While the rest of us worry until we're sick whether you're dead or alive, you go merrily on. But you're not bothered, because *you* know you're well. Your friends can go hang."

"Josette." The confusion in his eyes was unfeigned. "What happens to *me* is not important—don't you understand? It never has been. I never wanted to be duke, and I'll never be the caretaker of Kilmorgan that Mal is. I'm just Will. The spare. Doesn't matter what I get up to, does it?"

He spoke lightly, but Josette read the bitterness behind his words.

He'd told her this before—that he was the appendage Mackenzie. Duncan was the heir, Angus had looked after their father, Alec was the artist, and Malcolm kept the distillery running and the farm producing. Will had felt at loose ends, and ran off at an early age to see the world. He'd stayed in the world, finding exciting things to do, people who needed him—far better than kicking around at home in the way, or so he said.

"What happens to you is not important?" Josette heard her voice rise to the full-voiced shout that her daughter knew meant trouble. "Is that what you are telling me, Will Mackenzie, that no one will care if you live or die? Do we mean so little to you?"

She said *we*, but Josette meant herself. She knew Glenna would grieve hard if something happened to Will, and the men in this room would be sorry, but Josette would descend into a well of pain she might never climb out of.

To Will's steady gaze, she said, "You're a bloody selfish bastard, and I'm sorry I ever spared time for you."

"She's pegged you right," Bhreac said. "Don't fret, sweetheart. When he's swinging, I'll comfort you."

Josette seized her wine glass and dashed its contents into Bhreac's face. Bhreac skidded back in his chair in astonishment, coming to his feet and wiping his eyes. Then he burst out laughing.

"You chose yourself a vixen, Willie. Wise man. If you'll excuse me, your lordship, I'll go dry meself."

Without waiting for Wilfort's acknowledgment, he strolled from the room, mopping his face with a snowy linen napkin.

Wilfort studied Will with a hard expression. "You are now the heir, not the spare. Your father has been declared dead, and so has your oldest brother. Duncan had no issue. That makes *you* Duke of Kilmorgan, as next brother in line."

Will turned a slight shade of green. "I'll stay deceased, thank you very much. Malcolm loves Kilmorgan, and he has a wife and son. Give it to the Runt to pass on to his descendants."

"Yes, indeed," Josette said tartly. "Shove the responsibility onto Malcolm. Heaven forbid you take up any mantle of care. You might have to stay in one place more than a week, and acknowledge that your friends don't want you to leave."

Will's befuddlement changed to anger in the space of a breath. "Love, if I come back to life and claim the dukedom for myself, I'll be killed, and so will those who harbored me. No quarter given. That means you." He pointed a broad finger at her. "Malcolm is good at turning people up sweet. He'll have his house, his lands, his future. I couldn't stick bowing and scraping to the English bastards who gutted my brothers, and I'd be dead in a trice. Is that what you want?"

"And you turn an argument around to suit yourself," Josette snapped. "Your brave idea is to have Malcolm give you over to those same English bastards so *he'll* be left in peace. While you do what? Dive from a dock and swim back to the Continent?"

"If I have to." He tried a smile, the devilish smile that said he'd walk through hell and be fine. But he'd leave Josette behind to do it.

Josette slammed down her empty glass. "You go ahead. Bring Malcolm to Scotland. Have him give you over to the British army. But you'll get no good-bye from me, and no welcome if you manage to escape either. I am finished waiting and fearing for you, Will Mackenzie. If you go, you go alone."

She'd said more than she meant, but the words rang with conviction. Josette gathered her skirts and marched for the door without looking at Will or the other two gentlemen.

She heard heavy silence behind her, felt eyes on her back, but she opened the door and swept into the empty hall, the chill of it embracing her as tears flooded her eyes.

∼

"Mrs. Oswald is right," Captain Ellis said with a scowl once they heard Josette's rapid footsteps on the stairs. "It is a foolish plan. Do you care so little for her that you'd risk your life?"

Lord Wilfort said nothing, but his firm mouth told Will he agreed with Ellis.

"Excuse me, gentlemen." Will turned from their disapproving stares and went out the door Josette had left open.

The hall and staircase were empty. Will heard the click of Josette's heels above him then the slam of a door.

He took the stairs two at a time and managed to dive into Josette's bedchamber before she could lock the door. Not that she'd bothered. She was already gathering her few belongings into a bundle and didn't turn around when Will charged in.

"Josette, love, don't go."

Josette gazed at him through the mirror on her dressing table. "Why not? I've finished my mission. I have enough for the ladies to bribe their husbands' way to freedom and for me to take Glenna far away, out of Chadwick's reach." She patted the casket on her dressing table. "Or do you want me to stay because you know I'm taking the gold?"

"I don't give a damn about a box of coins. Take it, spend it, dump it into the North Sea if you want to."

Josette nodded, her eyes wise but so very sad. "You say that because you know you can get the rest from Mr. Macdonald or make him show you where it is."

"Will ye cease telling me my own plans? Particularly when you don't know them?" Will balled his fists and tried to rein in his temper. "Anyway, my idea thwarts Colonel Chadwick. He can't threaten you into giving me to him if I've already been surrendered to the British."

"I have half a mind to run to his house right now and shove you at him." Josette slammed the nightgown Henri had bought at the secondhand shop into the sack that served as her valise. "And how can I help speculating on your plans? I can only guess what you mean to do. Will trusts no one, not even the woman who loves him."

Will stilled. Josette turned crimson and quickly bowed her head over her packing.

Love? Will had never heard the word cross her lips. Josette loved her daughter. She tolerated Will and enjoyed being his lover—that was all.

He was across the room to her in the space of a moment. "What did you say?"

Josette wouldn't look at him, a lock of sable hair falling over her cheek. "Never you mind."

"I do mind." Will laid a hand on her arm, making himself keep his touch soft. "You can't love me, lass. There's nothing lovable about me."

"Don't I know it."

Will turned her to face him. Her cheeks were blotchy, her eyes wet, and she still refused to look up.

He rubbed a thumb across her cheekbone, and Josette's chest rose with a swift breath.

"I don't want to love you," she said rapidly. "It makes my life horrible—I'm always wondering whether you're dead or alive, if you're fine and haven't bothered to tell me. I try not to love you. I'd stop if I could."

Will's throat went tight. He stroked her cheek. "Lass."

"I'd never trap you," Josette said. "I don't want you to tie yourself to my side and live in my pocket like Sir William does with Anna—you're not that sort. But you care for no one, and that's cruel to your friends. We tear ourselves apart trying not to worry about you, but it's impossible."

Will gave her an incredulous look. "I care for no one? Why the devil do you think I've come here—to Scotland, Edinburgh, where it's death for me to walk? I came to beg for my brother, so he can live the life he deserves. I took myself to Sir Harmon's godawful house to help the women who turned to you. To help your daughter. To help *you*. If I don't care, then what the devil am I doing here?"

Josette remained stiff. "You're playing the gallant knight who charges in to save the world. You chose that silly costume for the masked ball for a reason. You rush about trying to put everyone's life to rights, never mind what *they* want. You've disappeared so many times—I am never certain whether I'm happy to see you again or dismayed."

Will caught her hand. "I always want to see *you* again, Josie. Always."

"How the devil do you think I felt when I saw the broadsheets proclaiming all those dead at Culloden? Listing your name? It was horrible. I couldn't eat or sleep for days—Glenna was terrified I would die."

Will kissed her fingers, pain a hard ball in his chest. "You know I sent word as soon as I could."

"And I was so angry." Josette at last looked directly at him, wells of fury and anguish in her eyes. "I received your cheerful note that told me you were well and on your way to France with your brothers. You could not bother to tell me in person—you were right not to. I wanted you to turn up so I could kill you myself."

"Lass." The word was a whisper.

Will hadn't known she'd react so to news of his death. Josette had always been brisk, matter-of-fact, understanding that Will had no choice but to depart when he'd prefer to linger, to breathe her in. *She'd* been the one to ask him to leave, several times.

He'd always been right to go, which kept his enemies from finding her or using her to trap him. Until recently, that is. Not that Colonel Chadwick was his enemy—the man was playing some kind of game, and Will would stop it.

When Josette turned from him, Will stepped behind her and slid his arms around her waist. "Don't go, love. Not this time."

She didn't lean into him but also didn't pull away. "I can't stay if you plan to let your brother hand you to the king's men. I can't be here to watch that."

"A temporary measure—"

"I know you believe you'll easily escape them, but what if you can't? Even if you manage it, you'll never be able to set foot in Scotland again. You keep saying you're fighting for your brother to return to the Highlands, that you need to be here, in your home, but you're ensuring that you'll have to flee. Far, far away—farther than your dad's house in Paris. So far I might never see you again."

"No." Will nuzzled her cheek, loving the silk of her hair. "You and I would come together, no matter what. We always do. The world hasn't been able to separate us so far, love. It never will."

"You also always believe you can do what you please," Josette said, her voice softer but no less sad. "With no consequences."

"Oh, there are consequences." He heard the helpless rage in his words. "I lost my brothers, my home, and my own name, because I didn't do enough. I can never do enough ..."

He didn't mean to break down. Will was always the tough one, the Mackenzie who had every situation under his control. He let men capture him so he could learn *their* secrets, vanishing from under their noses when he was done. He discovered their plans and fed them to the right ears so people wouldn't die.

But sometimes ...

It was never enough. Wars happened, and people died anyway. Will tried to make his words, his actions, save others, but he couldn't be everywhere, save everyone. He hadn't been able to save his young brother Magnus, who'd died from a weak heart, or Angus, trying to keep Duncan alive, or the arrogant Duncan himself.

"I took care of the family, because Duncan never would," he heard himself say. "Duncan was about glory and dreams. I had to be the practical one."

He felt Josette's touch, but the room had darkened for him. "I know," she whispered.

"I left home to make life better for them. Malcolm *stayed* home for the same reason. He looked Kilmorgan while I roamed the world, searching for the answer."

"There isn't one." Josette's words were as soft as her touch.

"I am learning that, my love. It's why everything's such a mess."

And there was no one in the world he could tell. Nobody who would understand like Josette Oswald, a woman who had stood against the world, alone, to protect her daughter.

No, not alone. Will would never let Josette be alone.

Josette turned in his arms to face him. "You're trying to put it right. But I can't watch you put it right by sacrificing yourself. I can't bear that. We must try a different way."

"We." Will tilted her face to him. "Does that mean you'll stay? Walk beside me every wretched step?"

Suspicion cut her softness. "Only if you give up this mad idea of having Mal hand you over. Promise me you won't do that, and I'll stay. For now."

"Only for now?" Will's heart felt suddenly lighter. "You said you loved me. Fickle woman."

"I was a fool to say so. You'll hold it against me, use it to your advantage—"

"You don't think much of me, do you, lass?" Will cupped her face. "What I'll do with your words is treasure them. Press them to my heart and keep them always."

"Charming me once more."

"I'm not the Mackenzie with the charm," Will said. "The charming ones are Malcolm and Alec. But what I have that they don't, is *you.*"

Josette stared at him, her dark eyes wet. "Damn you," she whispered, and then she rose on tiptoes and kissed him.

THE KISS LEFT JOSETTE'S CONTROL VERY QUICKLY. WILL CUPPED HER head in his hands, fingers loosening her hair as he opened her mouth with his.

He was impossibly strong, pulling Josette against him, one foot sliding between hers. He kissed her as though this was their last kiss for some time to come, and her heart squeezed, fearing it might be so.

Will eased back, but instead of finishing and walking away, he drew her closer, kissing her again, harder this time. His fingers bit down, lips commanding, the kiss growing fierce.

Josette fumbled at his coat, finding the buttons that held it closed, jerking them open. That barrier gone, she slid her hands inside, across the satin waistcoat that cupped Will's hard muscles. He was warm beneath the slippery fabric, fine to touch.

Will licked across her mouth and drew her lower lip between his. Josette made a wordless sound and let her hands move from his waistcoat down the breeches that hugged his backside. Will jumped, bumping her mouth, but he didn't break the kiss.

Only when she drew her hand to the front of his breeches, unbuttoning the flap did Will lift his head with a gasp.

"Lass," he growled, his eyes burning. "I warn ye—no."

Josette slanted him a smile, her lips raw from his kisses, and dropped the front of his breeches. Will dragged in a ragged breath as his cock tumbled free.

CHAPTER 22

*J*osette's smile undid him even more than her declarations.

The woman who loves him, she'd said. Admonishing him, but revealing her innermost thoughts without meaning to.

Now that woman closed both hands around his cock, and Will couldn't hold back a groan.

"Damn you, lass. How can I let you leave me, when ye do *that?*"

Josette didn't answer, only gave him her wicked smile. Long, long ago, when they'd become lovers for the first time, she'd smiled at him like that, though then her eyes had held trepidation.

Will had gone gently with her, marveling that this beauty of a woman had consented to share his bed. They'd come together tentatively at first, then as they grew to know and understand each other, with fervor and need.

Josette had grown more beautiful over the years, more daring. She made him want her, *crave* her.

As he craved her now.

Will knew he'd never have the patience for unlacing and unbuttoning. He seized Josette around the waist and turned her to the chair at the dressing table. She lost hold of him as he sat down and lifted her on top of him, but it didn't matter.

Her voluminous skirts were an obstacle, but she wore only an overdress and an underskirt, not the layers of garments many ladies of fashion put on. He lifted and shoved fabric until he found *her*, bare beneath them all, her thighs softer than any of the silks she wore.

Josette met his gaze as Will positioned her to straddle him, her dark eyes full of longing. She wasn't afraid of him, or what he'd do— she wanted the passion of loving as much as he did.

Will slowly slid her on top of him, his cock pushing up inside her. A small amount at first, then deeper, farther. Josette's eyes closed as she took him. Will sucked in a breath when she squeezed around him, more tightly than her fists ever could.

Was there anything better than being inside this woman? Josette surrounded him with her body, her scent, her heat. Will rocked back in the chair, desperate for more of her.

She opened her eyes, languor taking over. Harsh words and fluctuating emotions were behind them—the two came together in fluid harmony, erasing pain and sorrow—as always.

Will forgot everything but *her*, thrusting up into her with hot sensation, hearing her cries, watching her face as she fulfilled desire. Her hair, which he'd loosened, tumbled down, enclosing him in its silk.

Josie, love, I'd do anything in the world for you.

Including staying with her until the world ended. Which it might soon.

Josette opened her eyes. She looked down into Will's, the darkness of her velvet gaze erasing all that was terrible. She leaned to kiss him, then groaned as he thrust, Will holding her fast.

The fire sputtered, and candles burned low, and still Josette took her pleasure on Will, and gave him back that pleasure more than a hundredfold.

WILL ENTERED WILFORT'S STUDY THE NEXT MORNING, THOROUGHLY rested and feeling more alive than he had in a long time. He'd have preferred to lie in bed with Josette the rest of the day, feeding her breakfast, then dinner, making hot love with her in between. Not yet, but one day. Soon ...

While Will and Josette had dressed each other, a footman had brought Will a message that the earl wanted to see him in the study, alone. He added that the captain and Bhreac—the footman stiffly called him *Mr. Douglas*—were in the dining room and would await Josette there.

Will parted from Josette on the staircase where they exchanged a gentle kiss. Josette's fingers closed tightly on Will's hand a brief moment, then she turned away, composed, and descended to the dining room.

The earl stood at the window in his study, the man gazing over mist-enshrouded Edinburgh. He'd been in the same window yesterday when they'd arrived—he must like to keep watch from here.

"A beautiful old city," Wilfort said, keeping his gaze on the view as Will entered. "And now I can live here without fear."

"I wouldn't say *without fear*," Will said easily. "'Tis plenty dangerous in places."

"I know, but that spoils the sentiment." Wilfort turned to him. "I suppose there are many Scotsmen who'd throw me out of their city or cut my throat in a heartbeat."

"There are, but ye can't blame them for resentment. Culloden exacted a terrible price."

"I know. I regret that. Cumberland's orders weren't clear, but he interpreted them as pure slaughter, no accepting surrender. He longs for glory—his career in the French wars has not been the best. So far, Culloden is the only battle he's ever won."

"That tells me we ought to have had more Frenchmen in the Jacobite army," Will said. "But it's time for Scotland to join the world instead of hunkering behind our Roman-built wall and throwing everyone else out. Edinburgh is the place to do this joining with the world. We'll have our revenge, but in a different way than most people believe, I imagine."

"I agree." Wilfort's tone was dry. "There are formidable thinkers in

Scotland who aren't hidebound by the English tradition of clinging to old philosophies. I will watch with interest."

"Why did you send for me?" Will asked. "To talk about Scotland's future?"

"No, to talk about its present." Wilfort became brisk. "The list of names Captain Ellis gave me is unnerving. These gentlemen have connections to peers in the House of Lords, men on the King's Bench, and the Lord High Chancellor. The fact that I am on this list is even more troubling—I am one of the few men who can walked unchallenged into St. James's and chat with anyone I wish. Sir Harmon Bentley and Clennan Macdonald want to pry out our secrets, do they?"

"It appears so."

"And they sent the coxcomb you pretended to be off to gather them? A risk, I'd say."

Will shook his head. "They believe Sir William Jacobs too stupid to understand the intelligence he is to gather. That he's so desperate for money he'll do what they say without question. And that he is not high enough in society himself to realize who these gentlemen are." He tapped his lower lip. "Sir Harmon isn't too bright—wise enough to keep himself from his creditors, but he's more interested in growing rich from the work of others than coming up with plots against the crown. He just wants the money he can make. I'm certain Macdonald is playing him, promising him riches for his assistance."

"I've heard of Clennan Macdonald. We had an eye on him when Charles Stuart made his way to Scotland—we were certain he'd take up the Jacobite banner and be a formidable opponent. He turned the other way instead, to our surprise."

"He waits to see where the wind blows," Will said. "He guessed—rightly—that Teàrlach mhic Seamas wouldn't prevail, no matter how many determined Scots were behind him. Macdonald never liked Lord Murray, for instance. He probably nursed resentment that Murray had been chosen to head the army—Macdonald nurses many resentments."

"Including against Mackenzies, you said."

"Never forgave my mum for throwing over his little brother," Will said cheerfully. "Took it personally. Never mind that Horace married and lived happily in Edinburgh until his death. Clennan held the grudge. Still does."

"Macdonald has no idea you are involved in this?" Wilfort asked in a mild tone.

"I never showed my face to him, and we scrambled from Sir Harmon's abode before he could reach it. With luck, Sir Harmon concluded I was anxious to be off to earn my reward and invest the money, taking Captain Ellis with us for protection. If he and Macdonald gave chase, they did not do it with much determination."

"Or did not see the need to bother," Wilfort said. "They believe Sir William is under their thumb. But I believe Captain Ellis should remain here for a while. I'd like to keep his part in this quiet, plus away from any vengeance Macdonald might think to take once he realizes you betrayed him."

"He's a good man, is Ellis. He doesn't deserve to get caught up in Mackenzie schemes."

"And yet, he continues to," Wilfort said dryly. "I know he had a tenderness for my daughter, and I once would have been happy to call him son-in-law."

Will chuckled. "But Malcolm spoiled that by rising from the dead. Mary is deliriously happy with the Runt, I assure you."

"I agree. Which is why I bend over backward to help you and your trouble of a family. I risk my own neck doing so, by the way."

"I know," Will answered quietly.

They exchanged a look of understanding. Wilfort could have destroyed the Mackenzies at one time, and he had not, for love of his daughter.

Then Wilfort sighed. "But you are right about Macdonald's deviousness. He sold plenty of information to the British during the Uprising and hunted down Jacobites himself, but I know damn well he sold plenty of information to the Jacobites as well. But he was never caught at that. In return for his help to the crown, he was given amnesty by the king, as well as the pickings of the spoils of deposed Highlanders."

"Including Kilmorgan Castle and its lands."

"Just so."

"I will never let him have it," Will said in a hard voice. "I think you understand that." He shook his head and changed the topic before his anger could rise too high. "What about the Louis d'or?" he asked. "Was Macdonald given that for safekeeping? Or as payment for services rendered?"

Wilfort spread his hands. "That I do not know. No one ever found the gold—not the Jacobites waiting for it, nor the British sent to seize it, nor the French captain who ferried it from France. It was unloaded from the boat, and simply vanished."

"I believe Macdonald has it," Will said. "Or at least part of it. He might have stumbled upon it, or stolen it, or been entrusted with it, unbeknownst to you, and hidden it away. No matter what, he's decided the gold is his to do with as he pleases."

"I can have him raided," Wilfort said with a quiet authority that was chilling. "I can suggest to the right people that he might have been a traitor after all, and have his home searched, none too gently."

"I'd enjoy that," Will said. "Though I doubt he's hiding the bulk of it there. What he gave Josette and me was only a tiny part of the whole—if the sum a man in France told me was sent here is to be believed. Macdonald's too canny." He rubbed his hands together, cheered. "But do raid him. Should be entertaining. Do Sir Harmon's as well. I looked and found nothing, but I did not have time to search properly. Also … the lad, Henri. Sir Harmon stole that estate from a Scottish family called Dunbar, good people, according to Henri. They took in the lad when he had nowhere to go. They were arrested— Henri believes they were executed, but he's not certain. It seems they objected to Sir Harmon making his fortune on the backs of slaves, and this irritated him."

Wilfort nodded. "I can inquire. Sir Harmon himself is … irritating."

And when Wilfort was irritated, heads rolled—sometimes literally.

"About Malcolm," Will said. "It seems I won't be letting him turn me in. It was pointed out to me that this was not well thought."

Wilfort's cool stare said he agreed. "What you want is for Malcolm

Mackenzie to be the only survivor of Culloden. For it to be proved he was not a traitor, and for Kilmorgan to be handed back to him. You would forgo any claim to it."

Will lifted his hands. "Aye. Malcolm loves the place, and as embarrassed as a Scottish warrior is about softer emotions, I love Malcolm. The Runt deserves to be happy. Me, I'll do with a corner to tuck myself in. 'Tis easier for me *not* being Will Mackenzie, if you understand me."

"I think I do, though I've never really understood your motives. What about Mrs. Oswald?"

What about her? Will warmed as he remembered waking up next to her, nearly nose to nose, how her flush and smile had heated every space inside him. "If I have anything to say about it, Mrs. Oswald will be in that corner with me."

"I meant, will she be happy in that corner?" Wilfort said severely. "With a man of no name? Or should I invite her to stay with me as well, and make arrangements to send her wherever she wishes to go?"

No, was Will's instant thought. He did want Josette to be safe and sheltered, with her daughter, and he knew full well that Wilfort could arrange that. But after last night ...

Will wanted it all—Kilmorgan for Mal, the French gold to help all who needed it, Josette and Glenna free of threat, and Josette by his side. His *family.* It extended beyond the Mackenzies now.

"It will be up to Mrs. Oswald," Will said. "I promise ye, we'll have a discussion, probably a loud one, and she will do as she pleases. She always has," he finished proudly. "There's a man in Edinburgh, name of Chadwick. An English infantry colonel."

Wilfort gave him a nod. "I have heard of him. Widower. Wife was the daughter of Sir Rufus Addison, knighted for lending king and country an enormous sum of money and mustering a regiment to fight Louis of France. A formidable man—Addison. Chadwick is very much under his thumb. Why do you wish to know about him?"

"Keep a watch on him for me, will you? If he moves, send word."

Wilfort raised his brows. "Send word to where? And why are you interested?" His suspicion grew.

"Find Bhreac if you can't find me. The message will reach me. And

I will be sending word to *you*. About many things. My interest in the colonel is not for me, but Mrs. Oswald. He is a threat to her, and I want him where I can put my hands on him when I am ready. I'd ask for your help, but this is personal. Please see that he stays put."

Wilfort watched him carefully. He was a shrewd man, and probably was fitting pieces together. "Just so."

"Meanwhile, I'm back to a castle full of ladies—poor me. You'll look into their circumstances?"

"I can guarantee nothing, but I will make inquiries," Wilfort said. "If the men in question were coerced or threatened into taking up arms, as I know many in the Uprising were, a case can be made to release them. They might have to go into exile—are their ladies prepared for that?"

"They are. 'Twas not well done, some of the recruiting." Will had watched Jacobites threaten to burn down crofters' homes to force the men inside to join them in the fight. "These ladies need their menfolk —it's heartbreaking to see them remain so brave in their uncertainty. Besides," he finished briskly, "if they have to wait much longer, they might rush to London and tear down the Tower themselves."

Wilfort acknowledged this with a small smile. "I have become familiar with Scotswomen. If more of them had led the Jacobite army, I might even now be cowering in my home in Lincolnshire with a Scottish king on Britain's throne."

"Aye, you are catching on."

"One thing I do know," Wilfort said, sobering. "The husband of Lillias McIvor. I'm sorry to say, he has died. There was a fever in the prison where he was kept, and almost all the men there perished."

JOSETTE JOURNEYED BACK TO STRATHY IN THE COMPANY OF WILL, Bhreac, and Henri, but she did not share a horse with Will this time. She rode in a saddle that was more comfortable than the horse's rigid backbone, and had resumed the breeches and skirt. A packhorse carried the casket of gold, carefully hidden in their baggage.

She breathed a sigh of relief as they left Edinburgh behind. Will had not tried to find Colonel Chadwick either to kill him or give himself up or anything else nonsensical. He hadn't mentioned the colonel since their fierce argument, which was fine with Josette. She'd take Glenna out of the man's reach and then make sure he never put his hands on Will.

Captain Ellis remained behind as Lord Wilfort's guest. The captain had *not* wanted Josette to ride off with Will, but he did not stand in her way. He did agree to Will's suggestion to write to Sir Harmon and claim Sir William and his wife had indeed asked him to escort them for a while, and now they'd gone south to England.

Josette knew Will had given Captain Ellis as well as Lord Wilfort further instructions, but as usual was cryptic about them. How Will managed to wrap a cavalry captain as well as one of the foremost earls in Britain around his finger, she didn't know, but he'd done it. Whatever he'd asked them to do for him, they'd do.

Will and Bhreac wore the clothes of crofters, Will slouching under his broad cloak to make himself look smaller. Henri dressed as their servant, though it was clear Will did not consider him one. All three men packed and saddled the horses every morning and unsaddled them every night, none doing more work than the others.

On the first day, they passed several Highlanders and their families traveling toward Edinburgh. The men had packs on their backs, their breeches and homespun shirts threadbare. They'd draped themselves in cloaks pulled around their bodies like great kilts, but there was no tartan fabric in sight. The women looked ragged, exhausted from trudging.

Josette surmised they'd been turned off their land, or had fled when Cumberland's men came. The city might give them employment, or at least a place to huddle until they decided where to go next.

Bhreac addressed their leader. "Unwrap yourself, man," he advised. "They'll arrest ye even for *looking* like you're wearing a plaid. They mean to stamp out the national dress entirely."

"Should I take the word of a Lowlander?" the man asked in a flowing Highland voice, but he sounded more tired than resentful.

"He's right, lad." Will said, at last raising his head. "Go cautiously."

The Highlander gave Will a flinty look, and then he blinked, his eyes widening. Will shook his head ever so slightly, and the man dropped his gaze.

"God go with ye," the Highlander said in a low voice.

"And you, my friend."

Will and company reined their horses aside to let the Highlanders by, and they were gone.

Josette saw the lead Highlander glance back at them sharply. "Did he recognize you?" she asked in worry.

"He did," Will answered. "Not a surprise. He's one of me dad's crofters." His eyes burned with resolve. "It's why we need it all back, love. They shouldn't have to work in the factories and never see their lands again. At least I'll know where to find them when this is finished."

Josette reached across the space between them and caught his hand, squeezing it. Will drew their mounts close, and kissed her.

Their horses objected and jerked apart. Will laughed, true gladness in the sound, and led them up the road to the Highlands.

As soon as was possible, Will headed them off the Wade roads and over the mountains, moving westward.

They sheltered with crofters in hidden valleys, or beside rushing streams, or high on mountainsides, keeping well away from the British forts and encampments. The peak of Ben Nevis sported snow on its very top even in summer, the wind rolling down its slopes chilling.

Will turned north along Ben Nevis's eastern side and skirted the end of Loch Ness, just out of sight of Fort Augustus and the blue-black waters of the loch. From there they entered rough hills, making their slow way to the open Highlands and Strathy Castle.

The air had turned cold by the time the glen that held Strathy was in sight. Midsummer had passed, and autumn rapidly approached.

Josette heard Glenna before she saw her. The girl held the neck rope of a long-haired cow and was swearing at the beast in a mixture of French, English, and what Josette recognized as Erse.

The dog, Beitris, wandering near Glenna, caught their scent. She jerked her head up and let out an earth-rumbling *woof*.

"She'll not give up much milk if you yell at her like that," Josette called down the hill to her daughter. "You have to coax her, gentle like."

Glenna dropped the rope. "Mum!" she shouted and charged at her.

Josette slid from the horse, joy in her heart. She caught Glenna in a fierce embrace, and they held each other hard, Josette's world complete once more. Beitris gamboled about them, rushing from Glenna and Josette to the men and back again.

Glenna, her dark hair in a single braid, raised her head and scowled at Josette. "Why were you gone so long? I missed you!"

"We had to travel all the way to Edinburgh and back," Josette said, trying to sound as though such things were of no great moment. "I'll not ask you where you found the cow—I'm only happy you're safe and sound."

The ladies of the castle, hearing Glenna's shout and Beitris's barking, tumbled out the front door. At the sight of Lillias, Josette's heart constricted. Will had told Josette of Lillias's husband's fate.

Josette swallowed and gently pressed Glenna aside. "Lillias, love," she said. "Let us walk."

WILL HEARD THE MOAN THAT WRENCHED FROM LILLIAS AS SHE AND Josette moved into the heather, Lillias slumping against Josette's side.

A vision of Josette receiving the same news of Will came to him, Josette sagging as grief gripped her.

What a cruel world we were born to love in, Will said silently. *But it doesn't stop us loving.*

Henri shook his head as they led the horses into the courtyard, followed by a curious Beitris. "Poor lady."

Bhreac watched Lillias, sorrow in his eyes. He handed Will his reins and picked his way along the trail the two ladies had taken. His words floated back as he put his arm around Lillias's shoulders.

"There now, lass. I knew your husband. He was a good man. A good man."

Will watched the three a moment longer, his heart heavy, before he and Henri took the horses into the shelter at the back of the castle.

Later, when everyone was safely inside and the supplies they'd picked up along the way unpacked by the grateful inhabitants, Josette reappeared. She wore the practical but lovely gown Will had seen her in when he'd woken here the first time, and had dressed her hair in a tidy knot. No more frilly garments and jewels glittering in long curls.

"I put Lillias to bed and gave her something to help her sleep," Josette told Will in a low voice. He nodded, still angry he'd been too late to save the man.

They joined the ladies, Bhreac, and Henri, in the kitchen for a meal at the long table. Beitris gnawed on meat Will surreptitiously passed her. The mood was somber, though with an undercurrent of excitement. Will and Josette had found some of the gold.

"It will take some time to arrange things," Will said. "But I have the word of an honorable man that he will speak to the right people and try to get your lads released. He's got such a silver tongue, ye might not need the money to bribe their way free. Ye can use it to buy your-selves passage to the Continent and set up there."

"Thank you," Mysie said with true gratitude, and the others agreed.

"Don't expect them next week," Will warned. "Next month, perhaps, or the month after. Wheels turn slowly."

"Will it be enough for all of us?" Mysie asked glancing at the casket that sat in the middle of the table.

"Probably," Will said, "But don't fret yourself. I know where to find more."

He felt Josette's sharp gaze on him. He hadn't told her everything, and he had the feeling she'd be most unhappy with him when she discovered what he intended.

~

"Are you *mad*?" Josette demanded.

They stood alone atop the tower, in the same spot they'd argued upon Will's arrival. Will's golden eyes glinted in the dying sunlight as he finished relating his next insane scheme.

"I knew you'd be angry with me," he said, not looking very remorseful.

"How could I not?" Josette planted fists on her hips. "I *knew* when you were looking at that map I couldn't stop you from going. Even if it means your death."

Will's tone remained infuriatingly reasonable. "I didn't plan to print it in the newspapers and shout it in every village square, love. None will note my passing."

"Mr. Macdonald has been nosing about the place," Josette reminded him. "Or is that the true reason you want to go? To keep him from taking over Kilmorgan?"

"It is one reason," Will admitted. "I have several more. But no matter what those reasons are, my beautiful lass, I want you to come with me."

CHAPTER 23

*W*ill and Josette traveled to Kilmorgan alone, though Will decided at the last minute to take Beitris along. Bhreac, this time, chose to stay behind.

"The ladies need looking after," Bhreac said. "Protecting." His gaze strayed to Lillias, his expression troubled.

Henri asked to stay as well. "I can help here," he said to Will. "You won't let me kill Sir Harmon, and this is a good place. But hurry back." Henri's eyes sparkled with angry determination. "I won't wait forever."

"We won't be long," Will promised, meaning it. He was ready to destroy both Sir Harmon and Macdonald. That such men should be living in soft comfort while Lillias's husband had succumbed to a fever in a hard prison drove him on to the final stage of his plan.

He took Henri aside to explain a few tasks he had for the lad. Henri looked mollified when Will finished, and promised to do his best.

Will had spoken to Bhreac too, Josette knew, given him who-knew-what instructions. She knew Will wouldn't share these with her until he was ready, so she didn't bother to ask.

Glenna wanted to accompany them, and was furious when Josette refused. Will waited while mother and daughter argued in the courtyard, their voices echoing up to the hills and down to the loch.

Josette hated to leave her, Will knew, but Kilmorgan would be far too dangerous for Glenna. She'd be much safer in this remote ruin, with Bhreac and the fierce ladies to look after her.

It was far too dangerous for Josette to come as well, but Will didn't want her out of his sight. He also knew that he needed her help.

Glenna lost the argument. She burst into tears and stormed inside, but a moment later was back to fling her arms around Josette, her face wet.

As Will helped Josette mount her horse, Glenna turned on him. "If you get her killed or hurt, I will hunt you down."

"If I do," Will said, drawing the girl into his embrace. "I'll deserve it, lass."

Glenna's tears continued, but she waved them off with the others. Will turned them northward, his body humming with the knowledge that he was going home.

JOSETTE SENSED THAT THIS JOURNEY WOULD BE THE MOST IMPORTANT of all. It was also the most perilous. They went north into the heart of the Highlands, skirting villages, this time avoiding crofters. Not all men in this area had joined the Jacobites and might be happy to turn in a Mackenzie and collect their reward.

The other danger was from desperate Jacobites in hiding, ready to fight anyone who crossed their paths. Will muffled anything metal on bridles and saddles with strips of cloth, once going so far as to wrap the horses' hooves as well. Beitris seemed understand the need for stealth, and stayed close to them, watchful and silent.

They slept in hollows in the rocks, Will and Josette wrapped together in a worn plaid. Josette snuggled into Will, enjoying his kisses on her neck as he drifted to sleep. They didn't make love, needing to stay alert, but Josette gathered to herself the joy of simply lying with him.

Will approached Kilmorgan from the north, riding well around the firths, following the coastline south. The track he used was deserted, any house they passed either burned out or empty, its roof sagging.

Josette felt Will's sadness each time they passed one of these derelict cottages, and his anger. The people of his land had fled or been captured or killed. Will blamed himself, but Josette never would. She blamed the Highlanders who'd rashly joined a war they couldn't win, and she blamed the Duke of Cumberland for exacting his swift and cruel vengeance. Not for nothing did they call him The Butcher.

Will paused on the edge of a clearing several days after they'd departed Strathy Castle. Before them a hill covered in sapling trees and thickening brush stretched to the sunset sky. On the top of this hill sat the stump of a building, walls open to the wind, windows that had once held glass gaping and empty.

Kilmorgan Castle. Josette had visited it long ago, when she'd first known Will, when he'd invited her here to show off his ancestral home.

Their father, the duke, had shouted that he didn't want the castle overrun with "Will's women." But once the brothers, including Alec's twin Angus, had made Josette welcome, the duke had unbent.

The duke had taken to Glenna very quickly—Josette had caught him on his knees on the drawing room floor one day helping as tiny Glenna soberly built a wall out of books. The duke steadied the expensive tomes she'd pulled from the shelf as they built stairways and curtain walls, ready to defend their fort from all comers.

Josette's breath caught as she beheld the ruin, tears in her eyes.

"Aye," Will said, the word quiet. "'Tis a sad thing."

They studied the castle a few silent moments before Will turned down a hill, putting the ruin behind them.

He led them to a steep glen about a mile from the castle and down a narrow path along this. At the end of the valley they came to a house built into the sheer side of the hill—black stone like the cottages, but with whole glass windows and a stout front door.

This was the distillery, constructed to house the family at the end of the seventeenth century while the castle was modernized, later turned over to brewing whisky. Covertly at first, though the Macken-zies had never considered themselves in the wrong. The rules, they said, had been created so the government could take a hefty tax and leave little for the whisky makers.

The house was so hidden that even other Highlanders weren't aware of its existence. The family had moved here when the castle had been destroyed, setting up a makeshift home. It was inhabited even now, Josette sensed, feeling watchers from windows and from a crack in the stable's door.

As they clattered into the courtyard, Beitris looking around vigi-lantly, Josette felt the tension, people ready to fight. Then Will pushed back the hood of his cloak, revealing his face, and stood in his stir-rups, showing himself for all to see.

The stable door banged open and a boy streaked out. He screamed something in Erse and flung himself at Will as Will swung to the ground.

"Ewan!" Will caught him up, the boy's legs swinging, then thumped him back to his feet. "Your screeching could make my eardrums bleed. How are you keeping, lad?"

Ewan's grin lit the dying day. "Ever so glad to see you, sir." He stared at Josette in curiosity—he'd have been a babe in arms when Josette had visited nearly ten years before.

Others poured from the house as Will lifted Josette from her horse, about half a dozen in all, men and women both, surly looks turning to smiles of welcome. Beitris milled about them, tail wagging, happy to be meeting so many people.

"'Tis good to see ye home," one man said.

"Errol," Will greeted him. "Is there a room to be had for the lady?"

"Of course." Errol was a big man with a shaggy brown beard and giant hands, but his smile was almost shy as he glanced at Josette. "The wife will see to her, don't ye worry."

"The wife," was a woman half his size, who once had been plump but whose skin now sagged—Josette suspected that feeding them-selves this last year had been difficult.

"I'm Isla, this big lump's wife," the woman said. She might be small, but her voice was robust. "We're clan Mackenzie. A distant branch, but Mackenzie all the same."

She said it proudly as she led Josette inside, out of the wind and fine rain that had begun to fall.

The interior of the house was dark, lit only by a small lantern inside the front door. The main hall, which ran back into the hill, rose several stories, a staircase reaching far into the gloom. Another wide hall ran the length of the house, rooms opening from it.

Will had showed her this place briefly on her visit, and she remembered it bustling with activity, lights in every room.

Now the house echoed, the halls silent. The soldiers who'd razed the castle had blown up the still and destroyed many barrels of whisky, Will had told her, leaving the distillery to burn. The retainers had quickly doused the fire, and the house had been too solid to fall, but it was a ghost of what it had once been.

Isla led Josette up the stairs to a chamber that was cold but had been made comfortable. The boy Ewan soon had a fire flickering on the hearth, the air filling with the scent of burning peat.

Josette heard Will's voice below, but he did not come up as Isla assisted Josette out of her wet and mud-spattered riding things and into her everyday gown, lacing her with competence. A sip of ale and a bit of bread made Josette feel much better—along with finally being warm and dry, and she went back downstairs in search of Will.

She found him in the still room, a vault of a chamber set back into the hill. Will gazed at a heap of blackened copper, his man Errol mournfully beside him.

"No one has the means to make another," Errol was saying. "Getting enough supplies together—with no one being the wiser—isn't easy. Lord Malcolm knew how to pry things out of the right people, bless him."

"Aye," Will agreed. "But do not stand there and tell me, old friend, that there is no still here at all. A Scotsman will brew whisky in a kettle beside a creek, and you know it."

Errol looked abashed. "'Tis only for us," he said in a small voice. "To stave off the chill. It's nothing like Mackenzie malt—nothing you can sell."

"Ha!" Will bellowed in true mirth. "I knew it. Well, it's a start. What about the barrels? Cumberland's men didn't get *all* of them did they? They weren't exactly stored in the open."

Errol flashed a grin. "Funny you should ask. Come with me."

He made for a door in the back of the still room. A cool tunnel of natural rock opened behind it, the tunnel's roof high enough for a man like Errol to walk through without stooping.

Errol took up a lantern and led Will inside.

Josette hurried after them in curiosity. Will caught her hand, tugging her along as he followed Errol. No telling her to stay behind or admonishing her that this had nothing to do with womenfolk. Such thoughts never occurred to Will, another reason she loved him.

A long way back into the hill, the tunnel widened. Racks had been set into this open space and piled with small oak barrels, about thirty in all. Beyond them, the tunnel narrowed and twisted into the darkness.

"Now, here's a fine sight." Will put a fond hand on one of the barrels. "Not been broached?"

"Nay, lad." Errol waved a hand at the nearest rack. "These have been waiting three years—nearly ready. Behind those…"

"The twenty-year," Will said, his tone reverent. "Mal's special reserve."

"Untouched," Errol said proudly. "We'd not drink that up. That's Lord Malcolm's."

"Aye." Will's gaze went remote, which Josette knew meant wheels were turning in his head. "You're a good man, Errol. Before long you'll have new clothes to wear and plenty of food in your bellies."

Errol looked surprised. "Are you going to sell the reserve? Who to? Your license can't be worth much now that you're all dead."

Will sent him a knowing look. "Never stopped my grandfather, or his father before him. The rarer the malt and the more secretive a man has to be to get it, the more in demand it is."

Errol made a grave nod. "Aye, 'tis true."

"How's the barley this year?" Will caressed the stave of a dusty barrel. When Errol flushed and didn't answer, Will asked with alarm, "Are the fields lying fallow? Was there no seed at all to plant?"

"No, no," Errol said quickly. "There's a crop waving in the fields. We saved enough from the last harvest to sow this year."

Will watched him closely. "But ye planned to sell it for cash."

Errol bowed his great head, guilt-stricken. "We need to eat, m'lord."

Josette's heart squeezed in distress for him, but Will glared at Errol.

"Did ye think I'd begrudge the food in your mouth, man? Of course ye'd sell the crops. What else would ye do with them—let them rot? But save some grain for the mash, will you? I'll have this still up and running by harvest time, never you worry."

Errol sent him a doubtful look. "No one's got the copper," he said. "We have a small still, aye, but as you say, it doesn't brew much more than a kettleful, and the stuff's raw. We drink it for warmth."

"I didn't think ye were pouring your kettle whisky into good oak," Will growled. "Don't flog yourself, man. Ye've done what ye can. We have barrels, in any case."

Errol perked up. "Aye, the empties. Those can be rebuilt and charred."

"And I can have Alec and Mal send over more wine barrels." Will glanced at Josette. "Old wine barrels re-cooped are good for whisky. And if we have to drink up the wine to empty them, all the better."

Errol grinned, his moroseness gone. "'Tis good to have you home, lad."

"But it's not my home." The light of the feeble lantern threw Will's huge, broad-shouldered silhouette behind him. "I'll put it to rights, but the Runt gets everything. He's the one with all the ambitious plans."

"Best take care," Errol said darkly. "Gents dressed in dainty suits come around to the crofters, saying the Mackenzie land is for sale, and they'll soon have to move off or accept a new landlord. Even some Scots are trying to push you out, damn them for eternity."

"Scots like Clennan Macdonald?" Will asked in a deceptively mild voice.

"Aye, he's been 'round." Errol spat on the floor. "Loyalist, he calls himself. Bastard, I call *him*. If Prince Teàrlach had been sure to win,

Macdonald would have followed so close in the lad's footsteps he'd have stolen his shadow. Now the man's in thick with Englishmen, pushing Scots off their own land."

"I've heard," Will said tightly. "Do not worry, my friend—I have a notion he'll lose his standing soon. That is, if I have anything to do about it."

Errol flashed another grin. "I will watch with pleasure. I'll take ship to the far reaches of the world before I let myself be a tenant of Old Bastard Macdonald."

Will thumped his shoulder. "You'll do more than watch. "You'll help me reduce him to rubble. Now—let's take one of these three-year and a day casks and give it it's birthday."

WILL AND ERROL LUGGED THE CASK WILL CHOSE BACK TO THE distillery, gathered the Mackenzie retainers who bowed their heads a moment in prayer, then Will broached the cask.

He dipped the first cup, handing it to Josette to taste. Josette wasn't one for spirits, but she accepted it, closed her eyes, and drank.

A smooth liquid danced over her tongue before it burned a warm trail to her belly. She tasted wind and smoke, heather and rain—the wild lands of the Highlands.

"Excellent," she pronounced, then coughed.

Laughter and cheers burst through the hall. Will dipped cup after cup, filled glasses, goblets, tankards—whatever the men and women had to hand. He even gave what he called "a wee drop" to Ewan.

Ewan drank the whisky with a swift, practiced gulp. "If that's the three-year," he said in admiration. "The twenty will be mighty grand."

A festive mood took hold. Fiddles and drums emerged. The men and ladies linked hands and began dancing in a circle.

Josette found herself joining in, caught in the dance and holding tight to Will's hand. The tiring journey fell away.

For now, there was no struggle, no cold and hunger, no defeat. Families and friends came together to celebrate, sharing what food they had, the fiery whisky to wash it all down.

Will had resumed his plaid. They others brought theirs out as well, the Highlanders hidden from all eyes in the halls of the old distillery. Free of restraint, they danced, shouted, reveled. They embraced Josette as Will's lady, throwing Mackenzie plaid around her shoulders.

During the lull in the dancing, Josette bade everyone good night, her exhaustion taking over. She tiredly made her way to the chamber she'd been given, undressed herself from her simple garments, and climbed into the high bed. She drifted to sleep, hearing the strains of fiddles below.

Josette dreamed she floated over the Highlands. She gazed down at its fields of heather, rocky peaks covered with snow, dark green trees marching to the sea. She saw Will Mackenzie, wrapped in a great kilt with a sword at his side, striding through the land, the wind in his hair.

She liked this vision of him, and even better, of Will coming upon her as she touched to earth, gathering her up, and pressing her into his hard body. He laid her down in the heather, unwrapping the kilt to reveal his bare strength, then rolled the both of them in the plaid warmed by his body.

Josette swam awake to find that part of her dream was true. Will lay beside her, naked and strong, his plaid enfolding them both.

"I didn't mean to wake you, lass," he whispered, touching a kiss to her hair.

Josette rolled to him, took his face in her hands, and kissed him with quiet desperation.

CHAPTER 24

*W*ill, already half drunk on *uisge beatha* and exuberance, became fully intoxicated by Josette.

She kissed him with passion and hunger, her hands skimming to his hips, then closing over his already hard cock. Will returned kisses with as much hunger, tasting her mouth, suckling her lips.

He undid the tapes of her nightgown with swift jerks, pushing the garment away. She was softness everywhere, shoulders, breasts, belly, her hair flowing to brush his skin.

Holding Josette completed a part of Will he'd never known was unfinished. Unbelievable that he ever thought he could send Josette away so she could live in peace. He'd never be able to let her go—he'd turn up on her doorstep the next instant, begging her to let him in.

Will bunched her hair in his fist and kissed her mouth. Josette squeezed his cock, and Will drew a sharp breath.

"Careful, love," he whispered. "I'll be too quick."

Josette slanted him a coy look and squeezed him again. She wanted to torture him, did she?

Will eased her down into the bedding, hand cupping her full breast. He bent to her, taking her nipple into his mouth, tasting the warm velvet of her. Josette rose into his touch, letting out a faint moan.

Will slid his hand down her belly and between her legs, finding her wet and hot. He stroked her as she stroked him, her sudden gasp loud in the stillness.

They drove each other mad, Will sliding fingers into her, Josette softly raking her fingertips up and down his cock. She arched against him, her gasps turning to groans of pleasure.

When Will could take no more agony, he moved Josette's hands aside, rose over her, and slid into her.

Josette's next cry turned to a shout. Will wasn't much quieter, sound tearing from him at each thrust. The bed was hard, holding Josette firmly so Will could drive deep inside her.

They held fast to each other, kissed, cried out, laughed. At the last, Josette wrapped arms and legs around Will and rose to him, while he thrust until he spent himself in her heat.

Josette's cries began to quiet, spiraling down into heavy breaths, soft smiles, a sleepy murmur. Will kissed the damp warmth of her skin and settled himself to lie between her breasts, a satisfying place to be.

JOSETTE SAT AT THE DRESSING TABLE, TRYING TO STUFF HER HAIR INTO some semblance of order when Will woke behind her. He'd slept with her all night, both of them falling into profound slumber after they'd crashed together, spent and out of breath.

Now Will stretched, rubbed his eyes, and sat up. She watched in the mirror as he rose from the bed, not wearing a stitch. Arms and legs long and strong, abdomen flat, cock half erect. A delicious sight.

Will ran the heel of his hand over his hair, blinking himself awake. Then he shivered. He snatched up a plaid, which had tumbled among the blankets, and wrapped it around his bare body, tucking in folds to keep it in place.

Josette's hair fell from her motionless fingers as she watched the grace and charged sensuality of his simple act. He looked like a Highlander of old, a shadow of the past merging with the vitality of the here and now.

"Let me do that for you." Will stepped behind her and took up a hairbrush, drawing it through her hair, his touch tender. "Isla is a wise woman. She's put you in what was Mal and Mary's room. Most comfortable in the house."

Josette closed her eyes, enjoying the sensation of bristles against her scalp. Will set down the brush after a nice long time and began to plait her hair with strong fingers.

"Why did you promise Errol you'd rebuild the still?" Josette murmured as he worked. "And sell the reserve whisky?"

"Because I will." The note of surprise in Will's voice made Josette open her eyes. He met her gaze with one of frankness. "I'd not lie to them."

"What about the soldiers searching houses? And the lack of copper? And Mr. Macdonald trying to buy the land?"

"All will be taken care of," Will said with his maddening calmness. "Lord Wilfort is a powerful man. I know he can have Mal's name cleared, even if it takes time—without risk to his own neck or reputation. He has that much influence. Wilfort loves his daughter more than anything in his life, and now he has a grandchild to think of."

"How will you pay for your supplies?" Josette asked. "We left all the gold with Mysie and her ladies. That's not what the gold is for, anyway."

Will finished braiding her hair and reached for a ribbon to tie it. "I'm not worried. I believe I'll find the cash right here."

"Here? What are you talking about?"

Will sent her a slow smile. "There's more gold in the Highlands than coins, lass." Josette waited for him to explain but he only tied the ribbon and kissed the top of her head. "But I also believe the rest of the French gold is nearby."

Josette spun to face him. "What are you talking about? How can you know that?"

Will shrugged. "I'm not certain, of course—won't be until I look, but this is a good place to hide it. I realized that when Naughton told me about Macdonald wanting Kilmorgan. Macdonald has come here several times, both Errol and Naughton say, looking the place over. We know Macdonald looted the castle, damn the man. He'd have plenty of time to stash the gold in the cellars or the tunnels beneath it, even to bury it in the woods. I'm sure Macdonald will bribe enough officials sooner or later to let him purchase this land. Then he'll live over the gold and off it for years to come." He paused. "Or so he believes."

Josette had to concede this was possible, even logical. "But if we search and *do* find the gold, what then? How can we prove Mr. Macdonald hid it here, and not the Mackenzies? If a stash of French gold meant for the Jacobite army is found at Kilmorgan, that will condemn your family forever."

Will kissed her lips, then smiled at her, a wicked sparkle in his eyes. "I thought I'd let Macdonald himself tell me exactly where it is, lass."

～

When Will dressed and went downstairs, Errol regarded him with an open grin. The big man had drunk more whisky than anyone the previous night, and yet, he was upright, eyes bright, step animated.

"When's the wedding, my lord?" he asked.

Will feigned confusion. "Eh?"

"From the noises ye two made, Isla and I guessed bairns will soon be coming. Ye'd want to be wed for that, wouldn't ye?"

Will's face heated, but he clapped Errol on the shoulder. "I do. And we will. But first, we have a few tasks to take care of."

In a low voice, he told Errol what he intended, and what he needed the man to do. Errol laughed out loud. "You're a devious one, lad. Always said so. Your brothers are fine men, but you think in ways they never can."

"A gift," Will said. "From God, said my mother. From the devil, said my father."

Errol made a cross of his two forefingers and laughed again.

"You gentlemen are merry," Josette said as she glided into the room, followed by a curious Beitris. Josette had breakfasted and looked rested and well. Beitris did too, in fact.

Will slid his arm around Josette, liking her warmth in the crook of his arm. Errol watched with enjoyment. "We are," Will said. "'Tis a grand day."

Josette gave him a wary look.

"I thought we'd start in the tunnels," Will said. "Shall we?"

When Josette gave him a nod, still wary, Will guided her down the hall toward the still room, Beitris following. Errol left them to it, chortling.

When they reached the entrance to the tunnels, Will took up a lantern, opened the door, and stepped inside. He heard Josette's footsteps so close on his heels that it made him want to laugh. She was as anxious as Will to discover if his theory was correct. He heard Beitris as well, nails clicking on the floor, a snuffling sound as she investigated the walls.

"Do you really think Mr. Macdonald hid the gold here?" Josette asked as they reached the wide space containing the barrels. Her words echoed from the rock ceiling.

"I have no idea. Kilmorgan's a large place. It could be anywhere."

Josette impatiently pulled her skirt free from the end of a rack. "Am I here to help you search? Shouldn't I be in our chamber sewing your shirts?"

Will lifted the lantern high, its light falling on her pink face, rich hair, and brown and cream gown. "Why the devil would you sew my shirts?" he asked in perplexity.

"It's what ladies do," she said primly. "When gentlemen are out having all the fun. We mend your clothes and keep the house warm for when you bother to return."

Will blinked. "Do you?"

"Have you so few married friends? 'Tis the way of the world."

"I've never witnessed Mary or Celia staying home to keep the fires lit while Alec and Mal disappear," Will said. "Those lassies would never stand for that."

"They're aristocrats," Josette returned. "I am a commoner. 'Tis a different thing."

Will let his grin come as he traced her cheek. "Oh, there's nothing common about you, love."

"Stop," Josette said, her teasing tone evaporating. "You melt my heart."

"Good." Will brushed his knuckle over her silken skin. "You and I will never be common, my Josie. Trust me on that."

Josette flushed but pressed a kiss to Will's finger, setting fires alight in his blood. He needed to finish this, so he could take her in his arms and convince her to stay with him forever.

Will made himself turn away and continue walking. They tramped for a time without speaking, Beitris bringing up the rear. Josette didn't complain about the damp, the chill, or the darkness, or demand Will take her back to the relative comfort of the distillery. She was quite a lady.

"Does this tunnel come out somewhere?" she asked after a time. "Or lead to deeper caves?"

Will answered without turning. "It used to reach the hills beyond the castle, but I don't know if it's been blocked up. I haven't been down here since I was a lad. But we should be directly under the castle about now."

He glanced up as though he could see through the rock to the home where he'd spent his boyhood. The tunnel had been shored up by stones and wood pillars in ages past and seemed fairly solid.

"It had some duplicitous purpose, didn't it?" was Josette's next question. "Smuggling? Cattle raiding? Carrying off maidens from rival clans?"

Will chuckled. "You read too many stories, love. We never needed to steal our neighbors' cattle or our neighbors' women. Dad absconded with Mum, true, but she had her things packed and ready. Or maybe she didn't bring anything—I remember she was resourceful. But you're right about the smuggling. The excise men have always been the true enemy of Scotland."

"You'd take the whisky out through here?" Josette continued. "To waiting ships?"

"Your interest in crime is worrying, love. But you are right—Grandad took the whisky out and brought the brandy in. Kilmorgan is close enough to the sea that we could have boats in a little cove, ready to go out with the tide."

"A good place to hide contraband, then," Josette concluded. "But would Mr. Macdonald know that?"

"He would if he explored thoroughly enough. Which I hope he didn't. I don't want him discovering *all* our secrets."

The floor began to rise as they walked, a good sign. The problem was, the ceiling *didn't* rise with it. Before long, Will had to bend double. Josette, not as tall, had less trouble, but she stooped as she walked, gathering up her skirts.

Will moved with care—it wouldn't help if either of them fell or brought the stones down on them. He was out of breath and ready to rest by the time he caught a glimmer of light ahead.

A glimmer only—the horizontal opening they found into the hill was narrow. Will broke away loose earth around it, then set his lantern outside on grass and crawled after it.

It felt good to stand up in open air after the closeness of the tunnel. Will stretched, releasing the crick from his back, before he turned to help Josette out of the hole.

She had to tug her skirts free, but she clung to Will's hands and quickly gained her feet. Beitris wriggled out behind them, shook herself, and looked about interestedly.

They'd emerged at the base of a sheer cliff that rose above them, the burned shell of the castle just visible on top. The land sloped down from their feet to woods that had thickened since Will had been here, trees creeping toward unused cropland.

Beyond the woods lay clifftops that overlooked a cove below, perfect for Mackenzie smugglers. Will at one time in his life had come and gone from that cove on his trips to France, the Low Countries, or England.

Since Culloden, however, he'd ceased arriving this way. Now he entered the country in places far from here, usually innocuously as a passenger landing in Dover or Greenwich, under one of his assumed names, with masterfully forged papers.

Josette breathed the fresh air tinged with peat smoke. "Lovely. But I saw no gold as we came through. I had my face pressed nearly to the floor during that last bit—I wouldn't have missed it."

Will agreed. "No sign of digging either. Macdonald might never have found the tunnel. But there are plenty of hiding places at Kilmorgan. The cellars under the castle are extensive."

Josette gave him a weary look. "*How* extensive?"

"Don't worry, love. I don't expect you to help me dig up every inch of my ancestral home. I have other ideas."

Her tone remained doubtful. "You never explained how you'd have Mr. Macdonald lead the way. You plan to bring him here?"

"Messages are already going back and forth between here and Macdonald's home at Shieldag. Ewan is a swift and trustworthy lad, and Naughton will make sure the man comes."

Josette looked aghast. "You sent that poor little boy to Macdonald?"

"That *poor little boy* led Mary to safety under the noses of Jacobites who'd come to arrest her father and aunt. Plus, I have Henri playing his part, putting the fear of God into Sir Harmon and Clennan Macdonald that the precious stash might be lost."

"Henri?" Josette asked, startled. "I thought he was helping Bhreac protect the ladies at Strathy Castle."

"He needed something to do." Will shrugged at Josette's accusing stare. "Something that lets him work toward his revenge but without violence or risk to himself."

"That is admirable, but will he keep his temper and not try his hand at murdering Sir Harmon?"

"I think so. Henri is impetuous, but he's not a stupid lad. I explained to him, as you did, how much better revenge can be if those who did the terrible things are lawfully punished while you live to gloat."

"I see. He did not seem convinced."

"He has no intention of dying heroically." Will let out a breath, trying to ignore Josette's skeptical tone. "I gave him hope, which is what he most needed."

"As long as that hope is fulfilled."

"It will be. I told him that if I didn't bring Sir Harmon to justice, he could take his pound of flesh from me." He pointed down the slope. "Now, the path to the cove might be a bit rough, but I think we can manage it."

"Will!"

"Aye, lass?"

Josette stepped in front of him, hands on hips. "You told Henri he could kill *you*?"

"I might have said that, yes." Will tried to look innocent. "It won't come to anything, love. Wilfort dislikes Sir Harmon and distrusts Macdonald and is eager to take them both down. You might not have noticed this, because Wilfort looks the same whether he's delighted, seething with rage, or wants a cup of tea. Henri is a good lad, just grieved and angry. He won't hurt me."

Josette made a noise of exasperation. "You base every plan you make on your ability to turn people up sweet. Including me." Her glare could have crumbled the rocks around them. "Why do you believe Mr. Macdonald won't simply stay home drinking his wine and gazing at his paintings, pretending he knows nothing about the gold? Coming here will only give his secrets away."

"Because he's not that sort of man. If he indeed stole that gold and hid it here, he'll come racing to save it, especially if he hears that Will Mackenzie is back and nosing around."

"Damnation, Will," Josette said in a near shout. "When will you cease throwing yourself headlong at peril and take care to *live*? Instead of promising lads they can murder you, or telling a dangerous man you're alive and waiting for him?"

"That's easy to answer." Will closed his hands around her clenched fists. "I'll stop when I find the gold, and marry you."

CHAPTER 25

*J*osette's breath left her. She stared at Will, but he didn't vanish in a flash like the otherworldly creature he must be. He stood before her and told her he would stop rushing headlong into danger the day he married her.

"Does that mean you'll *never* marry?" she asked, throat dry. "As in, you'll settle down when it snows in hell?"

Will's grin flashed. "No, ye daft lass. It means I want to marry *you*. I told you I would if it turned out you carried my bairn. But I wish to, no matter what."

Josette's mouth opened and closed a few times. "But you can't."

"Why not?" he asked, as though this was not the most important conversation of Josette's life. "We're of age and reasonably in our right minds." Will laid a warm hand on her abdomen. "And the way we're at it, we're *guaranteeing* a bairn. I want it to have a da."

Josette tried to form more words, but she could no longer speak. Years ago Oliver Chadwick had seduced her, lavishing her with attention, charm, gifts. When it was discovered Josette was increasing, he bluntly told her he wanted nothing to do with his child. He'd revealed that he was married, and that his wife would never understand or forgive him. Then he'd vanished, back to his regiment and ultimately, England.

Josette's young heart had broken as she'd been harshly introduced to the ways of the world.

Will, with his golden eyes and ready smile, had walked into her life a few years later and changed it forever. Now he said that of course they'd marry, as though there was no question about it.

"But you're dead," she finally managed, the words coming weakly. "And if you're found alive, so many will endeavor to return you to your grave—Mr. Macdonald, Sir Harmon, not to mention King George of England ..."

Will skimmed his hands up her arms. "Do *you* want me dead, lass?"

She could tease him with, *Sometimes*, or *Do not tempt me so*, but Josette had to tell him the truth.

"No." Tears stung her eyes. "Never."

Will's smile vanished as he touched her lips. "Then the others do not matter." He traced her mouth with a blunt fingertip. "When I'm with you, Josie, the world can go to hell. I only want you."

Josette swallowed, her heart beating swiftly. "Then ... are you asking me to marry you?"

Will took a step back. "Mmm, not yet. The ground's muddy, and I want to go down on one knee, like a proper swain." He touched her lips one last time, as though he couldn't help himself. "After we have Macdonald and Sir Harmon arrested, and Wilfort keeps his promises, then I'll be doing some proposing. Properly."

"Oh." Josette wasn't certain whether to be disappointed, relieved, angry, or amused. "Well. Then I ..."

Will laid his fingers over her mouth. "No, don't tell me your answer. Not until it's right. Besides, I don't want to know if you're going to refuse. It will keep my heart light. Like I said, hope makes all things possible."

Josette drew a breath as Will lifted his hand away. Was he jesting? Or serious? With Will it was difficult to know, and growing closer to him only made her less certain.

But one look in his eyes showed her his fear, a pain he kept deep within himself, one he was afraid of fanning to life.

"Yes," she said, holding his gaze. "Hope does."

Will slanted her his warm Mackenzie grin, the one she'd fallen in love with all those years ago. "Good. Now, let us search for some gold."

WILL LED JOSETTE TO THE COVE, HELPING HER DOWN THE NEARLY sheer path to the shingle below. Beitris bounded ahead of them, her great paws occasionally sliding off the trail, but she reached the bottom without mishap, finishing the last few yards with a great leap. She waited for them on the rocky beach, tail waving.

The cove was as Will remembered it, a thin strip of shingle lined with caves. At high tide, the shingle was covered, water seeping into the lower levels of the caves. Boats easily slid into the openings when the tide was in, darting safely out of sight.

The tide was at the bottom of the ebb this morning, so Errol had informed him. Errol kept track of the tides, being an able smuggler himself.

For now, the cove was deserted. To the far left was a fairly large cave, which never was more than partially filled with water, its deeper areas always dry.

Will checked that cave first, though he didn't think he'd find anything there—it was too well used to be a good hiding place, but one never knew. A second set of caves beyond that, mere cracks in the cliff wall, easily missed by those who didn't know about them, were a better bet.

Beitris went straight into these narrow caves without fear, but Josette followed Will closely, taking care. She hadn't said much since Will had blurted that he wanted to marry her.

What a daft thing to tell her, Will admonished himself. Josette had been made unhappy by men throughout her life, and that included Will. She'd looked shocked, and no wonder.

He'd hastily deflected the question when he'd seen her stunned surprise, saying he'd ask her again later. Bloody hell, what was the matter with him?

At least she hadn't punched him in the nose, turned around, and marched off, showing him a flash of fine ankles. She'd let him run on like an idiot, while she watched him with her calm brown eyes, her lips parted in that fetching way.

To avoid kissing her, wrapping his arms around her and not letting go until she agreed to be his wife, Will had swung away and nearly ran for the caves.

And now here they were, both awkwardly pretending the discussion hadn't happened.

These smaller caves had been used as well, Will saw as he flashed his lantern about. Above the waterline, niches in the rock held bits of useful supplies—rope, candles, a dark lantern, a cask of water, and a small flask full of brandy.

Will sniffed the brandy, nodded in approval, and tucked the flask into his pocket. He then helped himself to a new candle for his lantern, lighting it with the old one that had nearly burned out. He left the stub in the niche next to the unburned tallow candles.

He searched the caves for a time, Josette looking about with Beitris, but he turned up no convenient casks of gold.

Will did find some interesting things, however, as Josette and Beitris wandered back outside to sunlight. Another flask of brandy, a sheathed knife with a jeweled hilt, and curiously, a few paintings that had hung on the walls of Kilmorgan. They'd been rolled up and covered with oilcloth, proving supple and intact when unrolled.

He also found more cracks in the wall that led to another set of shallow, but very empty caves. Hmm.

Will looked these over briefly and then re-rolled the paintings and carried his find to Josette.

"Booty from a lost ship?" she asked, touching the rolled-up paintings in wonder. "Or a robbery?"

"This was Duncan's." Will held up the *sgian dubh*, the bejeweled knife Duncan had worn with his best formal kilt. "No doubt filched from his chambers when the castle's rubble was picked over. Whoever took this also knew what paintings to steal and how to keep them from ruin." He'd recognized the face of Rembrandt van Rijn and a still life by another Dutch master.

Josette's eyes widened. "Did Mr. Macdonald take them? I

remember … he boasted to Captain Ellis and me that he'd plundered paintings from Kilmorgan Castle. I saw a few of them."

"Possibly." Will scanned the horizon. "But others could have come here as well." He let out a breath. "No sign of the French gold. I might be wrong, and Macdonald has a different hiding place entirely."

"He using Kilmorgan is a good theory," Josette said generously. "And he might be better at hiding things than the thief who took these." She gestured at his armful.

"True." Will handed her the knife, hilt first. "Hold on to that for me, Josie. I can only juggle so many things." He tucked the paintings securely under his arm and took up the lantern. "Better still, keep it for yourself. If I know Duncan, that blade is clean, well oiled, and sharp. Or sell it. It's worth a few bob." A lump came to his throat as he pictured Duncan and his exacting obsession about taking care of his weapons. It hadn't kept him alive, in the end.

Josette reverently examined the scabbard and hilt encrusted with blue and green stones—Mackenzie colors. "I could never sell your brother's knife."

"Well, he isn't using it at the moment." Will cleared his throat. "And though Duncan was a sour man with his brothers, he was gallant with the ladies. He'd rather you had it than me, I think."

"Thank you, Will," Josette said, her dark eyes holding gratitude. "I'll look after it."

Will wanted to kiss her. He wanted to so much that he made himself turn and head for the cliff path under the cloud-covered sky.

He led them upward, Josette a little way behind him, Beitris lingering to chase a few sea birds.

A Scotsman stood waiting for them at the top, gazing over the cliff's edge, his craggy face set in a scowl. He was alone.

"Bhreac," Will said in surprise. "Why have ye come? You didn't bring the ladies with you, did you? Far too dangerous yet."

Bhreac didn't answer. "Did you find it? The French gold?"

Will thought rapidly and took a chance. "Yes."

Josette said nothing—in fact, a glance out of the corner of Will's eye showed she was not yet in sight, the last bend of the path concealing the view below.

"Good," Bhreac said. He lifted the pistol he'd been holding behind his back and leveled it at Will's nose. "Ye can give it to me, then."

JOSETTE FROZE WHEN SHE HEARD BHREAC'S WORDS. SHE CROUCHED down, hiding behind thick brush, and peered upward at the two men.

Bhreac had a pistol aimed at Will's face. Will regarded him calmly, still holding the lantern in one hand, paintings under the other arm.

Beitris reached the top of the path and noticed Bhreac. With a deep *Wuh!* the dog rushed him.

Josette held her breath, worried the dog's attack would make Bhreac pull the trigger. But Beitris only danced around the two men, recognizing her old friend and seeing nothing wrong. Bhreac ignored her.

Josette remembered Will's answer when she'd first asked whether they could trust Bhreac. *I have in the past. Doesn't mean he's entirely trustworthy, but he has no reason to betray me at the moment.*

Now, it seemed, Bhreac had found reason.

"I'll show you the gold later," Will said. "I'm tired of climbing up and down trails. It will still be there."

"Your plan to lure Macdonald here so he'll try to save it is a fool's one," Bhreac said. "He'll simply kill you and take it. Then all that lovely gold will be lost."

"*You've* come to kill me and take it," Will said mildly. "Not much choice for me."

"We're friends, Willie. Give me the gold, and I'll leave ye be. I want it to buy passage for me and poor Lillias to reach the Continent. She needs someone to look after her."

Will didn't move. "Was this her idea? Has the taste of Lillias McIver in it."

"She might have agreed with me," Bhreac said without a blush. "She doesn't trust you much—she's somewhat bitter that you couldn't save her husband."

"No one could have saved him," Will said somberly. "I'm sorry that should be so." He spoke quietly, but Josette knew the man's death had cut at him.

She crept slowly and quietly across the side of the hill, staying out of sight, aiming to come out a little way from the two men.

"Aye, well, I know you're right." Bhreac shrugged. "Give me the gold, and we'll be gone."

"And if I told you I was joking, that I couldn't find it?"

Bhreac sighed. "Ah, Willie, don't make me shoot you. Josette will never forgive me, and I'm fond of the lass."

"She's fond of you too. I truly don't have it, Bhreac. Your journey was for nothing."

"Never trust a Mackenzie," Bhreac said. "I've always said—"

His words cut off as Josette, moving soundlessly behind him, brought the hilt of Duncan's knife down hard on the base of his skull.

CHAPTER 26

O w!" Bhreac stumbled, pistol wavering in his slackened grip. "Devil take ye, woman ..."

Will twisted the pistol from Bhreac and pointed it at him. Then he looked again in disgust. "Ye didn't even prime it."

Bhreac shrugged and rubbed the back of his head. "I told you I didn't want to hurt you. Och, get off me, ye great beastie."

Beitris had finally decided to be a guard dog. She jumped on Bhreac, but instead of biting, she licked his face. No wonder she hadn't attacked, Will reflected. She'd known Bhreac wasn't a true threat.

Josette, on the other hand, glared at the man. She had the *sgian dubh* poised to smack Bhreac again, and Will had no doubt she'd have the blade out of its sheath in a trice if she decided it was needed. She knew how to fight, did his Josie.

"Down, Beitris," Will said. The dog gave Bhreac one last swipe of her tongue then fell to her haunches, tail thumping. "Did ye truly think ye could stroll in here and take the gold I plan to restore my family with? And I'd tamely let you?"

Bhreac shrugged. "Not really. But worth a try. You really haven't found it?" He sounded so wistful that Will wanted to laugh.

Will slid the pistol into his pocket. There was no powder in its pan, nothing to spark the gunpowder inside and discharge the bullet —if Bhreac had even loaded the thing. The man knew his way around guns, so Will believed him when he said he'd meant to frighten, not hurt.

"We've just began searching. Josette, ye can put the knife away now, love."

"I'll keep it out." Josette said, not lowering her hand.

"She's a wise lass," Bhreac said. "Well, if ye didn't find it in the caves, where next?"

"House. This way."

He led them off, Bhreac and Beitris following readily, Josette behind Bhreac, she still holding the knife.

Will's heart warmed. With Josette as rearguard, he need fear nothing. She was as fierce a warrior as any Highland bride.

By "house," Will meant the cleared land where the foundations had been laid for Mal's great mansion. Mal had started the manor not long before the British soldiers had come. The soldiers had gone through the site, destroying all work done, and scattering the stones.

The locals, seeing no reason to let perfectly good building stone go to waste, had taken what they wished. Will didn't begrudge them. Crofters needed to strengthen their cottages and repair shelters for their livestock for the hard winter.

Even with the foundation in ruins, the outline of the house was clear to see. The front gallery would run the length of the façade, with large windows every few feet to illuminate the interior. The view from the second and third floors of this gallery would be breathtaking—so said Malcolm.

Wings would run back from the main gallery, each complete with drawing rooms, libraries, and sitting rooms, with bedchambers on the upper floors. Each brother could have his own demesne, Malcolm had decided. He'd planned six wings, one for each of his five brothers and one for their father. He'd sadly revised those plans, cutting the wings to four.

A great staircase would rise through the house. The duke's artwork would hang here, as well as Alec's paintings. In a place of honor they'd hang the portrait of Allison McKenzie, beloved wife and mother. Malcolm had saved it from the burning castle.

"'Tis enormous," Bhreac said in admiration. "Will be, I mean, if it ever is built. Not much chance, is there?"

Will kicked at a rock. "Remains to be seen. Mal has grand ideas, I'll give him that. Alec is designing the gardens."

"Huh." Bhreac gazed about, pretending to ignore Josette, who hadn't let him move far from her knife. "Will be worth looking at, if they manage it." He rubbed his hands together. "Well, I'd best be helping you find the funding. Where do we begin?"

The workers had dug out cellars, which would house foodstuffs and supplies as well as wine and whisky. Not much had been done, but they'd left one square hole in the north side, supported with beams. Some of the beams had been looted as well, but enough remained to hold the makeshift ceiling in place.

The three of them searched, but found nothing hidden in the cellar, and no signs of digging to indicate buried treasure.

Will hadn't thought Macdonald would leave the gold where the villagers and crofters could too easily stumble upon it, but then Macdonald might have hidden it there precisely because it *was* in plain sight. He was guileful.

The castle ruin would be more likely. They left the foundations behind and ascended the hill to the castle, Beitris gamboling along in their wake. From the top of the hill, Will looked out over the land, and his breath caught.

The sun had poked through the clouds to bathe the world in golden light. Beams caught in the mists, sporting rainbows across the glen. The outline of the new house was more clear from here—it would stand large and strong against the green-gray land. To the west and north, mountains stretched tall; to the east was a glimmer of the sea.

The silence was immense. Will had run in and out of the castle from this courtyard all of his life—and noise had prevailed. His brothers shouting, his father's bellows, his mother laughing. Music—Allison playing the pianoforte she'd ordered specially from Padua, fiddles and drums of the villagers, his brothers trying to sing. Will hadn't been bad at the pianoforte, and liked to play whenever he could find one.

Now the only sound was the wind in the trees, hawks crying as they rode the updrafts.

For a moment, Will fancied the castle was whole, windows glittering, the door banging as the tiny boy, Mal, tore out and flung himself down the path to the bottom of the hill. Alec or Angus would be chasing him, Will laughing as he got in their way, allowing the Runt to escape. Usually Mal had done something mischievous, but Will had always come to his defense.

"Are you coming in, Willie?" his mother's voice floated to him. "If not, shut the door. You're causing a great draft."

Josette touched his arm, and the past vanished, dissolving on the breeze. The castle was a ruin, his family dead or scattered.

Josette was real. Warm. Here.

Will swallowed, closed his hand around hers, and led the way inside.

JOSETTE'S HEART BROKE AS SHE FOLLOWED WILL THROUGH THE REMAINS of the castle. She remembered, from her long-ago visit, the lofty hall, the polished wooden staircase rising through the keep, the whitewashed stone rooms softened with paintings, books, and comfortable furniture.

The old duke had been testy, the brothers teasing and arguing, Alec and Mal flirting with Josette and treating her graciously at the same time. Duncan had been disapproving but polite. Glenna charmed every single one of them, turning the tough Highlanders to mush. The castle had been a bachelor's abode, kept neat by the small horde of retainers there to look after the Mackenzies, including rawboned Naughton.

But it had been a home. Men and women had loved here, lived, died, found great happiness, suffered loss. Birth and death, marriage and family, brothers, fathers, sisters, mothers, friends, lovers—moving through the centuries.

Now it was a wreck. Scorched beams lay across rooms, crushing furniture beneath them. The stench of charred wood prevailed. The staircase was no more, having fallen to shards when flames consumed it.

"Oh, Will," Josette whispered. "I'm so sorry." Tears filled her eyes, which already stung from the lingering odor of smoke.

Bhreac glanced around in sympathy. "Aye, 'twas a bad business. I pray those who did this rot in hell, I truly do."

Will squared his shoulders. Josette noticed that he kept his gaze averted from the destruction as he led the way to the rear of the castle, where a few stone walls were more or less intact.

"I've been back only once since it burned," Will said, his voice neutral, but Josette heard the strain in it. "The cellars are still accessible."

The taint of smoke was heavy at the very rear of the castle, but a small area had escaped the fire. Will pulled open a warped door to reveal a stone staircase.

"From the original keep," Will said. "Mackenzies of old could scramble up this staircase from the bottom of the cellars to the top of the walls."

He started down without worry. Josette waited for Bhreac to follow him—she didn't trust him behind her. Bhreac shot her a nervous grin before he started downward, Beitris after him. Josette brought up the rear, following the glimmer of Will's lantern.

"Is it safe?" Bhreac asked, his voice tight.

"Should be." Will's voice floated back to them. "The keep has lasted four hundred years. More than one enemy has tried to raze it, without success. Ah, here we are."

He stepped off the stairs to a vaulted room that echoed his footsteps. The light from Will's lantern caught a stone floor and empty shelves, but didn't penetrate far into the darkness.

Josette gathered her skirts out of the dust as Will led them along without hesitation, passing rows of racks similar to those in the distillery. No whisky barrels were in sight, however, probably looted by the soldiers or those like Macdonald who happened along afterward.

Whatever hadn't been stolen had been smashed—crockery, wooden boxes, crates, empty kegs. Nothing of value remained that Josette could see.

"I don't spy any gold," Bhreac said, words loud in the still air.

"We should be above the tunnels now," Josette said, remembering their walk through the dark. "Is there a way down from here?"

"Used to be a trap door for lowering the whisky for the ponies to carry away," Will said. "We never opened it, so it might have been bricked over."

"Would Macdonald know about it?" Bhreac asked.

"No idea," Will began, but Josette interrupted.

"It would be another way in and out, one less visible than the castle's front door," she pointed out. "If Mr. Macdonald needed to move the gold in a hurry, he would have an easy way to take it out of the castle."

"The woman has cunning," Bhreac said. "I'd watch her, lad."

"Josette is the wisest person I know," Will said, sounding proud. "Man or woman. You are right, love—the trap door was over yonder."

He headed off into the darkness, Josette and Bhreac following. Beitris nosed about in the dark, finding many things to explore. Josette heard her snuffling, then sneeze.

"Oh." Will's voice drifted back to them and Josette hurried to where he stood unmoving, his lantern high.

Bhreac surged forward, stumbling over debris in his haste. "Did you find the gold? Is it here?"

Will didn't answer him. "I thought you gone forever, my friend," he said softly.

The light from his lantern fell on a bulk of something shrouded in a dust-covered cloth. Will set the lantern on the floor and grasped the cloth with great care. He pulled it slowly away, the fabric slithering from an object about five feet long and four feet tall.

Josette's breath caught as he raised the lantern again, its light glinting on burnished mahogany and polished brass.

Bhreac sighed in disappointment. "No gold there."

"No." Will's voice had gentled to a note Josette rarely heard in it. "Treasure of a different kind."

Josette thought the piece of furniture was a harpsichord, top shut, keys covered, or a clavichord. Then she realized it was a pianoforte, and must be the one Will had told her his mother had purchased. Will folded the cover back from the keys. It shouldn't play, Josette reasoned, abandoned here. But the thing had been cared for, the wood oiled, the brass cleaned.

Will pressed his fingers to the keys. The sound that came out was off, the strings far out of tune, but they struck and rang.

"My father sent this down here after my mother died," Will said. He played a scale, then another, the notes quiet. "He couldn't bear to look at it. Naughton took care of it, though, and so did I, figuring that someday Dad might want it back. I used to come down here and play, too far from the rest of the house to be heard."

He brought his other hand to the keyboard and picked out a tune. It was nothing Josette recognized, but she didn't have the knowledge of music Will did. Whatever he played had full notes in the base and clear, sweet sounds in the treble—or would when the pianoforte was tuned.

"Lovely," Bhreac said. "Is the gold inside?"

Will lifted his fingers away, and the music faded. "My friend, you have no soul."

He gave Bhreac a deprecating look but opened the lid to reveal the instrument's innards.

Josette peered inside but saw only strings stretched along the soundboard, pads on the hammers looking slightly the worse for wear. Definitely a pianoforte. Harpsichord strings were plucked; pianoforte strings were struck.

"No gold," Josette said quietly. "I'm glad. Might have ruined it."

Will, at her side, slid an arm around her waist. "Aye, that would have been a pity."

Josette looked up at him. His eyes held sorrow, memories, fondness. When she touched his cheek, he leaned down and kissed her.

The kiss was heat in the darkness, as sweet as the music he'd played. Josette loved this man and his many facets, from his laughter to the tears he'd blinked away as he'd turned from the keyboard.

Bhreac waited patiently until the kiss eased to a close. "Anywhere else we should look?" he asked as Will brushed moisture from Josette's lips.

Will's answer rang through the stone chambers. "No, I'm weary of dusty darkness. We've earned a dram or two." He grabbed the dust cloth, and Josette helped him settle if back over the pianoforte. He rested his hand on top of it when they finished. "I'll be rounding up Errol and any able-bodied man I can find to carry this treasure back to the distillery, I think. It's been hidden long enough."

A FEW DAYS LATER WILL ACCOMPANIED MEN TO THE CELLARS TO BRING his mother's pianoforte into the light. In the intervening time he had made space for it in the chamber that had been a small sitting room, Josette very interested in putting the room to rights.

He and Josette, with Bhreac and Beitris assisting, had continued to search in likely places for the gold, but turned up nothing. Will thought he knew why, but kept his speculations to himself.

He did make Bhreac tell him why he'd been drifting around the Highlands to chance upon Will and the ladies at Strathy Castle.

"I was looking for you," Bhreac said, wistfulness in his voice. "I could not accept that my old friend Will was dead, and then I heard of a ghost causing strife for army men around the forts and camps. A spirit of a vengeful Highlander, the stories went. Destroying supplies, releasing animals, terrifying hardened soldiers. I concluded it must be you or one of your brothers. So I went searching."

Josette had heard the same stories and had drawn the same conclusion, she'd said. Will was not certain he believed Bhreac entirely, but he embraced the man.

"I'm alive, old friend. And will take care to remain so."

Will had much to live for, he'd decided. The melancholia that had snaked into his heart at Culloden eased as he beheld Josette plumping pillows and choosing pictures for what would become the music room.

Soon his mission would be finished. He looked forward to celebrating afterward.

Now Will chided the men to be careful as they carried the pianoforte from the cellar, lifting it down through the trapdoor Errol had known the exact location of, to a waiting cart.

Will himself hung on to one of the ropes. He fretted so much that Errol had growled at him to go away and wait for them to trundle it out.

Sweat stained Will's linen shirt as the pianoforte was leveled in the cart and the patient horse started the journey to the distillery. He'd get the thing cleaned up, the pads replaced and the strings tuned. He knew a man in Inverness who would be just the one to help.

Will and the men had just managed to maneuver the pianoforte into the sitting room at the distillery, when young Ewan dashed into the courtyard, shouting for Will.

"He's coming," he said breathlessly when Will emerged at a run. "Macdonald himself. He's only a few hours behind me."

CHAPTER 27

*C*lennan Macdonald tasted both rage and triumph.

A Mackenzie was alive. *Will* Mackenzie, an upstart, braggart of a spy, whose exploits had betrayed many a Highlander. His family had foolishly thrown their lot in with the Young Pretender, which had killed Mackenzies, Macdonalds, and hundreds of men in all the glens.

Duncan had been the worst, but he'd been felled at Culloden. Clennan had witnessed Duncan's death, wishing *he'd* been the one to cause it. Clennan had joined the gunfire at the rest of their bloody family, though he hadn't seen who'd fallen in all the smoke and confusion.

He'd later read with glee the names of the hateful Duke of Kilmorgan and his sons—Allison's children—dead and gone. Served her right.

The woman ought to have married poor Horace and borne many Macdonald bairns. She'd have been where Clennan could put his hands on her, either to use her to bring glory to the Macdonalds or to ease his physical needs, whichever he liked. Horace wouldn't have minded. He'd already indicated such.

But the bitch had to defy them and run off with a Mackenzie, the be-damned Duke of Kilmorgan, of all men she could have chosen.

After Allison wed, she'd gloated to Clennan, to his face, that she'd escaped his clutches.

The day Clennan learned that the Mackenzies were dead, he'd laughed out loud. He'd gone to the ruins of Kilmorgan and taken the best of the artwork and trinkets that he could find. Allison's money had bought the Mackenzie bastards soft luxuries that should have been Horace's and Clennan's.

And now, he'd been told that one of Allison's sons had survived. Figured it would be Will, the coward who always managed to be miles away from any true danger. Will Mackenzie stirred up trouble and then left others to clean up his mess.

Clennan would kill him, make sure the rest of the French gold he'd tricked away from the Jacobites was safe, and destroy every stone of Kilmorgan Castle. He'd take a sledgehammer to that harpsichord or pianoforte, or whatever it was he'd found in the cellars—he'd left it there in case he could later sell it, but he knew it had belonged to Allison. She'd loved to play pieces by that German fellow, Bach, or by Italian composers—silly skill for a Scotswoman.

When a message had arrived from Sir Harmon Bentley, the man giving him the incredible news that a Mackenzie lived and had returned to Kilmorgan, Clennan had been stunned, but not for long—he'd acted quickly.

If Will Mackenzie found the hoard of gold, he'd be unstoppable. He might try to virtuously return it to the French king for a reward—rumor had it that he'd had a hand in introducing Madame de Pompadour to Louis. Probably Will had been her lover too.

If the delectable woman who'd been Alec's artists' model was with him, as Sir Harmon assured him she likely would be, Clennan would take her as well. She'd serve him until Clennan was tired of her.

Poor lass probably was sick to death of Will anyway. Will had made her pretend to be his wife, and then sent her in with whoever that Englishman had been to dupe Clennan out of the money he'd given them. Clennan imagined Will had forced the lass to turn over the Louis d'or she'd come away with, probably forced her to do other things as well. Made Clennan ill to think about it.

His horse, sensing his master's urgency, increased his pace,

eagerly picking its way along the valley toward Kilmorgan. The lad
from the West Indies who'd been Sir Harmon's footman, the bearer of
the news that Will was alive and after Clennan's gold, rode some
paces behind him, borrowed to be a servant for the journey. Sir
Harmon, the idiot, had apparently harbored Will Mackenzie under
his roof and hadn't even known it.

The youth—whatever his name was—was a surly fellow. Really,
the slaves should stay in the New World and not clutter up the place.

Not that Scottish servants were much better, Clennan growled to
himself. The manservant Naughton had run off God knew where,
just when he was most needed. Never mind—let the standoffish man
go to the devil.

Clennan pulled up in sight of Kilmorgan Castle, what was left
of it.

The ruin never failed to move him. Old Scotland, destroyed, as it
should be. The world was moving forward with science, understanding, and reason, not superstitions from the past. Clennan's own
brother had believed in will-o'-the-wisps, demons, and ghosts,
ridiculous fool.

He liked the outline of the manor house the youngest Mackenzie
had started. Clennan would build there, and have every luxury of the
world imported for it. Women too, to warm his nights—ladies were
malleable when shown a bit of cash.

He'd offer some to Will's woman, and she'd leap at it. Clennan
understood her kind.

He bypassed the ruin and made for the distillery, where he
reasoned Will would be hiding. He knew the distillery remained in
spite of efforts to destroy it, and was manned by those faithful to the
Mackenzies. No matter. Clennan would start up the still again once
he owned Kilmorgan and sell the whisky—no reason to waste a
perfectly good commodity.

Will was the greatest hurdle—Clennan would need to kill him
quickly. He didn't trust anyone else to do it properly, which was why
he'd come himself.

The distillery's courtyard was deserted. Clennan dismounted,
tossing his reins to the youth, who pulled up behind him. Removing

his pistol from its holster, Clennan assured himself that the bullet was tightly packed into the barrel and the pan was primed. He had only one shot, but that was all he'd need.

He found the distillery's door unlocked. He shoved it open and stepped inside, ducking into shadows.

All was quiet. Dust motes hung in the one beam of sunshine that sliced from above.

Clennan moved in catlike silence down the hall to the chamber where the wreckage of the great Mackenzie copper still resided. He saw no one, heard nothing.

He lit a lantern that reposed on a shelf—flint and steel had been thoughtfully placed near the lantern so its candle could be ignited. Taking up the light, Clennan opened the door in the back of the still room and entered the tunnel, making his way to the wider space where he'd found barrels of whisky stashed. He hadn't touched any— the special reserve would bring him much income once he owned the land.

He found Will Mackenzie leaning against one of the barrels, sipping whisky from a fine crystal goblet.

"There ye are, man," Will said, lifting the glass to him. "What kept you?"

Clennan raised his pistol, and fired.

WILL WASN'T THERE TO BE SHOT. AS SOON AS CLENNAN MOVED, WILL did too, diving to the rock floor.

The bullet struck a barrel. Wood splintered, and a stream of whisky spewed out, scenting the air.

"You stupid bastard," Will said in true anger as he scrambled to his feet. "Bloody waste." He caught some of the stream in his glass he'd managed not to break, took a swallow, and let out a sigh of satisfaction. "Excellent stuff—I knew it would be."

Clennan glared at him in outrage. "Ye should be swinging from a noose. Or tied to four horses and pulled apart. Maybe I'll do that to you myself."

"Will ye now?" Will pointedly scanned the empty space behind Clennan. "Ye came alone, didn't you? That's the word I've had—you and one servant. Very confident of you. How do you plan to take me?"

"You're alone too," Clennan said. "Is the lady still with you? Or did she run first chance she had?"

"Josette? No, she's here. Well, not in this tunnel, because I wouldn't let her put herself into any danger." Will pinched the bridge of his nose. "And didn't we have an argument about that? The lass can shout like hellfire."

"So she has you wrapped around her finger, does she? I'm not surprised. She must have learned how to handle Mackenzies when she was Alec's whore."

Will's ancestral fury woke. He wanted to lunge at Clennan, gouge out the man's eyes, snap his spine. Shut his mouth forever.

But then he'd have a murder on his hands, for which others might pay, and that wasn't the plan.

Will's jaw went tight. It was difficult to coolly follow his scheme while Clennan begged every second to be killed, but he'd do it.

"I'll grind your face into the dirt for that later," Will said. "*And* for ruining a barrel of twenty-year-old reserve. I imagine you're here for your French gold."

"Actually, I came to kill you," Clennan said. "The gold is a secondary concern."

"Ah. I'm flattered. The trouble is, Macdonald, that *I* know where the gold is, and you don't."

Will had the satisfaction of seeing Clennan flinch. The man tried not to, but the slight pause, the blink, betrayed that Clennan had thought killing Will and walking away with his gold would be easy.

Will held his glass under the trickling stream of whisky and took another mouthful. Shame about this—Mal would rage if he knew what Clennan had just done.

"You are lying," Clennan said. "You have no idea where it is. You lured me here so I'd lead you to it."

Will only looked at him. Bhreac had said this would never work, that Clennan would see through Will's ruse. Josette worried that

Clennan would simply try to kill Will and go home, believing his gold safe.

They were both wrong.

"I'll take you to it," Will offered.

Clennan regarded him with narrowed eyes. "Why should I follow you anywhere? I'd rather kill you now."

"You've already fired off your pistol," Will pointed out.

"I have other weapons. I'm not fool enough to face you without them." Clennan made no move to draw one—not certain enough yet of his ground, Will suspected.

"If you want your gold, you'll come with me," Will said calmly.

"And have you lead me into a trap? Where are your loyal men? The ones who'd die for the Mackenzies?"

"My loyal men fled into the hills long ago." Will made an expansive gesture. "Look around you, Macdonald. There's nothing here anymore for them. Men like you took it all away."

"Men like me are loyal to the crown."

"Aye, when it's expedient to be," Will said. "When it's not ..." He made a dismissive gesture with his goblet.

"And you are the same." Clennan's long-nursed hatred came through his words. "The Mackenzies bend whichever way the wind blows, no matter how many you send out to die for your pleasure."

Will thought of Duncan, believing hard in Scottish independence, ready to defy his father to make it so. Duncan had died believing he fought for a better future for his sons and their sons. Angus had died trying to keep Duncan alive so he could keep believing in Scotland.

"You're not quite right about that," Will said, trying to keep his voice light. "Not all men think like you."

"Don't they? They will if they're not idiots. Where did you put it?"

Clennan brought out a second pistol from a holster under his coat, the gun no doubt loaded and primed.

Will eyed the weapon then shrugged and thumped his goblet onto a shelf. "Come on, then."

He bravely walked past Macdonald and back toward the distillery. He could have led him out through the tunnels to the cliffs, but Will was not about to trust the man in close quarters in the dark.

Will walked steadily through the still room and into the main hall, the light through its windows glaring after the tunnels. He continued without stopping to the courtyard, where the light was even brighter —the sun had chosen to show itself today.

The courtyard was empty. Macdonald looked around quickly, then swore.

"Where the devil is that boy?" he growled. "Bloody lad stole my horses. And people want to halt the slave trade. Sell them all to the mines, I say."

Will kept his mouth shut and his hands at his sides, resisting the urge to throttle the man. Henri had done exactly as instructed— taking away Macdonald's transportation and any provisions.

The fact that the plan was moving along calmed Will a bit. He'd have a chance to thrash Clennan soon enough.

"We'll go on foot," Will said. "'Tis not far."

He started up the path that led to the foundations of the new house and the castle ruins beyond. Macdonald tramped next to him, pistol pointed at Will's ribs.

The land was deserted. Birds called deep in the woods, and a hawk soared overhead. The hawk would be able to see exactly who was where on the Kilmorgan estate—Will hoped everyone had assumed their assigned places.

He trudged past the outline of the new house. Macdonald glanced at it, covetousness in his eyes. Will also noted Macdonald's satisfaction when they moved past the ruined castle. Truly it was difficult not to kill the man.

Macdonald looked surprised when Will didn't head straight for the ruins. He said nothing, however, and the two men hiked in silence to the clifftops over the smugglers' caves.

This was the tricky bit. If Macdonald suspected what Will had in mind, he could simply push Will over the edge and go home. Will gambled on the fact that Macdonald wanted control over everyone and everything—he couldn't leave until he saw for himself whether Will had taken the gold.

"Lead the way?" Will offered with a grin.

Macdonald motioned with his pistol. "Go on, Mackenzie. Try to steer me wrong, and I'll kill you. I don't mind shooting a man in the back if I need to."

Of course he didn't. Will started down the path, moving swiftly. Macdonald was older than Will by about twenty-five years, but the man was fit and strong and kept up without struggle. The easiest method of travel in the Highlands was on foot, and this kept Highlanders hearty. Parisians and Londoners who couldn't move a step without being carried in a sedan chair were astonished at Will's robustness.

Will leapt from rock to rock, dancing his way down the slope. Macdonald followed directly behind, never losing his footing. His ease with the path gave away the fact that he'd been down it before. Probably many times.

When the path leveled out at the bottom, Will made for the cracks in the cliff wall that led to the smaller caves. Macdonald was right behind him.

The tide was out, leaving damp sand in the lower half of the cave they entered. Will moved to the driest part and through one of the small openings he'd found the last time he'd explored. This slit opened into a shallow cave, the ceiling of which arched high, carved out of rock eons ago by the relentless beating of water.

Macdonald squeezed in behind Will so rapidly it was comical. He looked around at the very empty cave before he aimed the pistol at Will's face once more.

"Tell me your game, Mackenzie."

"This is where you hid it," Will said.

"I know that," Macdonald snapped. "Did you bring me down here to explain this to me? I'll kill you now."

"I didn't say it was still here."

Macdonald glared at him. Then he growled, stamped his way to the cave wall and scraped rubble from natural niches in the rock. Limestone carved well, and a man could easily chip out depressions until he had a nice set of footholds to climb to ledges above, then pile carving chips and rocks on the ledges to hide what he'd put there.

Only an observant man would note the tool marks on the walls, and only a determined man would discover if something had been hidden *above* him. Will was both observant *and* determined.

He watched as Macdonald scrambled up his makeshift ladder. Rocks clattered to the cave floor, and Will heard Macdonald cursing. The man slid back down, landing with a thump, pistol trained on Will.

"Where did you take it?" Macdonald demanded in a near shout.

"Never said I took it. I said I knew it *was* here, but now 'tis elsewhere."

"Where?"

Will started to laugh. He heard the pitch of Sir William somewhere in the laughter, but there was a bit of all his characters in Will's true self. "Did you really think it would be safe *here*? In a smugglers' cave?"

"These caves aren't used anymore. I made certain."

"Of course you did. It was a wise choice—or would have been if you were more careful. Too many other men poking about the ruins of the castle, the foundations of Mal's new house, and the tunnels of the distillery, but no one ever went to the caves. At least, so you thought."

"Where is my bloody gold?" Macdonald roared.

"So you admit you stole it?" Will asked without moving. "How did you, by the way? Mal was part of the group meant to retrieve it and take it to Teàrlach and his generals, and I was with them when they were ambushed. Gold disappeared. Were you waiting at the docks with pack horses? Telling them you were an agent of the prince's?"

Macdonald looked disgusted. "Don't be thick. Who do you think paid for that consignment to come from France, who convinced their simpering king to send it? I didn't have to intercept the gold. The men who carried it off the ship took it where I told them to. Easy to leave it be and retrieve it once Teàrlach was being chased around the western isles and his Highlanders rounded up."

Will's brows rose and so did his bile. He'd known Macdonald had somehow been on the spot to take the gold, but hadn't realized the man had tricked the King of France into sending him a boatload of it in the first place. If Macdonald hadn't been so contemptuous of the lives of others, and so utterly selfish, Will might admire the man.

"I admit, I hadn't thought of that," Will said. "You played the Jacobites' ambition right into your own hands."

Clennan gave him a tight smile. "It's a Highland tradition. Use your enemy's weakness."

"Eh? I thought the tradition was to charge headlong with your claymore over your head and kill anyone threatening your clan. But never mind. Why didn't you tell Cumberland what you'd done? Send word to King Geordie? You'd have been a hero."

Macdonald looked at Will as though he were a simpleton. "Because then I'd have to hand them the gold. I might get a minute percentage as a reward, but no more."

"And this way, you got to keep it all. So your plan was never loyalty to the crown, then."

"What are you talking about?" Macdonald sounded amazed. "I spotted an opportunity, and I took it. You've done the same, and don't tell me you're so virtuous that you wouldn't. Cumberland didn't need to know. As far as he was concerned, the gold was lost, and the Jacobites didn't have it. He cared for nothing else." Macdonald took a step toward Will, pistol leveled. "So where is it?"

Will shrugged. "Maybe Cumberland came for it. Sent men to see why you wanted the Kilmorgan lands so badly."

Macdonald shook his head. "Cumberland is a fool, and he's back in France trying to pour more glory on himself, but he'll never win there. Besides, he does as I tell him, and kept his hands off Kilmorgan once it became free. I'll have it, you know. I'll claim my reward from the king himself."

Will felt cold. He'd known Clennan was a scheming bastard, but he hadn't realized how far he'd go. Well, part of Will's plan was to keep the man talking.

"What do you mean, Cumberland does as you tell him?" Will asked. "He's a bold young man out to take the world by the horns and prove himself. He's a hero already for putting down the Highlanders, although even ordinary Englishmen are appalled at his butchery."

"He's impetuous and rash," Clennan said, not hiding his contempt.

"He prevailed at Culloden, because *I* knew when the Jacobites would come out and what they'd do. Cumberland thinks I'm doing the same for him in France, because I know where the French army will be and what *they'll* do. But he's never thanked me for my help, never once."

Will nodded as though in sympathy. "That must rankle. He's as young a pup as Teàrlach. Tell me, why do you think Butcher Cumberland will never win in France?"

"Because he can't plan his way out of his own front door, and relies on luck and the loyalty of his troops. Plus the information I send him." Macdonald paused to look self-satisfied. "What I *decide* to send him."

"So he fails because you don't give him the right information? Or enough at the right time?"

"He fails because he bites the hand that feeds him," Macdonald said impatiently. "He'd have lost at Culloden if not for me, but what does he do? Dismisses me out of hand, refuses the title I should have been given—*I* ought to be a duke, not your bloody father, who never did a damn thing in his life. Cumberland expects me to continue to give him information on French plans and troop movements, which I could do, but why should I? I have plenty of information to pass to the French army, who at least pay me. Cumberland acted on some of my dispatches but never once acknowledged what I went through to get them to him."

"Well, no one ever said the man overflowed with kindness. So you keep the gold as payment of sorts?"

"Of course. Stupid young whelp. Told him it was at the bottom of the sea." Macdonald darted a glance around the cave. "By rights, this hole and everything in it belongs to *me*. Including you and your life. Now, where is my gold?"

"You are a man obsessed, aren't you? To think, if my mum hadn't run from you, I might have to call *you* Dad." Will shuddered. "I'd have had to live with the shame that you betrayed not only your own people, but those you betrayed them *to*."

Macdonald's eyes glittered with renewed fury. "Don't talk to me about that ungrateful bitch. I arranged a perfectly fine marriage for Allison—she'd have had everything. Far more riches than your skinflint father gave her. And you mean my *brother* would have been your dad."

Will shook his head. "Mum told many tales—I overheard her talking to my dad far more often than they thought. Your dear brother couldn't sire children, could he? You'd have taken care of that detail, though. Carried on the line yourself without the bother of putting up with a wife. Plus, you'd have the pleasure of my mother." Will lost his amusement, his voice growing hard as steel. "Which is why you'll die, Macdonald. Think of her when you're dropping on the gallows with a rope tight around your neck."

CHAPTER 28

*J*osette raced through brush and bracken under the trees, thorns scratching the leather breeches she'd resumed beneath her skirt.

"Hurry," she said breathlessly.

Henri did not answer—rightly—that he was moving as fast as he could. The ground was wet and boggy, and neither of them knew these woods well. But on the other side of the trees were the cliffs they needed to reach.

Bhreac, Errol, and others had followed Will and Mr. Macdonald—but not too closely, Will had admonished them. Macdonald was sharp-eyed and had been raised to know when an enemy was near.

Josette did not like that Macdonald and Will were alone in the caves, but she'd lost the argument of having Henri or Errol, or even herself, accompany them. Macdonald would only use them as hostages, Will had said, and Josette knew he was right.

But not knowing whether Macdonald would shoot Will in his anger, or just because he chose to, made Josette frantic with fear. Macdonald had not struck her as a man with the most even of tempers.

She and Henri emerged from the woods near the path to the cove, but remained far enough back from the cliff edge that anyone looking up from the shingle below wouldn't immediately see them.

Boats waited out of sight—or should be waiting anyway—for Josette's signal that Will had Macdonald cornered.

She caught her breath at the top of the cliff, while Henri moved along the edge, swiftly and silently. He was to go north of the cove and signal the additional ships that were supposed to be *there*.

Josette waited until the lad had faded back into the trees before she hastily unfurled a scarlet flag—a bedsheet dipped in dye—and waved it hard. Drops of red that hadn't dried spattered her cheeks and hands like blood.

She saw nothing on the sea but the caps of waves under the wind. Josette continued waving the flag, her arms aching.

Had the ships not come? Will told her he'd extracted promises from Captain Ellis and Lord Wilfort, but perhaps they'd not been able to persuade their superiors to help.

A shot rang from the cove. Josette froze, more cold droplets landing on her face.

She had to keep signaling, to bring in the men from the ships, if they existed. But who had fired the shot? Will? Macdonald? Was Will lying on the ground, bleeding, dying? Or had he killed Macdonald and now *he'd* be the one arrested?

No ships appeared. Josette screamed through her teeth, dropped the flag, and bolted for the path.

She lifted her skirts and scrambled downward, skirting boulders along the way. She could see nothing of Bhreac, or of the men supposed to be keeping an eye on Will. Where were they?

Josette jumped the last few feet from the path to the shingle. Her boots splashed in water—the tide was coming in. She stumbled on wet rocks as she dashed for the cave where Will had found Duncan's knife, and ducked inside.

The outer cave was empty, but Will had showed Josette the entrance to the inner chamber. Waves lapped the sand inside the first cave, but the ground would be dry in the second.

She squeezed through the niche to the inner cave, and stopped in horror, a cry dying in her throat.

Mr. Macdonald, braced with feet apart, held a pistol at his side, acrid smoke floating from it. Will was on the ground, but not laid out. He crouched next to a shaggy body, curses streaming from his mouth.

"Ye pox-rotted son of a bitch," Will snarled. "Why'd ye shoot my *dog*?"

"Because it attacked me," Macdonald snapped back. "You are next, unless you shut up and take me to what you stole."

Beitris lay still under Will's hand, but Josette could not see whether the dog was bleeding, dying, or already dead. All she knew was that tears dropped from Will's eyes, streaking his exhausted face and falling on Beitris's fur.

Josette's fury erupted. Macdonald, the horrible, greedy bastard, cared so little for any but himself that he'd shoot a defenseless dog. He wanted to take everything from Will's family—their land, their lives, and their name—all because Will's mother had refused to have anything to do with him and his brother.

In spite of her rage, Josette knew how to move in silence—Will had taught her well. She had Duncan's *sgian dubh* in her hand, and was behind Macdonald before he knew it.

As Clennan sensed her and began to turn, Josette crashed the bejeweled hilt of the knife into his temple.

McDonald grunted in pain. Blood trickled from the wound Josette inflicted, but he didn't go down. His spent pistol fell to the sand as he staggered, and then he seized Josette's wrists in a crushing grip.

Josette kicked him. She fought and twisted, struggling to break free.

Macdonald clamped down hard, his eyes filled with rage. "Give me that knife, ye bloody bitch. What I am going to do to you ..."

Will rose behind him like a dark ghost. He roared an incoherent sound, one Josette had never heard come from his throat.

It was as if all the Highlanders Clennan Macdonald had sent to their deaths, including Duncan and Angus, screamed their fury, and their need to kill.

Will landed on Macdonald's back, one hand gripping the man's head, his other arm braced across his shoulders. Macdonald tried to twist, to throw him off without letting go of Josette, but Will clung fast.

He'd break the man's neck. Clennan would be dead, gone, and the British soldiers would rush in to find an outlawed Mackenzie standing over the body of a loyal Highlander. They'd lead *Will* off in chains, and end his life.

That could never happen. Josette refused to live in the darkness Will's passing would create.

Will was not the only one with ancestors who'd fought savagely. Josette came from a long line of men and women who'd had to battle to survive, in a country so many throughout the ages had tried to possess.

The cries of her ancestors streamed from her mouth as she wrested her hands free and battered Macdonald's face with the very sturdy hilt of Duncan's knife. Macdonald tried to seize her again, at the same time struggling to be free of Will, who transferred his grip to Macdonald's throat, squeezing hard.

Macdonald gasped for breath, clawing at Will as his legs buckled. Will continued to squeeze, and Josette crashed the jewel-encrusted hilt between Macdonald's wide eyes.

Macdonald fell more or less on Josette, who jumped backward, yanking her skirts out of the way as he crashed to the ground. Macdonald thudded forward on his face and lay still, blood seeping to the sand.

Josette didn't bother finding out whether he lived. She raced past Will and fell to her knees beside the unmoving dog.

She gathered Beitris to her, cradling her as Will sank beside them. Josette saw no blood on the dog's fur, but she ran her hands over Beitris's body, searching for broken bones. Will bowed his head, his cheeks wet with tears, and rested his large hand on Beitris's side.

The dog blinked open her eyes, swiveled them to pin Josette with a welcoming gaze, and thumped her tail. She betrayed no hurt or worry as she heaved herself onto her belly and thrust her nose into Josette's hand.

"Will!" Josette cried with gladness. "She's alive. She's all right."

Will rubbed his face with the heel of his hand, smearing dirt, blood, and tears across his skin. He took in the dog who shoved her head under Josette's arm, then he turned on Josette.

"And what the devil are *you* doing here?" Will demanded, voice like broken gravel. "You're supposed to be waiting at the top with your flag." His eyes widened as he took in the scarlet spatters on her face and gown, but she shook her head.

"This isn't blood. I heard the shot. I feared ..."

"Aye, the great bloody dog followed us, and tried to attack Macdonald. He fired at her, and she yelped and fell. I thought ..." Will dragged in a shuddering breath. "I thought he'd killed her."

Beitris climbed stiffly to her feet and then shook herself. Droplets of blood flew, scattered by her tail, which she continued to wag. Josette gently caught the tail in her hand.

"The bullet grazed her. See?" She showed Will the tip of Beitris's tail, which was stained red. "Poor thing."

Beitris jerked her tail from Josette and put her paws on Will's shoulders, giving him a grin before she began to thoroughly lick his face.

"Daft beastie," he managed as he climbed to his feet. "Ruining my plans and all. And *you*—" Will hauled Josette up to him, his eyes flashing golden anger. "Running in here alone. The man had a gun, knives. What were you thinking?"

"I was thinking of saving you," Josette returned. "I couldn't let him hurt you."

"Aye, she gave him a right tap," came the admiring tones of Bhreac. He stood just inside the cave behind Errol and Captain Ellis, who strode to bend over Macdonald's unmoving form. "About time too. I was tired of listening to him yap."

"Please tell me you heard everything he said." Will addressed Captain Ellis. "I doubt he'd confess to you, even under torture."

"I did," Ellis answered quietly. "That he purloined a treasure sent by the King of France and kept it for himself, and sells secrets to Cumberland when it suits him. That he sells British secrets to the French when that suits him instead. I will make certain my testimony is heard and noted."

"If any listen to it," Bhreac said skeptically.

"They'll listen to a hero of the Jacobite war," Will assured him. "And to Lord Wilfort. As long as Wilfort diverted those ships here, I'm happy. Or else, I'll just shoot Macdonald right now."

Shouts sounded without, and Josette heard boots on rock, then the clink of swords. The men from the boats—they'd come.

Errol and Bhreac shoved Macdonald through to the outer cave, which was fast filling with water. Perhaps that was why the ships had remained out of sight, Josette thought dimly as she slid out after them. They were waiting for the tide to rise, easier for them to land.

Macdonald began to wake when his boots hit the cold water. Beitris galloped past to play in the waves, as Macdonald opened his eyes.

Josette enjoyed the look on Macdonald's face as he beheld the cool, tight countenance of the Earl of Wilfort and the stern one of Captain Ellis of the British cavalry.

"Clennan Macdonald," Lord Wilfort said in his quiet voice. "I arrest you in the king's name for treason, for spying, and for other crimes against the crown. You'll be taken to London, where you can expect a trial. I will tell you now that a confession will bring an easier death than denial."

Macdonald threw his head back, but he stumbled, still dizzy from Josette's blows and Will's chokehold. "*I* a traitor? The traitor is *there*." He gestured at Will as well as he could with Bhreac and Errol holding him, and swayed again. "I give you Lord William Mackenzie, who took up arms against the king and never contradicted the lists that showed him as dead. But maybe you don't care about that, Wilfort, because you let your own daughter marry his brother. Maybe *you* are the traitor, my lord."

Wilfort regarded him with cool blue eyes. "You admitted treasonous activities and deliberate interference with British army campaigns before witnesses, who are of good character and willing to testify."

"Tricks and lies," Macdonald ground out. "Will Mackenzie's a damned trickster—everyone knows it."

"You'll be able to put your case in court," Wilfort said. Josette didn't know what was more chilling, the red-coated marines flanking

Mr. Macdonald, murder in their eyes, or Wilfort's calm assurance that justice would be done. She reminded herself never to make an enemy of Lord Wilfort.

Wilfort nodded at the soldiers to take Macdonald.

"One moment." Will calmly faced Macdonald, then balled his great fist and slammed it into the man's face. "*That* is for my mum." Another slam. "And *this* for my lady." He stepped close to Macdonald, an inch of space between them, Macdonald bleeding profusely from nose, lips, and temple. "I'd rather kill you, you bastard," Will said, voice low and vicious. "But I'll sacrifice that joy for my lady's sake. And for my family, and my home."

Josette saw the flicker of fear in Macdonald's eyes as he realized he'd underestimated Will and what he was capable of.

Then Errol and Bhreac relinquished Macdonald to the marines. The men half dragged, half shoved him toward a boat, which pushed off as soon as they were over the gunwale. Captain Ellis helped push then climbed quickly aboard, as though not wanting Macdonald out of his sight.

Will had turned to Lord Wilfort and was speaking to him quietly. Josette caught the last of Will's words as she approached.

"Just so you keep your part of the promise."

Wilfort looked offended. "I gave you my word, remember? All will be done."

Will nodded. "Good." He offered his hand. "I'm pleased to call you friend, Wilfort, even if you're an English aristocrat toady to the king."

"And you," Wilfort answered. "Though you are a barbarian Scot."

Will thumped the man on the shoulder. "Come to the house with us —whisky all around." Will shouted the last. "There's much to celebrate."

"Aye, and soon." Bhreac shook out a booted foot. "Me feet are getting wet."

Wilfort cleared his throat, a dry sound. "A moment, Mackenzie. What about the French gold? Where have you stashed it?"

Will burst out laughing. He lifted his face to the rain, mirth and joy erasing fatigue and sorrow. "It's not here. I didn't lie to Macdonald. It's gone. Long gone, I wager."

Josette regarded him in confusion. "You knew it was gone? Then what were you going to show Mr. Macdonald?

"Not a thing, love." Will smiled down at her, eyes golden and warm like Mackenzie malt. "That money is truly gone—who knows where? These are smugglers' caves, and they're still used, if the supplies left are anything to go by. Do ye think those men wouldn't go over every inch of the place when they came to ground?" Will brushed hair from his eyes as the wind picked up. "I imagine they couldn't believe their luck when they found an entire treasure of Louis d'or waiting for them. They'd have snatched it up and run off with it to the Continent to live the good life in a trice. Poor Macdonald. His home is nowhere near the coast, and he has no idea what desperate men will do to survive. He's never been desperate enough himself. Until now, that is."

Will gazed after the boat that was hauling Macdonald away, but when he looked at Josette, his smile was light. He'd finished with Macdonald, and it wasn't his way to continually savor his revenge. He'd put it behind him, and face the next thing.

"Shall we, love?" Will asked, and gestured her toward the path.

Josette rose on wet tiptoes to answer without words. Then she took his hand, and led him home.

WHEN THEY REACHED THE DISTILLERY, A FIGURE BROKE FROM A GROUP of women in the courtyard and raced for Josette, slamming into her and nearly knocking her over with a wild embrace.

Will kept mother and daughter on their feet as they hugged, then joined in the greetings with exuberance.

Glenna, it seemed, had traveled to Kilmorgan with the other ladies, who'd all disobeyed the order to remain at Strathy Castle. They'd been looked after on the journey by the tall Naughton. The ladies talked all at once, asking about the gold, about Macdonald, Sir Harmon, Bhreac, Henri, Josette.

Josette, taking over, got them all sorted, inside, warm, dry, and sitting with coffee or whisky—she firmly took a glass of Mackenzie malt from Glenna's hands and passed it to Will.

Questions were shouted, explanations demanded. Will told them all how he'd positioned Captain Ellis, Bhreac, and Errol, in the second of the small caves, where Macdonald's words had echoed to them.

The ships had arrived courtesy of the navy and Lord Wilfort, some of the same ships Bhreac had seen floating around Loch Broom weeks ago. The fleet captain had agreed to stay out of sight while Will lured Macdonald to the cave and got him to talk. Not difficult, Will said, as the man loved to boast about his cleverness. Josette and Henri had waved their signal flags once Will had Macdonald in the caves, and boats had slid from the ships and put in for shore.

Will spoke glibly, as though nothing had been difficult. However, he didn't like to think about how close he'd come to have his plans thwarted. How Captain Ellis had arrived very soon after Ewan's announcement that Macdonald was on his way, narrowly missing being seen by Macdonald himself. How Ellis told them Lord Wilfort should be coming by ship, but he wasn't certain that Wilfort had convinced his naval contacts in time that they were needed.

Will could only be relieved that it was done, and that the men, including Naughton and Henri, happily imbibed whisky, and the ladies rested, eyes shining with excitement. That Beitris, doctored by Josette and Glenna, would be right as rain.

As the celebration continued, Naughton beckoned Will into the still room and handed him a tightly rolled tube of oilcloth. "Thought you'd be wanting this. Or Mrs. Oswald would."

Will unrolled the cloth until he beheld a young Josette on a painted canvas, her head turned, dark hair flowing down her back. He quickly rolled it up again.

"Thank you, Naughton," he said in true gratitude. "She'll be delighted to have it back."

"I brought the other paintings Macdonald stole from Kilmorgan too," Naughton went on. "Thought I should retrieve them before the king's men take apart his house."

Will laughed. "You're a good man, Naughton. Thank you for conveying the ladies here safely."

Naughton rubbed his red hair with a long-fingered hand. "When I stopped at Strathy to check on them, as you asked, they insisted they come, most adamantly. 'Twas *I* who needed safe passage."

Will laughed again and handed the man another glass of whisky.

The revelry wound higher, laughter filling the house.

Back in the main hall, where dancing had commenced, Lillias approached Will in some trepidation to apologize for sending Bhreac to see what Will was up to, but she made it clear she'd done so for the best reasons—in her opinion. "I feared ye'd take what ye found and leave us. I know you too well."

Will gave her a stern look. "Not well enough, if you thought I'd desert lassies who were counting on me. Josette wouldn't have let me, even if I'd think of it."

"I know." Lillias flushed, ashamed. "I've been grieved, and afeared, for a long while. I'm not one to hide while others go out to fight."

Will laid a hand on her shoulder. "I am so very sorry for your husband, Lillias. Sorry I couldn't do more."

"Not your fault, I know." Lillias shook her head. "It was the bastard English who killed him. I'm finished with the Highlands, Will. Bhreac is taking me to Amsterdam. Not with the gold you gave us— I'm leaving that for the others. But I'll prepare the way for them to come. They'll be helped?"

Will nodded. "I have the word of a very powerful and honest man that they'll be reunited with their men and in safety as soon as they can be."

Lillias took Will's hand, squeezing it hard as tears filled her eyes. "Thank you, Will Mackenzie."

"There now." Will pulled her into a quick embrace. "You lift a glass to your husband, who'd be glad to know you are well."

Lillias pushed away, wiped her eyes, and left him with a sad smile. Bhreac fell into step with her, the two walking close together.

She would grieve, Will knew, but Bhreac would take care of her. The two might be journeying to the Continent as traveling companions for now, but Will guessed that within a year or so, they'd be much more to each other than that.

In the great hall, fiddlers and drummers began to play, and dancers joined hands. They'd celebrate far into the night—men and women who'd lost everything finding joy wherever they could.

Henri fell easily in with the circle, dancing Scottish dances with skill. Will, watching him, looked forward to reuniting him with his Scottish family. Wilfort would make it possible, Will knew, and Will would have the pleasure of seeing Henri's grief and anger flee.

The merrymaking continued, but as the others ate, drank, laughed, and danced, Will steered Josette upstairs. Glenna had already gone to bed in a chamber she'd share with Mysie, though she insisted she wasn't tired—Josette had taken her up when she'd found the girl slumped on a bench, fast asleep.

Josette's bedchamber was cool, empty, and relatively silent. Will shut the door against the noise downstairs, and put himself in front of Josette.

"I never thanked ye properly for helping me bring down Macdonald," he said. "Let me do that now, lass."

CHAPTER 29

*W*ill made love to Josette like a man desperate. He needed to be inside her, to soothe his hurts and anger, quench his fears. When he'd seen her struggling with Macdonald, something had broken open inside him, a berserker that had been simmering below the surface for too long.

But hadn't Josette been beautiful when she'd yelled some of the filthiest French words he'd ever heard and smacked Macdonald right between the eyes.

He drove into her, harder, faster. She met him thrust for thrust, her cries as fervent as his.

Her body was liquid heat, her hands finding his most sensitive places, lips and tongue performing magic. Josette opened to him, welcomed him. Loved him.

And he loved her. Will loved her so much he splintered with it.

The release was like nothing he'd experienced before. Will shouted her name while she cried his. The room spun around them, insubstantial and misty. Only Josette was solid, and real.

They wound down together, falling into slumber while Will covered them with a plaid.

Love you lass, he whispered, or thought he did. Then everything flowed away, and Will slept.

∽

JOSETTE WOKE TO DAYLIGHT, WRAPPED SNUGLY WITH WILL, SAFE IN Mackenzie tartan.

She blinked a little, stirred, and moaned. She ached all over, stiff from climbing about the cliffs, waving the huge flag, and fighting with Macdonald. Then the dancing, and to end it all, the wild love-making with Will.

"I am too old for all this," she murmured.

"You are barely past thirty and the most beautiful woman in the world." The deep, rich voice of Will Mackenzie caressed her, followed by a brush of his fingers on her cheek.

"And you are the most beautiful man." Josette ran her gaze over the hard shoulders and sculpted plane of chest the plaid bared. "Though I shouldn't make your head swell."

Will put his hand on the head in question, further mussing his hair. "It seems the right size for now." His lips twitched into a smile, the warm one that melted Josette to her toes.

"Did smugglers *really* steal the gold?" she asked him. "You didn't ferret it away for yourself, did you?"

"Ah, she still doesn't trust me," Will said to the room. "Not that I blame her." He pressed his hand to his heart, fingers splaying on his sun-touched chest. "Yes, it's gone. I never laid eyes on it. I did find, in its place, a scrap of paper, with one letter on it."

Josette blinked in surprise. "Did you? What was the letter?"

"*G.* I believe a man named Gair, a slippery devil, and his second, Padruig, found the stash unguarded and helped themselves." Will shrugged. "They knew the Mackenzies were long gone from here— they were the ones who sailed us to France after Culloden. They might have witnessed Macdonald poking about and wondered what he was getting up to. Gair would know I knew what the paper meant, if I ever found it. And if I didn't …" He opened his hands. "No matter. He and Padruig are probably enjoying themselves in France or the Low Countries by now."

Josette listened in wonder. "I do not recall you telling this to Lord Wilfort or Captain Ellis."

"Why should I? Let Gair have it. He and Padruig helped us quite a lot over the years, at great risk to themselves. They deserve it."

"So the King of France loses his gold," Josette said slowly, "and your friends are the richer for it."

"Louis of France can afford the loss. Probably doesn't even remember it, now that he has the lovely Pompadour to distract him." Will nuzzled her. "Speaking of distractions."

"No," Josette groaned, but it was difficult not to melt back into him. "I should get up. Glenna will be rising, if she's not rushing about already."

"Not yet, love." Will's smiled vanished, something more somber entering his eyes. "We have one more thing to speak of."

"Mmm?" Josette murmured sleepily. She ran her hand along his chest, absorbing his warmth, no longer interested in speaking, or rising, or doing anything but snuggling down with Will again.

"We need to see to Colonel Chadwick. I'll not have him be a continuing blight on your life."

Josette sat up, covers sliding from her and letting in the cold, but the air wasn't more chilling than her fears. "We forget about Chadwick. You said Lord Wilfort is working to restore Malcolm to Kilmorgan, which is what you came here for. We take Glenna and go to France or perhaps Switzerland like Sir William and Anna. Disappear. Be safe from him."

"No, love."

Will's voice was quiet, and Josette stared at him with sinking dismay.

"I'm not leaving Scotland again," he said. "France is well enough for Alec and Dad, but Kilmorgan is my home. Mal can have the dukedom and his manor house, but I'm staying here with him."

"Then Cumberland's soldiers will round you up and cart you off. Chadwick suspects you're alive—he'll tell the right men his suspicions. Clennan Macdonald has already shouted it to a naval fleet."

"Macdonald will be regarded as a raving madman, which Lord Wilfort and Captain Ellis will confirm. As for Chadwick, I don't intend to let him do a damn thing. But we can't spend the rest of our lives looking over our shoulders, wondering when he'll strike."

Josette balled her fists. "I will never let him take you. I can't, Willie. I've just found you again."

His smile, wicked and handsome, should have made her feel better, but it did not. "I'm not leaving you, my Josie. I want all of it, remember? You, my home, Glenna, my family. Even that bloody dog. She fits right in."

Josette swallowed, throat tight. "She's fond of Glenna, is Beitris."

"Good, then she stays. I'll tell Bhreac."

Josette regarded him limply. "I can go to Chadwick myself. Pay him off with my share of the gold. Explain he's to stay out of my life. I'm not afraid to. I realized after my first despair when he left me that he's a rather weak person. He's been dominated by his wife and her family all his life."

"And saw a pretty young woman as refuge from that for a while." Will ran a hand through her tumbledown hair. "I understand why he fell for you, love. If he'd been a wiser man, he'd have known what a precious thing he'd found and never let you go."

Will could flatter—Josette gave him that. She tried a smile. "Well, if he hadn't, I'd not have met *you*." And that would have been unthinkable. "I learned much about Oliver over the years. He owed his career to his wife's father, and he could not walk away from that. Even if he'd been madly in love with me and wanted Glenna, he couldn't. Family ties."

"Aye, I know all about *those*." Will kissed the top of her head. "I also know I'll win this argument. Best to confront the man and end it." A kiss to her temple, his breath warm. "I'll not let him take me, or Glenna. Ever. You won't be rid of us that easily."

Josette had also learned much about Will over the years. She knew that if she tried to go to Edinburgh and speak to Chadwick herself, she'd likely walk into the man's sitting room to find Will there before her. He'd never stay hidden and safe when she was in danger.

Josette cupped his face and made him meet her gaze. "Be honest with me, love. Will you kill him?"

She saw a flicker of old rage in his eyes, dark and impassioned. "For what he made you endure, I'd enjoy it." Will turned his head and kissed her palm, his whiskers scraping. "But I promise, I won't endanger you so. I'll only kill him if absolutely necessary."

From Will, that was a solemn oath.

COLONEL OLIVER CHADWICK HAD TAKEN ROOMS IN A FINE HOUSE IN AN elegant part of Edinburgh, though the abode was not quite as lavish as Lord Wilfort's. The landlady was haughty, and an even haughtier valet took Josette's name and eventually showed her upstairs. Both landlady and valet silently let it be known what they thought of a lone woman visiting the newly widowed colonel.

Chadwick received her in a parlor that had been decorated with fine taste. The charming young infantry officer who'd seduced the even younger and naive Josette had done well for himself, she could see. He'd lit no lamps, however, and gloom dulled the well-appointed chamber.

Chadwick, a straight and thin stick of a man, stood upright in the center of the room to greet her.

When Josette had met Oliver all those years ago, he'd been handsome and dashing, already a high-placed captain, thanks to his father-in-law. Now he was nearing forty, and the years had not been kind to him.

His face had a hollow, pinched look under a brown wig that did not fit him well, and his frock coat and breeches hung on a spindly frame. The hand he clenched was painfully thin, the knuckles swollen.

Josette realized with a jolt that his gaunt appearance came from more than grief at the recent loss of his wife. Colonel Chadwick was a very ill man.

"Mrs. … Oswald," he said. Chadwick's voice was deep, not scratchy and weak, but even the two words left him breathless.

"Colonel," Josette said, giving him a polite curtsy. "I have come to negotiate."

Chadwick immediately shook his head. "I told you my terms in London. Bring me Will Mackenzie or I take my daughter."

"*My* daughter is happy where she is. Always has been." *No thanks to you,* Josette forbore to add.

Chadwick took another breath, closing his eyes a brief moment, as though searching for strength. "She will be cared for," he said stiffly. "I am a wealthy man with connections to eminent families. Glenna will live in a large house, with servants to wait on her every whim. If I am correct, she is already of an age to make her debut. As she is illegitimate, she won't be presented at court, but I and my father-in-law can find her a good match. She will marry a man of decent means, have a house of her own, children. I can promise you all this. Surely you'd want that for your daughter."

Josette didn't bother to hide her incredulity as she listened to this speech. "I never took you for a simple man. She'll *not* be welcomed with open arms. She'll be shamed as a by-blow—a badge of your indiscretion. She'll be given a back room, hidden out of the way of your family, and married off to whomever your father-in-law can bully into the match. Yes, she'll have a home of her own, but I'll wager it will be buried in the country somewhere, her husband told what to do every day of his life. As you have been."

Chadwick's mouth pinched. "I assure you, I have already made plans for her, and they will be carried out."

"In your absence?" Josette softened her voice. "If I am not mistaken, Oliver, you are not long for this world."

He fell silent, the anger and resignation in his eyes telling Josette she'd guessed correctly.

She continued, keeping her tone gentle. "Once you're gone, there will be nothing to prevent your family from throwing her out again. They are indulging you out of pity. Surely you can see that."

The anger sparked. "Perhaps. But when I lay my hands on Will Mackenzie, the money I gain from turning over a Jacobite, a spy, and a killer, I will give entirely to Glenna. I will make a trust for her that no one can touch, not my father-in-law, not even a husband. Surely, Josette, you'd want *that*."

Josette kept her hot reply from her tongue, choosing her words carefully. "For my daughter to have money enough to keep the world from her, and for her to have a happy life? Of course I want that. But why do you not believe I can give that to her myself?"

Now Chadwick looked her up and down in derision.

The truth of what he truly thought of Josette showed on his face—that she'd been a distraction for him, an amusement, and as Will had concluded, a refuge from his wife's smothering family. Josette saw clearly now that Chadwick had never had any respect for her, any caring for Josette as herself. The evidence of that was blatant as he studied her.

The younger Josette would have been devastated by his dismissal. Now she only blessed her stars that she'd not been tied to this man for life.

"You run a boarding house," Chadwick said with slow disdain. "A common boarding house in a cheap part of London. You consort with Jacobites. You've been a lover to the notorious Will Mackenzie." He nearly spit the name. "You became an artist's model for his brother—with your daughter in the studio watching you parade about in nothing." He snapped his mouth tightly closed, as though upset he'd had to say such unseemly things.

The young Josette might have burst into tears, or at least given him the harsh side of her tongue and then wept in private.

The older and wiser Josette only watched him quietly, hands folded. "I do not recall you rushing to save Glenna from all that when she was a babe. When I truly had no means to keep her and had to pose for artists so I could keep food in her mouth, I never heard a peep from you, no matter how many letters I sent you begging for help."

Chadwick reddened. "I could do nothing then. My wife—"

"Would have shown you the door, yes. Or at least had her papa cut you off from everything you held dear, including his purse. I have the feeling that Mrs. Chadwick would never have disgraced herself with a divorce, but you'd have paid dearly for your indiscretion, wouldn't you?"

"Yes." The word was sharp. "I am pleased you understand."

"I understand you decided your soft life was more important than your daughter." Josette let her voice harden. "You could have supported Glenna in secret, had you any caring for her, but you were too afraid even for that. Your wife never bore you children, did she? Well, sir, I pity you, but I refuse to let you try to make up for that hole in your life with my daughter."

"*My* daughter, madam." The determination entered Chadwick's eyes again. "By law, she is mine, by-blow or no."

A new voice spoke from a dark corner, one quiet, rumbling, and Scots. "Are you sure of that?"

Will Mackenzie stepped into the light. "You'd stand up in court and swear Glenna was your offspring?" he went on. "Because that is what you'll have to do. Do you have a witness that says she's yours? Other than Josette, I mean?"

CHAPTER 30

*A*s Chadwick beheld Will standing before him, every bit of his bravado drained away. He looked vastly tired, weak, ill. "How did you get in here?"

Will shrugged. "I have my ways. I'm a ghost, me. Dead, according to battlefield records. And staying that way. Now, I asked you a question. Are you ready to stand before a judge and tell him you want to claim a daughter?" His lips curved to a smile. "How do you know Glenna isn't mine?"

Chadwick looked no less weary but his impatience crept back. "Because there was no one else. I was Josette's first."

"Ah, so pleased ye acknowledge her purity. Which you then ruined. But you couldn't own up to your guilt." A glint entered Will's eyes. "I say Glenna is mine. Will you battle me for her?"

Chadwick gave him a cold look. "You are an outlaw, and as you just said, dead in the eyes of the world." The look he shot Josette held venom. "I knew you were hiding him."

Josette spread her hands and said nothing. She had no idea what Will was up to but was willing to leave him to it. She also noted that Will made certain he did not go too near the windows or raise his voice enough to alert the landlady and valet downstairs.

"*I* was hiding me," Will said. "Josette is blameless. Well? Will you concede Glenna to me?"

"No," Chadwick snapped. "Josette never met you until years later. I know this. I kept an eye on her."

"How benevolent of you. Spied on her from afar but never sent her a penny, never a comfort, never a kind word. Now, let me tell you why I say Glenna is *my* daughter." Will advanced on Chadwick, who took a few steps back as Will loomed over him.

"She is not," Chadwick asserted, some of his courage returning.

Will shook his head, ignoring him. "When Glenna was a wee one, couldn't she get into mischief? I wore out my feet running after her— aye, she'd be in one place then another faster than ye could blink. When she wanted to know all about the world, what trees were called, how water pumps worked, why rain fell, I told her. I read to her, I told her stories, I carried her across roads so she wouldn't be run down. I held her hand when she was afraid, and I taught her how *not* to be afraid. And most of all, I loved her mother as hard as she did. And that, my friend, is why I am Glenna's father. Not you. It never was you."

Chadwick listened with a scowl. "It doesn't matter. I sired her."

"Oh, I think it matters to Glenna, and to Josette. Whenever I had to leave them—" Will broke off, bleakness in his eyes. "It shattered me. Knowing Josette and Glenna were alone nearly killed me every time, but I went because I knew they'd be safer without me."

Chadwick swallowed, his sallow throat moving. "They'd have been safer if they'd never met you."

Will regarded Chadwick with pity. "You know, I don't believe that's true. I thought so for a long time, chastising myself for wanting to be with Josette, yet causing her trouble when I was. But I never could quite walk away. I always made sure she and Glenna were well, warm, fed, happy. I'd never let Josette be desperate again, or let Glenna be afraid of anything. And she is not. Fearless, that's Glenna. She takes after her mother."

Josette couldn't breathe. She was glad Chadwick and Will focused so tightly on each other, because she was about to break down and weep.

It was true that as much as she grieved when she and Will were apart, as much as she pushed him aside in worry for Glenna, he'd never truly left them. Will's hand had been in Josette's life since the day she'd met him, even when he'd been miles away.

He'd sent Josette and Glenna money, or had a man of business keep them in funds, found them lodging, and made certain that artists who'd painted Josette paid her well. He'd had his brothers look in on them whenever he couldn't, and made it clear that anytime Josette wished to go to Kilmorgan or the Mackenzie residences in Paris or Edinburgh, she'd be welcome.

Josette and Will had been as one for nearly a dozen years now, though neither of them had openly acknowledged it.

"Will," she said.

Both men turned to her, as though reluctant to give up browbeating each other. "Yes, love?" Will asked.

"Leave him. The poor man thought to assuage his conscience by trying to look after Glenna at the last, not wanting any regrets." Josette faced Chadwick. "I thank you, sir, for giving me my daughter. She is a fine young lady, robust and strong, and so beautiful. She is well and happy, and I believe her future will be the same." She took a step toward him. "But I will not give her to you, and I will not give you Will. Nor will I hand you the money I had planned to, to make you go away. You had many chances to be Glenna's father, and you threw them aside. If you regret that, I am sorry. I pity you for what you face, I truly do."

Josette walked all the way to the staring Chadwick, took his emaciated hand, and squeezed it gently. "I admire you for attempting to make things right, in the end. You can go knowing you at least tried, and assure yourself that Glenna is happy and well looked after." Josette raised his hand and pressed a kiss to his dry fingers. "Goodbye, Oliver," she said softly.

She was finished with him. Forever. Josette turned and walked out of the room, leaving the two men to watch her go.

∾

WILL JOINED JOSETTE OUTSIDE THE GATES OF THE CITY AS THEY'D arranged. By the time he reached her, she was shivering, tears on her cheeks.

Will risked ruining his disguise as a downtrodden peasant and took her into his arms.

"'Tis done," he whispered. "My darling Josie, you are the bravest woman I know."

"Or the most foolish." Josette leaned against his chest. "What is to stop him sending men after you, even from beyond the grave? You shouldn't have showed yourself."

Will held her closer, his heart burning with leftover anger, and sorrow for what she'd had to face. "Couldn't help it. I hated the way he spoke to you. And though Chadwick boasts of his powerful connections, mine are even more powerful. I am owed favors by men and women from the loftiest positions who could grind Chadwick and his in-laws to dust if need be." He stroked her hair, wanting to warm her shaking away. "He is gone, Josette. The past is over."

"Yes." Josette looked up at him, sad but with the light of determination he loved so much. "It is done."

Will held her until they both calmed, then he kissed her, and started them on the path for home.

THAT NIGHT THEY STAYED WITH ONE OF THE CROFTERS THEY'D VISITED on their last journey, and were made welcome. Will had brought the family food and cloth from Edinburgh, which he hid, along with money, so they'd find it after he and Josette had gone.

Will was like that, Josette knew. Taking care of everyone, no matter how much in the shadows he had to remain.

They came together under a pile of plaids in the miniscule shed in which they slept, no room in the crofter's house. Josette was as comfortable and warm there as when she'd stayed in a palace. Warmer, she reflected, as the stoves in palaces rarely worked well.

Will loved her swiftly, thoroughly, while the Highland wind beat at the stones, trying and failing to get inside.

He brought her to the highest point, and joined her there, the two of them kissing, crying their release, defying the wind to be louder. They drifted down into laughter, contentedness, tired joy.

Will kissed her for a long time, then held her close. Josette drowsed, happier than she'd been in a long while. She felt free and protected at the same time. Will had given her that.

"Love," he whispered. They lay on their sides, face to face. Will traced her throat, the single lantern showing an uneasy light in his eyes. "I promised I'd do it properly, but I'm too tired to rise. So I'll ask ye now." He hesitated, then drew a resolute breath. "Josette Oswald, will ye do me the honor of becoming my wife?"

Josette stilled. Will watched her—she knew he waited for her to say no, to run from him and bury herself in her lonely life once more. Her heart beat with jubilation, but she'd been practical for too long to succumb instantly to emotion.

"Are you certain?" she asked softly.

Will's face creased with a scowl, and he rose on one elbow.

"Am I certain? What sort of question is that? I'm a roamer, a vagabond, a ne'er-do-well. I vowed I'd never settle down, or fall in love, or be a family man. Never thought I'd have the chance, so why bother?"

Josette touched his face, smoothed the lines of his mouth. "So why do you want to bother now?"

"Because I know how I feel when I'm without you." Will's voice was gravelly. "And I know how I feel whenever you walk into a room … or a castle, or a cave. It's as though light enters my life again, banishing all the darkness." He cupped her face, closing his eyes as if he looked for courage. "I love you, my brave Josie. I always have, even when I couldn't admit it to myself." He drew a breath, his golden eyes flickering open again. "All right, then? Will you marry me, or not?"

Josette kicked practicality aside and sent it packing. Elation and joy won. "Of course, dearest Will." The last word broke on a sob. "Of course. I love you so much."

Will gathered her close, his words vibrating with warmth. "Thank the Lord. I thought I'd have to argue. Though I warn ye, I was prepared to do it for years if necessary."

Josette held on to him, his nearness banishing all the cold, anguish, fear, and pain of the past. "I imagine we'll argue constantly. About everything."

"Good. I'm looking forward to that. And to making up the arguments afterward."

"Yes, that does sound fine." Josette began to tingle in anticipation. Nights wrapped in Will, laughing, making love, or simply lying together in silence, was what she longed for. "Others might try to dissuade us, you know. After all, I'm not highborn."

Will huffed, his body moving with it. "A boon, I call that. We Scots are practical, not like the stuffy English who trace a person's ancestry before they deign even to speak to him. Look how Lady Bentley grilled poor old Sir William before she unbent. It's clan that matters to us, and once you're Clan Mackenzie, that will be enough. Besides, there's a reason I asked Lord Wilfort to bring Mal back to life and make him duke, not me. I get to be carefree Will. Plain old Will. Pain-in-the-fundament Will—whatever you like to call me. That's who will be marrying you, not a bloody aristocrat."

Josette started to smile. "And I am French."

"Thank God." Will brushed her hair back from her face. "We need a reprieve from all the inbreeding."

Josette laughed at that, then she quieted. "Speaking of breeding ..."

"Mmm, I like the turn this conversation is taking."

"I've not had a chance to tell you for the last days." Josette kissed him softly. "But I believe I'm with child."

Will went quiet. He lay so still, Josette pulled back from him in worry. "Will?"

Will lifted his head, his gaze like hard sunlight. "Are ye? You're certain?" His voice cracked.

Josette touched his cheek. "Aye, Willie, you're going to be a dad."

Will's body quivered. Josette expected him to leap from the bed, perhaps drag her out with him to dance in the cramped room, but he only put his hand to his face. When he removed it, his eyes were wet, gleaming amber in the candlelight.

"Josette," he whispered. "Ye've given me the greatest of gifts."

"As have you." Josette wiped away his tears with her fingertips.

"You've given me *you*. It's an amazing thing." She knew how hard it was for this man to open himself, to let any person grow close to him. The fact that he'd done it for her stunned her. She held that gift to herself, and treasured it.

"The amazing one is you." Will looked at her, naked emotion on his face. "I love you, Josie."

"I love you, my Will."

Will closed his eyes on more tears, but when he opened them, they blazed in triumph. The smile that broke through shone even more.

Then Will began to laugh. He laid his head back on the hard pallet and roared with laughter, true exaltation. Josette laughed with him. She adored this man of adventure and promise, who loved with his whole being.

A gift indeed.

Will let out a whoop, his exhilaration ringing from the stones of the shed, built from the bones of his homeland.

He rolled Josette down into the bed, showing his love and happiness in a most satisfying way, as they tangled together in Mackenzie plaid.

EPILOGUE

Ten Years Later

*J*osette Mackenzie hurried out of the front door of the distillery, buttoning her gloves as she went. The wind tried to take her hat, but she caught it, tying its ribbons more firmly.

"Will!" she called. "Duncan! Abby! Shift yourselves. It's time."

From the shrieking, she deduced that her husband, son, and daughter were playing raucous games in the grass beyond the courtyard. Sure enough, in a few moments, all three came running up, breathing hard, gleaming with sweat, and looking a bit guilty.

The two children, Duncan nine, Abby seven, had already managed to stain their good clothes. So had their father. Josette sent them back inside to change to their second-best—*hurry.* When they emerged again, they fell in line to trudge the short way to the main house.

Beitris, the old dog, thumped her tail as she lay curled up on a blanket in the courtyard. These days, she preferred to nap in the sun rather than run about the lands. Her two pups, however, now five years old, gamboled behind small Abby.

The Mackenzie mansion gleamed golden in the soft Scottish sunlight. Malcolm and his engineers, along with the local men, had constructed it over the past ten years, and now it rose like a fine palace from the heather. Malcolm claimed work still needed to be done—it was a slow business—but he declared the house to be habitable.

Luxurious was a better word, in Josette's opinion, but Malcolm liked to be modest.

The front door hung open to admit the summer air. A tall and stately man welcomed them—Henri, who'd become the majordomo of Kilmorgan Castle, Naughton retiring to live with his daughter, son-in-law, and grandchildren.

Will and Lord Wilfort had long ago found and released the Scottish family who had been so kind to Henri. Now they also lived in peaceful retirement in a cozy cottage, leasing out the house Sir Harmon had been forced to vacate.

Henri had remained with the Dunbars for a few years, marrying another young woman the Dunbars had rescued, and accepting Malcolm's offer of employment when the Dunbars had retired. Naughton had trained Henri well, and he now ran the house as capably as Naughton had.

A table in the middle of the staircase hall held a vase of wildflowers—violets and wild pansies. The vast staircase wound upward, the walls covered with paintings saved from the old castle, many rescued by Naughton from Clennan Macdonald, others brought by Mal and Alec home from Paris.

On the first landing was the portrait of Allison Mackenzie, smiling down on her son Will as he strode inside.

His two children squealed when they beheld the young woman stepping off the last stair. "Glenna!" they shouted, and launched themselves at her.

Glenna, twenty-six, and married to a Mackenzie cousin, opened her arms to gather in her stepbrother and stepsister. Glenna had a wee one of her own now, and Josette's heart warmed with gladness as Dougal Mackenzie, Glenna's husband, carried him in. Small Michael had a tuft of dark hair and beautiful brown eyes, taking after his mother.

More voices beckoned Josette and Will beyond the staircase to a spacious dining room. There, Malcolm Mackenzie, flanked by his brother Alec, turned from a sideboard. "Will! About time. Welcome, Josette. Will, come here and tell me what you think."

Mal's wife, Mary, rolled her eyes. "They can't wait to get at the whisky. Dinner won't be long, but I think we should leave them to it."

She put one arm through Josette's, the other through Glenna's, and they stepped out of the dining room's long windows to the terrace.

The gardens—some parts still under construction—stretched from the bottom of the steps to the woods in the distance. The flower beds, laid out in Alec Mackenzie's designs, were filled with riotous color, summer at its height. Box hedges and more beds flowed around walks and fountains, encouraging a stroll.

Alec's idea was that gardens ought to be more natural, unlike the rigid formality of older designs. Walks should lead one casually to a shady bench, which would be a perfect spot to sit and read, contemplate the world, or kiss a beloved.

Celia, Alec's own beloved, joined them, and the four ladies ambled into the garden. "So fine to see you, Josette," Celia said in her gentle voice. "I am always happy when we can return to Scotland. It does Alec such good."

Josette squeezed her hand, happy to see Celia again.

About ten years ago, Malcolm Mackenzie had been declared officially alive, absolved of all charges of treason, and allowed to return to Kilmorgan and take up its title. Lord Wilfort, Mary's father, was a powerful man indeed.

The rest of the family remained listed with the dead. Alec and his father, comfortable with their lives in Paris, were happy in France. Alec painted for its king, and the old duke enjoyed the company of other Scots in exile—including Bhreac Douglas and his wife, Lillias— as well as that of a rather no-nonsense French lady. The duke had remained behind with her—Alec had already hinted that there'd likely be an announcement of an engagement by the time Alec and Celia returned.

Lord Will Mackenzie had officially ceased to exist. However, Willie Mackenzie, distant cousin and now steward of the Kilmorgan estate, lived in the distillery with his wife, Josette, and his son and daughter, his stepdaughter having married and gone to live with her husband. Will and Josette looked after the distillery and were consulted by Mal and Mary as to the business of the farms, the brewing, and the tenants.

The distillery had flourished under Will's and Mal's tender care. A new, gleaming copper still had been installed, and production had been going strong for years now. Will had been correct that Englishmen would purchase Scots' whisky with enthusiasm, and it sold well abroad too. Mackenzie Malt—once again legally brewed—was famous throughout the British Isles and the Continent.

Josette now understood what Will had meant when he'd said there was more gold in the Highlands than coins.

"Well, ladies," Mary said. "Life has certainly turned out differently than we imagined, has it not?"

The four glanced back through the terrace doors where Will, Mal, Alec, and Glenna's husband tasted whisky from a copper cup Henri passed between them. Will's voice rumbled something, and he laughed. Mal groaned, and Alec clapped Will on the back.

"Indeed," Celia said. "My parents expected me to marry a frightful boor of a man. Thank heavens for Alec, my scandalous art instructor. Though my mother would have fainted if she'd seen exactly what Alec wished me to paint. Or more likely, burst into flames."

She gave them a secret smile, and Mary, Josette, and Glenna laughed. Josette had heard the story many times of how Alec had decided Celia needed to learn to paint the male anatomy.

Celia had reconciled with her mother over the years, the woman mellowing as she'd aged. Celia and Alec's children—a boy, Magnus, and a girl, Catherine, as well as Alec's daughter Jenny, now twelve years old and keeping a keen eye on her siblings—had softened Celia's mother a great deal. Celia's father doted on them all extensively.

"I was engaged to a horrid man myself," Mary said, and shivered. "I was already contracted to the marriage when I discovered how cruel Lord Halsey was. Thank heavens for *my* Mackenzie who stole me away."

They shared another laugh. The Mackenzie men had a way of taking what they wanted.

Josette did not join with a tale of her own. Until Will, she'd never had a man wish to marry her, whether she'd wanted marriage or not. She'd been poor and desperate, abandoned by a married lover, and raising a fatherless daughter.

But Will had swept her up, pulling her into his adventures, relying on her, trusting in her, while at the same time making certain she and Glenna were always cared for and well.

"He's a good man, is Will," Glenna said. She'd mellowed somewhat since she'd fallen in love with and married Dougal Mackenzie and then born him a son, but she retained her cheeky smile and the glint in her eye—a young lady never subdued.

The brothers and cousin drifted out to the terrace with their whisky. The tall men no longer wore the outlawed plaid, but they were plenty handsome in breeches and boots, linen shirts, and coats that clung to broad backs.

They'd be Highland warriors no matter what they wore, Josette realized. Whether wrapped in a great kilt or formal suit, their strength and vitality couldn't be tamed.

Will spied Josette and Glenna and lifted his cup in salute. Copper caught the sunlight, as red as his hair, the glints as golden as his eyes. This morning, he'd looked down at Josette with those Mackenzie eyes as he'd slid into her, celebrating their waking with a lazy smile.

Children burst around the men, nearly knocking Alec over. They exploded from the terrace and ran shrieking down the paths, from Malcolm's oldest—Angus, who would be duke after him—to Catherine and Abby, born the same year and determined to keep up with their older cousins.

Glenna's babe toddled out, lowered himself determinedly down the steps, and waddled speedily after the others.

Will caught little Michael before he could go too far, lifting him to his shoulder. "Not yet, grandson," he said. "Too much mischief ye can land in, and wouldn't your Mum and Grandmum light into me for letting you?"

Alec and Mal charged after their respective offspring, and Glenna took Michael so Will could do the same.

Will slid his arm around Josette's waist as he moved to follow his brothers, pulling her close and landing a firm kiss on her lips.

"Dinner might be delayed, love. While we round up Mackenzies."

"As usual," Josette said in mirth. "You can make it up to me later. As usual."

Will's eyes heated, and his embrace grew more ardent. "Aye, I always look forward to that, Mrs. Mackenzie."

Josette's heart warmed with a steady glow of happiness as Will kissed her again, hands hard on her back. The kiss tasted of love, of laughter, of the spice that only Will Mackenzie could bring her.

"Love you," she whispered when the kiss ended.

"Love *you*, my Josie." Will brushed back a lock of hair that had escaped the confines of her hat. "The making up will be pleasing, I think."

"Go on with you now," Josette said.

Will flashed her a grin, gave her yet another kiss filled with hot promise, and spun away to run after his children.

Sunlight flashed on the solid house, Malcolm Mackenzie's pride and joy. A breeze flared through the garden, stirring skirts and hat ribbons and sending to Josette, her sisters-in-law, and her daughter the golden sound of Mackenzie laughter.

AUTHOR'S NOTE

$\mathcal{T}$hank you for reading!
This book brings to a close the three-book arc of the Mackenzie eighteenth-century ancestors:

The Stolen Mackenzie Bride (Malcolm and Mary)
Alec Mackenzie's Art of Seduction (Alec and Celia)
The Devilish Lord Will (Will and Josette)

When I began *The Stolen Mackenzie Bride*, about the character "Old" Malcolm Mackenzie the Victorian Mackenzies admired, I planned to write it as a stand-alone. However, I once I introduced Mal's brothers, Alec and Will, I fell in love with them! I knew I had to write more about them.

I'd originally planned to have Malcolm be the only survivor of the 1745 Uprising (the reason he becomes Duke of Kilmorgan, though he's the youngest), but I no longer wanted Alec and Will to die.

So my imagination spun out their stories, along with how on earth Mal could become duke though his two older brothers are still alive. I decided Alec and Will would officially remain listed among the deceased from the Battle of Culloden Moor (though they really survived), but Malcolm would be brought back to life.

When I met Will, I knew immediately he didn't want the job of Duke of Kilmorgan. He was far more comfortable with his role of spy and intriguer, but he would bend over backward to make sure Malcolm could inherit the title and restore the family home. Will can only accomplish this with the help of his soul-mate, Josette, of course!

Alec, likewise, wants to be an artist, not spend his time in politics, so he marries and settles down in France with Celia and children.

Malcolm returns to Kilmorgan with Mary, builds his house, and lives happily ever after.

The story about the missing gold is taken from history. France shipped a large sum intended to help the Jacobite army purchase weapons and supplies, but the Jacobites sent to retrieve it were ambushed and the gold vanished. I decided to write my own theory of what happened to it. Who knows?

I have enjoyed my foray into the early eighteenth century. The Jacobite Uprising happened on a cusp of great change in Scotland. Scotland was about to become the center of an Enlightenment movement in science, technology, architecture, art, and financial and political thought. The age produced James Watt, David Hume, Adam Smith, Robert Adam, Allan Ramsay, and many more. The industrial age would soon usher in a new way of life, for good or ill. It is an amazing period in history to study.

I hope you have enjoyed my step back into the past of the Mackenzie family. Alec, Will, and Malcolm and families will live long and happy lives.

You can trace Mal's descendants to the Victorian Mackenzies in the family tree in the back of this book.

All my best,

Jennifer Ashley

ALSO BY JENNIFER ASHLEY

Historical Romances
The Mackenzies Series
The Madness of Lord Ian Mackenzie
Lady Isabella's Scandalous Marriage
The Many Sins of Lord Cameron
The Duke's Perfect Wife
A Mackenzie Family Christmas: The Perfect Gift
The Seduction of Elliot McBride
The Untamed Mackenzie
The Wicked Deeds of Daniel Mackenzie
Scandal and the Duchess
Rules for a Proper Governess
The Stolen Mackenzie Bride
A Mackenzie Clan Gathering
Alec Mackenzie's Art of Seduction
The Devilish Lord Will
A Rogue Meets a Scandalous Lady

Historical Mysteries
Kat Holloway "Below Stairs" Victorian Mysteries
(writing as Jennifer Ashley)
A Soupçon of Poison
Death Below Stairs
Scandal Above Stairs
Death in Kew Gardens

MACKENZIE FAMILY TREE

Ferdinand Daniel Mackenzie (Old Dan) 1330-1395
First Duke of Kilmorgan
= m. Lady Margaret Duncannon
|
Fourteen generations
|
Daniel William Mackenzie 1685-1746(?)
(9th Duke of Kilmorgan)
= m. Allison MacNab
|
6 sons
Daniel Duncannon Mackenzie (Duncan) (1710-1746)

William Ferdinand Mackenzie (1714-1746?)
=m. **Josette Oswald**
|
Glenna Oswald (stepdaughter)
Duncan Ian Mackenzie (1748-1836)
Abby Anne Mackenzie (1750-1838)

Magnus Ian Mackenzie (1715-1734)
Angus William Mackenzie (1716-1746)

Alec William Ian Mackenzie (1716-1746?)
=m. Genevieve Millar (d. 1746)
|
Jenny (Genevieve Allison Mary) Mackenzie (1746-1837)

=m2. **Lady Celia Fotheringhay**
|
Magnus Edward Mackenzie (1747-1835)
Catherine Mary Mackenzie (1750-1836)

Malcolm Daniel Mackenzie (1720-1802)
(10th Duke of Kilmorgan from 1746)

= m. **Lady Mary Lennox**
|
Angus Roland Mackenzie 1747-1822
(11th Duke of Kilmorgan)
= m. Donnag Fleming
|
William Ian Mackenzie (The Rake) 1780-1850
(12th Duke of Kilmorgan)
= m. Lady Elizabeth Ross
|
Daniel Mackenzie, 13th Duke of Kilmorgan (1824-1874)
(1st Duke of Kilmorgan, English from 1855)
= m. Elspeth Cameron (d. 1864)
|

Hart Mackenzie (b. 1844)
14th Duke of Kilmorgan from 1874
(2nd Duke of Kilmorgan, English)
= m1. Lady Sarah Graham (d. 1876)
|

(Hart Graham Mackenzie, d. 1876)

= m2. **Lady Eleanor Ramsay**
|
Hart Alec Graham Mackenzie (b. 1885)
Malcolm Ian Mackenzie (b. 1887)

Cameron Mackenzie
= m1. Lady Elizabeth Cavendish (d. 1866)
|
Daniel Mackenzie = m. **Violet Devereaux**

Cameron Mackenzie = m2. **Ainsley Douglas**
|
Gavina Mackenzie (b. 1883)
Stuart Mackenzie (b. 1885)

"Mac" (Roland Ferdinand) Mackenzie
= m. **Lady Isabella Scranton**
|
Aimee Mackenzie (b. 1879, adopted 1881)
Eileen Mackenzie (b. 1882)
Robert Mackenzie (b. 1883)

Ian Mackenzie = m. **Beth Ackerley**
|
Jamie Mackenzie (b. 1882)
Isabella Elizabeth Mackenzie (Belle) (b. 1883)
Megan Mackenzie (b. 1885)

Lloyd Fellows = m. **Lady Louisa Scranton**
|
Elizabeth Fellows (b. 1886)
William Fellows (b. 1888)
Matthew Fellows (b. 1889)

McBride Family

Patrick McBride = m. Rona McDougal

Sinclair McBride = m.1 Margaret Davies (d. 1878)
|
Caitriona (b. 1875)
Andrew (b. 1877)

m.2 **Roberta "Bertie" Frasier**

Elliot McBride = m. **Juliana St. John**

Ainsley McBride = m.1 John Douglas (d. 1879)
|
Gavina Douglas (d.)

= m.2 **Lord Cameron Mackenzie**
|
Gavina Mackenzie (b. 1883)
Stuart Mackenzie (b. 1885)

Steven McBride (Captain, Army)
= m. **Rose Barclay**
(Dowager Duchess of Southdown)

Note: Names in **bold** indicate main characters in the Mackenzie series

ABOUT THE AUTHOR

New York Times bestselling and award-winning author Jennifer Ashley has written more than 85 published novels and novellas in romance, urban fantasy, and mystery under the names Jennifer Ashley, Allyson James, and Ashley Gardner. Her books have been nominated for and won Romance Writers of America's RITA (given for the best romance novels and novellas of the year), several *RT BookReviews* Reviewers Choice awards (including Best Urban Fantasy, Best Historical Mystery, and Career Achievement in Historical Romance), and Prism awards for her paranormal romances. Jennifer's books have been translated into more than a dozen languages and have earned starred reviews in *Publisher's Weekly* and *Booklist*.

More about Jennifer's series can be found at
https://www.jenniferashley.com
or join her newsletter at:
http://eepurl.com/47kLL

Made in the USA
San Bernardino, CA
12 January 2019